Five Little Peppers
in the Little Brown House

Five Little Peppers in the Little Brown House

By
MARGARET SIDNEY

Grosset & Dunlap

PUBLISHERS

NEW YORK

Preface

"WHATEVER BECAME of Polly Pepper's famous chicken pie, and also Phronsie's red-topped shoes?" the friends of the Five Little Peppers keep asking. "We have searched through all the Pepper Books and cannot find them. Please give us those two stories again."

At last all these requests are granted in this book, containing, first of all, those two stories that make the very beginning of all the records of the Pepper family. Indeed, there wasn't any Pepper family before they were written; nor any Little Brown House, not a sign of one; nor any Badgertown even, till Margaret Sidney one day wrote "Polly Pepper's Chicken Pie" and sent it to the *Wide Awake Magazine.*

And no one could be more astonished than was she—for the record was so simple—when the editor wrote for another one just like it. So "Phronsie Pepper's New Shoes" was written.

And then—well, the editor wrote that the *Wide Awake* must have enough stories for one year, to be connected. So Margaret Sidney had to go regularly after that to the Little Brown House and write down all the records just as Mrs. Pepper and the Five Little Peppers told them to her, and then those insatiable editors wrote that they must have a book—nothing more nor less—because the children's letters to them from all over the country demanded it. So that was the way it all began. And of course the two separate stories—the *motif*, as it were, for the book—had to be left out.

So here they are now in the post of honor—leading off in the very front of the volume, as is quite proper; the other stories (which are all just newly written expressly for this book) following humbly after in the wake of Phronsie's red-topped shoes.

MARGARET SIDNEY

Contents

I

Polly Pepper's Chicken Pie

To BEGIN with, it was the most remarkable chicken that was to have made the famous pie for Thanksgiving. But alas! A sad mishap befell the Pepper family.

In the first place none of the family ever knew where it came from. Ebenezer, or Ben, as he was usually called, found it one day in a swamp, down by the meadow as he was digging sweetflag to sell, in order to get some money to buy a pair of boots for the coming winter. It was not hurt, only it couldn't get out. The wonder is, how it ever got there. However, Ben didn't stop to think of that; he must set to work to get Master Chick out. So, forgetting flagroot in his eagerness, he took an old fence rail, and by dint of poking and urging it, and tumbling around in the bog till he was pretty wet himself, he at last had the satisfaction of obtaining his prize.

It proved to be a fine black chicken, a Shanghai, and grasping it tightly under one arm, its eyes protruding with fright,

1

Ben flew home, and bursting into the door of the Little Brown House, astonished them all by thrusting the long-legged black fowl before their faces, nearly upsetting Polly as he did so, who was helping her mother pull out the basting threads of the coat Mrs. Pepper had just finished on the edge of the twilight.

The chicken gave a shrill scream, and this was the first introduction to its future home.

"Goodness me, Ben!" ejaculated Polly, "you scared me 'most to death, and you've broken my box."

"What is it?" exclaimed Mrs. Pepper. "Is it a crow?"

"Ho! Ho! Crow, Mother?" replied Ben, holding the chicken firmly by one leg, "It's the—well, the most beautiful bird you ever saw! Hey, Polly, look!" he flapped the Shanghai over Polly's brown head as she disconsolately groped around on the kitchen floor for her scattered spools and the cover of her cherished box.

"I don't care for any old birds, Ben Pepper. See there!" and she brought to light from under her mother's chair the dilapidated cover.

"Oh, Polly, I'm real sorry. Come, I'll give you half of the chicken. See, he's real big, and won't he grow into a buster! And then, perhaps—hooray, Polly; why, then we'll have him for Thanksgiving, and you can make your pie, you know."

"Will you really, Ben?" relented Polly, as she sat on the floor.

"Yes, certain true, black and blue!" solemnly said Ben.

"Hooray, then!" screamed Polly, "and, Bensie, I'll make the crust awfully thick, and it'll be 'most all drumsticks," and she danced a whirligig in the middle of the old kitchen floor.

"Queer kind of crust, I should think; drumstick crust," retorted Ben.

"Oh, you Benny goose!" flung back Polly, as she went up

to hug her mother's neck; "Mammy, when *is* Thanksgiving? Is it more than six weeks, anyway, before it comes?"

"Let me see," said Mrs. Pepper, laying down her work. "Oh, yes, it's July now. Yes, you'll have to wait four months. But perhaps you can't have it at all, for if the chicken belongs to anybody 'round here you must give it back. Let me see it, Ben," and his mother grasped the leg of the bird, which all this time was squawking dismally, and amid the groans from Ben, and the wails from Polly, she repeated: "yes, if you can find out where it belongs, you've got to carry it back."

"What, and have no chicken pie!" exclaimed Polly. "Why, we *can't*, Mother, we've waited so long for our pie, and I've never tasted one. We can't give it back!"

"For shame, Polly," said Mrs. Pepper sternly, "the chicken doesn't belong to you, and I should rather you'd never taste a morsel of chicken pie than to get one underhand. But put him away now, children," she said in a kinder tone, as she saw the sorrowful faces before her. "He can sleep in the box the gray goose had in the shed, for tonight anyway, and then in the morning we'll send him home if he's got any to go to."

"And we won't have anything left but the old gray goose," mourned Polly. "I wish the old thing was dead, I do!"

"Why, Polly Pepper! And then we wouldn't have anything," said Ben, preparing to take his chicken out to its quarters for the night.

"Well, I don't care," said Polly, as she followed. "I'm tired of seeing her 'round, anyway."

Now, all this time, the younger Peppers were away by chance from the old kitchen, or there would have been more of an uproar still, over the advent of the chicken. The two small boys were busy on the edge of Deacon Brown's cowyard, where in a dirty pool of water they were having the highest glee over the sailing of a boat, composed of one of Polly's old shoes with a rag for a sail. Well was it for the chicken that they were missing at the reception, else it would have been almost torn to death with delight. And Sophronia, or Phronsie, had been put to bed early this afternoon, so she was tucked away fast asleep under the gay, patched bedquilt of the old crib.

There was no father in this Pepper household. He died when Phronsie was a baby, and Mrs. Pepper struggled along bravely, making coats to put bread into her own and her children's mouths. And the children, healthy and rugged, and happy-go-lucky, came up or "scrambled up," as Mrs. Pepper said, and fairly made the little old brown house ring with their cheery life.

Polly was ten, and Ben one year older, and it was the one great ambition of their lives "to help Mother." The only thing in which Ben could really boast superiority over Polly, aside from his being a boy while she was only a girl, was the fact that once on a great and memorable visit with his father to a neighboring farm he had eaten a piece of chicken pie; oh, so perfectly splendid! And to Polly, who had never tasted or even seen one, he dilated upon it, till she was nearly wild with curiosity and longing at the delightful vision he brought up.

"Oh, Ben, was it good?" she would say the five hundredth time, as in some interval when work "slacked up," perhaps when they crouched at dusk on the kitchen floor, the wink of fire from the old stove lighting up their absorbed little faces, they imagined or played they had all their fancied dreams or wildest wishes realized.

"Yes, you better believe!" Ben smacked his lips. "Seem's if I taste it now!"

"Well, how *did* it taste?" questioned Polly, still for the five hundredth time.

"Oh, like—well, like everything nice; there was fat, and wing, and oh, the wishbone, Polly, and a thick crust, oh, thicker'n my hand, and the juice was *prime,* and, well, it was all the nice tastes together you ever had in your life, Polly Pepper!"

"Oh, dear!" Polly would sigh, "don't you s'pose we'll *ever* have one, Ben? I could make one, I know; I can 'most see one now, you've told me about it so many times."

And Polly would shut her eyes, and give herself up to the delicious thought till she had to hop up to put the children to bed, or to help Mother in the many ways in which she knew so well how to save her steps. And now here was a fine chicken come right to their very door!

The Pepper family had no cow, nor pig, nor even a chick. The only thing of life in the animal kingdom belonging to the household was an old gray goose; too old and tough to benefit anyone by her death. She was just as cross as she could be, or at least she might have amused the children and been of some comfort. She had grown for ever so long in her present quarters, wandering around the poor Little Brown House and shed, picking up a scanty living and taking thanklessly all the bits that the children still conscientiously fed her.

Polly and Ben had glorious visions of the day when they would "buy Mammy a cow," and many were the talks and plans as to exactly what kind it should be. But nothing ever came their way, until this black chicken appeared right in the old kitchen, and all for Thanksgiving, too! That is, if they could keep him; for Polly and Ben, albeit the conflict within, conscientiously obeyed the commands of their mother and made inquiries far and near as to the ownership of Master Shanghai. Nobody knew anything of him, and he seemed indeed to have dropped down from the clouds. Clearly he was to remain at the Peppers', and, as day after day passed by and they were not forced to give him up, their spirits rose, until the gaiety over the future festival assumed the jolliest aspect. They already saw in imagination the glorious pie completed, and decking the festival board which Polly declared "must be trimmed with flowers."

"Whew! Where are you going to get flowers?" demanded practical Ben.

"I don't care; we must!" persisted Polly. "Folks always have them at a party, and we'll get them someway; you'll see."

But although Ben always stanchly pinned his faith to whatever Polly said, on this occasion he only gave a little sniff. It was too good to be true.

So time passed on. The chick was fed, often by the scrimping of Polly's, or Ben's, or Joel's, or David's, or little Phronsie's plate, or, as it frequently happened, by all of them, each stealing out secretly to do it. Consequently he grew and throve famously, his thin frame filling out, until he enjoyed his new quarters so well that he confided in a burst of delight one day to the old gray goose his pleasure and delight at the attention he was receiving.

"Humph!" said the old goose, with a knowing look, "you don't know as much as you will in a short time, say in November."

Now what these mysterious words of the cross old goose meant, or even what November was, the chicken was unable to tell, having never in his short life seen a November; so he went to work, digging and scratching over the old stony ground, and soon forgot all about it.

But as time passed on, the hints of the goose grew broader and deeper, till at last the Shanghai, politely but plainly one day, asked her to explain and tell him exactly what she did mean. This was the week before Thanksgiving, a cold, dreary afternoon, and the two inhabitants of the old worn shed were perched on a rail shivering with the cold, and engaged in a conversation that caused Shanghai to shiver even more with fright. Inside the house, the fun had commenced.

The plans were all made, it is true, weeks before, but there remained that mysterious consulting and "talking over" which is half the pleasure, and at last it was decided that Ben could actually go up to the store tonight when he carried home Mr. Atkins's coat, and buy half a pound of raisins for the pudding. For Mrs. Pepper, seeing the joy and excitement of the children, scrimped and twisted her scanty earnings till she could contribute to the feast, and "you shall have the pudding, children," an announcement which was received with a perfect babel of delight. And Joel stood on his head in the corner, and waved his feet in the air, unable to express his joy in any other appropriate way.

Now, nothing remained but to kill the black chicken, which Ben was to do on the morrow morning, for Polly declared, as that would be Saturday, it must be done that day, "and then we shan't have to think it's got to be done, over Sunday, you know, Bensie, dear."

The feathers, David said, must be for a pillow to put at the mother's back when she sewed; a proposition that made Mrs. Pepper beam an appreciative smile, for Davie was "Mother's boy."

"And, oh, Ben, you can't think how perfectly elegant the crust is going to be! Mamsie, now, don't I know?" and Polly began a rapid jargon of the directions her mother had given her of the way they made chicken pies when she was a girl.

Poor woman! Very few had come in her way during her

married life. Thankful enough was she when bread and milk were plentiful; and of late years mush and brown bread took the place of more elaborate fare.

"Oh, and I say," broke in Joel, "I'm going to have the wishbone—so there!"

"No, you mustn't, Joel; Davie's younger," said Polly decisively.

"Well, Phronsie's youngest," retorted Joel.

"Yes, you're right there," declared Ben. "Phronsie, you're the girl for the wishbone. Do you hear, Puss, and you must wish with me," tossing her up in the air.

"No, no, I spoke for you, Phronsie," screamed Joel. "Say you'll wish with me."

"What is it, Ben?" said little Phronsie. "What is a wissbone?"

"Oh, you little goose," began Joel, but Polly gave him a pinch to make him stop.

"Let her alone, Joel," said she. "Phronsie, you'll see when Thanksgiving comes, and that's next week. Come and see, now, if the flour is all right."

And Polly spun along to the little old cupboard in the corner, the whole troop at her heels, to inspect the precious materials. The flour had been measured out certainly a week or more, and there it stood in the bag in the old yellow pudding dish. Everything was in readiness. There was the lard near by in a cracked bowl, and to the five pairs of happy, expectant eyes directed to these festive preparations, no sight could have been more delightful.

"Well, children," said Polly, as she shut the cupboard door fast with an important air, "we must get up early in the morning, there'll be so much to do. Now, Phronsie, it's time for you to go to bed."

"Oh, no, I'm not one bit tired," protested Phronsie in an

injured tone. But while Polly went to bring the little flannel nightgown to undress her by the kitchen fire, Phronsie's little yellow head bobbed ominously, and she nearly fell off her stool, so that Ben had to carry her in his arms into the bedroom, after all.

All this while, in the thick dreary November twilight, the old gray goose and the black chicken were talking busily. The old goose was so jealous and determined to make the last hours of the chicken very miserable that she dilated at length and with great exactness on the dreadful fate that awaited him on the morrow; and painted in fearful words the awful ending of being baked in pieces in a pie!

"I've seen 'em!" she declared, with the air of one who knew what she was talking about. "Year after year, hens and chickens, yes, and geese, too, stepping around in the morning, oh, so happy and smart, and then at evening they would go past here to market all stiff and stark, with their heads off, and Mr. Brown's boy holding 'em by their legs! All for pies, and so that people may eat themselves sick. And they call that a Thanksgiving!"

How the chicken shook! It almost fell from its perch; but it was very dark, so the old goose couldn't see very well. Shanghai wouldn't, for all the world, have had her jealousy rewarded by a sight of the terror she had inspired, so he controlled himself like a brave little fellow, and although his heart was beating dreadfully, he commanded his voice enough to ask, "Well, why weren't you, then, baked in a pie along with the others?"

"What—why—well," stammered the goose, "they were going to kill me time and again, but, well, the fact is, they thought so much of me they couldn't bear to."

In spite of its fright, the black chicken couldn't help laughing softly to himself as he sat there on the rail.

"Well, come, you'd better go to bed," snapped the old goose. "They'll come for you bright and early in the morning. I heard 'em saying so."

"In that case," declared the black chicken, drawing himself up on his long legs, "they won't find *me* here; that's all I've got to say."

"Why, where will you go?" demanded the old goose, sticking out her long neck in amazement.

"Oh, I'm going to set out for my fortune," gaily replied the chicken. "At any rate, I can't fare worse than to be baked in a pie. *Baked in a pie,* forsooth! I think I see myself staying here for that! No, good night, Mrs. Goose. Thank you, for all your kindness; I'm off!"

"Yes, and be stuck again in a bog for your pains," scornfully hissed the old goose, seeing it was useless to remonstrate further. The black chicken had hopped off from the rail, and, its long legs going at a pretty smart pace down the hill, it was soon out of sight.

Brightly rose the sun next morning, clear and cold. The air smelt of everything spicy and suggestive of the approaching holiday. Ben sharpened the old hatchet, the other children running away, for at the last minute they declared they didn't want the chicken killed. They'd rather go without the pie. But Mrs. Pepper and Ben talked until they made them see it was no worse than if they had bought the chicken. Fowls had to be killed and eaten, and they couldn't afford to keep the black chicken any longer. And the mother stopped Phronsie's screams as she ran to hide her head in her lap, and wiped away the tears that ran down the little cheeks. Joel and David relented at last, and joined Ben as he hurried out of doors. And Polly, as she began to wash the breakfast dishes to be ready to help pick the chicken, tried to be gay, and to hum a scrap of a song to reassure Phronsie, when Joel burst into the old kitchen and after him, little Davie.

" 'Tisn't there!" shouted Joel. "No, 'tisn't either!" gasped little David.

Polly whirled around with the dishcloth in her hand, and stared. "What?" she exclaimed.

"No, 'tisn't, I say," screamed Joel, and then he began to cry as hard as he could.

"Oh, Joe, what *is* the matter?" implored Polly, and then Mrs. Pepper, thinking that Joel was hurt, dropped her work to hurry over. And Ben came running in, his ruddy face quite white and his blue eyes big with distress.

"Come, boys, quick, and help me look for him," and he seized Joel's arm. "The chicken's gone," he explained to the distressed group.

Joel gave a louder scream at that.

"Stop, Joel," said Polly. "Oh, isn't it under the shed, Ben?" and she rushed out, dishcloth in hand, followed by Mrs. Pepper and all the others.

"I don't believe he's there," said Ben gloomily, and so it proved. Neither there nor in any other hiding place, no matter how long and thoroughly they searched, could they see the black chicken. There was the old gray goose as usual, stalking around and stretching her long neck to see everything, while the children flew hither and thither calling the chicken. They searched adjoining meadows, and little David ran down to the brook to see if he had fallen in there.

At last, toward noon, tired and hot, they were obliged to give up all hope. And a most distressed little bunch of children went slowly into the Little Brown House; and oh, dismal enough, a pouring rain set in, splashing the small-paned window as if crying with them.

"Don't you see you're making Mamsie feel bad?" whispered Polly hoarsely to Joel, and she pointed over to the corner where Mrs. Pepper was trying to sew.

Little David, at that, went behind the door and struggled to keep back the tears. "I can't help it," sniffled Joel. "Now we can't—we can't—"

"Be still," said Polly, pulling his sleeve, and turning her back on the old cupboard, where the flour bag stood up so smartly, all ready in the old yellow bowl. "Oh!" Then she gave a jump into the middle of the floor.

"Oh, what is it?" they all screamed. Little Davie ran out from behind the door to hear.

"Why," and Polly's brown eyes grew very big, "oh, let's have the old gray goose!"

"The old gray goose!" they all echoed, dreadfully disappointed, while Joel cried harder than ever, and little Davie slipped off toward the door again.

"I shouldn't think you'd say so," said Ben in disapproval, and wondering at Polly, for she always helped out in any trouble.

"Well, now, I think Polly's plan is a very good one," said Mother Pepper, over in her corner. "You can't get the chicken, and you must have your pie; it's as good as commenced, and the old goose ought to be killed, anyway; she's getting so cross, it isn't safe to have her around after she bit Sally Brown the other day. So, as Polly says, why not try it? There'll be a pie, anyway."

"Oh, Mamsie!" cried Polly, flying over to her with rosy cheeks to throw her arms around her neck. "I'm so glad you think it's right to try it," smothering a sigh at thoughts of the pie they might have had.

"Indeed, I do, Polly," said Mrs. Pepper, with a little pat on the brown head; "there, child, now run off to your work," and she picked up her needle to make it fly faster than ever.

"It won't be chicken pie," said Joel disconsolately, who had wiped his black eyes at these first signs of cheer.

"Well," said Ben stoutly, and swallowing hard, "if we can't have chicken pie, why, we must take the next best, and that's goose," and he pretended to laugh heartily at his joke.

"And," said Polly, running back to the little bunch of Peppers in the middle of the kitchen, for Davie wisely concluding since Mamsie thought Polly was right, everything was coming out well somehow, had hurried back to the others, "it's all we've got left; but why didn't the old goose run away, I wonder!"

The idea of the old gray goose running away set them all into such a fit of laughter that when they came out of it the affair was as good as settled. The chicken pie was to be goose pie, and such a goose! The tables were turned decidedly; the old goose, huddling into the shed from the November rain and chuckling to herself, had called down on her own head a sure retribution.

The old gray goose was killed. Polly went bravely to work as if the pleasure of making the most beautiful chicken pie in all the world was before her. And the "children," as Polly and Ben always called the three younger ones in the Pepper brood, laughed and sang and danced about, through all the preparations when they couldn't help them forward, and almost forgot they had ever intended to have a chicken pie.

And they had a pudding on Thanksgiving Day. Oh, yes, and a famous one it was! And at the last minute, old Mrs. Beebe, whose husband kept a little shoeshop in Badgertown Center, stopped in their old wagon, with some beautiful asters.

"Here, children, 's some posies for your table. I've got more'n I want; I'm real sorry you had such a time about your pie." And afterward, in the midst of the festivities at home, she broke out, "I declare, I was 'most beat to see them little dears behave so nice, and flyin' round pretendin' they'd rather have a tough old goose than not."

So Polly had her flowers after all, and she dressed the pie gaily with them, stifling a sigh as she put them over the old goose; and they laughed and ate, to be sure, not so much as if tender chicken had been on their plates. However, it turned out better than they had expected, Polly having persistently boiled it before it was cut up to be baked in the pie. And so they hurried over that part of the repast; they were all in such a hurry to get to that elegant pudding. That was just magnificent, and done to a turn; and to Joel's great delight, fairly beaded with plums. Wasn't it splendid, though!

But at last the feast was all over, and they finally pushed back their chairs, leaving the biggest part of the goose pie untouched.

"Now," said Phronsie, "where's my wissbone, Polly? I want my wissbone, I do."

"Oh, darling," cried Polly, catching her up from the high chair, "You'll have to wait for next Thanksgiving for that. 'Tisn't our fault you can't have it, Phronsie; the black chicken ran away with it."

II

Phronsie's New Shoes

POLLY was working hard to make the fire burn. Something was the matter with the old stove that morning. There had been a big crack for some time at the back that let in the air alarmingly; but Ben had stuffed this up with putty the week before, and it had done very well; but just as Polly had washed up the breakfast dishes this morning, and was going to put her pans of bread into the oven, out tumbled the putty, the old black stove grew cold, and everything came to a standstill. The truth was, the poor old stove was about worn out.

"Oh, dear!" said Polly, "now what's going to be done! Why couldn't it have waited, and Ben's away, too!"

She flew around for something to stop up the hole with; she couldn't find any putty, of course, but nothing else appeared. So she got down on the floor before it and rattled the dampers, and put in more wood. She was kneeling in front of it, her face very red with her exertions, and trying to push a refractory smoldering log of wood into a more "burnable" position, when Phronsie emerged from the bedroom with a very injured expression. "Oh, Polly, I'm so hungry!"

"Why, Phronsie," said Polly, giving the log a push, "you can't be."

"Oh, but I am, Polly," said Phronsie, shaking her head decidedly. "I know I am very hungry."

"Well, wait just a bit, dear—oh, why won't you stay where you ought to! (this to the log). You won't act so when Ben comes, old log! Yes, Phronsie, in a minute!"

"Oh, let me get it, Polly," said the little girl eagerly. "Let me, do!"

"Do you think you can?" said Polly, resting a minute, her black hands stuck straight out before her as she sat on the floor.

"Oh, yes! just as nice," said Phronsie; "it's only some bread, Polly."

Phronsie's delight was to be thought big enough to help, to go to the bread pail that hung under the little old steps that ran down into a small shed or provision room where the Pepper family always kept their slender stock of eatables. "Provision Room" was a good name for it, Polly had once said, because "there's always plenty of room *for* provisions, even if there are no provisions." Polly knew there were some good bits from breakfast that Phronsie could easily get, so she said "yes" rather absently, and Phronsie trotted off.

As she passed the cupboard door, she spied the old bread knife lying on the shelf. "Suppose," thought Phronsie, "I should have to cut some bread—I know how—I do truly. I better take the knife, I think." So she reached up, took the knife, and proceeded to go down the rickety steps. Now, why she should have stumbled this particular morning is more than anybody can tell. Yet, she certainly did; and the first thing Polly heard was a knock, then a rolling, then a sharp and loud cry. "Oh, what *is* the matter, Phronsie dear! I'm coming!"

Springing up, leaving the stove door wide open, she flew over the old steps, finding Phronsie in a little screaming heap at the bottom.

"Oh, darling baby! dear little Phron! don't cry!" said Polly, gathering her up. "There, there."

Sitting on the lowest step with her in her arms, she saw the knife off at some little distance, where it fell on the floor. "Oh, Phronsie, you *didn't* take the knife! Oh!" she added faintly, as she saw a stream of blood roll over Phronsie's pink apron, and great dabs on her face. White as a sheet, Polly never knew how she looked Phronsie over; but she soon saw the trouble came only from her little fat thumb, which, after the first fright, Phronsie protested was the only place that "hurt."

Strange as it may seem, Phronsie had rolled over and over the steps, with the knife in her hand, and sustained no injury beyond a rather deep cut in her thumb, which, however, bled enough to have caused greater fears. Polly sopped up the tears from the child's bloody little face, and rolled the poor thumb in her handkerchief. Then she set Phronsie down, pulled out her feet, felt of her joints, and made her get up and walk back and forth. She drew a long breath. "Well," she said in the greatest relief, "there aren't any bones broken anyway. Oh, Phronsie, do you feel bad anywhere else?"

"No," said little Phronsie, "only my thumb." And she stuck up the little dingy wad, and when she saw it began to cry again.

"There, there, Polly's darling! Now, let's see what we can do!" Polly cooed away as she waddled up the steps with Phronsie in her arms.

The first thing that met her view was the old black stove,

now utterly hateful, with the fire all out. "Oh, you old ugly thing," said she, "think what you've done this morning!" And then she set herself to work over Phronsie.

In the first place, she knew she must get some court plaster, for the cut was bleeding pretty fast. "Now, Phronsie, you sit just as still as everything." Polly had put her in Mammy's old rocking chair. "And, childie, you can have this." A most magnificent thing it seemed to Phronsie, and it stopped her tears at once, for it was a piece of cake, rather hard to be sure, but still beautiful. Polly had saved it up, since it had been given them, as a treat, and the children were going to have it this very night.

There wasn't any court plaster in the house, but she knew old Grandma Bascom had some. Her cottage was just down at the end of the lane; so leaving Phronsie munching her cake, she sped over, and rushed in without knocking, for the old lady was deaf, and wouldn't have heard, anyway. "Oh, if you please, Grandma, Phronsie's got hurt! May I have some court plaster?"

"Why, for the land's sake! Your ma's got hurt, did you say?" said the old lady, stopping her sweeping in the middle of the floor, and leaning on the broom.

"No, marm; *Phronsie!*" screamed Polly in the old lady's ear. "Mamsie's away."

"She is, though?" said Grandma kindly; "now that's too bad; 'n what did you say you want?"

"Court plaster," said Polly, "and could you hurry?—for her thumb's bleeding so."

"Yes, yes, to be sure," said the old lady, laying down her broom and waddling to the cupboard. She brought a big cracked sugar bowl to the table, then adjusted her spectacles, and diving down into the depths brought up paper after paper of herbs, salve, etc., till Polly thought she would go wild.

"Oh, I don't believe you've got any," she said.

"Yes, yes, I have, child; don't be so fast. I remember where I put it; 'twan't in this bowl, after all! I give some to Jane Dusenberry's folks, when her pa got cut with a scythe. You know Jane?" And Grandma paused, and rested both hands on the bowl to relate the dreadful accident.

"Yes, yes," said Polly, "but I can't leave Phronsie. Oh, I can get it for you, if you'll only tell me where it is."

"Hadn't you better run right home, and stay along of Phronsie, dear, and I'll step over and bring it soon's I get on my cap, and," looking around the room, "get fixed up just a mite!" said the old lady.

"If you please, I must have it now," said Polly in utter dismay, who knew what Grandma's "settling her cap," and fixing up, meant.

So Mrs. Bascom finally produced a roll of ancient court plaster out of some unseen drawer in the cupboard, the requisite amount was carefully cut off, and Polly bounded over to poor little Phronsie, whose supply of cake had given out, and who, consequently, as she sat curled up on the old chair, was surveying the poor little bandaged thumb ruefully.

The cut was soon nicely stuck together; her dirty little pink apron taken off; herself washed, and the tangled yellow curls all brushed and stroked by Polly's kind hands. And then Polly began to look around. Her mother, she knew, wouldn't be back until night. She had a chance to make some jackets for the minister's boys, so she was at the parsonage for the day. Ben was chopping wood, one of the odd jobs he picked up now and then; he might be in any time, it only depended on the length of the job. Where Joel and David were, Polly, for the life of her, couldn't have told. Their whereabouts were often shrouded in mystery. In the midst of it, just as Polly was saying, while she gave the last curl a brush, "There, dearie, you're all right again; now I must get at my old stove, hateful thing!" the door opened and in walked Ben. "Oh, Ben!" she cried, and she almost burst into tears, "I'm so glad you've come!"

And Phronsie, with a most important air, began to announce, "I've cut my thumb, oh, and it bled. See, Bensie, see!" And the child held up the wounded little hand carefully wrapped up in a clean, old handkerchief.

"Whew!" whistled Ben, as he stood still. "What's been happening? What is it, Polly?"

"Oh, Ben, such a fall!" answered Polly, kissing Phronsie tenderly; and she then gave him the whole account, interspersed with Phronsie's corrections, when she considered anything left out.

Ben petted Phronsie to her heart's content, patted the poor little hand sympathetically, and tried to think of something he could give her to show his sorrow. But he could think of nothing, till Polly leaned over and whispered something in his ear.

"The very thing!" he shouted.

"Sh! sh! but isn't it?" said Polly, skipping, "if Mammy'll only say yes!"

"What is it, Ben?" said Phronsie. "I'm big enough now to know secrets, and besides, I've cut my thumb."

"I know, Pet, and you wait a little," said Ben, "and you'll know. Halloa, what's the matter with your stove, Polly?"

"Oh, I don't know," said Polly despairingly. "It *won't* burn! The putty fell out, Ben, and I've put in wood, but it won't do anything. And there's my bread, see! It'll be spoilt, and what'll we do, then, I wonder!"

"Shan't we have anything to eat then, Polly?" said little Phronsie, with big eyes.

"Yes," said Ben quickly, "I'll go out and bring home lots of chipmunks, Phronsie, a hundred, say, and we'll hang 'em up all 'round the kitchen, and they'll last us a year."

"I don't think I should like chipmunks, Ben," said the child gravely.

"Oh, Ben, do stop laughing," said Polly, "for it is really dreadful if we can't eat the bread."

Ben was already on his knees before the stove. He fussed and worked over it, and had recourse to his putty again, which Polly remarked might stay as long as he was putting it in; and finally the old stove concluded to make the best of it and try again. So in a short space of time there was a bright, cheerful fire crackling and snapping, the bread was in the oven, and Polly was flying around making up for lost time.

About dinnertime, Joel and David made their appearance, as hungry as two little beavers. Polly's bread wasn't done, so they had to content themselves with the old crusts in addition to their hasty pudding. What a fuss they made over little Phronsie! Everything had to be gone over again for their benefit, the handkerchief to be taken off, and the thumb exhibited, and Joel felt very bad because Polly wouldn't allow him to pull up the court plaster to see exactly what kind of a cut it was. "Just one little end, Polly, I should think you might; it'll stick down again just as easy." But Polly was firm.

Phronsie was the pet of the household. Anything harming her hurt them all. Into each heart she crept, though in a different way, making a place not filled by any other. She was the baby; and to see Phronsie hurt almost took away the boys' appetites, the most touching way in which they could show their grief. After dinner, Joel rehearsed Phronsie's adventure, trying to roll down the old steps, just as she said she did. "Phoh! it don't hurt any," he said.

"Well, but take the knife, Joe," said Davie, "take the knife; that'll hurt, I guess."

"No," said Ben, "we've had enough cuts today; don't let's make any more trouble for Mamsie. What'll she say now, I wonder?"

Nightfall brought Mrs. Pepper, tired with her toil; but oh! so thankful, while she held her baby in her lap, that the kind Father in Heaven had watched over the Little Brown House in her absence.

There was nobody to little Phronsie's mind like her mother. Cuddled up there to her warm breast, while Polly got the cup of tea that had been kept warm for Mamsie by the stove, she told over in childish way the story that Polly had already rehearsed so fully to the mother's anxious ears, not forgetting —and here the child hung her head—the recital of taking the bread knife and the sad consequences ensuing. And then it all came out—Polly and Ben's secret—and after its disclosure Phronsie was decidedly glad that she had been hurt.

For some time, ever since Phronsie could remember, she had been promised a pair of new shoes, very new, for her own; just as soon as the mother could get together money that could be spared for their purchase. She had never had a pair really bought for her. Joel's and David's were generally so worn and holely, long before there was a chance of their outgrowing them, that there was no hope from that quarter.

Once, Mrs. Pepper had made a mistake in buying a pair for David. They proved to be much shorter than at first supposed, and put him in so much pain when wearing them that they were put by for Phronsie; the beauty of them was gone, however, before David complained of them. And once a lady in the village gave Mrs. Pepper a half-worn pair of her little daughter's; so that no "new shoes" had ever come to Phronsie —that greatest delight in a child's life.

For a long time then she had had the promise. It seemed to her interminable, but she waited patiently; only sometimes when she got to thinking of them it seemed as if she couldn't wait any longer. And Polly caught her one day saying to Seraphina, her doll, when she thought no one was near:

"Well, do you suppose I'll *ever* get my new shoes? Not till I get to be a big woman, I guess!"

Polly couldn't stand that, and she privately told Ben that they must contrive some way and get them soon. And now Ben's wood-choppings had helped some, and Mrs. Pepper had been able to get more work than usual, so that Polly, during that dismal morning, had been thinking perhaps now they could do it. And when would they ever want to do more for poor little Phronsie! She wouldn't be able to play for some time, for the cut would be very painful. Oh, if Mammy would only say yes!

And Mrs. Pepper had said "yes!" and the children had shouted and shown in different ways their delight; only Phronsie, the one most interested, sitting there in her mother's lap, had just clasped her little hands together as tight as she could for the thumb, and given an ecstatic long sigh.

So it was all settled—"really and truly settled," as Phronsie said. Tomorrow Polly and Ben should take her to the town to be fitted, if Mr. Brown would let them have his wagon.

"Oh, mayn't we go, too?" cried Joel. "We can sit in behind. Say, now, Mammy, mayn't we?"

"Do, Mammy!" said David.

"Well, I don't see why not, I'm sure," said Mrs. Pepper. " 'Twon't cost anything; the wagon's going, anyway, and the horse is strong—if you'll be good, Joey."

"Oh, won't I, though!" said Joel, giving his mother a hearty kiss, while little David beamed his satisfaction.

Ben ran over to Deacon Brown's to ask him about the horse and wagon. The answer was all right, for the Deacon wanted him to do an errand in town; so the wildest hilarity reigned in the Pepper household that night.

"Oh, Ben, will they be red tops, do you think?" whispered little Phronsie privately.

"Yes, I guess so, Puss," whispered Ben, back again, inwardly resolving if there *was* a pair of red-topped shoes in the store, that were otherwise just right, Phronsie should have them.

So on the morrow, after they had their early dinner, the old wagon was driven up to the door with a flourish by Ben, who guided the ancient but tough old roadster with a dignity befitting a better horse. Joel and David had already secured reserved seats, having run over ahead to the Deacon's shed and got in first. And there they sat, dangling their legs over the back of the wagon as they laughed and crowed in utter delight.

Phronsie stood in the doorway holding Polly's hand. It was a decidedly solemn undertaking to her, this setting out on this great and weighty expedition, and the child's heart was about as full as it could hold of anticipation and happiness. Oh, the pains that had been taken to get her ready! Ben said that Polly began before they got up in the morning.

At any rate, everything had been brushed, patted, and pulled into place on Phronsie a dozen times by each member of the family before they were quite satisfied. But, at last, they had acknowledged that nothing more could be done; and, as Polly tied the waves of yellow hair back with a little blue bow, Mrs. Pepper stepped off, set her head on one side critically, and said:

"Well, I'm sure, child, if you only behave as well as you look, you'll do!"

And then Phronsie was told to go and sit in her little chair and not move till it was time to put on her hood and sack. Any other child than Phronsie would have hated all this fuss and trouble, but to her it was only part of the extreme delight; so she stuck out the patched, worn little shoes before her, and thought of the new ones.

"Oh, Ben's coming, Polly!" called Mrs. Pepper, from the window where she sat sewing. "He's just driving down the hill! Hurry, child! I'll put on Phronsie's things."

"Yes, Mamsie," said Polly, from the bedroom, in a great twitter, "I'm coming."

And now they were all ready, and Mrs. Pepper on the steps gave her last injunction to Polly, who held tightly the old leather purse, with the precious money, in her hand—"to be sure and take the right change," and "to get them plenty broad" (not the change, but the shoes), and "not to let anything happen to Phronsie"; "oh! and not to get them 'rights and lefts,' you know, but 'evens,' Polly"—all of which directions she had given carefully before. All this made great confusion, of course, but it only added to the general delight, while Joel and David were screaming in chorus for them to "come or they'd be late!"

But at last they were off, and Mrs. Pepper from the doorstep shaded her eyes with her hands—perhaps the sun was too bright for them. Her precious load of little ones; might she only have more sunshine to put into their lives! Well, at least, they should enjoy this, bless them!

Merry was the ride to town. Once Polly was afraid she had dropped the old purse when she leaned over to tie Phronsie's tippet a little tighter, and they were all aghast for a minute at this tremendous fright; but, on Ben's pulling up the old horse, she found it in her lap safe and sound. So they were merrier than ever out of contrast, and Deacon Brown's horse so far overcame his usual melancholy manner as to quite enjoy the jolly crowd behind him, and to gallop and plunge in quite a festive manner along the road.

At last they turned into the village street and came in sight of the shops. Then it was that Phronsie sat straight up and began to look eagerly from one side to the other. They passed the milliner's, gay with ribbons and spring bonnets, and two or three other stores of various descriptions, until they came to a little unpretending shop, crowded in between two others, over whose green door hung the modest sign of "J. Beebe, Boots and Shoes."

When Phronsie caught sight of the little window strung with shoes of every size, from the littlest wee ones up, she cried out, "Oh, there 'tis, Ben! there 'tis! Oh, do stop!" long before they reached it.

"Yes, yes, child," said Polly, "Ben's going to. Joe, now you mustn't! You know you told Mamsie you'd be good." For Polly saw premonitory signs of Joe's giving one of his awful whoops to announce their arrival.

The whoop died away in Joe's throat as he reflected he never should get another chance to come "to town" with Polly, who was quite fastidious as to manners, if he indulged too boisterously now.

So they bundled out and up the steps, Joel quite gallantly opening the door for his sisters, to atone; while Ben fastened the horse to the well-worn post.

Old Mr. Beebe, smiling at the thought of customers, came, rubbing his hands, out from his little room at the back that served his old wife and himself as both parlor and kitchen. Oh, how magnificent it all looked to Phronsie! Oh, so many shoes, and such beautiful ones! Where did all the people live who could want so many! Great green things, that she found afterward were boxes, had shoes and slippers hanging and dangling to them; and then, away up by the top of the shelf were boots—oh, as big as Ben's!—and all around the little dingy room were rubbers, shoes, and slippers wherever there was a spot big enough to contain them. And, over and above it all, such a lovely smell of leather. Well, it was the most delightful place!

"And now, my little dears, what can I do for you today?" said old Mr. Beebe, pleasantly looking from one to another of the happy group, including Ben who had now joined them.

"If you please," said Polly with quite a matronly air, "it's for Phronsie."

"Is it, though?" said the old man. "Then we must get her a nice pair, don't you think?" And he beamed at her so kindly over his old spectacles that he quite won her heart over again, for the Pepper children were always delighted when an errand took them to his little shop; he was such a kindly, fresh, little old man.

"Now if you'll sit right down here, my little girl, we'll see what we can do for you." And he brought a little wooden chair and placed it in the middle of the room.

Obediently, Phronsie sat down and confidently put her rusty little patched shoe upon Mr. Beebe's knee.

"So, so!" he said, "and you thought you'd have a new pair of shoes this morning, and you thought you'd see what I'd got for you, didn't you?" he added to make conversation, the others meanwhile encircling Phronsie and watching her with the most intense interest.

"Oh, I've never had a pair for my very own," said the little girl simply.

"Haven't you, now?" said the old man kindly. "Well, then, I don't see but we must make this the best pair you've ever bought," and he laughed and shook his sides till his spectacles nearly tumbled off; and all the children laughed with him, he was so jolly.

Then he got up and rummaged among some boxes over in the corner, until he emerged from them with two or three pairs of little shoes hanging over his arm.

"There, now, here's a pair," he said, and he proceeded to try on a beautiful shiny shoe over Phronsie's little red stocking. It just fitted; but Polly saw to her dismay that it was "rights and lefts."

"Oh, Ben," she whispered to him aside, "they won't do, and they're lovely; for Mamsie said, you know, we must be *sure* to get 'evens.' "

"Well, we can try again, then," said Ben, "he's got plenty more, I s'pose." And he told Mr. Beebe the difficulty.

But Ben was wrong. It wasn't so easy to fit Phronsie's little fat foot thus nicely again, and Mr. Beebe brought forward shoe after shoe until they were almost in despair.

In the meantime, Ben kept his own counsel. He walked around the shop to see if he could possibly spy out a pair of red-topped ones. If he couldn't, he wasn't going to take away Phronsie's pleasure in the plain ones by mentioning it. But no delightful red-topped ones appeared, or showed signs of appearing, and he had almost given up the idea, when—

"Stay! wait a bit!" said the old man. "Now I remember I made a pair once for the squire's little daughter down to the Point, but her ma didn't take 'em, she thought they were too small. Maybe they'll just fit. I shouldn't wonder, now."

And he ambled away to the farther part of the room; there, from underneath a shelf, he produced a pair, saying as he brought them toward the children, "But perhaps you'll object to them for being red-tops."

"*Object* to them!" Phronsie screamed right out. "Oh, Ben,

he *did* have them!" And then she was so ashamed she hid her face in Polly's cloak, while Ben explained to delighted Mr. Beebe, who began to try them on.

Ben and Polly both held their breath. What if they shouldn't fit! But on the little shoe went; snugly it buttoned up; and then Mr. Beebe told Phronsie to stand up.

"Stamp in it, child. Why, it looks as if 'twas made for her, don't it?" he said, pleased almost as the children.

The price, too, was just right. Polly didn't know, as she counted out the money into the old man's hand, that at least a quarter of their value was deducted. Phronsie wouldn't have the shoe taken off; so the old man cut the string, buttoned on its mate, and rolled up the poor little old ones in a bit of newspaper.

"There, now,"—and then he put into her hand a most beautiful buttonhook; it had a bright little handle that looked like silver, and it was just as cunning as it could be—"that's from me! And you'll come and see the old man again, won't you, dear, and tell him how the shoes go?"

And then Mrs. Beebe had to come in to see the "Pepper children" and to ask after their mother; and to hear all about Phronsie's accident of the day before; and then she must run out and get a doughnut apiece for them all, out of the big stone pot; and for Phronsie, a big piece of cinnamon candy extra.

And then they all said "Good-by," and "Oh, thank you!" added Polly, "ever so much!"

Out again and into the old wagon.

"I say," said Joel, "that's prime! Don't I wish some of us had to get new shoes every day!" And he settled back to a huge bit of his doughnut.

Over, back, and away they went home, only stopping to do Deacon Brown's errand. Phronsie would keep sticking her feet out from under the old shawl to be sure that her shoes were really there, despite Polly's fear that she would take cold; for it was getting toward evening and a little chilly.

Such an uproar as they had when they got home. The shoes were admired and admired again, Mrs. Pepper protesting that she couldn't have done better if she had gone herself; as indeed she couldn't. And she praised the children heartily for their good behavior. As for Phronsie, she danced around the old kitchen till the red-tops seemed only little specks of color.

"I'm going to have 'em to sleep with me anyway, Polly," she declared, as Polly insisted on taking them off at last.

So to bed Phronsie trudged, grasping the precious shoes tightly to her breast. And when Polly went to get into the big bed with her mother, she peeped the last thing at Phronsie and laughed right out. One small, red-topped shoe was clasped in the little well hand; the other, tucked up on the pillow, had settled right down over her nose.

III

The Little Tin Plate

"Oh, dear me!" exclaimed Polly, out in the Provision Room. "What's that?"

A loud noise struck her ear, and she dropped the end of the big bag, out of which she was getting some potatoes for dinner and stopped to listen. There it was again.

"Oh, my goodness me!" Polly gave a merry little laugh, "It's at the door," and dropping the tin pan she had brought for the potatoes, she skipped nimbly over the big bag. "P'raps it's somebody come to call"; for Polly dearly loved to be elegant, and nothing could have been so truly magnificent as to have callers in their very best clothes come and rap at the old green door. She had often imagined how they would look. And now, "Perhaps—just perhaps," she thought, as she skipped along over the rickety steps leading up to the kitchen, "that there is one really and truly come to see us!"

She raced through the kitchen and threw open the old door, the color flying up to her brown hair, and her eyes sparkling. A man was standing on the old flat stone, and pressed up close to the green door.

"Oh, Mr. Beggs!" cried Polly, the color dropping all out of her cheek in her disappointment. He wasn't a caller, not a bit of it, only the ragman who drove through Badgertown once in a while, and collected the rags and old bottles at the houses. And in return he gave tinware of every description and brooms and wooden pails. There, off by the old gate, was his big red cart, waiting in the road.

"Yes, I've come." Mr. Beggs pushed back his flapping straw hat from his forehead, and pulling out a big red cotton handkerchief from the pocket of his much-worn linen coat that flapped around his legs, he wiped his forehead vigorously. "Call'ated your ma was ready maybe to trade today."

"We don't have many rags, Mr. Beggs," said Polly, stifling her disappointment. "You know Mamsie told you not to trouble to stop often because—"

"I know—I know," said Mr. Beggs, interrupting. Then he leaned against the door casing to rest on one foot while he talked. "But then I alwus d'rather stop, for you might get ready to trade. An' tain't no trouble to me, cause it rests th' horse. Is the boys to home?"

"No," said Polly, "they went off to dig flagroot."

"Pshaw, now." The ragman pushed the old straw hat farther off from his head till it began to look like a new background for it. "Why couldn't they have dug flagroot any other day, pray tell!" he exclaimed in vexation. "I was a-goin' to take 'em to ride on my cart."

"Oh, dear me!" exclaimed Polly, just as much distressed, and clasping her hands, "now, isn't that too bad, Mr. Beggs!"

" 'Tis," said Mr. Beggs gloomily. "I got to go all down 'round about here, an' over to the Hollow."

Polly couldn't say anything. To go "all down 'round about here and over to the Hollow" on top of the red cart was such an enchanting thing, and now the boys must lose it all!

"An' I ain't comin' this way agin this summer," said Mr. Beggs, as if the other statement was not as bad as it possibly could be.

"Oh, dear me!" said Polly again.

"I s'pose you an' th' little gal wouldn't go, now." The ragman pointed a dingy thumb into the kitchen to indicate Phronsie.

For one wild moment Polly thought, "Oh, Mamsie wouldn't care, and I never get the chance if the boys are home." And she took one rapturous step to get Phronsie from the bedroom where she was washing "Baby"; then she turned and stood quite still. "No," she said.

"Well, you come right along," said Mr. Beggs, well pleased to see her start for Phronsie. "I'll wait for ye an' th' little gal," and he was already slouching down to the old gate.

"I can't go," called Polly after him.

"Yes, come right along," the ragman kept saying, so of course he couldn't hear anyone else talk.

"I can't go, and Phronsie can't either." Polly panted it out as she went flying down the path after him, and she took hold of the end of his old brown linen coat as he had one foot on the trace preparing to jump up to his seat.

"Pshaw, now!" exclaimed Mr. Beggs, pausing to regard her ruefully. "Ye can't?"

"No," said Polly. She couldn't trust herself to look at the dear, delightful tin things hanging all down the side of the cart. What a lovely music they must make jingling together as the old horse jogged along on his way! And the brooms stuck up at the corners, and smelling so nice and new, and the quantities of other things, they might be the most beautiful in all the world hidden within, that Mr. Beggs would take out when customers were ready to buy. And she must give it all up!

"Pshaw, now—yer ma won't care, an' I ain't a-comin' this way agin this summer." Mr. Beggs didn't take his foot from the trace while he argued it out. "An' I'm goin' all down 'round about here, an' home by the Hollow."

"Oh, dear!" Polly turned off and threw herself down on the grass just beside the road. "I must go," she cried passionately to herself. "I've never been, and I can't get the chance again." Then Mamsie's face seemed to hop right up before her, saying only one word, "Polly."

"So run along an' git your bunnit, an' bring th' little gal." Mr. Beggs, seeing everything now fixed to his satisfaction, mounted his cart, and took up the well-worn leather reins.

"No," said Polly. She was standing by the cart now. "I can't go, Mr. Beggs. I thank you, sir, very much, but Mamsie wouldn't like it; that is, I can't ask her." The brown eyes seemed to say more than the words, for the ragman, giving a long whistle to vent his regrets, clacked to the old horse, and away the red cart rumbled down the dusty road, leaving Polly standing on the grass by its side.

And the two little boys, hurrying around by the back way, found her so, just as the red cart turned the corner of the road.

"Joel!" cried Polly, turning around. "Oh, I thought you'd gone to dig flagroot."

"So we did," grumbled Joel, "but Davie forgot the knife."

"I did, Polly," confessed little Davie, hanging his head.

"Never mind, now," cried Polly, in such a twitter she jumbled up her words, "the ragman—Mr. Beggs—oh, Joe, run after him—"

"Where?" cried Joel, his black eyes roving wildly. To have Mr. Beggs with them was an event not to be missed. "Where, Polly?" twitching her sleeve.

"There," Polly cried, just as wildly and pointing in the

direction in which the ragman had disappeared. "Oh, run, Joe—he's been here to take you and Davie to ride on his cart."

It wasn't necessary to tell Joel to run after that, and even Davie showed a nimble pair of heels, and presently they were lost to view, and Polly was left alone to go in and get the potatoes for dinner.

Joel roared so hard at every step of the road in pursuit of the red cart that when he finally did come up with it he had little breath left. Mr. Beggs had slackened speed at the beginning of the hill, and was now ruminating sourly over his failure to give pleasure to the Little Brown House people, when he heard a faint piping sound that made him crane his neck to look around the stack of brooms to see where it came from. "We're going," gasped Davie, running to the side of Joel, both boys having anxious hands outspread.

"Jerusalem, an' th' natives!" ejaculated the ragman, pulling the old horse up straight. "I thought you was a-diggin' flagroot."

"We were," gasped David. But it wasn't until they were both fairly on the cart and beside Mr. Beggs on the seat that breath could be wasted to relate the whole, "Only I forgot the big knife."

"I'll drive," declared Joel promptly. To talk about digging flagroot was well enough when there was nothing greater as a subject, but now—and he made a dash at the leather reins.

"Not yit," said the ragman, holding them fast in his horny hand. "Well, I never!" and he slapped his knee with the other fist. "Ain't this just—well, Jerusalem, an' th' natives—'tis!"

"When can I, say?" Joel pounded Mr. Beggs's knee, and fastened his black eyes pleadingly on the face under the old straw hat. Little Davie had lapsed into a state of silent bliss, and was hanging to the edge of the seat where it turned up on the outside. "Say, Mr. Beggs, when will you let me drive?"

"You be still," said Mr. Beggs, turning a pair of ruddy cheeks on which a broad smile of satisfaction played. "I'll let you drive when the time comes."

"When is it coming?" asked Joel in impatience.

" 'Tain't never comin'," said Mr. Beggs, "if you ain't still, an' behave yourself."

Joel, very much alarmed at this, sank back in his seat, and kept still till it seemed to him that the ragman had forgotten his promise, so he slid forward and began to clamor again.

"Can I—you said you would," he teased, stretching out both brown little hands.

"I said when 'twas time," replied Mr. Beggs coolly.

" 'Tisn't ever going to be time," declared Joel, quite gone in despair.

The ragman burst out laughing, but seeing Joel's face, and also that little Davie on the other side was leaning forward much disturbed since something that Joel didn't like was being said, he added kindly, "Now, Joel, I'll let you take th' reins when we come to that house. See it?" and he pointed off with his whip.

"Where—where?" cried Joel eagerly, and jumping up to his feet.

"Sit down," cried Mr. Beggs, pulling him back. "Land o' Goshen, you'll be out an' break your neck; then you never'd go with me agin, an' what would your ma say?"

"Well, where is the house?" cried Joel, struggling to get a sight of it. "I can't see it."

"You will in a minnit—there, now, look."

It wasn't necessary to advise this as Joel's black eyes were doing their best to acquaint their owner with an idea as to how soon the little brown hands could hold those reins. And at last he squealed right out, "Oh, there 'tis—oh, goody! I'm

going to drive, Dave, I am, soon's we git up to that house,"
pointing to a red farmhouse set back from the road and in
between two tall poplars.

When they arrived, he was in great excitement, not caring
in the least for the pleasure of hearing Mr. Beggs calling out,
"*Ra-ags—Ra-ags,*" in a tone that began in a sort of a roar, and
ended in a little fine squeal that seemed to vanish into thin
air; but it always brought every farmer's wife and daughter
to the window or door, eager to turn the last year's or half
year's supply of carefully hoarded rags and old bottles to
good account. For sometimes, if Mr. Beggs could not dispose
of his tinware and brooms and pails which, of course, he
much preferred to do, he would count out pennies and five-
cent pieces, so that new ribbons or a bit of lace would be
possible for such as cared for finery.

But little Davie, if it were possible to add to his bliss as he
sat there clinging to the edge of his seat on the top of the red
cart, now experienced that increase of delight, and he hung
entranced as Mr. Beggs bawled again impressively, "*Ra-ags—
Ra-ags!*" as they came almost up to the poplars.

A woman thrust her head in a sweeping cap out of the side
door. "The ragman's here, Em'line!" she screamed. Then she
ran out to the grassplot. "Here, stop, Mr. Beggs," she called
frantically, waving both hands.

"All right, marm," said the ragman, pulling up his old
horse. "I'm a-stoppin'; you needn't screech so."

"You said I might drive when we got here." Joel turned
on him perfectly furious, his black eyes flashing.

"Well, an' so you may," replied Mr. Beggs composedly,
preparing to get down over the wheel. "But we ain't a-goin'
to run over Mis' Hinman. When we start from here, Joel, you
can have them lines. Now, then, both o' you boys can git down

an' stretch your legs, while I dicker with th' women folks."

Joel, seeing that this was all he could get, suffered himself to be helped down from the cart, and little Davie followed, for both of them hung absorbed over the exciting bargaining and exchange that now took place.

"There's another bag in the wood chamber," said Mrs. Hinman, as Em'line, a tall, thin maiden not over young, with her red hair done up in a hard twist like a doorknob on the back of her head, came hastily dragging after her a swelled-up bag over the grass. "You've forgot that."

"I hain't forgot it," said Em'line tartly, releasing the bag on the ground by the side of the red cart, "but I can't get 'em both to once. My arm's 'most broke with this one."

Mrs. Hinman's faded eyes took a new light. "You'll give us good weight, Mr. Beggs," she said greedily.

"I'll give you th' weight that 'tis," said the ragman, lifting out from under his seat the long iron steelyards.

Em'line ran her eyes, a second edition of her mother's, over the two little figures crowding up at the ragman's elbow. "Can't one o' them boys git that other bag o' rags?" she said.

"Oh, you don't want to let 'em in th' house," said Mrs. Hinman in dismay.

"They won't do no hurt," said Em'line carelessly; "it's in th' wood chamber."

"But they've got to go through th' kitchen," protested her mother, "an' you don't know who they be."

"Excuse me," said the ragman with great dignity, "but I don't take folks a-ridin' with me on this cart unless I do know who they be, Mis' Hinman."

"Well, they're boys," said Mrs. Hinman, holding to her point, notwithstanding her desire to get to trading.

"Yes, to be sure, they *is* boys," said Mr. Beggs; "I ain't a-denyin' that," and running the hook of the steelyards through the tied strings of the bags, "but they're Mis' Pepper's boys, an' that makes a difference."

"Not Mis' Pepper over to Badgertown, who lives in that little brown house!" exclaimed Mrs. Hinman.

"Yes, marm." With that the ragman lifted the steelyards and gave the bag a swing, endeavoring to slide the hook along the iron bar to adjust the weight, peering at it closely while he held the whole thing aloft.

"Take care—it's a-tetchin' you," screamed Mrs. Hinman, and trying to push the bag of rags away from the long linen coat.

Mr. Beggs turned on her an angry face. "When I weigh rags, I weigh 'em, Mis' Hinman," he said, "or else I never drive a trade with nobody."

Thus admonished, Mrs. Hinman folded her nervous hands across her apron, and held herself in check.

"Well, are those boys a-goin' in after that other bag?" said Em'line. "I know I ain't—my arm's broke almost, draggin' this one down." But Mr. Beggs, not appearing to hear, and certainly Joel and David, so absorbed over the excitement of seeing the rags weighed that they couldn't be expected to understand what was wanted of them, it really began to look as if Em'line would have to go after the other bag herself if she wanted it brought down.

"Twelve—twelve an' a ha-alf," said Mr. Beggs, slowly moving the hook along a hair's breadth.

"It's more'n that," broke in Mrs. Hinman, standing on tiptoe to peer over his arm.

"Of course it is," declared Em'line; "it weighs a lot more. It most broke my arm a-draggin' it along," she added, as if bringing out a wholly new statement.

"Th' bag's fairly busting, it's so full," contributed her mother indignantly.

"Rags weigh light; it takes a good many to make a pound," said Mr. Beggs oracularly, and squinting at the numbers on the iron rod.

"I don't care if they is, an' mine are good hefty ones—all them pieces after we got through with Sarah's jacket, you know, Em'line," she nodded across Mr. Beggs's big back.

"Don't I know, Ma?" said Em'line thriftily; "of course there's lots o' money in that bag o' rags."

"Twelve pounds an' half an ounce," declared Mr. Beggs, dumping the bag on the grass and slipping out the iron hook from the strings. "There's every bit as much as 'tis, an' if you want to sell 'em to some other ragman, why, I don't care," he added squarely.

"Oh, we ain't a-goin' to sell 'em to no one else, Mr. Beggs," Mrs. Hinman made haste to say in alarm. "Only we did think there was a little more weight to 'em—jest a leetle more."

"That's every scrap there is," declared Mr. Beggs, pushing back his straw hat from his forehead, and beginning to put up his steelyards under his seat.

"An' there's another bag, you know," cried Em'line. "Say, ain't one o' them boys goin' to bring it down for me?"

"I d'no, I'm sure," replied Mr. Beggs. "That's as they say. I don't invite folks to go a-ridin' with me on my cart an' then work 'em while they're a-visitin'."

"Well, don't they want to?" said Em'line; "say, don't you?" and she turned to Joel.

"Want to what?" demanded Joel, turning his black eyes on her, since the delights of weighing the rags was over.

"Go into th' house an' get another bag o' rags," said Em'line wheedlingly.

"May I bring 'em out," cried Joel, his black eyes sparkling. "May I?"

"Yes, if you're a good boy," said Em'line.

"Oh, whickets!" screamed Joel, springing off. "Come on, Dave."

"At th' head o' th' stairs from th' kitchen," screamed Em'line after him, in a jubilant little shriek.

"An' don't tetch nothin' in th' kitchen," Mrs. Hinman called shrilly. "You better go with 'em, Em'line," she advised anxiously.

"There ain't no need," said Em'line, yet she went lazily over the grass and disappeared in the kitchen doorway. And presently down came Joel and David carrying between them a bag as much bigger as possible than the first one.

"There, now, I guess you'll see rags, Mr. Beggs," said Em'line, triumphantly following them; "them's mine," as the boys deposited the bag on the grass, and then stood up to draw a long breath.

"Whew!" whistled the ragman, and then to fill up conversation, he added, "I guess you're goin' to git married, Miss Em'line—"

Em'line simpered, and hung her head with the little hard knob of red hair at the back. "How'd you guess, Mr. Beggs?"

"The Land o' Goshen, ye be!" exclaimed the ragman in great surprise. "Well, who's th' man, pray tell?"

"It's Isr'el Sawyer," said Mrs. Hinman quickly. "An' we better be a settlin' up this rag business, for I've got all my work a-waitin' for me in th' house."

The ragman smothered something in his straggly beard that, if heard, would not be very complimentary to Isr'el Sawyer's good judgment. "That's so, Mis' Hinman," he declared briskly. "Well, now, we must see what this 'ere bag weighs. 'Tis heftier, ain't it?"

"I sh'd think 'twas," cried Em'line, with greedy eyes and an expansive smile.

"Well, now, bein's you're goin' to git married, I s'pose we

must make these rags come to as much as possible. Goin' to take 'em out in tin?" All the while he was adjusting the iron hook in place on the steelyards and getting ready for the final swing of the bag.

"I guess not," snapped Em'line; "I'm goin' to have money an' nothin' else."

"I'd just as lieves," assented Mr. Beggs. "There she goes!" Then, when the bag ceased to tremble as it hung from the hook, and the final notch on the long bar had been decided on, "Fif—teen pounds an' a quarter—"

"There's twice as much," cried Em'line, with an angry twitch at the steelyards. "Let me weigh 'em myself."

"No, sir—ee!" declared Mr. Beggs, quite insulted. "No one does th' weighin' on them steelyards but myself. You can see all you want to, an' there 'tis, an' you can't make no more, not a mite, but fifteen pounds an' a quarter. But I ain't anxious to trade with you today, Miss Em'line," and he slid out the hook from the strings of the bag. "So after you've picked out your tinware, Mis' Hinman, or do you want a broom today, or do you want money, I ain't partic'lar which, why, I'll say good day to ye both."

"There, now, you see, Em'line," cried her mother, "how you bite your nose off to spite your face! Now you won't sell them old rags at all, for another man won't come along, like enough, who'll buy 'em, in a dog's age."

Em'line stood biting her lips and tapping the ground with an irritable foot. "You can have 'em," at last she said to Mr. Beggs.

"I ain't a-goin' to take 'em unless you're satisfied," said the ragman. "Land, I can't make 'em weigh more'n they do. You goin' to take tin, or a broom, or money, Mis' Hinman?" he turned around to her.

"I'll take a broom," said Mrs. Hinman; "I got to; mine's all worn down to th' handle. What you got new in tin, Mr. Beggs?"

"A full assortment." He threw open the side of the red cart, and she stuck in her head, still in its sweeping cap, to gloat over its shining contents. "My! I guess you have been stockin' up!"

" 'Tis a pretty good lot," said Mr. Beggs, affecting indifference. "You said a broom, didn't ye, Mis' Hinman?" He stepped up on the hub of the nearest wheel and handed down one. "That's prime," he declared.

"I d'no's I will take a broom," said Mrs. Hinman discontentedly, and not looking at it, but with her eyes glued to the shining interior of the cart, "but then I've got to, for by'm by I'll have to sweep with the handle. How much is that skimmer?" with an abrupt finger pointing to the article.

"Twenty cents," said Mr. Beggs.

"That's dretful dear," said Mrs. Hinman. "Well, let's see your broom," so she pulled away her head from its close proximity to the fascinating door and put out her hand. "Hain't you got one that ain't so thin along th' edge?" running her fingers over it. " 'Tain't near as good a one as th' one I bought last of you, Mr. Beggs."

"I thought this was pretty fair for a broom," said the ragman, who had stepped down from the hub of the wheel. He now hopped up again, and after careful examination of his stock in trade, so far as brooms were concerned, got back to the ground again with one in his hand. "There, if you like that any better you're free to choose," he said obligingly.

"This one's all uneven—seems so there ain't no two wisps alike," said Mrs. Hinman, turning the broom over and over and pinching it here and there. "When I buy a broom, I want one, Mr. Beggs."

"All right," said the ragman, so he mounted the hub of

the wheel again. "There," he said, coming down with a great clatter, "now, take your pick an' go over th' hull lot," and he deposited the entire bunch on the grass.

When the trading was done, so far as Mrs. Hinman was concerned, who went carefully over and over the collection of brooms laid out for her inspection on the grass, she finally decided that she wouldn't take a broom at all, but some article of tin. And it took so long to pick these over and select from the lot that Em'line finally broke in—"Well, I know I ain't goin' to stand here all day. Are you goin' to pay me my money or not, Mr. Beggs?"

"If you're satisfied," said the ragman.

"I'll sell 'em to you, anyway," said Em'line, "an' that's enough." So Mr. Beggs took out an old leather bag from his trousers' pocket and counted out the money, which she seized and stalked into the house, grumbling all the way over the grass.

"And now," said Mr. Beggs, stowing away the two bags of rags on his cart, "if you've got through turnin' over that tin, marm, I'll just start on my way."

"Can't you throw in that?" asked Mrs. Hinman, diving into the cart to hold up a little tin plate with big letters all around its edge. "I sh'd admire to have it to give John's little boy."

"No, I can't," Mr. Beggs shook his head decidedly. "An' John Hinman jest a-rollin' in money!" he declared wrathfully to himself.

"I'll take the skimmer," decided Mrs. Hinman, tossing back the little tin plate scornfully into the cart. "Tain't wuth twenty cents, but if you won't take no less—"

"I won't take no less," said Mr. Beggs, picking up his brooms from the grass and piling them up on the cart, "as I'm a-givin' it to you now 'most a cent an' a half off; your rags don't come to more'n a leetle over eighteen cents. I don't give skimmers *entirely* away, Mis' Hinman." Then he slammed to the door of the red cart. "Now, then, boys," to Joel and David, who had been standing quite still hanging on every word, "hop up lively."

"Are you going?" screamed Joel, all awake to the fact that now was the time when those leather reins were to be put into his hands, and beginning a wild scramble for the top of the cart, little Davie pitching after.

"I s'pose we'd better be," said Mr. Beggs grimly, "unless we spend th' mornin' here. Well, good day, Mis' Hinman."

But she neither saw nor heard him, busy as she was picking her way across the grass, her new skimmer grasped in her hard old hand.

"She beats th' Dutch *an'* Tom Walker!" exclaimed Mr. Beggs. It was all that escaped him, but as he repeated it over and over, perhaps no more was needed. And as the old horse had been somewhat revived by his long rest, he now concluded to show off his best speed. Joel sat up as straight as he could, his brown little hands thrust stiffly out, grasping the old leather reins in a great state of excitement, and crying out, "G'lang, there—g'lang!" while little Davie plunged into terror, clung with one hand to the edge of his seat, and the other to Joel's jacket to keep him from falling out.

"Ye're enjoyin' it, ain't ye?" Mr. Beggs leaned over to peer at Joel's red cheeks.

"It's prime!" cried Joel. "G'lang there—see him go, Dave, I'm driving," he announced.

"Isn't he going *very* fast?" asked little Dave timidly, not being able to look around, having all he could do to hold on with both hands.

"Gee—whiz!" sang Joel, wishing Polly was there to see him, and how he was exactly as big as Ben.

"Oh, don't, Joel," begged Davie, "make him go any faster."

"Phoo! that's nothin'," said Joel magnificently; "I'm going to take the whip," and he broke away from David's clutch to lean forward.

"Oh, don't!" screamed little Davie. "Oh, Mr. Beggs, don't let him," he implored.

"You needn't worry," said Mr. Beggs, settling Joel back with a big hand. "Nobody takes that whip on this cart but Peter Beggs."

"I don't want the whip," said Joel, grasping the reins tighter than ever. "G'lang there—see me drive, Dave!"

"An' you're goin' to drive on th' way home," said Mr. Beggs, leaning over to fling the words to little Davie.

"You're going to drive on the way home—oh, goody!" screamed Joel, as away the old horse jogged, so surprised at such unwonted jollity back of him that he forgot to slow down to his accustomed gait.

It was well along toward noon when Phronsie, who had been watching for a long time in the front yard, scrambled over the flat doorstone. "They're coming, Polly," she screamed.

"Oh, no, I guess not, Pet," said Polly, who had been summoned several times to hurry and welcome the boys—"we shall hear them fast enough. Run out and play, child."

"But they are, Polly, coming, really and truly," declared Phronsie in an injured voice, and her lip trembled. So Polly flung down the broom where she was sweeping and taking Phronsie's hand ran out to see. And, sure enough, there they were, the old horse coming up in front of the gate in grand style, and Joel waving both hands and hooraying with all his might from the high seat of the red cart, little Davie between him and Mr. Beggs, and—oh, most wonderful sight—holding the reins and driving! Polly and Phronsie ran as fast as they could to the road.

"I drove 'most all the way over there," screamed Joel, before he clambered over the wheel.

"Did you, Joey?" cried Polly, in a transport, while Mr. Beggs, now out on the ground, helped little David down. "And to think that Davie drove home!" as he ran up to her, his blue eyes shining with excitement and his cheeks as pink as could be.

"I didn't drive all the way," said little Davie, rubbing his hands together and trying not to think that they smarted.

"Well, you drove some," said Polly happily. "Just think of that, Davie."

And just then, whether it was that the old horse felt the excitement of the morning too much for his nerves, no one knew, but he started suddenly, and before Mr. Beggs could even shout out "whoa!" or clutch the leather reins dangling over the harness, away he went with a few clumsy jerks, and off flew Em'line's bag of rags, the strings untying and a good part of the ravelings and snippings of her wedding clothes scattered in the dusty road.

And away clattered Mr. Beggs after his horse, Joel whooping and hallooing at his heels, and little Davie following as fast as he could.

"Oh, dear me!" exclaimed Polly, clasping her hands. She longed to run, too, and help to catch good Mr. Beggs's horse, but there was Phronsie—no, she must stay and take care of her.

"Won't he ever come back?" asked Phronsie, and the tears began to come.

"Oh, yes, Pet," said Polly cheerfully. "There, I'll lift you up to the gate, so you can see better—"

So Phronsie put up her little arms, and Polly lifted her and set her in a good place on the old post. "Now then, says I, look sharp, Phronsie, and pretty soon you'll see Mr. Beggs and the boys coming back, and——"

"And will they bring the horsie with them?" asked Phronsie, folding her hands in her lap.

"Yes, of course, child," said Polly promptly, and keeping a tight hold of Phronsie's little gown. "Now watch, Phronsie—here they come!"

"Here they come!" piped Phronsie, clapping her hands. Then she threw her arms around Polly's neck. "Oh, they *are* coming back," she cried; "they truly are, Polly."

"Yes, and they're here," said Polly quickly setting Phronsie down on the ground, "and now we've all got to help pick up those rags and put them in the bags, just as soon as Mr. Beggs gets back and ties up his horse, so he can't run away some more."

"I'm going to pick 'em up now," declared Phronsie, running into the middle of the road and sitting down in the dirt among the pieces of Em'line's wedding gowns.

"Oh, Phronsie!" exclaimed Polly, hurrying after. And just then up came Mr. Beggs holding the bridle, with Joel on the other side of the horse trying to be big enough to do the same thing, and little Davie following the red cart.

"Oh, we'll help, Dave and me," cried Joel, when the old horse tied to the gatepost couldn't run any more, and seeing Phronsie and Polly busy over the rags scattered in the road, the two boys scampered off to the scene of action. And presently when Mr. Beggs got there, every one of the four pairs of hands was gathering up the pieces, oh, so fast—that there really didn't seem as if there would be anything for him to do.

"We'll pick 'em all up," screamed Joel at him, as he stood

in the road, and flying up to cram both fists full into the bag
as it flopped half empty where it had tumbled.

"Take care, Joe," warned Polly, "don't let any dirt get in—"

"I guess a little dirt ain't a-goin' to hurt 'em," said the ragman and very much pleased to think he didn't have to get
his fat body down to pick up the snips.

Phronsie, who was busy as a bee, picking up the smallest
pieces and carrying them one at a time to tuck in the bag, was
suddenly interrupted by Joel calling out, "Look at Phron!"
Then he burst out into a laugh.

"Hush!" said Polly warningly. "Oh, Joey, how could you?"
For Phronsie suddenly deserted her snip of cloth and ran to
hide herself in Polly's arms—"There, Pet—"

"I didn't mean to," cried Joel, with a very red face. Then
he threw down his bits of cloth, and raced off to where Polly
now sat on the grass with Phronsie on her lap. "Oh, Polly,
I didn't mean to—" and he burst into a loud sob.

When Phronsie found that anyone else could feel badly,
she lifted her yellow head, and two tears that had made up
their minds they were coming out, concluded after all they
wouldn't. "Are you sick, Joey?" she asked, patting his old
jacket.

"Now I tell you what, Joel," said Polly briskly, "you take
hold of Phron's hand. No—no, Phronsie, Joel isn't sick.
He's going to take you over to the bag, so you can help him
pick them up. And that will be helping good Mr. Beggs, too.
You must, Joey," she whispered in his ear.

So Joel lifted his stubby black head, and when he saw
Phronsie with a happy smile and heard her exclaim joyfully,
"I'm going to help you, Joey, and good Mr. Beggs, too," he
smiled too, and seized her hand and raced her over to the
big bag. And before long with all those brisk little hands,
why, how could those snips and bits of Em'line's wedding

gowns do anything but hop back into their bag again. And it was tied tightly together with the old strings, each of the children having a turn at pulling the knot fast, and then Mr. Beggs tossed it up to the top of his red cart. "There, I guess ye won't come down agin till I take ye down," he said.

"Now you're all safe," exclaimed Polly happily, looking up at it, and bobbing her head at the big bump where it had settled, "and you can't come down again."

"You can't come down again," shouted Joel, dancing a jig around the red cart.

"You can't come down again," sang little Davie, flying away after him, and then Phronsie had to pipe it out, as she picked up her red gown to make a cheese in the road.

"And I'm sure I'm obleeged to all ye children," said Mr. Beggs.

"You took them to ride—" said Polly; "oh, Mr. Beggs, you are so very good!"

"You took us to ride," said Joel and Davie together. "And can I go again?" begged Joel, racing up to clutch his arm.

"Oh, Joel, for shame!" cried Polly, her cheeks very rosy.

But Mr. Beggs only laughed. "Yes, *sir—ee*. I ain't comin' this way this summer agin, but sometime ye may. Well, thank ye all for pickin' up them pieces."

"I picked up, too," announced Phronsie, who, seeing all the others around Mr. Beggs, concluded not to make any more cheeses. So she got up, and spatted her hands together to get off the dirt, and made her way over to the group. "I picked up, too—I did—"

"That's a fact," Mr. Beggs bowed his old straw hat solemnly. Then he said, "I wonder, now, if there ain't somethin' in my cart that's just waitin' to hop out an' stay with you." And he threw open the door of the cart to that beautiful shining array.

"Oh—oh!" they all crowded around, Joel getting dreadfully in the way, until Mr. Beggs lifted Phronsie up and set her on his knee. "Now, then, I wonder what you'd like, little gal?"

"Are you going to give it to her to keep?" screamed Joel, looking up into the ragman's face.

Mr. Beggs bowed again solemnly.

"To keep always?" cried Joel, not believing his ears.

"Yes, forever an' ever. Amen," said Mr. Beggs.

"Oh, hooray!" screamed Joel. Polly, scarcely less excited, held her breath, unable to speak, while little David panted out, "Oh!" Phronsie was the only one able to gaze unmoved at the beautiful shining things.

"I guess this is about th' best thing for a little gal about your size," said Mr. Beggs at last, and reaching with his long arm over Phronsie's head into the interior of the cart he brought out the little tin plate with big letters all around its edge, from the corner just where Mrs. Hinman had thrown it, and put it into her hand. "There, that's for you," he said.

But it took some time to make Phronsie believe that the little tin plate was really and truly hers. When she did, she sat down on the grass by the side of the road, holding it tightly with both hands, and Mr. Beggs looked back from the top of his red cart, the last thing before he turned the corner of the road, to see her sitting there.

IV

In Deacon Blodgett's Barn

"Yes, you must come, Joe; so hurry up."

Ben slipped the last spoonful of mush and molasses into his mouth and pushed back his chair.

"Oh, I don't want to," whined Joel, scraping his saucer violently. "Polly, I'm awful hungry."

"Oh, you can't be, Joe," said Polly, hurrying off with her hands full of dishes to be washed. "You've had two big saucers full."

"They weren't full," said Joel, with an injured air, "only up to there," rapping his spoon against the side of the saucer. "See, Polly, only just that much."

"Well, that's full," said Polly, peering back over her armful. "If you put any more in, you'd splash over the molasses."

"I wouldn't splash molasses," declared Joel on a high key, "and I'm awful hungry."

"Do say 'awfully,' Joe," corrected Polly, with a little wrinkle in her brow.

"And you've just got to come along," said Ben, with a pat on his shoulder that meant it. "See Davie! Aren't you ashamed, Joe!"

Little David had laid down his spoon on hearing Ben, and, slipping off from his chair, was now over by the door, waiting.

"Oh, Davie," cried Polly, with a glance at his saucer of mush, as she set down her load by the waiting dishpan, "you haven't finished your breakfast. Wait a minute for him, Ben." And she ran over to the door. "Come, Davie."

"I don't want it," said little Davie. "Truly, I don't, Polly."

"Oh, yes, you do," contradicted Polly, taking hold of his jacket. "Come back and finish your mush."

"I wish I could have some more," said Joel enviously, as David, with one eye on Ben, who stood cap in hand, sat down again and made his spoon fly briskly.

"Don't eat so fast," said Polly. "Misery me, you'll choke yourself. No, no, Davie," as David pushed his saucer over toward Joel. "Joey's had enough."

"I haven't had near enough," declared Joel stoutly.

"Well, you aren't going to have any more," declared Polly decidedly. "Davie must eat all that up, else he can't go and help Ben."

So Joel, seeing he was not to get any more breakfast, flung himself on the old kitchen floor and waved his legs in the air, shouting to Davie to hurry up at every spoonful. Until at last, his face quite red, and swallowing the last morsel, Davie hopped off from his chair and ran over to Ben. "I'm through," he announced happily.

"That's a good boy," said Ben approvingly. "Now, then, we're off."

Seeing this, Joel took down his legs from the air, and

hopped up, racing after them, and banging the door as he went.

"Oh, dear me!" cried Polly, in vexation, "now Joel's forgotten to take the molasses can." Then she rushed over to a corner of the kitchen where Joel had thrown it. It was his turn today to take it to the store, to be filled, on the way to Deacon Blodgett's, where the boys were to work. Then on the way home it was to be called for, all ready with a fresh supply for breakfasts in the Little Brown House.

"Where are you going, Polly?" It was Mother Pepper's voice from the bedroom, where she was getting off Phronsie's soiled little pinafore, down which trailed a sticky stream of molasses.

"Oh, Joe's forgotten the molasses can, Mamsie," called back Polly, and starting on a run after the boys. "Jo-*el!*" she called, racing down the path. But Ben, who hated above all things to be late to his work, was hauling them along at a pretty pace. And the wind carried away her voice, so they didn't hear.

"Oh, dear me!—well, I don't care," gasped Polly, feeling every nerve tingle with delight in her healthy little body as she sped on, "if I don't catch up with them at all. If I only could work at Deacon Blodgett's," she mourned, at the thought of the old dishpan and the hateful tasks indoors that awaited her at home, where she would be cooped up all day. But she couldn't even reach Deacon Blodgett's, for just then Ben turned.

"My goodness me!" as he spied her.

"It's the molasses can," panted Polly, her brown hair flying, and swinging it at them as she raced up. "Joel forgot it—"

"Oh, Joe, how could you?" began Ben reproachfully, as the two little boys whirled about on the road.

"I didn't mean to," said Joel, digging his rusty little shoe into the dirt, while his fingers worked nervously together, and his face got very red.

"Oh, I don't mind," said Polly, wiping her hot face. "It was good to run"; while Ben took the molasses can with a "Here, Joe."

"I didn't mean to," said Joel, over again, and taking the can; "I didn't, Polly, truly."

"Oh, I know it," said Polly, smiling at him.

"Well, come along now," said Ben, beginning to stride off faster than ever to make up for lost time. So little David, divided between sorrow for Polly having such a long hot walk, and fear that Joel was going to cry, ran by the big brother's side, doing his best to keep up with him.

Joel, on the other side of Ben, hurried on, clutching the molasses can, to the turn in the road; then he suddenly spun around, and dashed back after Polly's fleeting footsteps.

"Wait!" he wailed. But Polly, all her thoughts intent on getting back to those waiting dishes—for Mamsie might stop and do them, oh, dreadful thought!—was going at her best pace. And presently Polly dashed up through the old gateway, up the path and over the flat doorstone, and after her Joel as hard as he could run.

"Oh, my goodness me, Joe!" she cried, and then she sat right down on the big old stone. "What have you come back home for?"

"I'm sor-ry, Polly," panted Joel, stumbling up to fling himself, molasses can and all, in her lap. "Oh, dear me!—Boo—hoo—hoo! I didn't—didn't—" He couldn't get any further, for the tears rained all down his round, hot cheeks.

"Oh, hush—Mamsie will hear you," warned Polly in great distress, and lifting his stubby black head. "Oh, misery me, Joe, how you look!" For Joe's face was streaked from top to bottom where his grimy little hands had frantically tried to wipe away the tears, a few drops from the molasses can oozing out as he had bumped it up and down in his mad run, adding themselves to the general effect. "Now you must come right around to the Provision Room door, and I'll bring out a wet towel and wash you up, for it will worry Mamsie dreadfully to think you didn't stay with Ben."

"I don't want to be washed up," began Joel, perfectly overcome with all this dreadful accumulation of woe, most of which was now the fear of Mamsie's being worried.

"Well, you are going to be," declared Polly, getting off from the doorstone; "the very idea, Joel Pepper; such a sight as you are! Just think of going down to Deacon Blodgett's in that way." So Polly hurried into the house, and Joel crept miserably around its corner, and presently out through the Provision Room door, there she was, towel in hand, and in less time than it takes to tell it, there he was, too, his round face all red and shining and spick-span clean.

"Now, Joe," said Polly, setting a kiss on each red cheek, "you run right straight down to Deacon Blodgett's like a good boy, and don't forget to leave the molasses can at Mr. Atkins's —and don't bump it."

"I'm sorry," began Joel, beginning again on what he had come back to say.

"Well, you've said that ever so many times," said Polly, "so don't say it again; only run along, because just think now you've been naughty to run away from Ben and Davie."

So Joel, feeling as if things that he'd got to be sorry for were piling up too fast for his taste, gulped down his sobs, and started off, this time holding the old molasses can up high with both hands.

"Oh, dear me!" cried Polly to herself, "now he'll tumble on his nose, I know. Joe—don't do so," she screamed after him.

But as well try to stop the wind. And at last, Joel had put the molasses can on the counter of Mr. Atkins's shop, and sped out again, wild to get to the work at Deacon Blodgett's that now seemed the loveliest thing in the world for a boy to do.

Ben turned a disapproving glance on him as he panted into the barn.

"Davie is up in the loft," he said. "He's picking over the nails. You go up and help him, Joe."

"I'm sorry," gasped Joel, flinging himself up against Ben sawing away for dear life on some hickory sticks.

"Take care—well, I sh'd think you would be, Joe, running off like that," said Ben, not stopping his work an instant.

"Oh, dear—dear!" Joel twisted his small fists into his eyes, whirling around so that Ben might not see him. And catching sight of this, Ben threw down the saw, thinking, "I'll tell Deacon Blodgett I stopped a bit"—and the next thing Joel knew he had two strong hands on his shoulders and he was spun about again.

"Now, says I," exclaimed Ben, "what's it all about, Joel?"

So the whole story came out, and at the end Joel scampered up over the crooked stairs to the loft where little Davie, trembling first because Joel had run away and then much worse because he had come back, and something dreadful seemed to be the matter, was suddenly pounced upon where he sat sorting out a big box of nails.

"I've come back!" announced Joel in the most cheerful of tones, and dropping to the floor by Davie's side.

David gave a little scream of delight, and throwing his arms around Joel upset the big box and away flew half of the nails, crooked and straight in the greatest confusion.

"There—now you see," cried Joel, springing after them, and succeeding in overturning the box again, thereby spilling out the most of the remainder.

"Oh, I'll pick 'em up," exclaimed Davie, in a transport, his little hands trembling in his efforts to recover them. Since

Joel had come back, the whole world might be upset and it wouldn't be any matter.

"So will I," cried Joel, pawing wildly about in the straw scattered on the floor. So the two boys worked like everything, and presently were obliged to say that they had found all that they possibly could. And then setting the big box carefully between them, they set to work sorting out the good nails from the crooked ones.

"They're 'most all crooked," observed Joel, shifting a handful in one grimy little palm and peering into the big box.

"There's some good ones," said little Davie, carefully picking out one as he spoke.

"I wish we could have the crooked ones," said Joel. "P'r'aps Deacon Blodgett'll give 'em to us. I mean to ask him."

"Oh, no, you mustn't, Joe," cried little David in alarm. "You know Mamsie told us never to ask for things."

"Well, I'll tell him we want 'em," said Joel, patting a long crooked nail fondly before he laid it aside, "to build our rabbit house with." The Pepper boys had never had a rabbit, nor was there any expectation that they ever would possess one, but since Joel had said they ought to get a house ready, and perhaps then a rabbit would come, little Davie had worked as hard as he could to achieve it. Every bit of board was saved, and there were not many, because Polly had to have all that would burn nicely in the stove, of course. But, oh, joy!—Mr. Atkins, the storekeeper, finding all this out one day, presented the boys with some old boxes. Nails were the hardest things to get, and every stray one that came in their way was hoarded as a great treasure. But they came in very slowly. And now here was the Blodgett big box, and Joel was not to ask for a single crooked one!

"No, no, no!" Little Davie dropped his work to bring his

hot face over toward Joel's. "You mustn't tell him, Joel; Mamsie wouldn't like it."

"That isn't asking," said Joel, bobbing his black head obstinately and picking away furiously at the assortment of nails in his hand.

"Yes, it is," said little Davie. "Oh, you mustn't do it, Joe."

"No, it isn't either," contradicted Joel, "and I shall tell him all about our rabbit house, Dave. So there, now."

"Then I don't want any rabbit," declared Davie, slipping back to his place on the floor and wringing his hands.

"Not want any rabbit!" reiterated Joel in amazement, and letting the nails stream through his fingers.

"No, I don't," said Davie, quite pale and sitting very still, "want any rabbit at all, Joel."

"Then I don't want any nails," roared Joel. "Not a single smitch of a one."

"Oh, I am so glad," said little Davie, his pale face breaking into a smile, " 'cause then, Mamsie won't be sorry, Joel. She won't, really."

"And you'll want a rabbit?" cried Joel, hanging on Davie's lips.

"Yes, I will," nodded David, "very much, if you won't want the nails, Joel."

"I won't want one of the old nails," said Joel, diving vigorously into the box-depths for a fresh handful.

"Boys!" called Ben from below. "Are you working up there?"

"Yes," screamed Joel quickly, and picking at the nails with all his might.

But little David's fingers got in each other's way so much, over this new panic, started by Ben's voice, that he made very little headway, and mixed up the pile of nails dreadfully.

"You're putting in crooked ones," said Joel, twitching out one from the straight specimens. "Hah—Hoh, just see that, Dave Pepper!"

"Oh, dear me!" exclaimed poor little David, quite overcome with mortification.

"I'll pick 'em out," said Joel generously. "There—there ain't a single bad one in, now."

So David, after assuring himself that this was really so, began to breathe easily once more, and the two pairs of small fingers kept busily on at their task, till the first thing they knew, heavy steps were heard ascending the crooked stairs and a long face appeared, its keen gray eyes spying them at once.

"Well, boys," said Mrs. Blodgett, walking along the floor of the loft, "now you must come in to dinner."

"Dinner!" screamed Joel, hopping up to his feet and making nails fly in every direction. Little Davie sat quite still, clasping his hands silently, "Oh, are we to stay to dinner, Mrs. Blodgett?"

"Yes," said Mrs. Blodgett, her long face, with its high cheekbones, taking on a smile. "I'm going to keep you to dinner. Come, Betsey is peeling the potatoes, so you must hurry."

"Did Mamsie say we're to stay?" asked David, trembling with delight, so that he could hardly get to his feet.

"No," said Mrs. Blodgett, "but I expected you to stay, only the Deacon forgot to say so, when he told Ben to bring you along to look over those nails."

"If Mamsie didn't say we were to stay, we can't," said little David, feeling the expected bliss dropping away from him at each step. Joel, cantering over the crooked stairs, hadn't heard, and he was singing at the top of his joy, and telling everybody within hearing that they were going to stay to dinner at Mrs. Blodgett's, as he raced into the house.

Deacon Blodgett, wiping his face on the crash towel that hung by the sink-room door, heard him as he came rushing in.

"So you be, Joel, so you be," he cried, almost as much pleased. "Well, now, Joe, come and wash up." He set the tin basin he had hung up on its nail, down again in the sink and pumped up some fresh water into it, as Mrs. Blodgett, with little Davie, came in.

"Where's Ben, Pa?" asked Mrs. Blodgett. "He wasn't in the barn."

"I sent him up to the wood lot," said the Deacon. "He'll be along at the right time. Dinner ready, Ma?"

"Yes." Mrs. Blodgett hurried into the kitchen, where Betsey was making a terrible clatter dishing up the hot things. At the good smells, Joel plunged his face down to the tin basin, and splashed the water all over his hot cheeks and into his eyes, then put out a hand blindly for the crash towel on its nail. "Hurry up, Dave!" he cried.

"We ought not to stay," said little Davie, huddling up to his side, the Deacon having followed Mrs. Blodgett into the kitchen.

"Mrs. Blodgett said we must," said Joel, mopping away like everything. "Oh, what do you s'pose they're going to have for dinner?" wrinkling up his short nose in an effort to distinguish between the delightful smells.

Little Davie tried not to smell at all, even burying his nose in one hand, while he held to Joel's jacket with the other. "Mamsie won't like it," he said, when the door opened, and there was Ben, his ruddy face now quite red. "Oh, boys! I ought to have told you to go home before," he cried, catching his breath, for he had run from the wood lot every step of the way.

"We are going to stay to dinner," announced Joel boldly. "Mrs. Blodgett said so."

"Well, you can't," said Ben shortly, "for Mamsie expects you home."

Joel didn't stop to think, but dashed wildly into the kitchen and up against Mrs. Blodgett's big blue-checked apron. "He's going to send us home, Ben is," he gasped.

"What's that?" Deacon Blodgett, catching the words, broke in. "Hey, Ben?"

"Yes, sir," said Ben, in the doorway, with little Davie hanging to his hand, "the boys ought to go home, for Mamsie expects them."

"Oh, let 'em sit down and eat," said the Deacon sociably. "There, Joel, stop feeling bad, you h'ain't got to go home. Come, Ben, set down, and here's your chair, Davie." He was dropping into his own, while he talked.

"No, sir," said Ben firmly.

It seemed as if he could never get the words out, when he saw the Deacon's face. Maybe he wouldn't give him any more work if he didn't mind him; for there was a little black cloud coming on the high forehead. And Ben shivered from head to foot as he stood there.

"Set down, set down," Deacon Blodgett, pointing with his fork, kept repeating.

But Ben shook his head, while Joel sobbed in the depths of Mrs. Blodgett's big apron, and Davie hung helplessly to Ben's hand.

"There, Pa, I guess I wouldn't urge no more," said Mrs. Blodgett at last. "Yes, you must go," to Joel, loosening his hold on her apron, "and some other time, maybe, I'll ask your ma beforehand to let you stay."

The Deacon jabbed a potato with his fork from the big dish of smoking hot ones, and carried it to his plate without another word.

"And you can stay and eat dinner, Ben," said Mrs. Blodgett. "No," said Ben, "thank you, Mrs. Blodgett, I've got my dinner same's ever; Polly put it up for me. It's in the barn." He kept talking, hoping the Deacon would say something, but he didn't even look up, and Ben stifled a sigh, and went out after the two boys.

And after they had started for the Little Brown House, Mother Pepper, not wishing them to work but half a day at a time helping Ben, he sat down on a log of wood and ate his dinner. But he didn't enjoy it very much, for thinking of them with every mouthful.

"Well, dear me, what did make you so late?" cried Polly, as the two boys walked into the kitchen. Then she hopped out of her chair, where she sat over in the west window, pulling out basting threads from one of the coats Mrs. Pepper had finished that morning before she went down to the parsonage to help the minister's wife, and hurried to take out the potatoes she was keeping hot in the oven. In that way she didn't see the two dismal little faces.

"Now, then, says I, haven't they got hot little jackets, though!" sang Polly, running over with the two baked potatoes wrapped in an old towel. "Hurry, and get into your chairs, boys, and I'll cut you some bread."

And she flew into the pantry. "That's fine," she sang, rushing out with it, when, catching sight of Joel's face, "What *is* the matter?" And she set the plate of bread down hard on the table, and stared at them.

"We couldn't stay to dinner," said Davie, as Joel, contrary to his usual custom, didn't answer.

"*Couldn't stay to dinner!*" echoed Polly.

"Oh, Polly!" Little Davie, finding it hard to keep up this one-sided conversation any longer, and not willing to show

Joel's part in the matter, now rushed to her, wailing, "Mamsie wouldn't have wanted us to," and throwing his arms about her, he burst out crying as hard as he could.

Now, all this time, Phronsie, who had come in tired from play, had eaten her dinner very early, and Polly had tucked her into the trundle bed for a long nap. So all was quite free in the old kitchen for the good talk that Polly now set up with the two boys. And she soon had one each side of her, and leaning over her lap, when, the whole story once out, she comforted and coddled them quite as much as Mother Pepper herself could have done, which is really saying a good deal. And so, although the baked potatoes, waiting on the table got very cold, the three little Peppers were bubbling over with happiness, and Joel really forgot he was hungry, until Polly sprang up, nearly upsetting the two small figures.

"Oh, my goodness me!" running over to the table and beginning to pinch the brown jackets of the potatoes, "they're as cold as two stones."

"I like 'em cold," declared Joel, rushing after her and seizing one of the potatoes. "Oh, ain't they good!" tearing off the skin to scoop out a mouthful.

"Put in some salt, Joe, do," said Polly. But Joel couldn't wait for such small matters as salt, and he dug his spoon violently back and forth in the potato jacket. "I'm going to eat it, every scrap," suiting the action to the word.

"No, no, Joe, you mustn't," commanded Polly, just in time, as the whole of the potato skin showed signs of rapidly disappearing.

"I'm so hungry," cried Joel.

"Well, if you are very hungry, you can eat some bread," said Polly wisely, and wishing she had something nice for them after their terrible disappointment about the beautiful dinner Mrs. Blodgett had wanted to give them. But what was there? Oh, dear me! Polly knew quite well, without looking into the cupboard, just exactly how bare she should find it.

"Now, I tell you, Joel and Davie, what I'll do. There isn't anything else to eat, you know, but bread. You may have as much as you want of that. I'll tell you a story, if you'll be good boys and eat it. Mamsie would let me, I know," said Polly to herself, thinking of the basting threads not yet pulled out.

"Why, it's the middle of the day, Polly," said little Davie in astonishment, for Polly never was able to leave the work that always seemed clamoring to be done, to tell stories to the children. That enjoyment had to be put off till the twilight hour, when it was too dark to see to do anything else.

"Yes, I know," said Polly recklessly, "but I'll tell you one now, Mamsie would say I could, if she were here."

"Then I want it," said little David happily, and reaching out his hand for a big piece of bread. And Joel began to cram down his slice as quickly as possible to get the sooner to the story which he felt quite sure would not be forthcoming until Polly saw the bread disappear, when the door opened so suddenly that they all three jumped.

Deacon Blodgett's round face appeared. "How d'ye do, Polly?" and without further ado, he marched in, and laid a bundle on the table wrapped in old newspaper, in between the potato skins and the plate of bread. "Somethin' Mrs. Blodgett sent, and I've got to go down to John Hines's, and if you'll let Joel and David go with me, I'll take 'em along. They can tend to what's in that bundle on th' way."

Joel had already torn off the old newspaper, little Davie quite willing to sit still and watch the proceeding.

There was disclosed a much-worn clean napkin with a red border all around it, and Joel's frantic hands soon got this open, and there were some of the slices of beef he had smelled just before dinner in the Blodgett kitchen, and thick pieces of bread with—really and truly there was, and plenty of it—butter spread all over them! And at last—and didn't Joel's eyes stick out then, and even Davie held his breath!— two little apple turnovers tucked in at the bottom!

"They can eat those in th' wagon," said Deacon Blodgett, when he could be heard for the shouts sent out by Joel, and Davie's crows of delight, "if you'll say, 'Yes, they can go,' Polly."

"Oh, yes, yes, yes!" cried Polly, saying it so fast, over and over, it seemed as if she were never going to stop. "Dear Mr. Blodgett, they can go, and oh, you are so good to ask them!" and it didn't seem a minute before they were all off and she was picking up the potato skins and clearing the table neatly, as the rattle of Deacon Blodgett's wagon wheels died away in the road.

V

Baking Day

"DEAR me!" said Jasper, standing on tiptoe and running his head well within the old cupboard, "how perfectly fine! I wish we had one just like this at our house," he added enviously.

"Isn't it!" cried Polly, with sparkling eyes, quite delighted that he should so approve. "And we keep our very best dishes here." She pointed up to a blue willow plate, and one or two cracked cups and saucers on the upper shelf.

"Good?" exclaimed Jasper heartily; "I should say it was! I just love it all, Polly."

"Phoo!" cried Joel, crowding in between, "that's nothing. We're going to have ever so many more; the shelves'll be all rammed, crammed full."

Little Davie, who couldn't possibly get nearer than the outside edge of the group, stared with all his might.

"What do you mean, Joel?" gasped Polly, hanging to the door of the old cupboard.

"We are," declared Joel, delighted to see the impression he had made, and pushing his way out to the middle of the kitchen to thrust his hands in his little trousers' pockets and strut up and down the old floor, "and they won't be such old things neither. They'll be spick-span new, every single one of 'em; plates and plates *and* plates—yes, sir!"

"Joel Pepper!" exclaimed Polly, deserting Jasper and the old cupboard to rush over and seize his jacket sleeve, "what are you talking about? We aren't ever going to have anything new."

"We are, too," declared Joel, and facing her.

"Oh, dear me!" cried Polly, "what *do* you mean?"

"We're going to have everything new," declared Joel confidently.

Then he took his little brown hands out of his trousers' pockets and waved them triumphantly around the old kitchen. "We're going to have a sofa like the minister's for Mamsie, and Dave and me's going to have a table and a gimlet and some jackknives, and—and a piano. Oh, Polly, you're going to have a piano," and Joel pranced about joyfully, "and our ship's going to bring 'em!"

"*Our ship!*" echoed Polly faintly, while Jasper ran over to this exciting center of things, joined by little Davie. Phronsie alone remained gazing up into the old cupboard.

"Um!" nodded Joel, "and they're coming here, and going to bring 'em. And Mirandy Peters is going to have some ships coming, too; I heard her mother tell her to wait for 'em. I did, truly, Polly, just the other day, when I went to work there, and they gave me some dinner, 'cause the dog eat mine up. And then Mrs. Peters told me to wait for it. So there, now!"

"Oh, dear me!" cried Polly. Then she sat right down on the old floor and little Davie sank by her side. "Oh, Jappy, do tell him that folks don't really have ships."

"See here, Joel," called Jasper.

But Joel, delighted that now he had explained everything to the complete satisfaction of Polly and the others, had dashed off and was now spinning around the old kitchen, whooping and shouting as if driving a pair of the most unmanageable steeds. "And I'm going to have a horse just like Mr. Beggs's. No, it's going to be like Mr. Tisbett's, and—"

"Oh, Joey," cried little Davie, getting up from the floor to run after him, "do have it like dear Mr. Beebe's horse; do, Joey," he begged.

"Phoo! Mr. Beebe's horse can't go any," said Joel scornfully, slackening his speed a bit.

"But he's so nice," pleaded David with tears in his eyes. "Please, Joel, I'd rather have one like dear Mr. Beebe's."

"Well, then, I'll give you one," said Joel magnificently, "but I'm going to have mine like—no, I'll have two—like Mr. Tisbett's, and I'll have a stage and go, flapperty jickerty, down the hill, just like this—g'lang, there, git up!"—brandishing an imaginary whip. And away Joel pranced, raising a dreadful make-believe dust, and making so much noise there was no chance for anyone else to be heard. And Davie, well pleased since he was to have a horse exactly like dear Mr. Beebe's, raced and pranced after him.

"You can't hear yourself think," said Jasper, laughing to see them go; "there's no use, Polly, in trying to talk to him."

"But just as soon as they stop a bit, oh, please, Jasper, tell him that we aren't going to have any ships coming in," begged Polly, clasping her hands. "It's so very dreadful for him to be expecting them."

"I'll try," nodded Jasper at her. "Don't you be afraid, Polly, and perhaps you will sometime have new things," and he sat down on the floor by her side.

"No," said Polly, shaking her brown head, "we're ever and always going to live in this Little Brown House, Jasper King, and we don't want new things, only—" and her face fell.

"Well, you've got a new stove," nodding over at it, said Jasper cheerfully; "that's good, Polly."

"Isn't it?" cried Polly radiantly, and her cheeks grew rosy

again. "Dear Doctor Fisher gave us that, you know, Jasper."

"Yes, I know," said Jasper, who had heard the story many times, the Pepper children never tiring of telling it over. "Well, and perhaps some more things will come, Polly."

"Oh, no," said Polly, heaving a sigh, "they won't, Jasper, and we don't want them, only—" she paused again.

"Only what, Polly?" begged Jasper quickly. "Tell me, Polly, do."

He looked so very unhappy that she hurried to say, "Mamsie ought to have a new chair to sew in."

"I thought you were going to say a piano," said Jasper abruptly.

"A piano!" cried Polly, springing to her feet. "Why, Jasper Elyot King, I'm never going to have a piano in all this world!" and her brown eyes opened their widest.

It was just at this moment that Joel paused to take breath and to let his pair of horses exactly like Mr. Tisbett's, go up hill comfortably, and the words "a piano" striking his ear, he threw down his reins, and plunged over to Polly.

"Oh, play for us now," he begged, for nothing beside Polly's stories ever gave so much joy as to hear Polly drum on the old kitchen table, running her fingers swiftly up and down along its entire length, while she hummed and sang the tune. "Play, Polly, do!" he teased.

"Oh, I can't," said Polly with flushed cheeks.

"Please, Polly." Little Davie, tired by driving a horse even exactly like dear Mr. Beebe's, jumped off from his wagon, and added his entreaties, so Polly allowed herself to be pulled and pushed over to the old table. "Well, what shall I play?" she said. "Oh, wait, I must put the dishes away first."

"Yes, clear off the piano," said Joel, sticking out two ready little arms to help; "that's Polly's piano," he announced, just as if stating an entirely new fact.

"No, no, Joe," cried Polly warningly, "I'll do it," and "I'll help; oh, let me," begged Jasper.

So the two older ones put away the pile of clean breakfast dishes left standing until the cupboard shelf—which Polly had just washed down, should be dry—was ready for them, which now being the case, they were all neatly set in place.

"There, now, that's all done," said Jasper, rubbing his hands in great satisfaction. "Come, Phronsie," and Polly started to shut the cupboard door.

"But I want to look at them," said Phronsie, in gentle remonstrance and putting up her hand to stop Polly.

"Oh, no, Pet," said Polly, "you've seen them enough; come away, child."

"But, I haven't seen them enough, Polly," contradicted Phronsie, "my dear Mamsie's dishes, and I want to look at them some more, I do."

"Don't you want to hear Polly play on the piano?" asked Jasper. "Come, Phronsie, she's going to."

"Is Polly going to play on the piano?" asked Phronsie, her hand dropping down and taking off her gaze from the old cupboard shelves.

"Yes, she is, Phronsie," said Jasper.

"Then, I want to hear her play very much indeed," said Phronsie, turning away from the old cupboard, "and I can look at my Mamsie's dishes tomorrow."

Joel, who had been clamoring for Polly to hurry and come, now set up a dreadful racket on the old table as he drummed his impatience. "I'm a soldier!" he cried. "Come on, Dave, I'm captain!"

"Oh, hurry, Polly," cried Jasper, bursting into a laugh, "he won't stop until you play. Hold up, there, Joe," he shouted, "Polly's coming."

"So I must," laughed Polly, "or the house will come down."

"Will the house come down, Polly?" asked little Phronsie anxiously, as she hurried over clinging to Jasper's hand.

"Oh, no, Phronsie," said Polly quickly. "I shouldn't have said so," she added reproachfully.

"Dear me, it couldn't ever come down," declared Jasper. "Why, it's as strong as anything. It's going to last just forever."

"And I'm going to live here, I am, just forever, too," declared Phronsie, hopping over the uneven floor.

"Well, now, what shall I play?" asked Polly, with quite an air, and pushing the sleeves of her brown calico gown up further over her wrists.

"Oh, play that jiggy-wiggly piece," said Joel, who never could remember the names of Polly's wonderful flights of melody.

"Oh, Joel, I don't want that today," said Polly, wrinkling up her cheeks in disdain.

"That was splendid," retorted Joel, "and I liked it when the organ man played it."

"Did another organ man come by here?" asked Jasper, in a whisper to Polly.

"No," said Polly in a low voice, and her cheek turned pale at the remembrance of the dreadful time when Phronsie followed one to see the monkey.

Jasper drew a long breath of relief.

"He stopped at Mr. Beebe's, one day when we were there, and dear Mrs. Beebe gave him five cents to play for us," finished Polly.

"Oh!" said Jasper, quite relieved.

"And I like that best of all," Joel was saying in a loud, injured voice, "and Polly won't play it."

"Oh, I will, I will," cried Polly, quite overcome with remorse, and then Jasper ran over to bring a chair and place it in front of the old table, and Polly sat down, and began with quite a flourish. And before she got through, she forgot all about how she hadn't wanted to play that piece, and there she was singing away for dear life, and presently she ended by gay little trills and a "bang,—bang!"

"Hooray!" cried Joel, capering about. "Now play another one, and we're going to dance. Come on, Phron!" trying to seize her hand.

"Hold on," cried Jasper; "you've had your choice, now let Davie say what he'd like, Joe."

"Yes, that's the way to do," said Polly approvingly, and trying to whirl around on her piano stool, which she couldn't do very well as it was a stiff wooden chair. "Each one just take turns and choose. But then, oh, dear me, we ought to have let you choose first, Jasper, 'cause you've come over from Hingham to spend the day with us; oh, dear me!" Poor Polly, who dearly loved to be hospitable, was now so mortified not to do Mamsie credit by having good manners that the color went clear up to her brown hair, and she sat quite still in distress.

"See here," said Jasper quickly, "I didn't want to choose first, for I'm not company, Polly; I'm just living in the Little Brown House today, and I'm your big brother."

"Oh, oh!" screamed Joel, forgetting all about his desire to dance, and deserting Phronsie to rush over to Jasper, "are you our big brother, Jappy? Are you really?"

"Yes," said Jasper eagerly, "I am; that is, if you'll all have me," and his gray eyes shone.

"Oh, we will, we will," screamed Joel. "Oh, Dave, Jappy's our big brother. Now we've got two."

And presently, the three younger little Peppers were clinging to him, for Phronsie was soon acquainted with the blissful news by Davie screaming it rapturously into her ear. And

Polly hopped off from her piano stool to seize Jasper's hand, declaring, "Oh, how fine! Jappy's really to be our big brother. Ben'll be so glad," and so the compact was signed at once.

"Well, now, we must begin and choose what Polly is to play," said Jasper at last, when this was all settled, and feeling very fine and big to be considered one of the Little Brown House family. "Who's next—Davie?"

"Yes," said David, "I am," and he came over to the old table, where Polly was seating herself again before her piano. "Please play that little brook piece, Polly," he said softly.

"Oh, how nice," said Jasper approvingly. "What's the name, Polly?"

"Oh, I don't know," she said with rosy cheeks, and beginning to play.

"She just makes it," said little Davie, and coming around back of Polly, to gaze up into Jasper's face, "and then she plays it, and the water runs all over the stones; you'll see," and having communicated this piece of information, he hurried back to slip up close to Polly on her other side again.

"Did you make it up in your head, Polly?" cried Jasper admiringly. "Oh, dear me, I wish I could ever do that. All I can do is to play stupid old pieces that I learn."

"Oh, this isn't much, Jasper, only Davie likes it," said Polly, all in a tremor at having Jasper find out that she made it up.

"Well, I don't like it," said Joel, hanging back discontentedly from the group. "It's dreadful soft and squashing; I'd rather have something nice."

"Look here, sir," Jasper turned on him, "you've had your piece, Joe. Now I just know that I shall like this best."

To have Jasper like the new choice best invested it at once in Joel's mind with new interest, and he drew nearer, not taking his black eyes off once from the new big brother's face.

And Polly, since she must play her own piece, made up in her head, remembered what Mother Pepper always said, "Do everything just the best you know how, Polly." And so she sat quite straight, and sang away, and made her fingers run up here and there, all along the old table front, and she even put in a great many more tumbles of the water over the stones than little Davie had ever dreamed of. And then she sat back in the old wooden chair and drew a long breath.

"Oh, dear me!" exclaimed Jasper excitedly, "I'd give anything, Polly Pepper, to play like that; and to think you made it up out of your own head. It's too splendid for anything!" and his eyes shone.

"Isn't it?" Little David ran out of his place by Polly's side over again to Jasper. "Isn't it, Jappy?" he cried, his blue eyes very big, and hopping up and down in front of him.

"I should say it was!" cried Jasper, taking Davie's hands for a good spin in the middle of the floor. "It's just too splendid for anything, Davie Pepper," he repeated enthusiastically.

"I like it," said Joel, veering around. Then he ran over to the two whirling about. "He's my big brother's much as yours, Dave Pepper," and he crowded in to get hold of Jasper's hand, and spin too.

"So you shall," declared Jasper, well pleased to be adopted into all the comradeship of the Little Brown House. "Now, then, Joe; I'll give you a spin that is one!"

And Polly flew off from her piano stool and ran over with Phronsie for the fun, and there they all were, capering about, until, flushed and out of breath, the whole bunch of children stopped short.

"Oh, dear me!" exclaimed Polly, pushing back the little rings of brown hair from her forehead, "that was just splendid, only I'm afraid we've tired Phronsie to death," throwing her arms about her.

"I'm not tired, Polly," panted Phronsie, her cheeks very pink. "Please do so some more."

"Come, now!" cried Polly, "you mustn't dance any more. You're all tired out. Mamsie wouldn't want you to."

That Mamsie wouldn't want her to was sufficient reason why Phronsie shouldn't dance any more at present, so she dropped her little pink calico skirt that she had gathered up, and stood still obediently.

"I'll tell you," said Jasper, seeing her face, "what you might do, when you're rested; when it's my turn to choose a piece for Polly to play, then you can dance to it."

Everybody shouted at that, they were so pleased to find that Phronsie was not really to be disappointed, and Phronsie, dreadfully excited, began to hop up and down, "Polly's going to play, and I'm going to dance, I am."

And then she chose her piece, for of course it was her turn next. And it was just what Polly and the two boys knew it would be, the good-night song Mrs. Pepper used to croon to her baby, "Hush, my dear, lie still and slumber."

"Oh, yes, Phronsie, I'll play, 'Hush, my dear,'" said Polly, who saw the words coming long before Phronsie opened her red lips. And Phronsie very gravely stood close to her side, while Polly sang it through and through; each time that she tried to stop, Phronsie would say "again" and pull Polly's brown calico gown.

At last, Joel was worn out waiting for Polly to get through, and Davie was in a condition that was not much better, so Jasper broke in, "Now it's my turn to choose" and the one he begged for was "Old Kentucky Home."

"I think that's beautiful," said Polly, pushing back her sleeves, to begin afresh, while Phronsie, seeing that she was not to get any more "Hush, my dear," went off to sit down on her little stool and think it all over. She was only roused by

Jasper singing out, "Now, then, for your dance, Phronsie!" and there he was holding out his hand.

So Phronsie hurried off to her dance, and Polly began on the liveliest of jigs, every now and then looking over her shoulder, to be sure to keep good time; for Phronsie, who always wanted to make cheeses when very happy, would puff out, without a bit of warning, the skirt of her little pink calico gown in the very midst of the measure, and down she would sink to the old floor, to bob up and dance again.

"It's perfectly awful to keep time to her," said Polly, who dearly loved to be exact about things, especially with a tune.

"I know it," said Jasper sympathetically, "but, oh, she's so sweet!"

"Isn't she?" cried Polly with shining eyes, and beginning to play away with new vigor.

But at last Phronsie must be stopped, for Mamsie would surely say so if she were home. And then Polly had to hold her, as with flushed cheeks she begged to be taken up into her lap, and then the music stool was taken away and the grand piano became an old kitchen table once more.

"And now," said Polly, "if Ben would only come, we could have our baking, Jasper. Oh, dear, I wish he would!"

"I'm going to watch outside," said Joel, prancing off to the door.

"That won't make him come any quicker," said Jasper. "Can't we help about something, Polly?" He wrinkled his brows and gazed around the old kitchen.

"No," said Polly, following his gaze, "there isn't anything to do, but—" then she stopped.

"Oh, what?" cried Jasper eagerly, and hanging over her chair where she sat with Phronsie.

"Oh, you can't do it," said Polly, wishing she had bitten the end of her tongue before she had spoken.

"But we can, Polly," insisted Jasper, "I know we can. Do tell what it is," he begged.

"Why, Mamsie is going to ask Ben to fill the tub in the Provision Room with water to wash tomorrow, and I'm going to help her."

"Oh, Polly, do you wash things?" asked Jasper, looking admiringly at her fingers, now smoothing Phronsie's yellow hair.

"Yes, indeed!" answered Polly proudly. "I can do them real nicely, Mamsie says." Then she blushed at her own praise and hung her head.

"Oh," exclaimed Jasper, "how I wish I could help! Does Ben wash things, too?"

"Oh, yes, indeed!" said Polly. "You ought to see him. He ties on one of Mamsie's aprons. Ben washes all the sheets; they're the biggest things, you know. And he wrings them out, and then we all go outdoors and have great fun pinning them to the line. And Phronsie has a little string; haven't you seen the hook out on the side of the woodshed? And we fasten it up for her, and she washes all her doll's clothes. Oh, it's such fun!" Polly clasped her hands around her knees and drew a long breath.

"You do have such good times," said Jasper enviously. "Oh, dear me, and I've never had a sister or brother."

Down dropped Polly's hands, "Oh, I forgot," she said.

"I mean a little sister, or near my own age," corrected Jasper. "Sister Marion is just as nice as she can be," and his gray eyes glowed. "You ought to see her, Polly; you'd love her dearly, but she's ever so much older than I am."

Polly regarded him sorrowfully. Then she brightened up. "Well, Mamsie will let you come here all the time you can," she cried, meaning from this minute on to do everything she could to make a boy happy who hadn't any sisters near his own age, nor any brothers at all. To do this nothing was so good as to let him join them in a baking frolic. "Oh, I do wish Ben would come," she said again, for about the fifth time, just as Joel, out on the path, screamed out, "Oh, here he is!" and dashed off, Davie, as usual, at his heels to meet Ben.

Jasper was just springing over the rickety steps leading down into the Provision Room. "Polly," he called, "where's the pail to fill the tub with?" And Polly, racing after to get it for him, where it hung behind the door, of course, they didn't either of them hear Joel's cry nor see him run down the road with Davie. So the first thing the two knew, Ben's face appeared. "Halloa!" he cried. "Oh, are you filling that old tub?"

"Yes," said Polly, "we are; and now you won't have to break your arms over it, Bensie."

"Well, I guess I'm not going to let you fill that tub, Jasper," said Ben decidedly. "No, sir—ee!" and he made a lunge at the pail now in Jasper's hand.

"And I guess I'm not going to let you have this pail," cried Jasper merrily, and squaring off, "No, sir—*ee!*"

And there they were going 'round and 'round in the middle of the Provision Room, the pail swinging wildly out from Jasper's arm. At last, in one unlucky moment, down he tripped, and Ben rolled over him, and the pail flew off and ran away by itself.

"Hooray!" Joel and David, who had both run after Ben, now seized it together. "Let me have it," screamed Joel. "I'm going to fill Mamsie's tub."

"We didn't either of us get it, you see," said Jasper, bursting into a laugh and sitting still on the earthen floor. "Oh, Ben, to see your face," and he laughed harder than ever.

" 'Tisn't worse than yours," said Ben; "it can't be, Jasper. Yours is dirty from top to bottom."

"Well, that's because you rolled me in the dirt," said Jasper coolly, and rubbing his face. "Well, I think we'll need to get into the tub, instead of the clothes," he added.

"Oh, I'll get you a towel and the basin," said Polly; "then you can wash your faces. Misery me, how you both look!" she exclaimed, as she ran out to get it all ready for them.

"Joe," called Ben, as Joel and David hurried off dragging the big pail, which banged over the rickety steps, "don't you get that water. Jasper and I are coming out for it."

And in a minute or two, there the two boys were, all washed up, fresh and clean, out by the big barrel into which a rainspout ran to collect the water so that Mrs. Pepper could wash the clothes, with Polly and Ben helping her.

And between them they made very quick work over filling the big tub. And then—after the hands were all washed up spick and span—"Oh, now for the baking!" exclaimed Ben with great satisfaction, and hanging up the towel by the sink.

"Yes, now for the baking!" they all exclaimed. And soon the old kitchen was the scene of a great excitement, till it thrilled with life in every corner. And the fire burned with clear little winks of light that seemed to say, "Go right ahead, and be as jolly as you want to, I'm with you in everything!"

And the flour bag was brought out from the old cupboard. It took two of the boys to get it, although it wasn't a big bag by any means, nor was it anywhere near being full. It was brown flour, to be sure, but Jasper declared that was ever so much nicer than if it were white. And the little tins—they were just as clean and shining as they could be, for Polly always kept them so. Besides, she had given them an extra rubbing over that very morning to have them ready. But now, of course, they must have the dish towel whisked over them again, to be actually sure that they were all right. Oh, the old kitchen was a very busy place, anyone could see, with something for all the fingers to do. Even Phronsie was provided for in that respect, for she was polishing up the little tin biscuit cutter most carefully.

"But, dear me!" Polly stopped in the midst of all this merry bustle. "Oh, how could I forget!" Then she dashed into the bedroom and threw open the middle drawer of the old bureau, just above the one where Phronsie's red-topped shoes were always kept. And she pulled out one of Mrs. Pepper's clean blue-checked aprons. "Here," as she ran back to Jasper, "I must tie it around your neck—Mamsie said so—before you began to bake."

"That's fine," exclaimed Jasper, as the big apron fell down in folds almost to his feet, and Polly tied the strings around his neck. "Now, says I, you'll see what biscuits I'm going to make!" and he brandished the rolling pin.

And then Phronsie must sit up to the table and have a small piece of dough to make little biscuits all alone by herself. And she patted the lump into shape, turning it over and over to push it here and there before she cut one out with the top of the small tin salt shaker that Polly took off for her, and singing softly to herself all the while. This she did so many times that at last Joel looked up from his end of the table. "Look at Phron," he cried, "she hasn't cut one single one out yet!"

"Hush, Joe." Polly, with a tin plate covered with small lumps of dough that were going to be the most beautiful biscuits in good time, in her hand, turned quickly as she was just going to slip them into the hot oven, and ran up against Ben. "Oh, dear me!" as he put up his hand, but away went the tin plate, falling bottom upward, and all the little lumps hitting the floor.

"Oh, dear, that's my fault," cried Ben in great distress. "Polly, I'm dreadfully sorry—" and getting down to pick them up.

"Oh, no, it isn't," cried Polly. "Never mind, Ben," as she saw his face. Jasper and the others immediately left the baking table to hurry to the scene.

"We can scrape them off," said Ben ruefully, and getting a knife to begin operations.

"But they've been on the floor," said Polly, "and they'll never be so nice," and she sighed.

"Well, let's make some more," said Jasper, "and throw these away, Polly. That's easy enough."

"But we can't throw them away," said Polly in horror, "and we haven't very much flour in the bag," and she leaned over to look into it. "Mamsie said that was all we could take."

"Then we must cut off the tops of the biscuits, Polly," said Ben; "there's no other way."

"And Dave and I'll eat 'em," said Joel briskly.

"Well, you must have a sharp knife then, Ben," said Polly. "Wait, I'll get it." So she ran and got Mamsie's special one in the little drawer under the sink that Mrs. Pepper always used when there was any meat (which wasn't often) to cut up, and all the bunch of children watching, the tops of the little biscuits were slowly cut off by Ben.

"They're dreadfully small," grumbled Joel, who thought it a great waste. "You might have given them to Dave and me."

"For shame, Joel!" said Polly; "you couldn't ever have eaten them unless Ben had pared them. Oh, dear me, they are small," her face falling, "but I guess they'll be good."

"I'm sure they will," said Jasper, "and, Polly, they'll be so cunning on the plate. Do put them on the blue one that is up in the cupboard there." He nodded his head over to the corner where the few best dishes were kept.

"Oh, we couldn't take that down, Jasper," said Polly quickly, "not unless Mamsie says we may."

"And if you don't hurry and get those biscuits in the oven, you can't put them on any plate," broke in Ben wisely.

"That's so," laughed Jasper. So Polly started again with her tin plate of little lumps of dough. And the oven door was flung wide, and in they slipped, and then the door banged, good and hard, and all they had to do was to bake as nicely as possible till they were a lovely brown.

"Oh, I hope they'll be good," said Polly, anxiously coming back to the table to oversee operations.

"Oh, I guess they will," said Ben comfortingly.

"I can't do anything with mine, Polly," said Jasper, patting and punching the lumps of dough in his hand at a great rate. "It sticks dreadfully—see there! It's in no end of a mess."

"That's because you want some more flour on your fingers," said Polly, holding out the little bowl in which was a sprinkling of flour for just that very purpose. "There, Jasper, stick them in."

"Is that so?" cried Jasper, freeing one set of fingers to get the others in a worse plight. "Ow; it's all sticking to my other hand. I've just spoiled it, Polly." He held out the little wad hanging to his thumb and finger and gazed at Polly in dismay.

"Oh, no, it isn't," said Polly, picking it off to set it on the breadboard. "It'll come as good as can be after you get some more flour on your fingers, and—"

"Your biscuits's burning!" screamed Joel, sniffing. "They are—burning—Polly!"

But she didn't need this second shout to make her run and fling the oven door open, Jasper hurrying after, his fingers all over dough, and all the others following.

"Oh, dear, dear!" he mourned. "Now I made you stop. Oh, Polly, I *am* so sorry!" kneeling down beside her. "Here, let me pull them out."

"Oh, Jasper, you'll burn your hands," she cried. But he

already had the tin plate out; "whew!" dropping it just in time on the old table.

"Oh, did you burn you?" cried Polly. "Oh, what would Mamsie say to have such a thing happen to any one spending the day at the Little Brown House! Oh, dear me!" She was quite gone in distress.

"Only just the veriest bit," said Jasper, blowing on his thumb. "There; that's all right now. Don't worry, Polly."

And Ben was as much distressed to have anything happen to Jasper. "Come over and stick it under the pump," he said, leading the way.

"Don't want to," said Jasper. "It's all right now, I tell you, Ben."

Meantime, Joel had been hanging over the tin plate with the little lumps of dough and loudly protesting that they were all burned up, and that now nobody could eat them. Finally, Polly and Ben satisfying themselves that Jasper's thumb was really as he said, "all right," turned off to investigate for themselves the state of the biscuits.

"Indeed, they're not burned at all," declared Jasper. "They're just a lovely brown, and they'll taste awfully good, I know they will."

"So do I," said Ben.

"Give me one—just one," begged Joel.

"Get away," said Ben, as Joel lunged at the tin plate. "You just said they were all burned, Joe."

"Well, they aren't," said Joel. "Do give me just one, Ben," he whined.

"No," said Ben firmly, "you can't have one till we all have some; and we aren't near through our baking. Why, just look at Phronsie! She hasn't finished hers yet."

"Phronsie never'll get hers done," grumbled Joel. "She turns it over and over all the time."

"Well, you've got to wait," said Ben, and that ended the matter. And then they all set to work busier than ever, around the table, and the little brown biscuits that were baked were slipped off from the tin plate, and another batch slipped on it; Jasper's being given the place of honor in the middle. And Ben brought out a pan that Mamsie and Polly always baked their bread in. "There, Polly, let's put some in there," as he set it on the table.

"That's good!" exclaimed Jasper, beaming in approval. "Oh, Polly, my apron's coming off—"

"Oh, dear me!" exclaimed Polly, "I'll tie it up again, Jasper," and she dropped the dough she was patting deftly, on to the breadboard.

"You keep still, Polly," said Ben; "I'll tie him up," suiting the action to the word. "There, I guess you won't get that out in a hurry, Jasper."

"You'll have to untie me, old chap," said Jasper, "when the baking's over. Oh, Polly, this plate is all full now. Let me put it in the oven."

"And I'll open the door," said Ben, hurrying over. "That's just fine," he said, regarding the biscuits admiringly.

"Let me see—let me see before you put them in!" cried Joel, getting from his chair to run over to the stove. "I want to see them, Ben."

"Come on, then," said Ben, as Jasper paused, resting the tin plate on the sill of the oven.

"Oh, aren't they splendid!" exclaimed Joel, his fingers itching to get hold of one of them, "and those others are little bits of squinchy ones—"

"You be still, and not abuse those other biscuits," said Jasper, slipping the tin plate carefully into the center of the oven; "they're just splendid, too—" and Ben shut the oven door with a clang.

"They're dreadfully little," said Joel, clambering up into his chair.

"Well, now they're all done but Phronsie's," said Polly, as the tin bread pan was ready to slip into the oven on its last journey. "I've saved a place for hers, right here in the middle."

"Come, Pet, aren't you ready?" said Ben, going over to her high chair.

"I will be, Bensie," said Phronsie, "in a minute," and turning over her pat of dough again.

"That's just the way she's been doing all the while," said Joel.

"Never mind," said Ben. "Well, now, Pet, I guess that's done."

"In just a minute—please wait, Bensie," she begged, pushing up the little lump of dough softly. "See, it isn't nice like Polly's," and she turned it again.

"Oh, dear!" groaned Joel impatiently.

"Phronsie," said Jasper, running around to the other side of the high chair, "see what a cunning little place Polly has saved for you, in the pan—to put your biscuits in."

"Has Polly saved a place for me?" asked Phronsie, in gentle surprise, and pausing as she was turning her little dough pat again.

"Yes, indeed," cried Polly, running over to show her the bread pan, "right there, Phronsie—see, in the very middle; and your biscuits will be next to Jasper's and Ben's."

"And mine'll be there, too!" screamed Joel, interrupting. "Tell her, Polly; mine'll be there, too."

"Yes," said Polly, "Joel's will be there, too, and Davie's. I declare, almost every single one of us are in that pan; our biscuits, I mean. So put yours in, Phronsie."

"Are yours there, Polly?" asked Phronsie, stopping with

her hand holding the small pat of dough almost over the pan.

"Er—no," said Polly. "I didn't have any in this pan, Phronsie."

"Then I don't want to put my biscuits in," said Phronsie, pulling back her hand. "I want them to go in next to yours, Polly, I do."

"Oh, dear me!" said Polly, "now whatever shall we do, Ben?" over Phronsie's yellow head.

"I don't know," said Ben, at his wit's end. Still, something must be done, for Polly was dreadfully worried, and to have Polly troubled was about the worst thing that could possibly happen, in Ben's estimation.

"Now, Phronsie," he said, "if you don't put your biscuits in the pan, there, just where Polly has said, you'll make her feel very bad."

"Will it make her sick?" asked Phronsie slowly, a worried look coming over her face.

"I don't know," said Ben honestly, "but she'll feel very bad, I do know that, unless you put your biscuits just in that very spot." He pointed to the little place in the center of the pan.

Phronsie gave a long sigh. She wanted dreadfully to put her little biscuit in next to Polly's and have it bake alongside of hers. Still, it never would do to have Polly feel very bad, as Ben said she would, so she reached out her hand and laid the little dough pat just where she was told to.

"Now that's a good child," said Ben, with an approving pat on her pink apron.

"And when they are done," said Polly, waving the bread pan on her way to the oven, "we'll—"

"Take care, Polly," warned Ben, "or you'll spill them—"

"Why, we'll spread them all out and have our party, and eat them all up," sang Polly gaily, "but first we must clean all our baking things away."

VI

The Little White Cat

PHRONSIE was crying bitterly. Everything had gone wrong in the Little Brown House that morning. In the first place, it was snowing—not a cheery, white fluffy shower, but a sour, comfortless downpour just on the edge of becoming a drizzling rain that sent the chill in between the clapboards and under the old doorsill, and made Polly run every few minutes to put more wood in the stove. And as luck would have it, this was the very morning when the stock in the woodbox ran low. Ben, just before he hurried off to work, told Joel to be sure and fill it up, but Joel, frantic with delight at the approach of what he persisted in calling a snowstorm, had rushed off with little Davie, dragging their homemade sled of rough boards merrily after them, and forgot all about it.

"Dear me!" exclaimed Polly in vexation, as she poked the fire up and put on a fresh stick; "there are only two more left," with an anxious glance into the big box back of the stove.

"I'm so cold," said Phronsie, laying Seraphina down on the floor and coming up to Polly, and she held up her fat little hands.

"Goodness me, so you are, Pet," said Polly, feeling of them

in great concern. "Well, you must have on Mamsie's shawl."

So Polly ran into the bedroom, Phronsie following quickly, and humming: "I must have on Mamsie's shawl. Yes, I am, Polly, so cold"—in great glee at the mere mention of Mamsie's shawl.

"Now pin it," she said, standing on tiptoe as Polly got it out of the bureau drawer. It was a little brown and black plaid woolen one that the parson's wife had given Mrs. Pepper to lay over her shoulders when she sat by the west window to sew on cold winter days. So Polly took one of the biggest pins sticking up in the red-flannel cushion on the top of the bureau and drew the little shawl together, making it fast around Phronsie's neck.

"There, now, Pet," she said, giving her a kiss, "Mr. Jack Frost will have to go away, for you've got on Mamsie's shawl."

"Mr. Jack Frost will have to go away, for I've got on Mamsie's shawl," echoed Phronsie, and folding her arms closely together so she could hug the little shawl the tighter she ran out into the kitchen after Polly, who was now busy over the stove again.

"Misery me—now there's only one stick left." Polly was cramming in some wood, and she set the cover back in a great hurry. "Now I've got to go out to the woodpile and get some more. You keep away from the door, Phronsie; I'll be back in a minute." And she threw on her sack and hood and dashed out of doors.

But she didn't come back, and it seemed to Phronsie it was too long to expect anyone to wait. She couldn't see the wood-pile from the window, although she plastered her little face against it and tried as hard as she could to find out what Polly was doing.

"I must get Polly," at last she decided, so she went over to the door and opened it, huddling up into Mamsie's little shawl as the wet, clinging snow struck against her.

But Polly was nowhere to be seen, and Phronsie, stumbling over to the woodpile and peeping behind it, couldn't find her anywhere.

"Polly—Polly," she called in a grieved little voice, but there wasn't a sound except the soft dropping of the wet snow that was almost like rain. And presently Phronsie's tears were falling fast and she could hardly see because of them.

"Well—well!" It was Doctor Fisher coming around the side of the Little Brown House because he had been to the big green door and there was nobody to say "come in." He had a bag in his hand that he was carrying carefully. "Child, what are you doing out here?" he cried in astonishment.

"Polly isn't anywhere," wailed Phronsie, running over to him with the tears streaming down her face.

"Polly isn't anywhere!" repeated the little doctor in aston-ishment. "Take care, child," holding the bag at arm's length in one hand, while he gathered Phronsie within his other arm. "Oh, yes, she is. We'll find her just in one minute. Now, then, I must get you into the house."

"Will you find Polly?" cried Phronsie, looking up through her tears, as the little doctor, the bag in one hand, hurried her along with the other.

"Yes, sir—ee!" declared Doctor Fisher, nodding so violently that his big spectacles tumbled down to the end of his nose; "wait a minute." He released Phronsie and set them straight. "Now, then, Polly!" he called in a loud voice.

But of course there wasn't any Polly to answer, and Phronsie was just going to burst into another wail, when a funny little noise struck her ear and she paused in astonish-ment.

"I don't suppose you know what I've got in this bag," said

Doctor Fisher artfully, as he set it on the floor, then got down on his knees beside it.

But Phronsie couldn't get her mind off from Polly, so she turned a sorrowful little face to the window.

"Please get Polly," she begged.

"Yes, yes, all in good time," responded the little doctor in a cheery fashion, as if it were the easiest thing in all the world to get Polly. "But you must see what is in my bag first, because, you see, I don't know what will happen if I don't let her out soon. She may die," said the little doctor in an awful whisper, as he untied the bag, put in his long fingers and carefully drew out a fluffy white kitten, who blinked on being drawn out to the light, and then said very indignantly, *"Fuff—siss!"*

"There—there!" exclaimed the little doctor, holding the fluffy little ball very gingerly, with a great regard for possible claws, while Phronsie squealed with delight. "Oh, give her to me—I want her!" holding out both hands from beneath Mamsie's little plaid shawl.

"Well, you shall have her, for I brought her to you," said Doctor Fisher, depositing the fluffy little ball in Phronsie's arms. "Take care, now, or she may scratch you. Such a piece of work as I had to get her here."

"Fuff—siss!" said the little white kitten again, just as there was a rattle at the door, and Polly came in quite slowly, because her arms were full of wood, and she couldn't walk fast.

"Oh, Polly!" screamed Phronsie, "you've come back!" And she hurried over to her, kitten and all, the little doctor following quickly.

"See—see!" said Phronsie, dreadfully excited, and holding up the fluffy white ball that was spitting dreadfully, while little Doctor Fisher precipitately seized the wood out of Polly's arms and dumped it in the big woodbox back of the stove.

"Now, says I," he exclaimed, with a quick eye at the stove, "I guess some of those sticks want to go in here." And in a minute he had the cover off, and before long the wood was crackling merrily away, and Polly was rubbing her cold hands together, thinking how good it was to be in such a nice warm place.

"And so you've been out working at the woodpile," said the little doctor, with a keen glance at her red cheeks.

"Oh, I didn't get it at the woodpile," said Polly, flinging off her hood. "Isn't that the dearest little kitten in all this world!" she cried rapturously.

"You didn't get it at the woodpile!" said Doctor Fisher, straightening up to look at her in astonishment. "Where in the world, Polly—" he began.

"Oh, Grandma Bascom gave it to me," said Polly, with a little laugh. "You see Ben split her wood all up—a whole lot of it—for her, and ours is too big, and I couldn't find the hatchet, and—"

"No, no, I should think not," assented the little Doctor Fisher hastily. "Well, now, you are all right, Polly," with a glance at the stove.

"We're all right," said Polly, with a merry little laugh and skipping around the kitchen, Phronsie huddling up the white fluffy kitten tightly, and flying after her.

"And if you are a good girl," said the little doctor, opening the door and looking back at Phronsie, "why, then the little white cat shall stay with you always."

"The little white cat shall stay with me always,—he said so," declared Phronsie, trying to keep up with Polly's flying steps.

"Yes; isn't he good to bring you that dear sweet kitty!" exclaimed Polly, seizing it to give it a good hug, whereat the small fluffy ball said *"Fuff—siss!"* again very loudly.

"Oh, dear me!" exclaimed Polly, drawing back. "I didn't hurt you, you funny little thing, you; you needn't scream at me so."

"She's only talking, Polly," said Phronsie, anxiously watching Polly's face.

"Talking?" said Polly, with a little laugh. "Well, never mind, I guess she won't hurt me, Pet."

"She won't hurt you, Polly," said Phronsie, shaking her yellow hair positively. "I won't let her."

"And did you ever see such a nice place as this!" said Polly, glancing approvingly around the old kitchen and over to the stove where little winks of the bright fire could be seen, and the wood was crackling away as hard as it could. "Phronsie, I don't believe ever anybody had such a dear Little Brown House as this is—ever in all this world!"

"It's my Little Brown House," said Phronsie, coming to a sudden stop and looking all about her very intently, "and I shall live here forever."

"Well, come on," said Polly, every nerve tingling for another spin, she was just beginning to feel so nice and warm and cosy, and holding out her hands. So Phronsie, although she would have preferred to sit quietly and play with her new treasure, hugged it up tighter to her little bosom and let Polly dance her about to her heart's desire, the little white cat spitting and mewing her discontent, until the two children, tired out, sat down, flushed and panting, to rest.

And just at that moment the door opened and in plunged little Doctor Fisher, his spectacles gleaming behind a big armful of wood.

"Oh—oh!" cried Polly and Phronsie together, as they rushed across the kitchen to him.

"It was such good fun!" declared the little doctor, depositing the big armful with a rattle and a clatter in the woodbox.

His eyes sparkled, and a smile of great satisfaction spread all over his face. "You can't think!"

"You've split up all that wood!" exclaimed Polly in dismay, going back of the stove to peer into the big box; "and where did you find the hatchet?" rushing back to him.

"Oh, that's telling," laughed Doctor Fisher.

"And Ben won't like it, to have you do this, because you have to work so hard to cure sick folks," said Polly, with a very flushed face.

"Ben isn't to know anything about it," retorted Doctor Fisher.

"He would have filled it," began Polly, and the rosy color flew all over her face deeper yet, "only—" And then she stopped suddenly at the thought that she would have to tell about Joel.

"Ben's all right," declared the little doctor with emphasis. "Now, Polly, don't think anything more about it."

"You see, Joel—" And Polly clasped her hands. She had almost let it out, for Ben mustn't be blamed unjustly—Oh, dear, what could she do!

"And because Joel ran off and forgot to fill the box," said little Doctor Fisher gaily, "is that any reason, I should like to know, why I can't have the fun of splitting up a few sticks? Well, Phronsie"—and he whirled around to her—"don't you want to know where I got that little white cat for you, before I go, hey?"

"She's my little white cat," declared Phronsie, too excited to think of anything except that the kitten was really hers.

"Yes, I know," Doctor Fisher nodded at her. "Well, now, I'm going to tell you how I got her. Polly, you come over and hear it, too."

So Polly obediently went over. "Oh, you've been so good, dear Doctor Fisher; you've saved my eyes, and given me my

stove, and now you've brought Phronsie a little white cat."
Polly clasped her hands tightly together. Oh, if she could
only do something for him!

"Well, now, let's hear how I got that little white cat," said
Doctor Fisher briskly. He never could bear to be thanked,
but he was very much gratified, all the same, at Polly's words.
"You couldn't guess, children," he cried with great animation.

"Phronsie," said Polly, "he's going to tell how he got your
little white cat."

At that Phronsie was greatly excited, and she piped out,
"Oh, tell me!"

"Why, I didn't get her at all," said Doctor Fisher.

"You didn't get her at all—" repeated Polly in amazement.

"No," the little doctor burst into a laugh at her face; "that
is, I didn't go after her. She came to me."

"She came to you!" echoed Polly. "Oh, do tell us, Doctor
Fisher," hanging on every word breathlessly.

"Why, you see I had been around considerably on my calls
yesterday," said Doctor Fisher. "Never had so many it seemed
to me; so I got home late and I had bundles in the top of the
gig—had it pushed back, you know. And after I had Dobbin
out of the shafts, and in his stall, I just reached in to get the
parcels, and the first thing I knew—see there!" The little
doctor held up one hand, and there was a long, red scratch
running halfway across it.

"Oh, dear me!" cried Polly in great distress.

"That's the first thing I knew about that little white cat,"
said Doctor Fisher ruefully. "Although I'd been on the look-
out for a kitty for Phronsie, and a white one, I never expected
she'd come to me. But there she was, as fine as a fiddle, and
she sprang up on top of those bundles. I'd waked her up,
you see—and she puffed up twice her size and hissed and
spit and scratched at me like all possessed!" He threw his

head back, and laughed long and loud at the remembrance.

"And didn't you find out where she came from?" cried Polly, with big eyes. Phronsie, divided between her joy at the story and her sorrow at the long scratch on Doctor Fisher's hand, only hugged the little white cat tighter without a word.

"No, not a bit of it. You see, I'd been in so many places yesterday, how could I?" said Doctor Fisher, wrinkling his brows. "I suppose Miss Puss thought my gig top was about as nice a place to sleep in as she ever saw—so in she went without asking anybody's leave—"

"Phronsie, just think—your little white cat walked right into Doctor Fisher's gig top," laughed Polly, her worry over the wood dropping off for a moment. "Oh, how funny!"

"How funny!" laughed Phronsie, and the little doctor laughed. And the door swung open suddenly, and in burst Joel, staggering under a load of wood very much too big for him, and after him panted little Davie, and he had an armful, too.

"Oh, Joel," exclaimed Polly, dashing over to him.

Joel's face was very red, but it wasn't from carrying the load of wood, and he couldn't drop it into the woodbox, because that was full, so down it went with a clang on the kitchen floor.

"I didn't mean—oh, I—oh, dear me! Polly, I didn't mean," he blubbered. Then he broke down and ran into Polly's arms to hide his tears.

"Oh, I know—I know," said Polly soothingly, and rubbing his stubby head. "Oh, Davie, put down your wood, do," for little Davie seemed to be paralyzed, and stood quite still in his tracks.

"And I forgot," sniffled Joel, perfectly oblivious of Doctor Fisher and everything else. "Oh, dear me, and Ben told me." Here he gave a fresh sob.

"Well, Ben thought there was some wood split," said Polly,

with another pat on his black hair. Still, in her own mind, she was very much perplexed. When did Ben ever forget anything like that? "Never mind; we've ever so much now," she added brightly.

"But there was lots," declared Joel, lifting his head to look at her, "lots and lots all ready, and Ben told me—" Here he burst out crying again, and down went his head.

"Joel, stop crying," said Polly, getting her hand under his chin. But he burrowed deeper yet into her gown, mumbling, "I forgot—"

"Where was the wood?" demanded Polly. "Joel, you must tell me this minute."

"In the Provision Room," wailed Joel. "Oh, dear me!"

"In the Provision Room," repeated Polly faintly.

"Yes, Ben put in in there to have it dr—dry," whimpered Joel; "in the Cubby Hole—Oh, dear me!"

There was a broken place on the outside of the Provision Room, called by the children the "Cubby Hole," and Ben had tucked the split wood in there, telling Joel to fill the box behind the stove; then he had hurried off to work for Deacon Blodgett.

"Well, never mind," said Polly again. "Don't cry, Joel, you didn't mean to forget."

"No, he didn't," said little Davie, who had set down his wood on the floor by the side of Joel's armful, to come anxiously up to Polly's side. "He didn't mean to, Polly."

"I know," said Polly, nodding over to him, "and we have plenty of wood. See there, boys," she pointed over to the big box.

"Where'd you get it?" Joel raised his head to sniff out the words between his tears.

"Oh, Doctor Fisher brought in the most of it," said Polly.

"No, I didn't," said the little doctor, who had heard every

word, and whirling around toward them. "Polly brought in the first lot."

"Oh, dear me!" exclaimed Joel at that, ready to burst into fresh sobs, for the boys never allowed Polly to bring in any wood, each one vying with the others to be the first one to fill the big box.

"Oh, no," said Polly, so anxious to keep Joel from feeling badly, she forgot she was contradicting. "I only brought in a little, Joey; Doctor Fisher brought in all the top part."

"Well, now," said the little doctor cheerily, "the wood's here, and, although it was very bad of you, Joel, to go off and forget what Ben told you—I'm not denying that—it didn't hurt Polly half as much to bring it in, as to see you cry. Come, wipe up; you're 'most a man, Joel." And that long speech over, Doctor Fisher whipped out his big bandanna and mopped Joel's red face from top to bottom.

"Fuff—siss—meow!"

"What's that?" cried Joel, emerging from the big handkerchief with dry and shining cheeks, and pricking up his ears. Little Davie whirled around to listen, too.

"Oh, that?" said the little doctor, bursting into a laugh. "Well—run over and ask Phronsie. Good-by, children," and he skipped to the door and hurried out to climb into his gig and rattle off.

Joel plunged over to Phronsie, little David racing after. "Give her to me, Phron," screamed Joel, catching sight of the little white ball.

The kitten, quite accustomed now to Phronsie's fat little arms, had snuggled down, thinking it wasn't such a very bad place, after all, that she had come to, but at Joel's loud cry she sprang upright and glared at the two boys—the very things, if the truth must be told, that she had fled from when she jumped in that old gig standing in the front of her home down in the Hollow.

"Oh, Joel, don't—you're scaring her to death," said Polly, while Phronsie screamed in dismay, and struggled, her face very pink, to hold the little cat.

"Phoh! I ain't scaring her," said Joel, poking his stubby black head up closer.

"Don't, Joey," begged David, trying to pull him back, but the little white cat, considering it wiser all around to look out for herself, struggled out of Phronsie's arms and leaped across the kitchen floor, and in a minute there she was, perched up on top of the old corner cupboard and glaring down at them out of two big, angry eyes.

"Now see what you've done, Joel," exclaimed Polly in vexation. "There, Phronsie, don't cry; your kitty can't get away."

Phronsie, since Polly said so, stopped her screams, and running over to the cupboard—"Come back, my little white kitty," she begged, holding up her arms.

But the little white cat looked down at her, as much as to say, "No, indeed, you don't catch me as long as those dreadful boys are there."

"I'll get her," shouted Joel, running across the kitchen to the old table and preparing to drag it over.

"Stop, Joel!" commanded Polly, running after him.

"I'm going to put a chair on it; then I can reach her," screamed Joel, with a very red face, tugging away at the table.

"No, no, you mustn't, Joe," commanded Polly.

"Oh, dear—dear!" Little Davie was wringing his hands helplessly and turning first to Phronsie and then to Joel in distress.

"We must just let her alone; she'll come down herself by and by." Polly ran over to say this to Phronsie.

"But I want my little white kitty now, Polly, I do," said Phronsie in a sorrowful little voice.

"I know, Pet, it's too bad she's up there—but she'll come down by and by," said Polly reassuringly, and craning her neck at the little white cat, who sat serenely on her perch. "Let's go off and play something," she proposed suddenly.

"Oh, I couldn't play, Polly," said Phronsie reproachfully. "I want my little white cat."

"Well, I could get her," declared Joel in a loud, wrathful tone, "if Polly'd let me; just as easy as pie—"

"Well, I'm not going to have you tumbling off from that chair on top of the table," declared Polly firmly. "Besides, Joe, the kitty wouldn't be there when you'd climbed up."

"Then I'd jump down and catch her here—gee—whiz!" said Joel, slapping his little brown hands smartly together and stalking up and down in front of the old cupboard.

"Well, you mustn't try," said Polly. "Now, Davie, you and I will play with Phronsie, if Joel doesn't want to. Come on, Pet. Oh, wait a minute; you must take off Mamsie's shawl."

"Oh, I don't want to take it off, Polly," cried Phronsie, edging off and clutching the little plaid shawl with both hands.

"Yes, you must," said Polly; "you'll get so hot." So the little shawl was unpinned and laid carefully on the table. "Now, then, come on," said Polly.

"I don't want to play, Polly," said Phronsie again, and surveying her with very disapproving eyes.

"Oh, yes, come on, Pet," said Polly cheerily, holding out her hands, "and you too, Davie."

So Phronsie, who never really thought of disobeying Polly, went slowly over to Polly; and having Davie on her other side with a very solemn face, as he much preferred to see how things were coming out with Joel, Polly spun out with the two children into the middle of the kitchen floor.

"Now let's play Ring—around a rosy," she said gaily. "Come on."

"I want to play Ring around—a—rosy," cried Joel in a loud voice.

"Ring a—round—a rosy," sang Polly, skipping off bravely. "Take care, Phronsie"; for Phronsie's gaze was fastened on the little white cat, who sat up stiffly on the top of the old cupboard, with her tail lashed around her legs, and staring down at them. "You almost tumbled on your nose, then, child."

"I want to play Ring a—round—a—rosy, I say," screamed Joel, as the little circle swept by in the middle of the floor as fast as they could go, and singing at the top of their voices.

"Joel wants to come—Polly, stop," begged little Davie breathlessly, as they whirled around.

"Oh, dear me!" panted Polly, and stopping suddenly. "Do you really want to play, Joel?" she asked. "Really and truly?"

"Yes, I do," said Joel. "Oh, Polly, let me," and he rushed up to crowd into the ring.

"Then you may, if you really and truly want to, Joel," said Polly. "There, now, says I, take hold of Davie's hand."

Little Davie, only too glad to have Joel in the ring, joyfully tried to seize his brown little hand.

"I want to take hold of Phronsie's," said Joel, pulling away, "and yours, Polly," running over to get into that part of the little ring.

"No, no," protested Phronsie, hanging to Polly's hand for dear life.

"No, you can't, Joel," said Polly decidedly. "That is Phronsie's place. Come the other side."

"I'll let him take my place," said little Davie, swallowing very hard, for he very much wanted to hold Phronsie's hand, but he dropped it at once, to let Joel slip into the ring.

"Oh, Davie, that is so good of you!" exclaimed Polly, beaming at him, but she didn't look at Joel, as he seized Phronsie's hand. "Well, now, come on," sang Polly. "Ring—a—round—a rosy." And off they skipped.

"I don't like it—stop!" roared Joel. "Polly, I don't—I say—"

But Polly, not heeding, pulled them around and around till everything in the old kitchen spun before their eyes, and Phronsie couldn't even see the little white cat sitting stiffly up on top of the old cupboard.

"Stop!" roared Joel, and "Oh, do stop, Polly," implored little David, tugging at her hand.

"Why, what's the matter?" Polly brought the little circle up suddenly with a laugh. "Oh, dear me, wasn't that a fine spin!" And she brushed her brown hair off from her hot face.

"I'm not going to take hold of Phronsie's hand," said Joel, dropping her fat little fingers and running over to squeeze in between Polly and David. "Dave can have the place."

"Oh, I'd rather you'd have it," said little Davie, but his heart gave a happy little throb.

"Now, that's so nice of you, Joey," said Polly approvingly, and she dropped a kiss on his stubby black hair. "Well, if you don't want to play Ring a—round—a—rosy any more, why, we won't."

"Oh, I do—I do," said Joel, whose feet actually twitched to be spinning again, and he pulled at Polly's hand.

"I'd rather play the Muffin Man," said Phronsie, beginning to feel a bit easier about her little white cat, since she sat up there on top of the cupboard so quietly.

"Oh, no!" roared Joel, horribly disappointed. Then he looked at Polly's face. "Yes, let's play the Muffin Man," he said.

"So we will, Joey," cried Polly, smiling at him.

So Joel, feeling as if the Muffin Man was just the very nicest play in all the world, since Polly looked at him like that, scrambled into his place in the line, quite contented to let Davie be the Muffin Man and fill the post of honor.

"Phronsie ought to be that first," said Polly, "and then Davie can be next—"

"All right," said little David, tumbling out of the post of honor. So Phronsie was set there, but she didn't like it, because then she had her back to the old cupboard, so of course she couldn't see her little white cat. When Polly heard that, she gave the order for all the line to whirl over to the other side of the kitchen, with a "Hurry up, children," to the two boys. "Now, then, Mr. Muffin Man, we're going to see you; you must scamper and be ready for us—" which Phronsie did as fast as she could, but she didn't pay much attention to her approaching guests, all her thoughts being on her little white cat. At last she could bear it no longer, and as the line was advancing, "We all know the Muffin Man—the Muffin —Man—the Muffin Man," Joel shouting it out above the others with great gusto, she broke out—"Isn't she ever coming down, Polly?"

"Oh, dear me!" exclaimed Polly, who had almost forgotten the little white cat in the general glee. "Oh, yes, sometime. Now, let's begin again. We all know the—"

But the Muffin Man suddenly deserted the post of honor and ran wailing over to the middle of the line coming to visit him. "Oh, I want her, Polly, I do!" in such a tone that Polly knew that something must be done to try to get the little white cat down from the top of that cupboard.

"Well, now, says I, I must get that kitty," said Polly, gathering Phronsie up in her arms, and at her wit's end to know how to do it. "Yes; there, don't cry, Phronsie; I'll try to get her down for you."

"Let's take the broom," cried Joel, running over to get it where it hung on its nail behind the door. "That'll shoo her good."

"No, no, Joel," said Polly, shaking her head in disapproval, while Phronsie screamed at the mere thought of the broom touching her little white cat, "that would be the worst thing in the world. It would make her cross and hateful, and then Mamsie would have to send her away and Phronsie couldn't keep her at all."

"Well, then, how are you going to get her down?" asked Joel, standing still to regard her impatiently.

"You must let me think," said Polly, wrinkling up her brows. "Now, Phronsie, if you cry so, I can't ever get your kitty down. Oh, you bad, naughty little thing, you!" this to the small white cat sitting stiffly up on the cupboard.

"She isn't a bad, naughty little thing, Polly," sobbed Phronsie. "She's my little white cat, and I love her."

"Well, I don't mean really she's bad and naughty," said Polly with a sigh, "but I do wish she'd come down, Phronsie."

And then the very strangest thing in all the world happened. "Mee—ow!" said the small white cat, but it was in a soft little voice, and she unlashed her tail from her legs and there she actually was digging her sharp claws into the side of the old cupboard to assist her descent to the floor!

"*Hush—sh!*" whispered Polly, her brown eyes very wide, and seizing Joel's blue cotton blouse; "keep still, all of you. Oh, Phronsie, don't stir—she's coming—she's coming!"

"*Mee—ow!*" said the little white cat, stepping gingerly along into the middle of the floor, and beginning to believe that the children hadn't wanted her before so very much after all, and she came up to rub herself against Polly's brown calico gown.

"Oh, keep still—don't touch her!" warned Polly, holding

her breath. Joel twisted his brown fingers together tightly, and little Davie and Phronsie, not thinking of disobeying Polly, didn't stir.

"Mee—ow!" said the little white cat, this time in displeasure and beginning to walk all around the small bunch of Peppers. "Mee—ow!"

"Now you all keep still," said Polly. "I'll catch her." And, sure enough, in a flash, Polly had the little white cat in her arms. "Oh, you're hungry, I do believe, you poor little thing, you!" stroking her fur gently. "Joel, keep your hands off. Yes, Phronsie, you shall take her in a minute. There—there!" And Polly cuddled her up, and that little white ball of fur began to purr and try to lick Polly's face and snuggle up to her like everything!

"Now, boys," said Polly, after a few minutes of this delightful proceeding when the old kitchen was fairly alive with happiness, "I do believe you must go and ask Grandma Bascom to give us just a very little milk in a cup": for the little white cat, although apparently much pleased to be the center of attraction, did not cease to bring out every now and then the most dismal "Mee—ows!"

"Oh, I don't want to go," whined Joel, at the mere thought of missing any of this pleasing entertainment.

"For shame, Joe!" exclaimed Polly. "The poor little thing is almost starved."

"Mee—ow!" said the little white cat.

"And there isn't a bit of milk in the house and she's only just come," finished Polly, feeling it a very poor way to entertain a newly arrived guest, while Phronsie hung over the new treasure, telling her she was going to have some really and truly milk. Joel hung his head. "I'll go," he said. "What'll I get it in, Polly?"

"Take one of the cups," said Polly, pointing to the dresser, "and Davie, you run too with Joel, that's a good boy."

"I'll run, too," said little David with alacrity. So Joel took down one of the cups and the two boys hurrying with all their might, raced off, Polly calling after them—"Don't spill it."

And before long back they came. "Oh, dear me!" exclaimed Polly in dismay; "Grandma needn't have given us all that. Didn't you tell her just a very little, Joel?" as Joel, gripping the cup with both hands, not daring to take his eyes off from it, walked up carefully to Polly's side.

"I did," said Joel. "Oh, yes, he did," declared little Davie loudly, while Phronsie gave a little shout of delight. Then she laid her yellow head close to the little white cat, still snuggled up in Polly's arms. "You are going to have some really and truly milk, you are, kitty," she whispered.

"Now you may hold her, Phronsie, a minute," said Polly. "I must pour the milk into a saucer." For the little white cat's nose was poked up toward the cup, and trembling violently in her eagerness to get some. "Oh, she'll upset it all," cried Polly. "Hold her tightly, Phronsie."

"Mee—ow!" cried the little white cat in disappointment, as Polly hurried off, two or three drops of milk trailing down the side of the cup.

"Yes, yes—you shall have it," promised Polly, over her shoulder. "Poor little thing, you—do keep still; I'll be right back."

And in a minute there the little white cat was before a saucer, both eyes closing blissfully, and her small pink tongue, darting in and out, was busy enough carrying the milk to her mouth, all four of the little Peppers in a ring around her on the kitchen floor.

VII

Spending the Day at the Beebes'

"ALL day," whispered little David, in a rapture. "Just think, Joey, all day!"

"I know it," sang Joel. "Whoopity la! Ow—you pulled my hair, Polly."

"Well, I can't help it," said Polly, "you jumped so, Joel. Do stand still."

"I can't," said Joel, giving a long stretch. "Ow! Mamsie, Polly is hurting me dreadfully," he whined to Mother Pepper, out in the kitchen.

"That's because you don't stand still and let her brush your hair as it should be done, I suppose," said Mrs. Pepper coolly. So Joel, getting no comfort there, wisely determined to make the best of things, and he wrung his hands together, trying his best to keep still, only interrupting the proceedings by teasing to know when Polly was to get through.

At last it was over. "Oh, dear me!" exclaimed Polly, sinking into the first chair quite exhausted. "I'm so glad I'm through, Joey."

"So am I," echoed Joel jubilantly, and beginning to prance about; "now I'm going to do Dave's hair," and he made a lunge at the old hairbrush in Polly's hand.

"No, you're not," declared Polly, clinging tightly to it. "You go right away, Joel Pepper; the very idea! Davie's hair would look just like everything if you brushed it."

"Oh, I don't want Joel to do it," cried David in terror, and running over to Polly's side—"don't let him, Polly."

"Indeed I shan't," said Polly with vigor, and waving the old hairbrush defiantly. "Now come, Davie, and I'll fix yours, and then you can all start for dear Mrs. Beebe's. Phronsie is so good; just look at her!"

There she was in her little chair, as still as a mouse, her eyes fastened on the red-topped shoes stuck out straight before her, and her hands folded in her lap. She had been patted and pulled into shape by Polly, and then told to sit down and wait till the boys were ready. The getting-ready process, when the Pepper children were going out visiting, was always full of delight to Phronsie, who wouldn't have had one of the many details left out that Polly considered were so important.

"Umph, I can fix it as good as pie," grunted Joel. Then he capered out into the old kitchen, snapping his fingers. "I don't care—I don't want to. Whoopity la, we're going to spend the day at Mr. Beebe's shop!"

"Misery me," exclaimed Polly in dismay, "do stop, Joe! You'll muss up your hair dreadfully. Oh, Mamsie, he won't be fit to be seen," she wailed.

"Joel," said Mrs. Pepper, "stop this minute," as Joel capered by, "and go and sit down in that chair"; she pointed to the other side of the kitchen.

"Oh, dear me!" grunted Joel. "I don't want to sit down, Mamsie."

"Go and sit down at once, Joe," said Mrs. Pepper firmly.

"Can't I take the chair into the bedroom and sit next to Phronsie?" asked Joel, who always tried for some alleviation of his punishments, and he began to drag it into the bedroom.

"Yes, you may do that," said Mrs. Pepper, "but you must sit down on it and keep still." Then she went back to her work.

"And just think how you've spoilt your hair," said Polly in exasperation, "and it did look so nice." She heaved a great sigh. Little David ducked under the brush swiftly going over his own head, to peer into her face. "Never mind, Davie," she said, smiling at him. "Dear Mrs. Beebe will think you look good anyway."

"Won't she think Joel looks good, too?" asked Davie anxiously.

"Oh, yes, maybe," said Polly, stifling the sigh. "Well, hold still, dear. I'll brush him again before he puts on his cap."

Joel, who luckily hadn't heard this, now crowded up as closely as possible to Phronsie, and sat up on his chair as stiff as a ramrod. And at last everything was pronounced by Polly all ready for the children to set forth on the visit; "Except this," said Polly, flying over to Joel and giving his stubby black hair the final attention amid his violent protests. And then they were hurried out to Mother Pepper in the kitchen to see how nice they all looked, as they stood in a row, and for her to give them their final charge before setting forth.

"You know, children," she said, running her black eyes over the line in satisfaction, "that you are to be very good, for Polly and Ben can't go to Mrs. Beebe's till afternoon. Just think, this is the first time you have ever been out in company alone!" She surveyed them proudly. "But Mother trusts you, and I know you will be good."

"I'll be good," said Joel promptly. "I'm always good."

"I'll try, Mamsie; I will," said little Davie; "I will, truly, Mamsie."

"I know you will," said Mother Pepper, beaming at her boys, "and Phronsie, too—I know she'll be good."

"I'll be good," piped Phronsie, putting up her little red lips to be kissed.

So Mrs. Pepper took her baby in her arms, and gave her a good hug and a good-by kiss all at once, and then Joel crowded in between them insisting on the same attention, and of course little Davie couldn't be forgotten. But at last the three were out on the flat doorstone, and Mother Pepper and Polly in the doorway to see them start.

"Now take hold of hands; let Phronsie go in the middle," said Mrs. Pepper, "and walk along nicely. Be careful, Joel, don't run—remember—" as the children went down the path to the old gate.

"Doesn't it seem funny, Mamsie," said Polly, cuddling up close to Mrs. Pepper's side, "to have them go alone out visiting?"

"Yes," said Mrs. Pepper, "but they're old enough now. And you're going, and Ben, too, in the afternoon, so it's all right," yet she cast an anxious glance after the three little figures now going solemnly down the road.

"Yes, I'm going in the afternoon and so is Ben, down to our dear, sweet Mrs. Beebe's," sang Polly, with a hop, skip, and a jump, getting back into the middle of the old kitchen floor. "Mamsie," as Mrs. Pepper came in and shut the door, "isn't it just lovely that we're really going to supper there?"

"I wish you could have gone for all day," said Mrs. Pepper with a sigh, and pausing a minute before taking up her work, "just like the other children—you and Ben."

"Well, I can't," said Polly, flinging back her brown hair

where it tumbled over her forehead, "I'm going to help you, Mamsie—Oh, misery me!" catching sight of herself in the cracked looking glass. Then she burst out laughing and raced into the bedroom. When she came back, every hair was in place, and two braids hanging neatly down her back. Mrs. Pepper looked up and smiled approval that seemed to hop right down into Polly's heart, making it glow with comfort.

"I do think this is just the nicest place, Mamsie," she burst forth in the midst of flying about to do the belated morning work, left in order to get the children ready for their visit.

"So it is, Polly," nodded Mrs. Pepper. "It's home, and the Little Brown House is—"

"The very sweetest place," finished Polly in another burst, and guilty of interrupting.

And just then there was a little scrabbling noise outside the door, and the latch was lifted, and in stumbled Joel, and after him Davie holding fast to Phronsie's fat little hand. Mrs. Pepper dropped her work, and sprang up, her face very pale, for she didn't see any one but the two boys, and Polly let the teakettle she was carrying over to fill the dishpan, clatter down to the floor—and away raced the hot water.

"Oh, goodness! Oh, here's Phronsie!" cried Polly, all in the same breath. Then she sprang over the puddle of hot water to throw her arms around the little figure, but Mrs. Pepper was there first.

"Phronsie would come home," said Joel in a loud, injured key. "Her sunbonnet's untied, and she wouldn't let me or Davie tie it up—she wanted Polly to."

"Please, Polly," begged Phronsie, holding up her hot little chin and hanging with both hands to the strings of the pink sunbonnet, "tie me up, 'cause I must hurry to go and see my dear sweet Mr. Beebe and my dear sweet Mrs. Beebe."

"She's been saying that all the way back," said Davie,

sitting down on the kitchen floor, "and we couldn't hurry to go and see 'em, 'cause she made us come back for Polly to tie up the strings."

"And now we've got to go clear back there," cried Joel wrathfully; "I mean to run every step of the way this time."

"Oh, no, Joe, you mustn't," said Mrs. Pepper. "You'll be a good boy and take hold of Phronsie's hand, and walk nicely, or else you'll have to stay at home."

"And that old sunbonnet is going to stay tied this time," declared Polly, getting down on her knees to make a wonderful bow of the strings. "There, says I, Pet, that won't come out! Now, Mr. Sunbonnet, you behave yourself!" And she gave a pat on Phronsie's head.

"Mr. Sunbonnet, you behave yourself," gurgled Phronsie. So the three children all took hold of hands and started again, Mrs. Pepper and Polly watching them as before, until they were lost in the turn of the road.

All this made them somewhat late at the little shoeshop down on Badgertown's Main Street. Old Mrs. Beebe, in one of her best caps with flying pink ribbons, had been out to the old green door at least three times, shading her eyes, and peering down the narrow cobbled pavement to come back in disappointment.

"You are sure Mis' Pepper understood 'twas today th' children was to come, Pa?" she asked at last.

"Did you ever know Mis' Pepper to make a mistake?" answered the old gentleman, calmly sewing up a rip in one of his own old shoes that had been waiting for just such a spare time. He was just as much put out as was his wife at the threatened loss of the visit, but it never would do for both of them to show it at the same time.

"How you can, Pa, go right on sewin' an' mendin' same's every day," exclaimed old Mrs. Beebe, sitting down heavily on the settee running the length of their little shop where customers sat to have their boots and shoes fitted on, "I don't see, when we're 'xpectin' those blessed children every minute." She smoothed down her black silk apron with her plump hands in vexation.

"It's just because I am 'xpectin' of 'em every minute to come in," said old Mr. Beebe, "that I can set an' be comf't-able," and he drew up his thread with slow, careful fingers.

"Well, I can't," said the old lady, twitching the pink flying ribbons on either side of her cheeks into better place. "Dear me, I wonder if I got out enough doughnuts; they'll be awful hungry when they first get here," and she hurried off into the pantry opening into the room back of the little shop. For this reason, she didn't hear the small steps on the cobblestones underneath the little-paned window, nor the rattling of the latch, nor any of the bustle of the entrance of the little Peppers. And when she got back after replenishing the doughnut plate, there they were surrounding old Mr. Beebe's chair!

But didn't they get a good welcome, though! And Phronsie's pink sunbonnet untied and hung up carefully in Mrs. Beebe's bedroom, she soon had a doughnut in her hand while she sat on Mr. Beebe's knee; and Mother Beebe regaled the two boys with a sugary one apiece, and then they each had a cup of real milk.

"I like it," said Phronsie very gravely, when the old lady set down the cup and wiped off the white drops that trailed away from the little lips, "very much indeed, dear Mrs. Beebe. Why don't I ever have truly milk at home?" And she put up her mouth for some more.

"I shall let her drink all she wants to," said old Mrs. Beebe, nodding furiously over Phronsie's yellow head to the old gentleman, who put up a protesting hand. "There, honey bird, so you should have some more. It won't hurt her a mite," she finished to her husband. And then away she went to see about getting dinner ready and to set out the table with the three extra little plates.

"Now, Phronsie," said old Mr. Beebe, when the doughnut was all eaten, "I'm a-goin' to show you some o' my shoes I have for little folks, an' where I keep 'em."

"I wore my new shoes," said Phronsie, sticking out both feet to regard them affectionately.

"So you did, to be sure," exclaimed old Mr. Beebe in a tone of great surprise, not having been able to see much else besides Phronsie's face since she had perched on his knees.

"And I must wipe them off," said Phronsie, regarding with great disfavor the dust from her long walk that had clung to them, and trying to slip down from his knee.

"No, no—you set still," said old Mr. Beebe. "I'll clean 'em, child." With that he whipped out his big bandanna and softly patted and rubbed the little shoes quite bright again. "There —they're as good as new. How nice you keep 'em, child!"

"They're shut up in Mamsie's drawer," said Phronsie, following his every movement with great satisfaction. "And I wrap 'em up, dear Mr. Beebe, every day."

"So you do," laughed the old man. "Well, that's a good child."

"And I love my new shoes—I do, dear Mr. Beebe." Phronsie put both arms around the black silk stock encircling his fat neck, and whispered in his ear.

"Do you so?" whispered back old Mr. Beebe.

"Yes, I do, very much indeed," whispered Phronsie again, nodding her yellow head at every word.

"That's a good child," repeated the old gentleman. "Well now, Phronsie, I must show you where I keep the shoes for other little girls who are good an' come in to buy 'em," and he set her gently on the floor.

All this time Joel and David had plastered their faces in among the rows of shoes and rubbers dangling from strings running across the shopwindow, to see the passers-by in the narrow street, an occupation of which they were never tired, but now hearing old Mr. Beebe and Phronsie opening drawers and undoing little boxes, the two boys deserted their perch in the window and ran across the little shop.

"Oh, let me," cried Joel, throwing himself into the center of operations—"let me, Mr. Beebe, take 'em out," while little David edged up on the other side of Phronsie just as eagerly.

"Softly—softly," said the old gentleman; "take care there, Joel, you mustn't touch 'em till I tell you to—" as Joel seized a small pair of shiny black slippers out of a box.

"Oh, can't I see 'em?" begged Joel dreadfully disappointed, and having a hard time to keep the tears back.

"Maybe," said old Mr. Beebe, "but I'm going to show Phronsie some of 'em first, an' she's goin' to help me fit 'em if any little girl comes in to buy."

"Oh, may I help you to fit shoes?" screamed Joel, with very red cheeks, and even Davie cried out too, "Oh, *please*, dear Mr. Beebe, let us help you fit shoes."

The old gentleman burst into such a merry fit of laughter at this that even Phronsie, although she didn't in the least know what it was all about, laughed and clapped her hands in glee, Joel and David whirling all around the two, begging and teasing so that old Mrs. Beebe left the little apple turn-overs she was filling and ran out into the small shop, her spectacles pushed up to her cap border. "Gracious me, Pa," she exclaimed, "I thought some of 'em was hurt!"

"There ain't no one hurt, only me, Ma," said old Mr. Beebe, shaking and chuckling and wiping his eyes, "There—there, boys, maybe I'll let you help me. I d'no but Phronsie's goin' to—leastways, if there's a little girl comes in with her ma for a new pair of shoes."

When this was really explained to Phronsie by Joel's screaming it out several times, and Davie's repeating it carefully to her, she sat right down on the floor, quite overcome.

"Look at Phron!" laughed Joel, pointing at her.

"You let her alone," said old Mr. Beebe. "Now, I tell you what you can do, Joel, if you really want to help me."

"I do; I do!" cried Joel. If he couldn't fit on shoes to possible customers, he could at least be of some importance in that delightful shop, and maybe sometime, if he were very good, old Mr. Beebe would really let him wait on folks fortunate enough to have money to buy shoes with.

"That's good," said the little shopkeeper, rubbing his hands in great satisfaction. "Now then, I guess I can find some work for a boy of your size to do. Yes, just the very thing." He went over to the further side of the little shop and lifted the chintz valance hanging down from the lowest shelf. "See those boxes, Joel?"

"Yes, I do," said Joel, getting down on his knees and peering under the valance, little Davie doing the same thing in confidence that something was going to be found for him to help, too.

"Well, I want those all taken out and piled on that shelf." Old Mr. Beebe, who, after all, much preferred them where they were, pointed off to the side of the shop he had left. "Think you can do it, Joey?"

"Yes, sir—ee!" cried Joel decidedly, and beginning at once.

"See here," said old Mr. Beebe in alarm, lest his hard work in finding something for Joel to do should result in injury to his beloved goods, "you mustn't knock off the covers so."

"I didn't mean to," said Joel, his cheeks in a blaze, and

speedily clapping the cover of the green box fast again.

"I know you didn't," said the old gentleman kindly; "but you mustn't go so fast, my boy. There—that's it," as Joel carefully set one box on another and marched across the room with them. "And now, Davie."

David's blue eyes sparkled with delight. "You can help me ever so much." He led the way over to a set of drawers that ran around the side of the small shop to meet the little-paned window. "I've wanted these done ever so long, and now only to think, one of you Pepper children has come to help me out!" And he took up a large snarl of shoestrings of all lengths, very much tangled up.

David's face fell, but the old gentleman, not perceiving it, had him sit down on the settee. "Now, says I," and he laid the bunch in Davie's lap, "if you'll pick that out for me and lay 'em straight, you'll be a good boy as ever lived."

To be "a good boy as ever lived" was such a dazzling outlook that little Davie, smothering his sigh as he saw Joel marching importantly across the shop with his delightful armful of green boxes, took up the snarl, and began at once to pick at the first shoestring end that presented itself.

"And now, Phronsie." Old Mr. Beebe by this time was over by her side, where she still sat on the floor, quite lost in the delightful thought of the little girl to whom she was to help to fit on her new shoes.

"Oh!" she screamed, clapping her hands, as the old gentleman bent over her with—"Now, Phronsie." "Has she come, dear Mr. Beebe?"

"Not yet," he said chuckling, "but you and I are to look out for her, for we never know when customers are comin' in, Phronsie."

"I suppose she's on the way," said Phronsie in grave happiness, and getting up to her feet to smooth down her pinafore. "And she'll sit right here, dear Mr. Beebe, won't she?" running over to pat the old settee.

"Yes, maybe," said the old gentleman, "or I rather think, Phronsie, she'd better sit in that little chair where you did when you got your new shoes."

"Yes, she better have my little chair," cried Phronsie in great excitement, deserting the old settee at once to run over and drag the small wooden chair away from its corner up beside it. And everything being now ready to fit on new shoes to some little girl who needed them very much, old Mr. Beebe and Phronsie now began to watch earnestly for footsteps outside, and to see if the latch on the green door should fly up.

But the latch didn't fly up, and no one coming, Phronsie at last drew a long breath. "The little girl doesn't come, dear Mr. Beebe," she said in a tired voice.

"Well, I declare," Mrs. Beebe's voice broke in upon them. "I declare, how busy you all be! An' dinner'll be ready in ten minutes: I've come to get th' childern to wash their hands an' faces."

"Oh, supposing the little girl should come, dear Mr. Beebe," Phronsie clutched his plump hand and held back as old Mrs. Beebe waddled across the little shop.

"I guess she ain't a-comin' till aft'noon," said the old gentleman soothingly, and just then the big iron latch clicked and the green door was thrown open.

"I've come," said a woman, hurrying in, a black crocheted bag dangling from her arm, "to see if you've got a pair of shoes to fit my little girl. Oh, how do you do, Mis' Beebe?"

Phronsie screamed right out, "Oh, she's come—she's come!" and pulled the little shopkeeper's hand as hard as she could.

"So she has," said old Mr. Beebe, every bit as much excited.

"Yes, indeed, Mis' Phipps, I've got a splendid fit. Walk right in an' set down." He waved her over toward the settee and the little wooden chair close to it. "An' you come along with me, Phronsie, an' we'll pick out some to suit this little girl."

Everything now settling down to business old Mrs. Beebe turned to Dave. "Well, well, an' what has Pa set you to doin'?" she cried, bending over him and his snarl of shoe-strings. "I declare, I never see sech a boy; you're pickin' out those dreadful things jest splendid. Yes, this is Mis' Pepper's boy, Mis' Phipps, that lives in the Little Brown House, an' that's the other one," nodding over to Joel, now down on his knees, prowling under the old chintz valance.

"And that's Phronsie," added David, afraid she would be forgotten and left out in the enumeration, and laying down his strings long enough to point to her over with the old gentleman.

"Is that so?" said the customer, regarding him with great interest. "An' how is your ma?" turning off from the small girl on the little wooden chair, who was following Phronsie and the little shopkeeper with her intent eyes. And without waiting for a reply, her gaze roved over to Joel and at last switched off to Phronsie and the little shopkeeper.

"I'm in a great hurry, Mr. Beebe," she said importantly, "an' if you hain't got any shoes for Marianna, why, I must go somewhere's else. We are to meet her Pa at Simmons's; he's come to sell his grain, and he'll be all put out ef we ain't on time. I've sold my eggs and butter," she volunteered, shaking the black crocheted bag on her arm, so that an old pocketbook could be seen dancing about within the meshes.

"We'll get Marianna's shoes es quick 's we can," said old Mr. Beebe composedly, "but ef you'd rather go somewhere's else, Mis' Phipps, why, I'd advise you to."

"Oh, I didn't say as I was goin'," replied Mrs. Phipps hastily. "You mustn't get mad, Mr. Beebe," she added in an injured tone.

" 'N' I'm glad you've had good luck," said the old gentleman, beginning to feel that perhaps he had used unkindly speech.

"Oh, I hain't had such very good luck," cried Mrs. Phipps in great alarm, lest the price of shoes should go up. " 'Tain't no easy matter when all is counted up, to make much out o' a few hens that do nothin' all day but eat fit to burst."

"Well, here's a pair, now." Mr. Beebe took the two little shoes out from the box, turned them over several times in his big hands, felt of the leather of each upper, then finally placed them in Phronsie's hands. "You run over and show 'em to that lady," he said, nodding over to the settee.

Mrs. Phipps eyed Phronsie curiously, dividing her interest between her and the shoes, Marianna doing the same, so that when the little shopkeeper advanced to them, there wasn't much progress made toward a trade, and old Mrs. Beebe, smothering a sigh, waddled out to see if by chance the stewed beef set back on the stove could have caught.

"It's good leather," said Mr. Beebe. "You needn't pinch it so hard, Mis' Phipps; that shoe'll wear like iron."

"It can stand a few pinches now, then," said Mrs. Phipps grimly, and nipping up another portion between her hard nails.

"Now let's slip on that shoe," cried Mr. Beebe quickly, "an' see how it fits. Maybe it won't do at all."

"I want it," said Marianna suddenly, the first word she had spoken, and leaning over her mother's arm, her mouth watering for the possession of the coveted treasure.

"Stick out your foot then," said old Mr. Beebe cheerily. "Now, Phronsie, you sit down on the floor. Then, says I, that shoe'll fly on. Tee—hee—hee!"

"That child ain't a-goin' to try on shoes!" gasped Mrs. Phipps in amazement. "Why, what are you thinkin' of, Mr. Beebe?" She hitched her black crocheted bag up farther on her arm, throwing aside her shawl ends nervously.

"Ef I fit shoes," observed old Mr. Beebe, "I fit 'em as I please in my shop. As long as they *fit,* I dunno's folks can complain."

But Phronsie took her gaze off from the customer's face, and got up from the floor where she had obediently seated herself. "The lady doesn't want me to, dear Mr. Beebe," she said gravely, and her mouth quivered.

"Oh, yes, she does," said old Mr. Beebe confidently, "or else, you see, Phronsie, there ain't goin' to be *any* shoes fitted in this shop."

"I want them shoes," screamed Marianna in a loud cry, and pointing a red little finger at the one now dangling from Mr. Beebe's hand. It was so piercing that Joel dropped a green box and sprang across the little shop to see what was the matter. David had long ago laid down his snarl of shoestrings to give absorbing attention to his neighbors on the settee, and the little wooden chair.

"Stop your noise," commanded her mother angrily. "I hain't any objection to her, I'm sure," turning to old Mr. Beebe, "so long's you're there."

"There, you see, Phronsie, th' lady's willin'," said the old gentleman.

"Is she, dear Mr. Beebe?" asked Phronsie, clinging to his hand and wishing very much that Mamsie was there.

"Yes, indeed; so sit down, child, and pull on th' shoe."

So Phronsie got down on the old shop floor again, and Marianna in a perfect tremor of bliss tore off her old shoe, and stuck out her very much darned brown cotton stocking. And Phronsie, with both hands trembling in delight and with

a great deal of fear lest the terrible lady staring at her from
above might not like it after all, pulled on the new shoe, old
Mr. Beebe only having to give a helping hand once when it
stuck on the heel.

"It fits—it fits!" screamed Marianna, her black eyes protruding. Joel joined her in a crow, but that was at Phronsie'
success in helping dear Mr. Beebe so well.

"Keep still; you can't tell nothin' till it's tied on," said Marianna's mother. So Phronsie began on the long strings. Thi
was greater enjoyment even than to fit the shoes.

"Here, let me help you," Joel dropped to the floor by he
side.

"No—no," protested Phronsie, "I must do 'em all myself
Joey."

"You let her be," said the old gentleman, "an' get me
chair, Joel."

"She's doing 'em all in the wrong holes," said Joel, running
for the chair which he dragged up to the scene of operations

"Never mind; there, Phronsie," old Mr. Beebe seated him
self in the chair, and leaning over Marianna's foot, somehov
or other each little hole soon had the right string in it, and
bow was neatly tied, and Phronsie, with very pink cheeks, wa
regarding her work. "I did do it," she cried in a joyful littl
voice.

"'Taint done yet," announced Mrs. Phipps—"not till sh
stamps in it." So Marianna stamped up and down in front o
them all till even her mother had to be satisfied, and then th
other shoe was put on and tied up, and everything was don
but paying for them. At last the old pocketbook was draw
out of the black crocheted bag. "I suppose you'll mend thes
up for nothin', seein' I've bought a new pair," said Mrs. Phipp
suddenly, pausing before opening the pocketbook flap, and
pointing to the old shoes on the floor.

Old Mr. Beebe picked up one of Marianna's old shoes. "I couldn't do that," he said. "An' besides, Mis' Phipps, there ain't nothin' to mend. She's run 'em all out."

"Humph—that's all nonsense," ejaculated Marianna's mother. But seeing that she couldn't get anything out of the little shopkeeper but that one statement, she had the old shoes done up in a newspaper, and counting out the price of the new ones in quarters and ten-cent pieces she took her departure, saying, "I shouldn't let her wear those home ef I warn't goin' to make a call on th' way this aft'noon." Then she peered into the room back of the shop, "I must say good-by to Mis' Beebe."

This took some minutes, as the smell of the dinner and the table all set made it impossible for Mrs. Phipps to leave it without a strong effort to include herself and her daughter in the family for that one meal, but old Mrs. Beebe, not looking at it in just that way, Mrs. Phipps twitched Marianna's hat straight and hauled her off without any good-by after all.

But oh! what a good dinner the little shopkeeper had sitting at the head of his table, with old Mrs. Beebe, her pink cap ribbons flying, at the other end, and the three little Peppers, their plates filled with splendid pieces of stewed beef and dumplings. How the spoons and forks flew! till even Joel couldn't eat any more, and Davie was obliged to give up the effort to see the bottom of his plate cleared. And after dinner —well then, why, Phronsie must have her nap. "For we can't have Polly come running in, and not have this blessed little creeter's eyes as bright as buttons," said the little old lady.

"Oh, I'm not tired," protested Phronsie vigorously.

"No, that would never do," declared old Mrs. Beebe, just as decidedly. "Now then, Phronsie child, you shall curl up on Pa's sofa, an' I'll cover you with my plaid shawl; then, says I, you'll be asleep in forty winks."

To curl up on Pa's sofa, and, best of all, to have spread over her dear Mrs. Beebe's plaid shawl, was after all something well worth thinking about. So Phronsie allowed herself to be patted into place, and Mrs. Beebe pulled down the old green paper shade and waddled softly out. In five minutes she thrust her cap in around the half-opened door. There lay Phronsie, one little hand grasping tightly the old frayed fringe, fast asleep as anything.

Meantime, old Mr. Beebe had a hard time enough with the two boys! Joel's task of carrying the green boxes from under the chintz valance to the shelf was soon finished, but as he wouldn't do anything till Davie could join in it, and the snarl of strings was apparently (no matter how diligently worked over) not much nearer unraveling than when begun, and little David could not be persuaded to leave it, the old gentleman was in despair.

"Come, Davie," he said for the third time. But David shook his head and kept picking away. He didn't mean to be disobedient, but all his mind intent on helping dear good Mr. Beebe, it never entered his head to leave his task until completed.

At last Joel flung himself flat on the floor, and waving both feet in the air gave a loud cry of disapproval. "He's a naughty boy," he said, "and I shall tell Mamsie he wouldn't mind you."

Down fell Davie's snarl of shoestrings to his lap. "Oh Joel," he cried, slipping from the old settee to the floor beside him, "don't, don't tell Mamsie."

"I will," said Joel, seeing his advantage with great delight and cocking one black eye at him. "I'll tell her Mr. Beebe told you one—two—ten—'leven times to stop those old strings, and you wouldn't mind him—so there!"

"Joel," cried little David in the greatest distress and clasping both hands, "I'll stop this very minute. I will, Joel, truly I will."

"Won't you go at 'em again?" demanded Joel, thinking it just as well to have it settled definitely.

"No, I won't," said Davie, swallowing hard, "not till dear Mr. Beebe lets me, if you only won't tell Mamsie."

"Then, I won't tell Mamsie," promised Joel, springing to his feet. "Come on, Dave. Now, what'll we do, Mr. Beebe?" he cried.

"Well, now, I tell you," said the old gentleman, wrinkling up his forehead in thought, "you've got to stretch your legs outdoors else you'll be sick. S'posin' you run down to th' butcher's shop an' tell Mr. Hanks I may want, in th' mornin', a slice o' ham. Don't say as I will, remember, but I may. An' then come right back, an' you can set in th' window, an' see th' passin', an' watch fer Polly an' Ben."

"All right," shouted Joel, and seizing Davie's hand he bore him off, and the two little figures clattered off over the cobblestones. Presently there they were back again, and crowded up in among the dangling shoes and slippers, their faces pressed against the small-paned window.

But it seemed as if Polly would never come, although they knew she would get through her work first; it always took Ben a good while when he was tackling any work at Deacon Blodgett's, and they were nearly turning away in despair when, "Hooray!"—Joel spied her first, and he jumped so quickly he knocked down one of the strings and away flew a whole lot of rubbers into the middle of the floor.

"'Tain't hurt 'em a mite," said old Mr. Beebe, as Joel paused in his mad career. So off the two boys dashed to meet Polly, flying up over the cobblestones, her cheeks as rosy as anything and her brown eyes dancing.

"Oh, I'm so glad to get here!" she exclaimed, seizing them both. "Oh, dear me, I thought I should never get through my work. Where's Phronsie?"

"She's asleep," said Joel, "and you've been awful slow." All the while he clung to her hand tightly.

"I know it," laughed Polly, "but I'm so glad dear Mrs. Beebe made her take her nap. Well, Mamsie sent you her love, and she knew you'd been good children."

Little David hung his head. That affair about the shoestrings still troubled him, and he meant to tell Mamsie as soon as he got home, but Joel saved him all words at present.

"We've been as good as pie," he declared. That made him think of that delightful dinner. "We had some, Polly," he cried, "little ones," and he smacked his lips.

"And they were all juice," said little Davie reflectively, from the other side.

"Yes, and Mrs. Beebe has saved one for you and one for Ben 'cause you couldn't come to dinner," said Joel.

"Has she?" cried Polly radiantly. "Oh, isn't that too good of her! And Ben does so love little pies."

"I wish she'd saved me one," said Joel. "So do I love 'em."

"Why, you ate yours up, Joey," said little Davie, craning his neck around Polly to regard him with surprise.

"I know it," said Joel, bursting into a laugh, "but I wish I had another."

"Well, if you've had one of dear Mrs. Beebe's little pies, Joe," said Polly, laughing too, "that's quite enough," as they scrambled up to the green door.

And Phronsie opened her eyes the minute they all swarmed into the room back of the little shop, old Mr. and Mrs. Beebe joining the ranks, and sat up quite straight on Pa's old sofa, and put out her arms with a little crow—"Oh, Polly, take me!" tangled up as she was in the old plaid shawl. And then after they had all sobered down after the delight over Polly's coming, the old lady exclaimed suddenly, "Dear me, I must set th' table for supper, so's to be all ready for Ben."

"Oh, let me help," cried Polly, putting Phronsie down and flying after her.

"Let me too," piped Phronsie, stumbling after.

"And me—and me!" echoed Joel and David.

And old Mrs. Beebe laughing and saying "Yes, come along all of you," the whole bunch of Peppers rushed here and there quite overcome with delight, all getting hold of the tablecloth at once, so that nobody could pull it straight.

"See here," said Polly, when she had whirled around and around the table, first pulling one corner and then another straight, to have it immediately whisked away, "we can't ever do it this way. Now, only one of you must help me, and the others stand still. Take care, Joe, you'll tear it!"

"It's all hanging on the floor," declared Joel.

"Well, that's because you twitched it so," said Polly in vexation, and running around the table again to examine it for herself. "Oh, dear me, so it is. Well now, Joel, you let it alone, and Davie and I will straighten it."

"I don't want to fix it," said Joel, quite well pleased to have nothing to do with it, and only longing for the time to come when the dishes should be placed on the table. So Polly and little David patted and pulled it quite straight and smoothed out all the crinkles. "Now," said Polly with a long breath, stepping back to review the work, "doesn't that look just fine though!"

Then Joel made a rush for the pantry door. "I'm going to get the dishes," he shouted.

"Oh, no, you mustn't, Joe," cried Polly in alarm. "I'm going to take them down; you might break them."

"I ain't goin' to have those dishes for supper today," said old Mrs. Beebe. "I'm goin' to set out my best chiney."

"You're going to set out your best china!" gasped Polly, and looking over at the corner cupboard, not believing that she could have heard straight.

"Yes," said old Mrs. Beebe, nodding till her pink cap ribbons trembled violently, "I am, for I hain't used 'em since th' minister took tea here when he first come to Badgertown, an' that's ten years ago; an' I was thinkin' th' other day I wish't I had a chance to set 'em out."

"But s'posing we should break them." Polly came over to say this in an awe-struck voice, while the boys, quite impressed with all this, crowded up to hear the whole of it, Phronsie was spinning around the room making a merry little cheese and humming softly to herself. It was quite enough for her to be at supper at her dear sweet Mrs. Beebe's and to have Polly safely there.

"Oh, you won't break any of 'em," said the little old lady confidently, and going over to the corner cupboard. "I shall give th' childern some mugs, but you and Ben shall have a nice cup an' saucer, an' we'll have th' cake plate and th' glass pudding dish," and her eyes shone.

Polly turned quite pale. It was perfectly splendid, but oh, if anything should happen to those two cups and saucers that Ben and she were to have! But she had no time to worry about it, as old Mrs. Beebe now handed down from one of the shelves a china mug. "There," she said, "that's for Phronsie's place. I used to drink out of it when I wasn't any bigger'n she is. 'From a Friend,'" read the old lady, turning the mug around so that they all could get the best view.

"Let me see—I want to see 'From a Friend,'" screamed Joel, crowding up, while little Davie edged up to gaze at the faded gilt letters.

"Yes, my mother's uncle give it to me. He said I was a good girl. I warn't no bigger'n Phronsie, an' she's a good girl, so I'm goin' to let her drink out of it today."

"Phronsie, you're going to drink out of 'From a Friend,'"

screamed Joel, deserting old Mrs. Beebe and the china mug to run and twitch her pink pinafore.

When Phronsie understood that she was really to have her milk in that splendid china mug that her dear sweet Mrs. Beebe used to drink out of when she was a little girl, her delight knew no bounds. And she went and stood by the table edge, quite satisfied not to move, so long as she could look at it where Polly had placed it ready for supper.

"I wish I could have a 'From a Friend' to drink out of," grumbled Joel.

"Hush, for shame, Joe!" said Polly. But old Mrs. Beebe had heard. "Well, now I must see what I can get for you, Joel," she said kindly. "An' then Davie must have one, too."

"Yes, you must get Dave one, too," said Joel, hopping from one set of toes to the other in delight.

"You can take Pa's cup; he hain't used that for years," said Mrs. Beebe. She handed down a great coffee cup. The handle was snipped and the flowers around the edge were much worn.

"The saucer's broke, but you don't need one," said Mrs. Beebe, setting the cup within Joel's awe-struck hand.

"What's that?" asked Joel, running one finger over the edge of the cup that covered the top a little way.

"Oh, that was when Pa had a beard. He used to wear his hair all 'round his mouth," said old Mrs. Beebe, "but he shaved it all off a good many years ago. An' the saucer's got broke, so we set th' cup up on th' shelf. But I'm goin' to let you drink out of it, now, Joel."

Joel, vastly pleased to have something used by a big man with hair all 'round his mouth, marched with it to the table. "There, that's mine," he announced. "It's a great deal better than any old 'From a Friend.'"

Little Davie held his hands closely clasped together. Would

the corner cupboard hold any more such splendid things to drink out of as Joel and Phronsie had received. He scarcely breathed when—"There, says I, Davie, now what do you think!" and a little mug was held before him. It had two shining luster bands running around it and between them was a yellow band, and on it, for all the world, was in big letters of gilt *"For David."*

When David saw those words, he seized the little mug, and screamed right out, "It's for me to drink out of!" and held it close to his blue eyes big with joy.

"That was my grandpa's," said old Mrs. Beebe in as great a delight. "An' his name was David—David Brown. An' now to think you are goin' to drink out o' it today, you preety creeter, you!" and she beamed at him.

"Oh, David!" exclaimed Polly, hurrying over to him, "do be careful. Oh, dear Mrs. Beebe, I don't believe he ought to have it." But Davie hugged his treasure tightly to his bosom, and went unsteadily over to put it on the table.

"He won't break it," said Mrs. Beebe; "an' besides, I'm goin' to give it to him 'cause o' th' name, when I get through with bein' able to look up an' see it up there in that cupboard. An' now you come an' help me set out th' cups and saucers for Ben an' you."

"Oh, here he comes!" cried Polly, with a glance through the glass door opening into the little shop. "Oh, Ben!" and with a bound she flew off to meet him.

"Hooray!" Joel deserted his treasure, but little Davie and Phronsie had been so absorbed in theirs that they hadn't heard a word.

"Well," cried Ben, his cheeks glowing and his big blue eyes alight, as he came in with Polly and Joel hanging to him, and old Mr. Beebe, rubbing his hands in satisfaction, bringing up the rear. And he had hardly spoken to dear old

Mrs. Beebe before Joel dragged him off to the table. "I've got a cup all to myself; see, Ben, see—see—and a big man used to drink out of it with hair all 'round his mouth; and it's mine. And Phronsie got a 'From a Friend,' and I like mine best."

"Hulloa!" exclaimed Ben, "and so Pet has got one, too," and he bent to kiss her.

"Yes," hummed Phronsie, putting a little finger gently on it, "and I like it, Bensie, very much, I do."

"Well, see Davie's," cried Polly, getting hold of Ben's jacket to pilot him around the table; "only think of this 'For David,'" and she held the shining little luster mug up.

"Well! well!" exclaimed Ben, quite overcome; while old Mr. Beebe nodded and smiled over the heads of the Five Little Peppers as pleased as the children themselves.

"And see our cups," cried Polly at last, pointing to the corner cupboard where the whole array of ancient flowered china was spread forth. "You and I are each going to have one of those! Dear Mrs. Beebe told me so her own self."

"An' now, says I, I must get 'em down, an' then you an' me, Polly, will set on th' supper. We'll have it early 'cause Ben must be hungry."

"I am," said Ben, "awfully hungry. I believe I could eat a bear—every bit of him!"

"Oh, Ben," screamed Joel, swarming over him excitedly, "not his head, Ben, and his legs, and every single smitch of him."

"Yes, *sir!*" declared Ben recklessly. "I'm so hungry, Joe, there wouldn't be any bear when I got through."

VIII

At the Peters Farm

"HALLOA, Joel!" Mr. Atkins left the bundle of brown sugar he was doing up for the Widow Smollett, and hurried around the counter to the door. "Wait a minute." But Joel was off on the wind.

"I never see such a boy for getting over the ground," the storekeeper exclaimed, discomfited, turning back to his customers.

"I'm goin' by the Little Brown House, an' I'll tell Mis' Pepper anythin'," volunteered a man, waiting his turn to be served.

"Well, you tell her I've got a job for Joel," said the storekeeper, getting nimbly back of the counter again, to resume work on the brown-sugar bundle.

"Pshaw!—what can that little chap do?" said the man, jamming one hand deep in his trousers pocket and laughing.

"He's little, but he's smart as a cricket," said Mr. Atkins.—

"No, I hain't had any eggs brought in today, Miss Bassett.—Good land o' Goshen, Hiram, all them Pepperses have got git up an' git to 'em.—No, I said I hadn't had any brought in today. I was just a-tellin' Miss Bassett so."

"And I sh'd as soon set a cricket to work," said Hiram, still laughing, "but I'll take th' message all right to Mis' Pepper."

"An' them children'll do more someday for Badgertown 'n all o' us folks put together. That's my Bible belief," declared Mr. Atkins, snapping the string off short.—"There's your sugar, Mrs. Smollett, four cents a pound; it orter be four an' a half, but I hain't riz on it yet.—I'll wait upon you," in reply to an irate question, as to how long he was expected to stand there "doin' nothin'," from an impatient applicant for saleratus.—"Yes, well, you tell Mrs. Pepper I've got a job for Joel; that's all you've got to do, Hiram.—Now, I'll 'tend to you first; you've ben waitin' some time." And he turned off to a customer at the end of the counter.

And Hiram's several bundles having been done up, and deposited in his wagon, Mr. Atkins felt quite relieved in his mind, and very sure that Joel would be down as soon as ever the message got to him.

Which happened exactly so. There he was, with David at his heels, and pounding on the counter. "What is it, Mr. Atkins?" he cried, his black eyes sparkling in excitement. It was the very first time in his life that a job had ever been waiting for him in this important way.

"There's a person been in here, Joel," said Mr. Atkins, "this morning who wants a boy to help him; and I thought of you, 'cause I knew you wanted to be like Ben an' help your ma."

"Yes, I do," said Joel, standing very tall, "and I'm going to have a job and be like Ben; just exactly like Ben, Mr. Atkins," and his black eyes shone.

Little David could not conceal his admiration, and beamed on him affectionately.

"So you shall," declared the storekeeper with great enthusiasm, "and I got you this job, Joel. I expect you're goin' to be master smart at it."

"I'm going to be. Oh, what is it—what you said?" declared Joel with energy, and getting up now to his tiptoes.

"Master smart," repeated Mr. Atkins with emphasis. "Well, now, Joel, you've got to begin your job tomorrow at Old Man Peters's."

"What?" Down went Joel to stand flat, and his hands left off pounding the counter to fall to his sides.

"Old Man Peters was a-goin' to get another boy"—Mr. Atkins was talking in a perfect stream, now—"but I spoke for you, Joel. An' you've got to go an' take that job, 'cause it's the only one there is to be had," and he shot a keen glance into Joel's black eyes.

"I ain't going to work for Old Man Peters," declared Joel in a great dudgeon, and marching to the door, his hands now thrust into his pockets and his head quite high. "Come on, Dave."

"See here, Joel." The storekeeper leaned over his counter. "You come here a minute."

"I ain't going to work for Old Man Peters," declared Joel stoutly, standing quite still to regard the storekeeper with anything but pleasure.

Just as decidedly, "Yes, you will," Mr. Atkins said. " 'Cause if you don't, you can't help your Ma, and be big like Ben."

"I ain't going," began Joel. Then his voice died down, "Oh, dear me, I ain't—I ain't."

"I don't blame ye," broke in two or three voices. "I wouldn't do a stroke for sech a skinflint," added another. The storekeeper cast a reproachful glance in that direction, and aid sharply, "I'm a-talkin' to Joel Pepper just at present."

Joel was wringing his small hands now, the picture of distress as he stood in the middle of the store, with little Davie quite gone in despair at this dreadful state of affairs, huddling up against him.

"To help Mamsie." He could do it if he would only take this job that Mr. Atkins had gotten for him, and "be big like Ben." "Oh, dear me!" Joel didn't see any of the men, nor the one sympathetic woman who hovered on the edge of the group to see how matters would turn out. He was lost to everything around him. And when at last Mr. Atkins said very coldly, "Oh, well, if you don't want to help your Ma, Joel, why—" He burst out, "Oh, I do, I do," and dashed up to seize the storekeeper by the arm, and hang to it screaming, "I'll go to Old Man Peters's, Mr. Atkins, I will!"

"That's a good boy, Joel," said the storekeeper, quite mollified, who had really been quite put to his wits to find something that one of the brood in the Little Brown House might do to help eke out the store of pennies that kept the wolf from the door. And lately, when Mrs. Pepper brought back the coats she made, he was struck with dismay to see how white her cheek was, and how tired the bright eyes looked.

"She's getting all beat out," he said on one such occasion to his wife as he locked up for the night and went home, which only consisted in going into the extension of the store built on to accommodate the growing needs of his family.

"Can't you find her somethin' for th' boys to do, 'Biah?" said that good woman, setting the teapot down after taking off a cupful for herself. "No halfway stuff for me," she always said; then it must be filled to the brim for Mr. Atkins, who couldn't bear it strong.

"Ben's doin' all he can," said the storekeeper, sitting down heavily. "Well, I never have ben on my legs so much as to-day, Jane."

"I don't mean Ben," said Mrs. Atkins quickly, and taking up the teapot to pour the boiling water in. "I'm sure that boy'll work himself to death if somebody don't stop him. I'm talkin' of Joel an' David."

"Them little chaps," cried her husband. "What are you thinkin' of, Jane? The idea o' settin' them to work."

"Now, there's lots o' work small fingers can do," observed Jane nowise dashed, and tipping up the teakettle deftly, she poured the boiling water in. "That won't keep you awake, 'Biah," she said, with a glance of scorn for the cup she set beside his plate.

"An' if Mrs. Pepper breaks down, why, I can't tell what would happen to those Little Brown House folks." She suddenly took up one corner of her brown checked apron, and do what she would to prevent it, Mr. Atkins distinctly heard a sniffle as she abruptly disappeared in the pantry.

"I can't help it, Jane; I'm sure 'tain't my fault." The store-keeper turned uneasily on his chair, put in a spoonful of sugar too much in his tea, then tried to cover up the mistake by getting in a double portion of milk. "You'll have to get me another cup, Jane," at last he called to his wife, who on that summons hastily emerged from the pantry, trying to look gay of countenance as if the conversation had been of the cheeriest description.

"Now, 'Biah," she said, her heart smiting her at a sight of his face, "don't you worry no more about th' Pepperses; th' Lord'll provide," and she twitched up his cup, poured off the contents in the sink, and came back with a fresh one steaming hot.

"Th' Lord ain't a-goin' to take care o' folks in Badgertown, so long as He's put other people here to look after 'em," said the storekeeper, this time with a careful hand to deal himself the right seasoning for his cup, "an' I do b'lieve I better find somethin' for Joel to do. He's awful smart, Jane."

"That's so," said Mrs. Atkins, getting into her seat opposite her husband. Then she wiped her eyes again, for Jane had a tender place in her heart. "But don't let it be too hard," she begged.

"I'll have to take what I can get," said Mr. Atkins stirring his tea, and beginning to feel a bit relieved at the prospect of lightening the burden settling down on the Little Brown House.

"I'll ask every one who comes into th' store tomorrow, Jane, an' somewhere's there must be a boy wanted to do chores, I'll be bound."

"So do," nodded his wife, and, delighted to see him more cheerful, she took a long draught from her black-looking tea, and switched the conversation to more entertaining gossip.

But no matter how much Mr. Atkins pushed his inquiries among his customers to unearth the needs of a small boy to do chores in or around Badgertown, not only tomorrow but several days thereafter passed, and no one seemed ready to acknowledge any such need. At last the storekeeper was reduced to despair, and to cudgel his brains for some other plan to give timely assistance to a person who would not accept money.

At this moment, the rattle of wagon wheels and a sudden plunge as a long-suffering horse was brought to a quick stop by a loud and angry "Whoa!" proclaimed the arrival of a rich but by no means desirable customer.

"Now I suppose 'Old Man Peters' will want a pail o' lard for nothin'," muttered the storekeeper, his vexation noways alleviated by the sight of a customer who usually brought into his shop more plague than profit.

When the trifling matters of trade that always lengthened out by long dickering were at last brought to a conclusion, and Mr. Eli Peters buttoned up in his waistcoat pocket his wallet that had not suffered greatly in the business transaction, much to the storekeeper's disgust, he paused, and said in a sharp high key, "You don't know of a boy, d'ye, Atkins, that I can hire?"

"What kind of a boy?" demanded the storekeeper irritably.

"Oh, a smart, likely one; he don't need to be big. Ye don't know of one, do ye?"

"I know a smart, likely boy as ever stepped," said Mr. Atkins, determined not to give any names, "but I don't know as he could do your work, Mr. Peters."

Old Mr. Peters's little ferret eyes gleamed. "Hey, well, who is't?" He tapped on the floor with his stick that he always carried in the wagon to help his progress as soon as he stepped on the ground. "Who is't? Come, speak up lively, I hain't no time to lose; time's money."

"I guess it is," said the storekeeper with a snap to his thin lips, and a lively memory of the half hour wasted over this unprofitable customer, whom, after all, it never would do to offend.

"Well, this boy I know of is smart enough, my gracious, but he ain't big enough to work hard. What you want to set him at?"

"Oh, little odd jobs," said the old man carelessly; "some of 'em in th' house to help th' women folks."

"Oh, if that's the case," said Mr. Atkins, who was friendly to Mrs. Peters and Miss Miranda—"as different from that old Scrooge," he had said in the privacy of his home, "as light is from darkness"—"why, I'll give you his name; it's Joel Pepper."

"Oh, that boy." Old Man Peters's eager face fell, and the

light in the ferret eyes went out. "I d'no's I want him," he said slowly.

"*Not want one o' them Pepper children!*" exclaimed the storekeeper in astonishment, as if the greatest blessing the earth could yield had been ignored. "Well, I never!"

"I don't think I like that Joel," said Mr. Peters, beginning to work his way to the door.

"Well, I can tell you that Joel Pepper is th' smartest boy around here for miles and miles," cried the storekeeper, taking up quick cudgels, "an' I don't b'lieve his ma would let him come to you, anyway," he added with venom. "So, we'll say no more about it; she's awful particular where any o' 'em go," he added, not caring if his words did lose him, for good and all, the chance of seeing the rich old man darken his door again.

"Hey, what's that?" squeaked Old Man Peters, this quite deciding him, and suddenly whirling about. "Well, I'm willing to try Joel, only he come to my house once, his ma sent him on an errant, an' he was awful sassy."

"Sassy, was he?" Then Mr. Atkins laughed; he couldn't help it. "Well, I guess that's all right; you don't mind what a shaver as little as him says, I s'pose."

"I d'no's I do," replied the old man grudgingly. "Well, send him along; tell him to come tomorrow." And he stumped out, untied his old horse, upon whom, as soon as he got into the wagon, he bestowed a stinging blow from the whip, and rattled off at a smart rate down the road.

The storekeeper leaned his hands on the counter. "Sassy, was he?" he ejaculated with delight. "Well, I guess Joel can take care o' hisself wherever he goes. An' it's th' only place there is. Yes, I'll advise him to try it."

And on the morrow, sure enough, Joel, as tidy as possible (for although the material might be well worn down to its bones, Mrs. Pepper always kept the clothes of the children clean and wholesome), set forth on his long walk to old Mr. Peters's house. The worst of it was that David was not allowed to go. He had not been asked by the prospective employer, so, of course, he must stay at home, and he now plastered his face against the small-paned window as Joel went out of the old kitchen and off to his work. He felt very big, and he tried to walk just like Ben, pushing up his little shoulders sturdily, holding his head high, and clutching his bundle of dinner, that Polly had put up for him, under his arm.

"Make it a big one, do, Polly," he had begged, prancing after her as she went to the bread-pantry.

"Yes, I will, Joey," she cried. "Oh, dear me!" she was just going to say, "you mustn't go to Old Man Peters's." Then she remembered what the mother had said, "We can't choose our work, Polly, and we'd ought to be thankful that Joel has got the chance," and she stifled the sigh, and cut off a generous slice, bemoaning all the while to herself that it wasn't cake.

"If we only had something nice to give him, Mammy," she mourned, hurrying over to Mrs. Pepper's chair when Joel had raced off to wash his face for the last time.

"It's the best we've got," said Mrs. Pepper bravely. Yet she looked tired, and a little white line was beginning to come around her mouth.

"Sometime, we are going to be rich; oh, awfully rich, Mamsie," cried Polly, when she saw that. Then she danced off to the old breadbox again, and pretty soon Joel's dinner was all ready, and he was kissed and pulled into shape by Polly, and then Phronsie had to be hugged, and last of all, Mamsie, because little Davie was not to be counted, as he clung to Joel through the whole time.

"Joel," Mrs. Pepper laid down her needle and looked into his black eyes, "we're going to be very glad that you're working for Mr. Peters."

Joel squirmed at the name, but he never took his gaze from her face.

"And the Little Brown House is never to be ashamed for anything, Joey."

"I'm going to be good," declared Joel with a smart bob of his black head.

"See that you are," said Mrs. Pepper firmly. Then she took up the needle again, because that had to fly in and out, or else the wolf would surely get in at the door; and off Joel sped, to whirl around and wave his hand at the turn of the road.

"Don't feel bad, Davie," cried Polly, gazing over his head at the little figure disappearing down the thoroughfare. "Oh, dear me! Davie, don't," for little David, quite beside himself with grief at this first separation from Joel, threw himself on the old kitchen floor, and burst into a passion of tears.

"Never mind, Polly." Mrs. Pepper got out of her chair, "you can take Phronsie out of doors to play—there, there, Davie, Mother's boy," and she was down on her knees stroking the soft light hair away from his forehead, as Polly took Phronsie's hand and led her softly out.

"What is the matter with Davie?" asked Phronsie in a troubled voice. "Oh, Polly, I don't want to go out and play."

"Well, you must," said Polly in a thick voice, and a desperate feeling at her heart. Supposing David was going to be sick! Oh, it might kill him to be kept away from Joel! And there was Joel going to work for that dreadful hard, cross old man. Oh, how cruel he was to keep Joel and not pay him on that day when Mamsie had sent him with the coat and told him to wait for the money. She sank down on the grass under the old scraggy apple tree, and buried her face in her hands.

Phronsie tugged at her apron. "Polly," she said gently, but Polly did not hear.

"Polly!" This time the voice was a very grieved little one, so that Polly flung down her hands, and seized her hungrily, covering her face with kisses. "Oh, I'm a bad, selfish old pig, Phronsie," she cried remorsefully.

"You are not a bad old pig, Polly," said Phronsie, "and I love you very much, I do."

"Oh, yes, I am," declared Polly. "I'm just as bad as I can be, when Mamsie sent me out here to play with you. Oh, dear me, come on, Pet." She sprang to her feet so suddenly, she nearly overthrew the little figure, and held out her hands.

"But I don't want to play," said Phronsie, now standing quite still and regarding her gravely. "I want to go into the kitchen, and see what is the matter with Davie; I do, Polly."

"No," said Polly in her most decided fashion. "You can't do that, Phronsie, and I can't go in there either, for Mamsie sent us out. Oh, dear me! I'm going to play tag. Come on, Phronsie!" and she dashed around the old apple tree, and in a minute, there was Phronsie, merrily flying after her, little peals of delight sounding all through the dismal old kitchen.

"Now, then." Mrs. Pepper was wiping off the last tears from Davie's little cheeks as he sat in her lap. "Mother's boy is going out to play with Phronsie, and let Polly come in and finish her work."

David shivered at the word "play" and crouched down lower within her arms. "Must I?" he said.

"Not if you don't want to," said Mrs. Pepper, "but you'll help Polly ever so much, and that will help me."

David gave a long sigh. "Then I'll go, Mamsie," he said, and slid out of her lap.

"Now, that's Mother's good boy," cried Mrs. Pepper, kissing his pale cheek into which a little pink color began to come at her praise. "You can't think what a comfort you'll be to me for doing that, Davie."

"Am I a comfort?" asked little Davie, the pink beginning to get very bright, "am I, truly, Mamsie?"

"Yes, indeed!" declared Mrs. Pepper in her heartiest fashion, and with another kiss. "You're just as much help as Joel is. Remember that, Davie."

"Oh, Mamsie!" Little David was so surprised, he stared at her in wonder. "Joel's earning money," at last he said.

"Well, and you're helping me to earn money," said Mrs. Pepper cheerily; "so run along and play prettily with Phronsie, so that Polly can come back to her work," and she dismissed him with a little pat on his shoulder.

"Dear me, I ought to fly off to mine." And she burst into a merry little laugh, so like to Polly's own, that Davie felt his heart grow light at once, and he laughed, too, and ran off as fast as his feet would carry him.

Meantime, Joel, who had trudged on happily, every step of the way feeling big and important, the minute he saw the big, rambling, old red house, known as the Peters farm, felt his feet begin to lag, and when he reached the gate hanging by one hinge, why, he almost turned right straight around to fly home to Mamsie! But there sat Old Man Peters on the porch.

"Hey, so you're here at last, you Pepper boy," he called out, "a quarter of an hour late."

"I'm not late," said Joel in a loud voice, and trudging in at the gate feeling big at once, and able to defend himself. "Mamsie said I had half an hour, and if I didn't stop, I could get here in plenty of time. And I didn't stop a single bit, but I walked on and on." Joel brought this out wrathfully, and sank down hot and red on the lower step.

"Don't you contradict me, you Pepper boy," snarled Old Man Peters, knocking with his cane the well-worn piazza floor, "and I don't care what your mother says. My time's what I go by."

"My mother is always right," said Joel proudly, and fixing the wizened face above him with his black eyes.

"Pa, don't badger the boy when he's first come," said Miss Miranda, making her appearance in the doorway. "Look how red his face is; he's awful tired."

"You go in an' 'tend to your work," commanded her father, shaking his stick at her, "an' I'll see to my business. Now then, boy," he got out of his chair, "I'll set you to doin' somethin'. Mebbe that'll stop your sassy tongue."

So Joel got off from the lowest step and followed the old man as he stumped off over the patchy grass, and the remains of a once good vegetable garden, where everything straggled off in its own sweet will, trying to hide behind its neighbors as if ashamed to be seen in Old Man Peters's domain.

At last, behind the big barn, many of whose shingles seemed about to part acquaintance with their fellows, while the big door, and the shed tacked on to the rear partook of the general decay, the old man paused and pointed with his stick. "That's your work, Joel, or whatever your name is, and the sooner you set at it, the better it will be."

Joel stared on all sides and burst out, "I don't see any work."

Old Man Peters broke into a laugh that was more of a cackle than anything else, and that showed all his gums, for most of his teeth were gone long ago.

"Ha, ha! It's there all the same. You're to clean out th' pigpen."

Now, the pigpen at old Mr. Peters's place hadn't been cleaned out for so long that no one could remember the exact time, and it wouldn't have been done now, only for the reason that the owner had at last made up his mind that if the big barn were not strengthened by some good work being put out on it, it would result in a great loss to him, for it was sagging dreadfully in that corner, and, besides, when the work of putting in new timbers was being accomplished, then was the time, if ever, to put on an ell, and increase its size. But, first of all, the pigpen must be cleaned out; and, to do this, a small boy, who needn't be paid very much, was the best sort of a person to set to work on it.

"Get down, Joel, and go at it," said Old Man Peters, now in a very good humor indeed. "I've taken the pigs to t'other shed, so you can set to work at once."

"I shan't," said Joel wrathfully, and the color flying all over his cheek, "do it ever; not a single thing."

"You won't?" cried the old man in a passion, and he raised his stick. But as Joel looked at him without even so much as a glance from his black eyes at the stick, he thought better of it, and his hand carrying it dropped to his side. "You engaged to come and do my work," he snarled.

"I didn't," said Joel stoutly, "say I'd come and do your pigpen; so there, now."

"You're a pretty boy," said Old Mr. Peters, shaking with wrath at the prospect of losing him. "What kind of a mother have you got, I'd like to know, to bring you up like that?"

"She didn't bring us up," cried Joel, his black eyes blazing, and advancing on him so furiously that the old man stepped involuntarily back against the barn.

"No, I sh'd say not," he cackled.

"And you aren't going to say anything about my mother," declared Joel, doubling up his small brown fists and throwing back his head.

"Stop—get off," said Old Man Peters, edging farther away. "Well, she didn't teach you to keep your promises," he sneered.

"She did—she did," cried Joel wildly, "and you're a bad old man, and I hate you."

"Well, I sh'd s'pose if you think so much of her, you wouldn't want to worry her," said Mr. Peters, seeing his advantage. "How'd she like it to have you go home and say you'd shirked your work, hey?"

Down went Joel's angry little fists to his sides, and his black head dropped.

"An', beside, see," said the old man, now quite elated, "that if you go home, an' say you wouldn't do my work, like enough she won't ever let you take another job. Then, says I, Joel Pepper, where'd you be?"

Where Joel would be in such a dreadful state of affairs was more than he could say. And by this time he was beyond reasoning, so he dropped down to his knees on the edge of the dreadful mess in the pigpen and began to crawl over the sill of the barn.

"I'll throw you a broom an' a shovel," said the old man in great glee. And presently that was done, a worn-down broom and an old shovel with a broken handle tumbled in, and then, after minute directions how the work was to be done, Mr. Peters stumped back to the house.

"Well, I've set that lazy boy to work," he said, rubbing his hands in delight as he sat down in the kitchen.

"What's he doin'?" asked Mrs. Peters, rolling out piecrust on the baking table. It didn't in the least look like what Mrs. Deacon Blodgett considered worthy to cover her "apple filling," Mr. Peters not allowing any such waste of lard and other necessary material. But it was called "pie" and as such had to be made regularly—so many a week.

"Never you mind," Mr. Peters stopped chuckling to emit the sour reprimand. Then he sank back in his big chair and rubbed his hands again harder than ever.

Mrs. Peters exchanged a glance with her daughter, who caught the last words, as she was coming into the kitchen, her dustpan in her hand. "Hush, don't say nothin'," she said as Miranda passed her to throw the sweepings into the stove, and she shook her head over in the direction of Mr. Peters in the big chair.

"I'll find out for myself," determined Miranda, and going out with her dustpan for another accumulation. "Beats all what makes Pa act so like Kedar; what's he ben up to, I wonder."

Meantime, Joel worked on like a beaver; not only his hands and face were grimy, but his clothes were smeared from head to foot, while as for his shoes, well—they were so covered with mud and straw and the general mess of the old pen that no one would have known that they were shoes. But after he was fairly at work, Joel thought nothing of all this, but pegged away, his face streaming with perspiration, one happy thought running through his mind—"I'm earning money, and helping Mammy"—and he actually forgot his dinner, tucked away by Polly, in the paper bundle that he had carried under his arm, and set down carefully by the side of the barn before beginning his work. It was only when he heard a voice that he looked up.

"Oh, my!" it was a boy considerably bigger than Joel looking over the pigpen rail.

"What you doin'?"

"Working," said Joel shortly. He didn't like this boy, and Mamsie didn't approve in the least of him, so Joel had strict orders, whenever they met in the village on errands to the store, to keep as good a distance off as possible. So now he bent over his work again.

"Hah! he goin' to pay you?" demanded the boy, pointing with a dingy thumb toward the house.

At the word "pay" Joel straightened up. "Yes," he said, feeling very big and important.

"How much?" the boy looking over the railing cried eagerly, his green eyes glistening.

"I don't know," said Joel.

"Hah, hah, hah! You *are* a greeny," cried the other boy. Then he doubled up with laughing and slapped his patched knee.

"Stop your laughing," cried Joel, lifting a face that would have looked very red could it have been seen for the mud.

At this, the other boy laughed harder than ever.

"If you don't stop laughing, I'll come up and punch you," cried Joel, forgetting all about Mamsie and what she had told him, and he lifted black, wrathful eyes that snapped vengeance.

But the other boy, preferring to keep on laughing, did so, until he rolled on the mangy grass, holding his sides, only to hop to his feet, when he saw a small but determined figure advancing dangerously near.

"I'm going to punch you," announced Joel, his fists in two hard little knots; "I said I would."

"Hah!" began the other boy, but he hadn't time to finish, for Joel, having announced his intentions, did pitch in, and the visitor, who began by thinking it an easy matter to whip the smaller boy, was now principally occupied in trying to see how he could best avoid the hard thwacks the sturdy little fists were dealing him.

"Ma! Ma!" cried Miranda, at last spying them as she was shaking out her dustcloth. "There are two boys fighting down by th' barn," she screamed over the stairs.

"Oh, you don't say so," cried Mrs. Peters back again. "Dear me, I hope they won't go near th' Pepper boy. If anythin' sh'd happen to him, his ma never'd forgive me."

"It *is* th' Pepper boy who's fightin', Ma," proclaimed Miranda, running her head out of the window. "Oh, goodness me!" Then she pulled it in, and hurried over the stairs.

"You go right straight out an' separate them boys," commanded old Mrs. Peters in a dreadful state of mind. "Here, take th' broom, Mirandy, and tell 'em—I d'no what you will tell 'em, but you git 'em apart anyway."

Miranda, having a pretty good notion of her own what she would say when she got there, sped over the grass, waving her broom as she went.

"Here, you," at last, as she reached the spot, her long light braids of hair streaming out behind, and her breath almost gone, "stop!" and she shook her broom at them. "Oh, dear me, Joel Pepper, I *am* s'prised!"

"There, you see," exclaimed the other boy, getting up from the grass where Joel had just neatly deposited him underneath himself, "what she says."

"Oh, it's you, Jim Potts, is it?" said Miranda, with a look of scorn. "Well, if you ever let me see you here again, I'll pitch into you myself. Get out!" and she shook her broom at him, and not caring to make the acquaintance of Joel any further, he slunk away, first calling to a yellow dog, nosing around the barn.

"You take that miserable dog away," screamed Miranda Peters after him; and the dog seeing the broom, for which household implement he had no special fondness, at once set into a lively run in which his master joining, they were soon lost to view.

"If ever I see such a sight in my life as you be, Joel Pepper," exclaimed Miranda with extreme disfavor. "My, and phew! What have you been doin'?" She wrinkled up as much nose as she possessed, and pulled her calico gown well away to be sure it couldn't possibly hit any part of his muddy clothes.

"Cleaning out the pigpen," said Joel, pointing a very grimy finger at it.

"Cleanin' out th' pigpen!" exclaimed Miranda Peters. "Oh, my, *and* Oh, my! What will Mrs. Pepper say?"

"Oh, don't tell Mamsie," pleaded Joel, crowding up closely to her.

"Oh, you get away!" cried Miranda, edging off and whipping her gown tighter than ever around her feet. "Don't you dars't to come no nearer, Joel Pepper. Well, first I must clean you up," and she took up the broom she had dropped in her agitation.

"Oh, I'm going back," said Joel, preparing to descend again to his work.

"You come right straight here," commanded Miranda shrilly, "an' don't you stir one step into that nasty hole. Oh, dear me, I'm afraid as death of what Mrs. Pepper'll say."

"I must finish it," Joel began.

"You come here," and back he had to go, and then she swept him all over with her broom, knocking off the clinging straws and pigpen litter, all the time exclaiming: "Oh, dear me! What *will* Mrs. Pepper say!"

"Mamsie wouldn't want me to stop my work," said Joel wrathfully, who didn't like this sort of proceeding at all.

"You be still." Miranda whirled him about picking at his sleeve gingerly, wherever she could find a place least besmeared, "That ain't your work, an' Pa ought to have ben ashamed to set you at it. Oh, dear me, what a scrape he's got us into," she said to herself; "for Ma an' me has got to get this boy clean enough to go home. Oh, mercy, do stand still," she said aloud.

"My mother won't want me to leave my work," said Joel loudly, his black eyes flashing, "and I ain't going to, so there."

"Well, you keep still; I'll give you some work to do."

"Will you?"

"Yes, yes, do stand still; oh, mercy, what a mess!"

"What shall I do?" demanded Joel, smiling now. It was all right since he was going to work, and carry home some money to Mamsie. "Say, Miss Miranda, what'll I do?"

"Oh, I don't know. Do be still," she twitched him into position again.

"You said you had some work for me," said Joel loudly. "You said so, your very own self."

"Well, so I will give you some," promised Miss Miranda, pushed into a corner. "There, you're brushed, all I can get off of the nasty stuff. Now, you must come into th' house."

"Will you give me the work, then?" asked Joel, determined to have that settled before starting.

"Yes, yes."

"Well, wait, I'm going to get my dinner," for the first time this now coming into his mind, and he ran off to the side of the barn, where he had tucked his paper bundle.

"Why, where—" he began, getting down on all fours. Then he sprang up. "It's gone!" he shouted, with a very red face, over to Miss Miranda.

"What's gone?" she screamed back.

"My dinner—my whole dinner; and Polly did it up."

Joel by this time was prancing about and shaking a piece of brown paper violently, but no dinner appeared. It was gone as completely as if there never had been any in the bundle.

"What was in it?" asked Miranda, leaning over to scrutinize the empty paper.

"My dinner!" choked Joel, waving the paper wrathfully.

"Well, what was it?" said Miranda contemptuously.

"Bread."

"Bread! Oh, dear me, well, I wouldn't cry about that," said Miranda.

"I'm not crying," declared Joel passionately.

"And was that all?"

"No, there was a potato and nice, nice salt."

At this, Joel, remembering how he had seen Polly put it up, and how very hungry he was at this present moment, turned away and began to sob, trying to keep it all back, so that Miss Miranda shouldn't see.

"There, I wouldn't feel bad, Joel," she said not unkindly. "I'll give you some dinner. I s'pose Jim Potts's dog eat it up."

All the sorrow went out of Joel's face, and he whirled about, dashing off the tears from his black eyes. "I'll punch him for that," he said.

"No, you won't, either," said Miranda, and picking his sleeve again. "You let that Jim Potts alone, Joel Pepper. He's a bad boy, an' as for that poor dog o' his, he's hungrier 'n you be. Come along, an' I'll give you some dinner."

And presently Joel was seated before a plate on which were scraps of cold corned beef, very red and stringy, it is true, but tasting perfectly delicious, and a little pile of cold cabbage and potatoes. He wasn't in the kitchen, it is true, because neither Mrs. Peters nor Miranda thought it the least desirable that Mr. Peters should meet him. But in the washshed, back of the big tubs, he sat on a little stool, and ate away with only one thought—"Oh, how good it was! And wouldn't it be prime if they could ever have such splendid things at the Little Brown House for dinner!"

"We must give him something to eat before we clean him up, Ma," Miranda had whispered out in the kitchen, after closing the washshed door, "for he's half starved. My, what *will* Mrs. Pepper say, an' how could Pa git us in such a scrape!"

But after the last morsel was carefully scraped from his plate, Miranda, remarking that it looked as if it had been washed, Joel straightened up and clamored for work again.

"What'll we put him at?" she whispered, carrying out the plates and knife and fork to the kitchen sink.

"My land, I'm sure I don't know," said old Mrs. Peters helplessly. "There's enough work, goodness knows, in th' house to do, but nothin' to set a boy on. It beats me, Mirandy."

"Well, there's some that's got to be found," said Miranda decidedly. "Meanwhilst, we'll just whip off his clothes, an' I'll run 'em through th' tub."

"What'll he put on?" cried the old lady, aghast.

"Why, there's John's things up in th' attic," said Miranda. "I'll run up and fetch 'em."

Which she did, and although John, when he left home to go to sea, was a lad twice the size of Joel Pepper, and his garments left behind had been hanging in the garret ever since, to the great delight of the moths, Joel not only made no objections to being inducted into them, but his face actually shone with pleasure at the prospect. Now, he was big, indeed!

"I can roll up your sleeves," said Miss Miranda reassuringly, as the well-worn edges dangled over his hands.

"Did John roll 'em up?" asked Joel, regarding her movements with suspicion.

"No, of course not," said Miranda briskly, "but he was bigger'n you be. Why, he was almost a man."

"Then, I don't want 'em rolled up," said Joel, trying to get away from her long fingers, "and I'm almost a man, too. See how big I am, Miss Miranda."

But notwithstanding, Miranda went on pinching and rolling the sleeve ends, and at last she threw Joel's little blue cotton jacket and trousers into the nearest tub. "There," she said, surveying him and her work, "at least, you're clean."

"An' I've thought of some work he could do," said old Mrs. Peters, looking in at the door.

"That's th' best thing of all," said Miranda, soaping the

stains vigorously; "I can wash an' iron, but I can't pick out work for a boy. What is't, Ma? It's got to be somethin' not near to Pa," she said in a lower tone.

"Your pa can't hear nor see this," said Mrs. Peters. "It's to pick over apples down cellar. They're all a-rottin' an' spilin' like all possessed."

"The very thing!" exclaimed Miranda joyfully. "Now, you run along, Joel, with Ma. She'll set you to work."

It was impossible for Joel to run in the garments that he now was in, but that seemed to him of small importance, since a man was not supposed to run down the cellar stairs.

So down he went, and presently he was seated in the Peterses' cellar on an old butter tub, turned upside down, and before a great pile of apples, from which he was to pick out the decayed ones.

"And mind, Joel, don't put any specked ones in there." Old Mrs. Peters pointed a long thin finger over to the big basket set for the purpose.

"No, I won't," said Joel, all his eyes on the great pile of apples, and his mouth watering.

"An' you may have one." The old lady leaned over John's coat sleeve, to whisper it, as if afraid that the ceiling above would tell the story to Pa, snoring in his big chair in the kitchen.

"Can I?" cried Joel. "Oh, goody!"

"Hush, hush," said Mrs. Peters, catching his arm. "Yes, you may have two, only you must take specked ones, Joel."

"Well, that boy's fixed." Mrs. Peters came toiling up the cellar stairs and into the washshed. "So he's quiet about some work to do. But how'll we pay him, Mirandy?"

Mirandy leaned her soapy hands on the rim of the tub. "I s'pose I'll have to break into that egg money," she said.

IX

Over at Grandma Bascom's

"No, CHILDREN," Mrs. Pepper shook her head, and bent closer over her sewing in the west window.

There was an awful silence in the old kitchen. Only Phronsie moved uneasily and put her hand up to Polly's chin to turn the face down, so that she might see into the brown eyes. But Polly wouldn't look.

"Oh, we can't give it up, Mamsie," at last she burst out passionately. And that set Joel off.

"No, no," he howled, "we can't, Mamsie." And then little Davie blubbered; he couldn't help it on hearing Joel, and he hid his face on his sleeve.

"Can't is a very poor word to use, Polly," said Mrs. Pepper dryly, "when folks know what ought to be done."

"But, Mamsie," cried Polly, deserting the ring of children sitting on the floor to rush tumultuously over to the sewing corner. Phronsie immediately got up and pattered after her,

Joel following after, little David sitting quite still, and sobbing softly into his sleeve, "don't you see, oh, don't you see, Mamsie, that we've never had a chance to go—to go to Cherryville before, and we've wanted to for so long."

She thrust her face with a little white line around the mouth, up against the buttonhole where Mrs. Pepper was setting fine stitches.

"We've wanted to," cooed Phronsie who didn't yet half know what it was all about, only that Polly wanted something dreadfully, and she patted her mother's knee to attract attention.

"Take care, Polly," warned Mrs. Pepper. "You almost stuck that needle into you."

"Oh, I don't care," said Polly recklessly, and brushing back her hair from her flushed face. But she dodged the busy needle. "You see, Mamsie."

"Yes, you see, Mamsie," shouted Joel.

"I see," said Mrs. Pepper gravely. She lifted her face for a minute, and Polly's heart smote her when she saw how very pale it was; then the stitches were set as quickly as ever.

"And if we've got to give it all up—" Polly really couldn't stop by this time, but the words came rushing out over each other for all the world just like a noisy little brook tumbling over the stones in its way, "All the fun driving in Miss Parrott's coach, to stay with Grandma Bascom all day—why, we can't, Mamsie!" Down went her brown head in Mother Pepper's lap; and she sobbed as if her heart would break.

"No, we can't," cried Joel in a loud voice. "See Polly cry, Mamsie!" He pointed a surprised and shaking finger at the brown head buried in Mother Pepper's work. At that, Phronsie gave a sharp little scream. Mrs. Pepper put aside Mr. Atkins's coat with its last-but-one buttonhole half done.

"Joel!" she said.

When Mother Pepper spoke in that tone, it was not necessary for further reproof. And Joel immediately hung his head and blubbered out something. But Phronsie continued to scream on, and flung her arms around Polly's shaking figure.

"Now Phronsie's Mother's little girl." Mrs. Pepper drew her off to the side of her chair. "Stop crying and look up here, child."

Phronsie raised her head obediently and wiped off the tears on her fat little hand. "Polly's crying," she announced, her lip still quivering.

"I know it; Mother'll take care of Polly," said Mrs. Pepper; "now you go with Joel, and play out of doors till I call you."

"Dave must go, too—can't he, Mamsie?" broke in Joel.

"Yes, Davie can go, too," Mother Pepper tried to smile over at him where he crouched on the floor. "Now go along and be good children."

"I want Polly," said Phronsie, with a lingering glance at the figure still half-hidden in Mamsie's lap.

"No, Polly must stay with me. Go along, Phronsie, and be Mother's good child."

"I will be Mother's good child," hummed Phronsie. So Joel took her hand, and somehow little David found his feet, and stumbled out after them, and shut the green door fast.

In about half an hour, "tap,—tap," on one of the little windowpanes. There was Mrs. Pepper rapping with her thimble.

"Hi—yi!" screamed Joel, catching sight of her face in the midst of a merry game of tag. "She says, come in!" and off he plunged for the house.

"We must wait for Phronsie," said little David. But Joel was already in the old kitchen, and at last David found Phronsie on her knees watching the progress of a fuzzy yellow caterpillar in the middle of the grassplot. She had forgotten all about "tag," in which she was supposed to be an active participant.

"See, Davie, one of his legs is sick," she cried, "poor little thing."

"Oh, no, he isn't sick," said David; "he's only slow. Come, Phronsie, and leave the old woolly boy alone."

"No, he's sick, the poor little woolly boy," persisted Phronsie, "and I'm going to take him in to Mamsie."

"Well, Mamsie wants us to come in," said David impatiently, "so do hurry, Phronsie."

"Does Mamsie want us to come in?" asked Phronsie.

"Yes, she does. She called us from the window."

"Then I shall go in," declared Phronsie, getting up from her knees and patting her hands clean, "but I'm going to take my little woolly boy in, Davie." So she picked him off gently from the grass, and setting him on her other hand came slowly after David, who was running on before.

"Do hurry, Phronsie," he begged, coming back to hasten matters. "There, don't you see your woolly boy isn't lame? He's walking up your arm like everything."

"He likes it," said Phronsie, subduing all desire to get free, since this promenade appeared to be so well suited to the caterpillar. "He's getting all well, Davie."

"Well, he isn't going to walk up your arm like that," declared Davie, unceremoniously picking off the caterpillar. "Now, Mister Woolly Boy, I'll carry you."

"Oh, no, no, Davie, let me," cried Phronsie, holding out her hands. "He's my very own woolly boy, and I like him."

"Well, hold him in your hand, then—like this." Davie doubled over Phronsie's fat little thumb and the fingers. "Not too tight or you'll squash him."

"What's squash?" asked Phronsie, trying to peek in the cracks between her fingers at her treasure.

"Why, smash," said David; "you'd smash him all to bits, and then there wouldn't be anything left of him but his fur coat and the juice."

"What's juice?" asked Phronsie.

"Oh, that's his insides," said Davie. "Take care now, don't squeeze him."

"Wouldn't there be any little woolly boy inside of his fur coat?" asked Phronsie, stumbling along with the greatest difficulty, both eyes fastened on her closed hand.

"No, not a single thing," asserted Davie positively. "Why, here's Polly!"

"Well, children," said Polly, running down to meet them, "why didn't you come in when Mamsie called?"

"Oh, Phronsie found an old caterpillar," said David discontentedly. To have missed any of Mamsie's calls put him out dreadfully.

"No, he's a woolly boy," corrected Phronsie; "see, Polly, and he's sick." She held up her hand for Polly to look through the cracks.

"Well, never mind, Pet," said Polly. "Mamsie wants us now, and we must hurry, for we are all to go to Grandma Bascom's."

"Aren't we going to—" began David.

"No," said Polly quickly. "We are going to Grandma's, and we are going to have a real good time, Davie."

With that she took Phronsie's disengaged hand, "Come on," and away they all sped into the Little Brown House.

And in five minutes it really seemed as if no such wonderful invitation had been received as that which Miss Parrott had sent down in a prim little note this morning. It had begged Mrs. Pepper to allow the four children (Ben was away at work on Deacon Blodgett's woodpile) to drive over to Cherryville, under the care of her coachman, who had to take the big family barouche there for some slight repairs. Was ever such a wonderful treat! And just the day before they had promised Grandma Bascom, who was sick in bed with the rheumatism, to spend this very morning with her. Polly was to bake the bread and tidy up the little cottage, and the two boys were to split the kindlings and feed the hens; Phronsie's part being to sit on the gay patched bedquilt by Grandma's side and read aloud to her, the old lady being deaf as a post, and the book generally upside down, never making any difference in the enjoyment.

"Now, then," Mother Pepper had deserted her sewing, and was bustling around helping to get the children started.

"You better take Grandma a piece of that butter, Polly," she said. "Put it in the blue bowl."

"Not the butter Mrs. Henderson sent us, Mammy?" said Polly, pausing in getting Phronsie's clean pink pinafore over her head.

"Yes, and you can toast her some bread," said Mrs. Pepper. "And, boys, you must hurry. You better start first, and tell Grandma that Polly and Phronsie are coming."

"Tell Grandma I'm coming," piped Phronsie, as Polly whirled her around to button up the back of the pinafore.

"Hooray—come on, Dave!" shouted Joel, banging out of the doorway with little Davie at his heels.

And at last, Polly and Phronsie were on the flat doorstone, ready to start.

"Oh, dear me!" Polly, the little blue bowl in her hand, turned back. "Oh, Mamsie, I'm *so sorry!*" and she hid her face in Mother Pepper's neck.

"There—there, Polly!" Mrs. Pepper patted the brown head with firm fingers, "that's all been settled now; remember it only wastes time to fret over the past. Hurry along to Grandma; she needs you."

"I will, Mamsie," promised Polly, struggling with her tears. "Come, Phronsie."

But Phronsie had to turn back, too. "Oh, Mamsie," she begged, just as if she hadn't said the same thing a dozen times before, "do take care of my poor little woolly boy, ple—ase, Mamsie!"

"I will, I will," nodded Mother Pepper, smiling at her baby. So hand in hand Polly and Phronsie hurried off, and Mrs. Pepper went back to the kitchen window to watch for the Parrott coach, which having in any case to pass on this road to Cherryville would waste no time in stopping at the Little Brown House.

"So I can give him the message, as well as to send word to Miss Parrott, that the children can't go," she said, as she picked up her neglected work to fly at it faster than ever; for that coat and the other three finished ones must be taken to Mr. Atkins just as soon as all were completed. Notwithstanding her hurry, Mrs. Pepper stopped once or twice to brush something away from her black eyes that seemed to trouble her. At last she said, "Bless them—pleasure and good times will come to them sometime—they must!" And then her needle flew faster than ever, to make up for lost time.

"Now, boys," said Polly, when the four children had scampered down the lane, bringing up breathlessly at the door of the little cottage, "you must go right to work, after you've said 'Good morning,' to Grandma, on splitting the kindlings in the shed, and pile 'em up nicely. And, Joel, don't ask her any questions; you know how to do it all."

"Grandma may want 'em done different today," said Joel stoutly.

"No, she won't," said Polly decidedly. "Shoo, there!" this to an old hen who stepped out to the flat doorstone as Polly opened the door.

"Let me shoo 'em! I'll do it," cried Joel excitedly, pushing past Polly and flapping his arms. "Shoo, there; scat you!"

"So will I," cried David following suit, and screaming with all his might, the poor old hen flying wild and squawking dismally.

Phronsie sat right down on the old flat stone. "Don't let 'em do it, Polly," she begged. "Grandma's poor old biddies; Polly, please stop them," lifting a distressed little face.

"Boys—boys!" called Polly. But they had raced around the cottage. Meantime a big white hen stepped out from under the old kitchen table and hopped leisurely out past Phronsie sitting on the doorstone.

"Misery me!" exclaimed Polly, "there's ever so many in here. Grandma didn't see them probably when she shut the door. There, make her go off, Phronsie. Shoo—shoo!" and Polly flew around the little old kitchen brandishing a dish towel, thereby making two or three other hens waddle and squawk in great distress.

"I'll help you," cried Phronsie, diverted from her lively interest over the white hen, and slipping off from the doorstone she ran into the kitchen. "Biddy—biddy—biddy," only succeeding in getting dreadfully in the way, so that the hens squawked and flew about worse than ever.

"It's a mercy that Grandma can't hear them," said Polly, pausing a minute to wipe her hot face. "Oh, you stupid things, can't you see the open door? There, Phronsie, you stand over in that corner, that's a good girl, and drive them this way. There, says I!"

But despite all this nice plan, the big clumsy creatures preferred to hop and dive under the table and chairs, and back of the woodbox, and any and everywhere but out of doors.

At last Polly sank down in a chair. "They won't go out. Oh, dear me, what shall I do!"

"Won't they ever go out of Grandma Bascom's kitchen?" asked Phronsie, deserting her corner to run over to Polly. "Say, Polly, won't they ever?" as Joel with Davie at his heels whooped in.

"Oh, whickets!" exclaimed Joel at sight of the hens. Then began such a lively chase that Polly had all she could do to restrain the boys and comfort Phronsie, while the little old kitchen rang with the noise. At last, out flew and plunged the hens over the flat doorstone and Joel screamed with delight, "There, sir, they're all gone!" And Davie wiped his hot face and panted out, "Yes, they're all gone!"

"No, they haven't, Joel!" Polly exclaimed. "There's one going into the bedroom. Oh, dear me!"

"I'll drive her out," cried Joel in huge delight, and prancing across the little old kitchen.

"No, you mustn't, Joe," declared Polly, seizing his arm. "You'll scare Grandma to death. Here, give me that broom."

"You can't do it as good as me," grumbled Joel, while they all followed Polly, broom in hand, into the bedroom.

"Oh, you pretty creeters, you," cried Grandma, raising her head in its big ruffled cap from the high pillow of the four-poster, and beaming at the whole bunch. "So you've come to see Grandma, haven't you?"

"There's a hen under your bed," announced Joel without any preamble, and marching up to the bedside.

"Hush, Joe," said Polly. Then she laid her rosy cheek against the withered one under the big flapping ruffles.

"Good morning, Grandma."

"You needn't sweep up just yet," said Grandma, with an eye for Polly's broom.

"I'm not sweeping," said Polly, rosier than ever.

Then she tried to lift Phronsie up on to the gay patched bedquilt by Grandma's side.

For the first time in visiting Grandma Bascom, Phronsie pulled back. "I want to tell poor old biddy to go out," she whispered, struggling violently. "Let me tell her, Polly, do," she implored.

"No, no, Phronsie," said Polly, holding her fast, "you must do as I say, Pet, or else you'll have to go home."

So Phronsie, two big tears splashing their way down the pink cheeks, was set on the bed by Grandma's side.

"Oh, dear me!" exclaimed the old lady in the greatest distress at the sight of these. "What in the world is the matter? Didn't she want to come to see Grandma?" So Polly had to lean over and scream as much of the whole story about the hens as was possible into the old lady's ear.

Meantime, Joel had determined to see to the old hen himself; so he had crawled under the bed, and by dint of wriggling smartly back and forth had at last caught her by one leg; since forgetting how she had crept in under the valance, she ran round and round in a vain effort to get out.

And presently amid a terrible squawking out he came, flushed and triumphant, dragging her after him.

"I did get her—bad old thing!" he cried jubilantly, his black eyes flashing. "See, Polly, see, Grandma!" and he swung the poor bird up before them.

Phronsie gave a loud scream.

"Joel Pepper!" cried Polly, bounding after him. But Joel was already out through the kitchen, and with a wave of his hand sending the clumsy old hen over to the grassplot in front of the door. "Shoo, now, scat!" he said, which being just what best suited the hen at this time, she plunged in under the currant bushes, to relate her story to some other hens who came running to the spot.

All this delayed the work of the morning. But at last Polly saw the two boys splitting and piling the kindlings neatly, and

Phronsie was reading most importantly aloud to Grandma, who alternately dozed and opened her eyes, saying, "You pretty creeter, you!" while Polly herself was busy as a bee over her housewifely tasks.

At last the bread was baked (Mrs. Pepper having run over and made it the night before) and Polly drew a long breath, then ran into the little bedroom. "Well, Phronsie, Pet, now you must hop down and play, and I'll stay with Grandma," and there was Phronsie fast asleep, one hand up across Grandma's little plaid bed shawl, while Fox's *Book of Martyrs* had slipped to the floor.

"She's tired to death," cried Polly to herself. "Well, now she shall have a good nap. And Grandma is asleep, too, so that's a comfort."

And she went out softly and closed the door; then ran around to the woodshed where the boys were.

"Oh, Polly!" cried Joel, pitching a stick of kindling over on the pile. "See what we've done!" and his round cheeks glowed with delight. Little drops of perspiration were rolling down Davie's face.

"Oh, I never saw such a pile!" exclaimed Polly, "and Grandma'll be so pleased. Now you two boys may stop working."

"Goody!" cried Joel, picking up another stick to give it a good fling and prancing off to the door, "Come on, Dave.— Oh, Polly, I'm so hungry."

"So you must be," said Polly sympathetically. "Stop, Davie, didn't you hear me say you needn't work any more? Dear me, how hot you are!"

"I just want to finish this stick, Polly," said little Davie, holding it up, while Joel kept calling: "Oh, come along, Dave," ending with, "I'm so hungry, Polly."

"Well, just that one," said Polly, relenting, "then you two

boys are to go home and wash your hands and faces, and you'll find the bread and the mush and molasses in the pantry, Mamsie said."

"Have we got to come over here afterward?" asked Joel with impatient black eyes.

"Yes, of course," said Polly, "but you are not to split kindlings any more. Mamsie said only do that once. And you've such a nice pile, boys."

"It's just a bully pile!" cried Joel, running over to regard it affectionately and kicking a stray stick with his foot.

"Joel, what did you say?" cried Polly in dismay.

Joel hung his black head, and dug the toe of his old shoe into the woodshed floor.

"Mamsie wouldn't like that," said Polly soberly, "so you must never, never, as long as you live and breathe, Joel Pepper, say it again."

"Oh, I won't, I won't," promised Joel eagerly. "Polly, I won't, truly."

"That's right," said Polly. "Now run along and get your bread and mush, and then come right back here." And off the boys clattered.

And as soon as Phronsie woke up, then she was hungry, so Polly took her hand and raced down the lane, for Mother Pepper had told the children to come home for anything to eat, and there Polly found the two boys sitting by the kitchen table busy over their mush bowls.

"It's good," declared Joel, just putting in a big spoonful, and he smacked his lips.

"Oh, misery, what a face, Joe!" exclaimed Polly with a grimace. "The molasses is all up to your ear."

"That's because Dave jogged my arm," said Joel composedly, and going on with his consumption of mush.

"Well, go and wash it off," said Polly; "yes, yes, Pet, I'll get you some mush, but you must have on your eating-apron first."

"I don't want to wash my face yet," grumbled Joel, eating away faster than ever. "It'll get all dirt again; Dave'll joggle me some more."

"Oh, no, I won't," declared little Davie in distress, "and I didn't mean to before, only I was trying to get the molasses pitcher. Truly, I didn't, Polly."

He laid down his spoon, and his blue eyes filled with tears.

"I know, Davie," Polly stopped to smile at him as she came back with Phronsie's eating-apron and tied it under her chin. Then she lifted her up to her high chair.

"Yes, Joel, for shame to want to sit still and eat with such a sticky face."

"I'm going to kiss Phronsie, first," said Joel, dropping his spoon and springing out of his seat.

"No, indeed, Joel Pepper," cried Polly, putting up both hands, "the very idea; you'll stick her all up."

"Then I'll kiss Dave," declared Joel, bursting into a laugh.

But little David, ducking his head beneath his arm and Polly saying, "Joel Pepper!" in a way that he never remembered disobeying, Joel marched off to the sink, and presently came back, his round face red and shiny, to bestow attention again on his mush bowl.

But they didn't go back to Grandma Bascom's after all that day, for just then in came Mother Pepper, her black eyes shining.

"Mamsie!" they all screamed in joy, Phronsie laying down her spoon and beginning to clamber out of her high chair.

"There, there, baby, sit still." Mother Pepper put her hand on the fat little shoulder. "All of you children stay just where you are. No, no, Polly, I'll take off my bonnet. Yes, Mother's got home sooner than expected, for Mrs. Blodgett has had company come; so when I got there, after taking back the coats to Mr. Atkins, there wasn't anything to do."

It was a long speech for Mrs. Pepper to make, and then she went into the bedroom and the children's spoons clicked faster than ever.

"Now we must be good as can be," said Polly to the others, "and run right back to Grandma's without making any fuss."

"I shall tell Mamsie I don't want to go," announced Joel, having eaten as much as he could and giving a long stretch, "I'm awful tired, Polly."

"Awfully," corrected Polly, who was very particular about her speech as well as other matters. "You do say such perfectly dreadful things, Joel."

"It is awful," persisted Joel obstinately.

"No," said Polly, shaking her head, "it isn't; you must say 'awfully,' Joe."

"But I don't want to," said Joel, setting his little white teeth together firmly.

Davie at that turned to him in a worried way. "Oh, do say it, Joe," he begged.

"What is it?" asked Mrs. Pepper, coming out from the bedroom and looking from one to the other.

"Oh, I will," cried Joel, swallowing very hard. "I will, Polly. It is awfly; Polly, it is."

He got out of his chair, and ran around to her side.

"Polly," he whispered, pulling her ear down to his mouth, "it *is* awfly."

"All right." Polly turned and set a little kiss on his red cheek.

"Well, now, children," Mrs. Pepper was saying, with a happy smile over at the two, "I don't want any of you to go back to Grandma's, for I am going myself."

"Oh, Mamsie!" exclaimed Polly in dismay, "do let us. Really and truly, Mamsie, we want to."

"No, I don't think it's best," said Mother Pepper decidedly. "You've all been good children I know, and—"

"We've made the biggest pile of kindlings, Dave and me," cried Joel excitedly flying over to her. "Look in the woodshed, Mammy."

"So I believe," cried Mrs. Pepper in a pleased way. "I'll look in the woodshed, Joe and Davie," and she beamed at them both.

"And I read to Grandma," said Phronsie, bobbing her yellow head over her mush bowl at her mother. "I did; and Grandma, she liked it, she did."

"That's a good child," cried Mrs. Pepper, going over to her baby.

"Well, now you may all have the afternoon to play in, for I am going to take care of Grandma myself."

"Oh, whoopity!" screamed Joel, making for the door.

X

The Stage Ride

"G'LANG there, whoa!" Mr. Tisbett brought up in fine style with one of his best flourishes in front of the well-worn gate to the Little Brown House, and swept it with a confident gaze.

But instead of seeing Joel and David, nearly overcome with joy, rush out of the house and run wildly down the pathway, there was absolutely nobody stirring that he could see, and all was quiet except the droning of the bees in the meadow across the road.

"Beats all nature where they be." The stage driver, unable to get any satisfaction by staring, took off his old straw hat and violently scratched his head. This afforded him some peace of mind, but the silence continuing, except for the bees and the twitters of an inquisitive bird or two hopping to a near-by branch by the roadside to see what it was all about, he sat back on the old leather-covered seat and drew a long breath.

"Whew!" Then he laid the well-worn reins down and clambered from his perch to the ground, and with a "Stand still there," to his horses—a command they were always perfectly willing to obey —he slouched up to the old green door and gave two emphatic raps, but nobody answered them.

Now by this time Mr. Tisbett was convinced that the most important business in all this world was to get Joel and David and start them on that long-promised ride over to Cherryville on top of his stagecoach. The invitation, with a message "to be lively and not keep me waiting," had been sent to them only the afternoon before. Mr. Tisbett had left it at the village store to be delivered to one of the Pepper children or their mother, it being the day when Mr. Atkins expected some coats to be called for. But Phronsie had been sick and fretfully clung to Mother Pepper, and as Polly had a great deal more work to do than usually fell to her share, the coats were not called for, of course. And as a consequence, Mr. Atkins promptly forgot all about the matter until shutting-up time came.

"Oh, good gracious, Jonah!" he exclaimed, slapping the counter and looking up with a very distressed face, "if I haven't clean forgot all about Mr. Tisbett's takin' them Pepper boys to ride tomorrow." He ran to the door and looked up and down the long dusty road. There wasn't a sign of a person, to say nothing of a stray boy.

"They'd be thick as a swarm if you didn't want 'em," said the storekeeper, discomfited. "I declare, I'll go myself." He pulled off his old linen coat on the way to his home, which was entered by a door from the shop leading into the ell.

"I'm goin' out, Sarah," he said in a high sharp key, not made pleasanter by smelling the hot beefsteak pie he knew was being borne to the supper table at this very moment.

"Hey?" Mrs. Atkins set down the pie in its place before his plate and stared at him.

"I said I was goin' out," repeated the storekeeper irritably, and turning his back to the pie, while he wriggled into his out-of-door coat hanging behind the kitchen door.

Mrs. Atkins deserted the supper table to run over and look at his face. "You goin' out before supper?"

"Yes," said Mr. Atkins sharply, and pulling his coat sleeves down; " 'cause I know I won't do it after, for no one," it being the storekeeper's nightly habit to fall asleep after his evening meal in the big easy chair, and when he awoke from that, he would have neither inclination nor time to make evening calls. "I'll tell you about it when I get home, Sarah," and he crammed his hat on his head and started for the door.

Sarah Atkins ran around him to get there first. "You'll tell me now, Silas," she said quietly; "where on earth are you goin' without your supper?"

"Down to Mis' Pepper's," said the storekeeper, brought to bay.

"Down to Mis' Pepper's?" repeated his wife. "Has anything happened there?"

"No," said Mr. Atkins, and then the story came out.

Just then there was a vigorous knocking set up at their front door. It was so imperative that both the storekeeper and his wife hastened with all speed to answer it.

"I thought you was never comin'." Little Sally Brown stood there on the step with a very injured countenance.

"You only just knocked," said Mrs. Atkins, exasperated. "Now what do you want?"

"Some sugar—" said Sally; "two pounds—" Mr. Atkins, when he saw who the visitor was, had retreated a few steps with premonitions of a call to the store.

"Sugar?" he now cried sharply; "at this time of night—the store's all shet up."

"Yes," said Sally, "we've got comp'ny."

This piece of news, ordinarily exciting enough to be fol-

lowed up, was cut in twain by Mr. Atkins suddenly crying out as he pressed forward eagerly, "See here, you'll go to Mis' Pepper's for me, Sally?"

"No," said Sally decidedly. "I'm goin' home."

"You'll go to Mis' Pepper's for me, or you'll get no sugar *from* me," declared the storekeeper just as decidedly. Mrs. Atkins during this colloquy exclaiming—"So she can—Sally can tell Mis' Pepper," joyfully to herself, as she followed the other two all the way through the kitchen to the shop door. For Sally, wisely concluding to take the best that was offered her, finally assented to Mr. Atkins's proposal and seized the paper of sugar, saying, "Yes, I'll go."

"Be sure you've got the message right," said Mr. Atkins, holding her arm until she had gone over the message three times to make certain that there could be no mistake. "Mr. Tisbett is comin' tomorrow mornin' to take Joel and David to Cherryville. Be ready sharp at eight o'clock."

At last the weary storekeeper and his wife were back in their kitchen. "Now that's done," and he took off his out-of-door coat and hung it up with an air of relief.

"The pie's all cold," declared Mrs. Atkins in vexation, and she twitched it off the table.

"Bring it back, Sarah," said her husband. "I'm hungry as a wolf."

"It's cold as a stone," said Mrs. Atkins, pausing to turn a vexed face.

"Well, cold or hot, I'm goin' to have some," said Mr. Atkins, dropping into his seat at the supper table and laying hold of his knife and fork.

So the beefsteak pie was dumped down on the table in front of his plate once more, and Mrs. Atkins slipped into her seat to pour out the tea.

Meantime Sally Brown ran like a good one up the hill

and down again, fully intending to drop the parcel of sugar at home and then off over cross lots to the Little Brown House, but dashing into the kitchen she found herself in the midst of the entire family gathered around a common center, so, dropping the brown-paper bundle on the table, she burst in among the group to hear what the excitement could be.

"Oh, ain't it too cunnin' for anythin'!"

"Yes," said another voice, "it's cute as can be!" And there was Cousin Callena's little girl, part of the company, simpering and bridling with delight, and holding up a big doll in a pink satin dress and a red hat and white lace veil.

Sally's mouth opened wide, but she had no time nor breath to scream. The minute Cousin Callena's little girl saw her, she lowered the doll immediately to put both arms around it. "You shan't see it," she declared, with all the triumph of possession.

"For shame, Flora!" cried her mother, "when you've come visitin'."

But Flora, not considering it necessary to part with her usual manners just because she was visiting, kept on hugging her doll and swaying back and forth, repeating in a singsong voice, "You *shan't* see it—you shan't."

"I will," declared Sally, passionately, and with very red cheeks trying to thrust herself nearer for a better view.

"And so you may," said Cousin Callena, very much ashamed, and reaching over she first bestowed a smart slap on Flora's shoulder; then she twitched the doll out from her arms. "There, now, I'll take it myself. Come over here, Sally, and I'll show it to you."

Flora gave a loud scream, but, seeing it was useless to follow her mother, she threw herself flat on the floor and sobbed and kicked her heels all the while the resplendent doll in the pink satin dress and red hat and white lace veil was being exhibited in another corner of the kitchen.

And when Sally Brown next remembered the message to the Peppers, it was along toward the middle of the following morning. She had "eaten and slept" on nothing but that magnificent doll, being unable to get it out of her thoughts for a moment. When the message did flash through her mind, she started, and without a word to any one, raced off across lots as fast as she could to the Little Brown House. It was as silent and empty as when the stage driver had visited it.

"Oh, well, Mr. Tisbett's taken Joel and Davie," said Sally to herself, running all about the Little Brown House, and peeping into the west window where Mrs. Pepper usually sat sewing. "An' the rest have gone, too," she added enviously. "An' I hain't never been a stage-ridin'," and she disconsolately got herself back home.

It was just about this time that Mrs. Pepper, sewing away for dear life over in Grandma Bascom's cottage, looked up.

"It's time to make Grandma some tea, Polly," she said.

"Oh, dear me, so it is," said Polly, setting up the broom neatly and drawing a long breath. "Mamsie, it wouldn't be near so hard to get this floor clean if these old hens wouldn't keep coming in. There's one now!" and Polly flew for the broom again to brandish it wildly after the marauder. "They get the feathers all over everything."

"Shut the door then, Polly," said Mrs. Pepper.

"Oh, they come in just as easily in that hole over by the corner." Polly pointed to it with her broom.

"Is there a hole there, Polly?" asked Mrs. Pepper in surprise.

"Yes, Mamsie," said Polly, "there is. I'm going to put that

box up against it," which was no sooner said than done, Polly dragging up an empty soap box for the purpose. "There, now, old hens, I guess you won't get in," she cried, rubbing her hands in satisfaction.

"Ben must mend that hole just as soon as he has a chance," said Mrs. Pepper, snipping off her thread, while Polly set back the broom and ran over to the stove to get Grandma's tea.

"Isn't it good that Phronsie sleeps so long, Mamsie?" said Polly at last, while she was waiting for the old kettle to boil, and coming up to her mother's chair.

"Yes," said Mrs. Pepper. She looked tired and worried, but she smiled. "She'll be all right, I think," she hastened to say.

"I guess she's better because you brought her over to Grandma's," said Polly, with a happy little laugh, and balancing herself first on one set of toes and then on the other. "Isn't she, Mamsie?"

"Maybe," said Mrs. Pepper, then she laughed too, a sound that made Polly happier yet. "I think the kettle has boiled, Polly."

"I believe it has," laughed Polly, skipping back to the old stove.

And then when Grandma had had her tea and eaten the toast that Polly had made to go with it, and Polly had washed and wiped the dishes, Phronsie on the other side of Grandma's big bed turned over and put out her hand. "I'm so hungry, Polly," she said.

"Oh, Pet, are you awake?" Polly ran around the old bed and covered her face with kisses. "And you're all well, aren't you, Pet?"

"No," said Phronsie, shaking her yellow head as well as she could for Polly hugging her, "but I'm very hungry, Polly. I am truly."

"Well, and you shall have something," declared Polly, flying off into the kitchen to tell Mrs. Pepper all about it.

So Mamsie dropped her sewing and went in to look at Phronsie to see how she really was. And everything had to be told to Grandma, who by this time was in a bad fright lest Phronsie were worse. And then Grandma said Phronsie must have toast, too, and so Polly ran out to make that. And presently Phronsie was sitting up, proped against a pillow close to Grandma's, and eating with great satisfaction all around a crispy, crinkly slice of toast that Polly brought to the side of the bed with a great flourish on a piece of paper, pretending it was a napkin.

And then Polly curled up at the foot of the bed and laughed, and told Phronsie a merry little story about Parson Henderson's chickens that Phronsie always considered part of the eating process. And Grandma ohed and ahed through it all, although she hadn't heard a word, and everything was getting on as fine as could be, and Mrs. Pepper out in the kitchen gave a sigh of relief as her needle flew faster than ever. "It surely hasn't hurt Phronsie to bring her over, and Grandma needed us after that chill"; for Polly had run back through the lane after an early visit to the cottage, saying that "Grandma is awfully cold, and she can't get warm, and she's all huddled up over the stove." And Mrs. Pepper had bundled up Phronsie in an old quilt and carried her over, telling Polly to bring the coat she was trying to finish and the workbasket. And then Ben and Joel and Davie had all hurried off to work together, for the two little boys were to help Ben at Deacon Blodgett's on this morning.

"It's so funny to lock the door," said Polly to herself, as she swung the old key on her finger and skipped down the lane. "Oh, dear me, wouldn't it be nice to ever go off into the woods and pick flowers, and run—Oh, dear me—and stay as long as I wanted to—just think—oh!" But here she was at Grandma Bascom's, and ever so much work to be done.

"I'd stop for them boys tomorrow, I declare I would," said Mr. Tisbett to himself, rattling off on the way to collect his customers, "ef I warn't engaged to bring up them folks from the city to the Potter farm. That's jest it—this busy season— it beats all to know when I can git another chance so good as this was today, and no one to take this ere seat with me." He slapped his knees with his horny hand in his vexation, and set about his day's work in no very pleasant frame of mind.

"John!" An old yellow wagon, drawn by an older horse, rattled around a curve. "I say, John, stop, will ye?"

"I'm a stoppin' as fast's I kin with my horses," said Mr. Tisbett, pulling up his pair with a superior air. "What d'ye want, Mr. Potter?"

Mr. Potter guided his old horse up against the stage driver's pair, and bawled out, "Say, those folks ain't a-comin' to-morrow."

"Them city ones?" asked the stage driver.

"Yes—a-comin' Friday; just had a tel'gram." Mr. Potter drew himself up with dignity to see the effect on the stage driver. " 'Twas brought by Hiram Pendleton's son, an' he come lickety-split—thought someone was dead, an'—"

"I don't care about that," said Mr. Tisbett, dismissing the narration by a wave of his hand as of no consequence whatever. "I'll fetch 'em from Cherryville deepo Friday insted of tomorrow; that's the idee, ain't it?"

"Yes, ye see—" Mr. Potter stood up in his wagon, he was so anxious to get all the details of this change of plans in his city boarders well before the stage driver's mind, but that individual was already a good piece of his journey down the road, his horses kicking up a great dust while he cheered them on, for his spirits had risen very much indeed.

"Now I'll take the Pepper boys tomorrow to Cherryville," he declared, "an' I've got to go round there tonight when I come home, so I'll tell Mis' Pepper." This new plan almost made him forget his worry that otherwise would have seized him when he thought of the Little Brown House all so shut up and silent.

So all this is the reason why Joel and little David didn't hear before that night that they were really and truly going to Cherryville on the morrow. Then the Little Brown House more than made up for being silent in the early morning!

"Oh, I wish you were going, Polly!" said Ben the next morning, when she ran out to the woodpile where he had to work that day to get some ready for Mamsie, and he rested his busy saw a moment.

"Oh, I'm going sometime," said Polly, tossing back her brown hair and trying to speak cheerily.

Ben's face didn't lighten a bit as he took up his saw.

"And it's too bad you can't go," said Polly. "Dear me!" and she clasped her hands tightly.

"Oh, I'm going sometime," said Ben, repeating her words. Then he burst into a laugh. "But I've got to have this wood sawed first."

"And I've got to wash those old breakfast dishes," said Polly, skipping off to the kitchen door. "Misery me!" for there was Joel in a dreadful state of distress. He couldn't find his cap; search for it high and low, it was nowhere to be seen.

"Oh, I thought you were all ready, Joel!" cried Polly in surprise.

"He was—he was," gasped little Davie tearfully, and getting in everybody's way in his efforts to help along the search.

"Here comes the stage," said Mrs. Pepper, looking out of the window. "Joel, run out and ask Ben to let you take his cap."

"Oh, Mamsie," began Polly in dismay, who dearly loved, whenever any of them were going visiting, to have everything as fine as possible. But seeing Mrs. Pepper's eyes, she didn't finish with "Ben's cap will be ever so much too big for him," as Joel dashed off to ask him.

"You mustn't keep Mr. Tisbett waiting," said Mrs. Pepper, "so run along, boys," as Joel raced back, cramming Ben's worn cap on his head as he pranced down the path to be pulled up over the wheel by Mr. Tisbett, who performed the same good office for little David. At last a crack of the whip—and off they went.

Down to Badgertown Center the old stagecoach swung along, the horses now at a "pretty pace," as Mr. Tisbett called it, for he always made a good showing down the main street, till a sharp scream struck his ears.

"Halloa there, what you about," he called, "scaring the horses to death!" and he pulled them up shortly, and craned his neck at a woman running along the sidewalk and shaking a small bandbox tied up with a cloth cover at him. "Stop—stop," she gasped faintly.

"Ain't I a-stoppin'?" said Mr. Tisbett, leaning both hands holding the old leather reins on his knees. "Gracious, ye don't need to screech so, Mis' Sprigg."

"I was afraid," panted the woman, coming up to the stage, "that—you—wouldn't stop, Mr. Tisbett." Her face was very red and the drops of perspiration rolled down either side.

"Well, I'm a-stoppin' now," said the stage driver, while Joel and David peered around him to get as much as possible of the interview. "So if you'll state what you want, I'll be obleeged to ye, Mis' Sprigg."

"How much is't to Cherryville?" asked Mrs. Sprigg, depositing her bandbox on the grass by the side of the road, and pulling out a big handkerchief to mop her hot face.

"Just what it always was; a quarter," said Mr. Tisbett. "The price ain't changed any since yest'day when you asked me, Mis' Sprigg."

"I didn't know but what you'd take less when you'd had a chance to think over what good customers we'd been when we lived over to Cherryville," said Mrs. Sprigg, scanning the stage driver's face with her beady eyes. "We alwus traveled with you, Mr. Tisbett," she added wheedlingly.

"And how much did you travel?" said Mr. Tisbett scornfully, shifting his quid of tobacco to the other cheek. "Once in a dog's age, ye come over to Badgertown."

Mrs. Sprigg drew herself up to her greatest height, which wasn't much, and her beady eyes snapped.

"Well, I can't stop here with my horses coolin' their heels *all* day," said the stage driver. "Are you goin' to get in for Cherryville or stay where ye be?" And he shook the reins suggestively.

"I've got to go to Cherryville," snapped the little woman, snatching up her bandbox from the grass. "My sister's husband took sick, an' Eliza—"

"I can't stop to hear about Eliza," retorted the stage driver impatiently, and dropping the reins to clamber down over the wheel. "I've got some customers to pick up, an' some passels, an' I hain't no time to waste in talk. Now, then, Mis' Sprigg." He set her bandbox inside with a hasty hand, then took hold of her arm to help her into the coach. "Step lively, there!"

"Wait a minute—" she shook him off to peer down the road. "Oh, here she comes!"

Mr. Tisbett flew around also to see coming down the road, making the dust fly well at every step, a small girl holding a basket which she swung back and forth vigorously.

"Hold it straight," screamed the little woman, and she stamped her foot on the grass. "Martha Sprigg, don't you know no better!" But Martha not hearing, as there were several noises emanating from the basket, kept up the swinging, and at last reached her mother, who first gave her a smart slap, and then, after getting the basket away from her, a shake.

"You've pretty near killed him, I 'xpect," declared Mrs. Sprigg, bending over the basket in concern, from which a loud and indignant "Mee—ow!" pealed forth. "Now you go right straight back home, you naughty girl, you, and sew up that seam to that sheet, just as I told you."

Martha looked longingly at the stagecoach, and the two boys perched up on top, then her gaze fell down to her mother. "I want to go," she said boldly.

Mrs. Sprigg, with her foot on the step, having first seen Mr. Tisbett deposit her precious basket inside, turned in astonishment. "Well, I never!" she ejaculated.

"Let th' little girl go, can't ye?" said Mr. Tisbett good-naturedly on seeing Martha's face. " 'Twon't cost nothin'. I'll take her without charge."

For one second Mrs. Sprigg relented, being unable to pass anything by that did not cost. "No, indeed," then she cried decidedly; "it'll cost over there to Eliza's for eatin', an' Martha's got to do th' work to home. Go right straight back!" She whipped her skirts about her feet and skipped into the stagecoach.

"Well, there, ye see, I can't take ye; your ma won't let me," said Mr. Tisbett apologetically to the little girl, who stood twisting her small red hands together and wistfully regarding his face.

"Oh, let her come, do let her come," begged Joel, leaning forward on his high seat at the imminent risk of falling off on his nose; Davie crowding up close to his shoulder trying to see, too, and crying, "Please, Mr. Tisbett, let her come—"

"Can't," said Mr. Tisbett, swinging himself up to his seat. "That cantankerous old woman won't let me—" the last under his breath.

Martha, seeing her last hope which had flamed high at Mr. Tisbett's words, disappear, gave a loud scream of disappointment and flung herself face downward on the grass. The stage driver, just picking up the old leather reins, paused and looked over his shoulder. "See here, Marthy, don't cry. I'll take ye some other day."

Mrs. Sprigg poked her head, with its green veil tied carefully over her Sunday bonnet, out of the window to listen greedily. Martha sat up on the grass suddenly to brush away the tears.

"Yes, I will," said Mr. Tisbett. "You be a good girl an' run home now, an' I'll come for ye some other day," and he whirled back in his seat. "G'lang!" And Mrs. Sprigg was picking herself back from the opposite leather-covered seat and straightening her bonnet after the jerk of the old coach as the horses sprang off.

"Oh, we can't leave her," screamed Joel at the end of the seat, trying to see Martha; little Davie in just as much distress, huddled up in the middle.

"Look out—you set still," roared Mr. Tisbett at Joel. "If you don't, I'll put you off, an' you won't go neither," which had such good effect that Joel crowded up closely to Davie. "Oh, I will sit still, I will, Mr. Tisbett," as they rumbled off, trying to make up for lost time on the way to the store where they were to pick up the other passengers and the parcels.

When this place was reached, there was a little detention to allow an old gentleman with crutches to get helped in and settled comfortably by his daughter, who was the only other passenger. And then their trunk, a small black leather one, was swung on behind, and the various parcels (for Mr.

Tisbett, of course, carried the express to the different families between Badgertown and Cherryville) were packed in, and with a "good-by, Joel and David," from Mr. Atkins, who came out on the steps to see them off, away they went again, not to stop except once or twice to give the horses a breathing spell, until they drew up at Cherryville Center.

"It's a dull day enough," observed Mr. Tisbett sociably, on one of these resting spells, and crossing his legs leisurely, "for trade, that is. Beats all how that Mis' Sprigg's tongue goes," he pointed backward with his hand toward the open window.

Joel, who cared little for Mrs. Sprigg's tongue, now began to use his own, clamoring freshly to be allowed to drive, or at least, to hold the reins when the horses were resting.

"When you're bigger, ye may," said Mr. Tisbett, pushing back his straw hat from his forehead.

"I am bigger," said Joel, straightening up.

"I see," said the stage driver with a loud "so ye be."

"Then can't I take 'em?" cried Joel triumphantly.

"Well, ye'll be bigger yet in a little while—you wait and see," said Mr. Tisbett. "You'll grow faster ef you're quiet."

"Will I?" cried Joel eagerly.

"Yes, indeed," the stage driver nodded emphatically "You'll be as big as Ben if you don't look out. That's his cap ain't it, you've got on your head?"

Joel, at this, reminded of his head and what it carried clapped his hands to it. "Yes, 'tis," he nodded.

"Well, now, seein' you've got Ben's cap on your head, you ought to have some sense like Ben has, *in* your head." The stage driver, at that, raised the reins and "g'langed" to his horses, and away they went once more settling down to work.

Suddenly all three up on the top seat began to be aware that there was a lively commotion down within the old stage and a long crutch waved out of the window, besides various cries in as many different voices, made Mr. Tisbett think he must pull up his horses and get down and investigate, which he did at once, thrusting his red face in the window. "What in creation—" But he got no further, the young woman who had waved her father's crutch to attract attention and stop the coach, vying with Mrs. Sprigg to make herself heard. The old gentleman said nothing, but his eyes blazed.

"One of you ladies, at a time," begged Mr. Tisbett, waving his hands deprecatingly. "I'd be delighted to hear it all, if one of you would wait for th' tother—"

But that was precisely what neither would do, but Mrs. Sprigg got her story in shrilly above the other woman.

"My cat's gone—he's let it out o' th' basket."

"Indeed, I did not." The old gentleman was so indignant, he found his voice.

"Pa hasn't touched her old cat," cried the young woman angrily. "The very idea!"

"He's done nothin' but poke th' basket all the while with his crutch," declared Mrs. Sprigg, "ever sence he got in, an' th' cover's flew up, an' see there!" She held up the basket, and, sure enough, the cover was up, and no cat there.

"Well, the cat's under th' seat prob'ly," said Mr. Tisbett in the midst of the babel of tongues. "I'll wait while you get down an' get her, Mis' Sprigg, but you must hurry up." With that he rested one foot on the step and his hands on the window casing, while with many mutterings about neighbors who wouldn't keep their meddling sticks and crutches to themselves, and just as emphatic answers that there hadn't been any meddling sticks and crutches, and that the rickety old cover was to blame for the whole performance, Mrs. Sprigg slid off from the old leather swinging seat and began to prowl about in the dark corners for her straying pet, when, without

a bit of warning, out shot something big and furry over M
Tisbett's head, clawing the straw hat as it went, to land
dozen feet away on the roadside, and disappear over the ston
wall.

"My land o' Goshen!" exclaimed the stage driver, pushin
back his straw hat where it had been thrust over his eyes, a
Mrs. Sprigg's face came up to the window. "Oh, my cat!" sh
screamed wildly, and rattling the door to get out. "Catch hir
—catch him!"

"I'll catch him," cried Joel, tumbling off from his seat an
down over the wheel, followed by Davie, who never stoppe
to think of what had seemed to him before to be a dangerou
proceeding, and racing after Joel's heels, both boys were soo
over the stone wall.

"They'll scare him worse," cried Mrs. Sprigg, now dow
by the side of the road, and in a thicket of straggling black
berry bushes, and she wrung her hands.

"Plague take your old cat!" exclaimed Mr. Tisbett, in
panic over the boys. "Come back here—your ma won't like it,'
he shouted, but he might as well have saved his voice, for i
was carried off by the wind long before it could reach the twc
little flying figures, as they dashed up to the edge of a clump
of bushes. But just here the unexpected happened—the ca
with long leaps was making her way within the thicket, wher
a dog running through the bushes came face to face with her
nearly knocking her over, and Joel, seizing that instant, hac
her, though kicking and struggling dreadfully, held fast in hi
arms.

"I've got her—I've got her!" he yelled clear across the field
his black eyes shining in triumph, and running as fast as he
could for her kicking and clawing, Davie stumbling along by
his side, begging him to let her go, and wild with fright as he

saw a long bloody scratch on one of the little brown hands.

"No, sir—ee!" declared Joel. "There, now, I've got your other old hind leg," this to the cat, and gathering up the long paws with a good grip. "You can't scratch me any more," and presently he somehow got over the stone wall.

"Now give that pesky animal to me," commanded Mr. Tisbett. So Joel, although he much preferred to put the cat himself into the basket, was obliged to hand it over and stand quietly by, while it was crammed into its prison. And then Mr. Tisbett remarking—"We won't have no more stoppings out of *this* stage till you get to Cherryville," produced a rope from underneath the seat and securely tied on the cover, making it fast with a generous number of knots, and no one but Davie took any notice of Joel's bloody little hands.

It wasn't till they got to Cherryville and stopped at the Inn for dinner, Mrs. Sprigg and her cat and her bandbox having been dropped at "Eliza's," that the old gentleman as soon as he was helped up to the long piazza to sink down in one of the big chairs, said, "Hey, look at that boy," and he rapped on the floor with his crutch; then pointed to Joel.

Joel put his hands behind his little blue cotton blouse. He had wiped them pretty clean, but couldn't succeed in getting off all the dingy stains.

Mrs. Christy, the landlady, was bustling in the doorway, preparatory to ringing the big dinner bell. "What's that?" she said, peering at Joel.

"Nothing," he tried to say, squirming worse than ever. But little Davie piped out, "It was the cat."

"Let me see your hands," said Mrs. Christy, giving up all thoughts just then of ringing the dinner bell. So Joel had to show them. "Oh, dear me!" she exclaimed. "Now that's too bad, the cat must have hurt you just awful."

"Phoh, she didn't hurt much," said Joel, trying to edge off, little Davie having the hardest work not to let the tears roll down his cheeks.

"You come right here," said Mrs. Christy, "an' wash 'em good an' clean, an' I'll give you some court plaster. Then, says I, you'll be all ready to set down an' eat when Mr. Tisbett is. Come along and take off you cap," she said to David.

Joel clapped his hands up to his head, then stared at Davie, his black eyes getting bigger than ever. Little Davie, having been unable all this time to look higher than Joel's poor hands, now stared back at him.

"Oh—oh!" he screamed in the greatest consternation. "It's gone—it isn't there. Oh—oh!" and in a minute the whole long piazza was in an uproar that brought every lodger to the scene. Ben's cap was not only not on Joel's head—it was nowhere to be seen.

Joel cried steadily all through dinner, the tears running down his round cheeks, without the slightest thought of the boarders staring at him, as he sat back in his chair; and all attempts to make him partake of the nice things that the landlady and "Mandy" piled on his plate, failed, while little Davie softly sobbed next to him, until good Mrs. Christy and the stage driver were almost at their wit's end. Finally the old gentleman at the other end of the long table laid down his knife and fork, and exclaimed "Hem—" in such a loud voice, everybody knew he was getting ready to say something quite important.

"Here, boy—look here. *Hem!*" It was so very loud now and commanding that even Joel stopped a moment. Seeing this, Davie listened with all his heart. Could anything help them out of this dreadful trouble? *Ben's cap lost!* "I've got something for you that you'll like a great deal better'n your old cap; it was too big anyway for you."

"I wouldn't like it better," screamed Joel, a great deal worse than before; "this was Ben's and I've—lost—it!"

"Lavinia," said the old gentleman, giving his daughter a little key out of his waistcoat pocket, "you go to my trunk and get out that little black cap." He dropped his voice so that no one else could hear.

"Not the one you're taking to Jim!" said Lavinia, whispering back.

"You do as I say," commanded the old gentleman fiercely. If he could have reached his crutch, he would have pounded the floor with it, but it was left in the corner of the big dining room. So Lavinia went off with the little key in her hand, and presently she came back with a brand-new black cloth cap in the other hand.

"Now stick that on that boy's head," said the old gentleman. "Now, says I, whatever your—name—is, boy, you take Ben, whoever—he—is, that cap. He'll like it a great deal better because it's a new one. And then come back and finish your dinner, Lavinia."

So Lavinia stuck the new black cap on Joel's head as she went by his chair, and was just slipping into her own, when out jumped the stage driver from his seat and picked it off, going up to the old gentleman at the head of the table. "Thank ye, sir, kindly, but all th' same, it's me that's goin' to get a new cap fer Ben Pepper, seein' his'n has blew off from Joel's head while he's my comp'ny," and he was just going back to his place when a frowsy-headed stableboy walked right into the dining room without waiting to ask anyone's leave.

"He said," pointing with his thumb out toward the road, "I was to give you this to once't. You dropped it when you was chasin' th' cat, and him an' his dog found it," and he held out Ben's cap.

XI

A Little Yellow Chicken

"POLLY," said Phronsie, "I wish we could have cake every day." She held carefully, a small bit saved after nibbling slowly around the edge of the piece in her hand, "Why can't we, Polly?"

"Why can't we what, Phronsie?" Polly, rushing around the old kitchen, the dishcloth, which she had forgotten to put down, still in her hand, picked up a small bowl from the table and, knocking off a spoon that it had concealed, sent it clattering to the floor. "Oh, dear me, I do wish Joel would ever put his things up," she exclaimed in vexation.

"I'll pick it up," cried Phronsie, forgetting her cake crumb so that it went flying off to the floor, too. "Let me, Polly, do," she begged, running over to the table.

"Oh, no, never mind, Pet," exclaimed Polly, very much ashamed of her impatience. "There, I have it—well, oh, what did you want, Phronsie? Oh, dear me," she cried again, "I wonder when these old dishes will ever be done!"

"I'll do them," cried Phronsie, running after her eagerly as she bore them off to the big pan of water waiting for them, the dish towel flapping from Polly's arm. "Please, Polly, I'm so big; do let me."

"Nonsense, you're no bigger'n a chicken," exclaimed Polly, merrily setting down Joel's mush bowl and spoon among the other things the Pepper family had used at their simple breakfast.

"I'm not a chicken," said Phronsie in a grieved little voice, and standing quite tall.

"Oh, yes, you are," declared Polly gaily. Then, as she caught sight of Phronsie's face, she turned her back on the big dishpan and seized her for a good hug. "A sweet, puffy little chicken—there, and there, Phronsie Pepper!"

"Am I just like Mrs. Henderson's chickens?" asked Phronsie slowly, a light breaking over her face.

"Yes, as like as two peas," declared Polly, shaking her head decidedly. "Oh, you can't think, Phronsie. You're just exactly like one of Mrs. Henderson's chickens, every single bit." With that she gave her another hug.

"Am I like the little yellow one, Polly?" asked Phronsie, as Polly at last set her free, and flew off to her long-delayed dishwashing, only to find the water cold. "Am I, Polly?"

"Eh, what?" asked Polly, wrinkling up her brow in dismay. "Now what shall I do—that old stove! And the fire's out, of course. Oh, dear me, Pet, what is it?"

"Am I like the little yellow one, Polly?" asked Phronsie, thrusting her face in between Polly and the dishpan. "Am I, Polly?"

"The little yellow what?" asked Polly, all her thoughts on her delayed morning work, and her hurry to pull out all those basting threads on the coats Mamsie had just finished for Mr. Atkins, to surprise Mrs. Pepper when she had come home from Deacon Blodgett's where she had gone to help in the spring cleaning.

"You said I was like Mrs. Henderson's chickens," said Phronsie, her lip beginning to tremble, "and can't I be like the little yellow one? Please make me, Polly." A big tear she was trying to keep back wouldn't stay in its place, but ran down over the round cheek.

"Dear me, yes, of course, you can be like the little yellow chicken, Phronsie," promised Polly, bursting into a merry laugh, and throwing her arms around her again, quite in dismay at the tear. "Now, then, just think, Phronsie, how cunning he was when he hopped all around after his mother, and—"

"Just like this," laughed Phronsie, her tears all gone; and tumbling to all fours, she began to bob over the kitchen floor as a very fat, yellow chicken would be supposed to get along on its quite new little legs.

"Hah—hah!" scud—scud, scamper,—and two boys came bounding in. "See Phronsie!" screamed Joel to little David, who came plunging after.

"I'm Mrs. Henderson's little yellow chicken," announced Phronsie, lifting a flushed face, and having very hard work to keep her pink apron from tripping her up.

"Hoh—hoh, come on, Dave," screamed Joel, flinging himself flat on the floor. "We'll be the old hens. No, I'm going to be the rooster. Cock-a-doodle-doo!" With that he gave a terrible crow, and sprawled after Phronsie.

Little David, who very much wished to be the rooster, smothered a sigh, and immediately became one of Mrs. Henderson's old gray hens. And being perfectly familiar with their proceedings from the many visits the children had been allowed to make to the parsonage hen coop, he was soon clucking at a great rate, and following Joel and Phronsie about till the old kitchen rang with the noise of a farmyard.

"Goodness me!" cried Polly, turning away from the dishpan

where she was trying to believe the water was hot enough to make the dishes as nice as usual. "Oh, what fun!" She rested her hands for a moment on the rim. Dear me, didn't she just long to be down on the floor, and be an old hen with the others rampaging around the kitchen! But Mamsie was coming soon, and there were those basting threads—and beside, the dishwater would then be cold as a stone. It would never do even to think of it. So she flew back again, and made a great bustle with the cups and bowls and spoons trying to shut out the delightful noise. This was the reason she didn't hear what followed.

"Oh, whickets!" Joel couldn't help saying what Mamsie had reproved him for. Here was what looked like a piece of cake. It couldn't be, really, for cake didn't come to the Pepper household often enough to be found on the floor. But it surely looked like it; and Joel lost sight of the fact that he was a rooster, and rubbed his eyes. Yes, it surely was, and white cake, too, with even a bit of sugar frosting clinging to it. And yes, really and truly, there was half a raisin hiding in the corner. And Joel forgot still more that he was Mrs. Henderson's rooster, and he sat down an gobbled up the bit, wishing that his farmyard would always yield such rich pickings. If it would, he'd be willing to be a rooster forever.

"Let's play Mrs. Henderson is going to feed us now," David was saying, over in the other corner, to the little yellow chicken.

"Yes," gurgled Phronsie in delight; forgetting how tired she was, if only Mrs. Henderson was going to give them all their breakfast, and beginning to hop again.

"Look at Joel," cried Davie, pointing a finger over where the rooster still sat, absorbed in the delightful memory of swallowing that cake bit. Then the old gray hen flapped over there, followed with very uneven plunges by the little yellow chicken who tried desperately to keep up. "We're going to have some corn," he shouted. "Hurry up, Joe, Mrs. Henderson's coming with our breakfast."

Joel at that was brought to. "Huh!" he sniffed, "I've had cake," just as Phronsie came tumbling up, a very sorry-looking, hot little chicken. She heard the word "cake." "Oh, Joel," she cried in a pleased little voice, and, trying to sit straight, only succeeded in rolling over in a heap. Both boys hopped over to her and pulled her up.

"Oh, where is it, Joey?" she cried, holding out both hands.

"Where's what?" cried Joel, "—oh, the corn. Come on, Dave, Mrs. Henderson's calling us. Cock-a-doodle-doo!" Away he hopped, and David, supposing Phronsie in the merry chase, hopped after, flapping his wings and calling to his chickens in just that motherly way he had admired so often in the parsonage old gray hens. Phronsie left alone, sat quite straight for a moment, then, despairing of being heard in the babel, began to search diligently for the precious cake bit, that had been slowly saved till the last, because of that very corner of frosting and that half a raisin.

"Where's Phronsie?" cried David, missing her from the corn breakfast. Joel whirled around, sending keen glances over the old kitchen. "There she is," spying her pink apron back of Mamsie's big calico-covered rocking chair. "Come on, Phron," he called.

Phronsie put out a worried little face around the calico valance. "I can't find it," she said.

"She's lost something," said Davie. With that he forgot he was an old gray hen, and sprang to his feet and ran over. Joel preferred to still be a rooster, so he hopped after, reaching the spot to hear David say, "She says she's lost some cake."

"Cake?" cried Joel, tumbling back to sit on his heels, and his black eyes stuck out.

"Yes," said Davie, but he looked puzzled enough. "Oh, Phronsie, when did you have any cake?" he demanded incredulously. "We never have cake, you know. You're playing."

"No," said Phronsie, shaking her yellow head very positively. "I did have some, really and truly. Polly gave it to me, and I lost it." With that she began to feel carefully along the depths of the chair valance.

"Oh, dear me!" it wasn't in the least like a brave "Cock-a-doodle-doo!" that the big rooster now emitted, as Joel roared out something, and flew for Polly.

"Take care, Joe!" she warned, with her hands full of the dishes she was just going to pile on the shelves. "You 'most knocked off Mamsie's cup!" and she turned pale with fright.

"I've eat it up!" wailed Joel, burying his black, stubby head in Polly's apron.

"No, you haven't broken it," cried Polly, "don't worry, Joe, I didn't mean to scare you."

"It's eat, and I can't give it back," screamed Joel, burrowing deeper into her apron, thereby making all the dishes in Polly's hands tremble violently.

"Joe Pepper," cried Polly, "stop this minute. Oh, dear me, every single thing will be smashed! What will Mamsie say?" At mention of Mamsie, Joel, although he still wailed on, stopped his struggling so that she was able to set the dishes safely on the table. "Now, see here." She grasped his two shoulders and made him turn his face. "Oh, dear me, what is the matter?" she cried, aghast.

"I've eat it," cried Joel, breaking into a roar, and not looking up, his black eyes raining tears.

"Eat what?" cried Polly in great distress. "Stop screaming, Joe, and tell me this minute. What have you done?" She gave a great gasp, and instinctively turned a quick eye over to the corner where she could see David and Phronsie moving about, probably still as chickens, and not disturbed by Joel's roars, supposing it a new phase of his playing at being a rooster.

"Oh, I've eat it—don't you understand, Polly?" screamed Joel in a fresh burst, and stamping in his impatience. "And I can't give it back."

"Eat what?" demanded Polly in bewilderment.

"The cake!" roared Joel. This time it was so very loud, no one could possibly think it was a rooster. So little Davie cried joyfully, "Oh, he's found it, Phronsie," and they both scuffed over.

"Oh, don't let her come," screamed Joel in terror, and trying to hide behind Polly's apron. But it was too late.

"He's found it!" piped Phronsie in a gleeful little voice, and holding up both hands. "Oh, give it to me, Polly, do."

"Oh!" screamed Joel, huddling around Polly's other side and twirling her apron.

"Take care, Joe, you'll break the strings," she warned. "Now, children, you two go and sit down," pointing to the wooden chairs ranged against the wall every day after breakfast was over, and the floor swept up, "just a minute, and I'll come over to you."

"But I want my cake, Polly, I do," said Phronsie reproachfully, and very much astonished at this delay, for Polly always attended to her at once. "Please, Polly, give it to me now," she begged.

At this, Joel, on Polly's other side, began to struggle in and out the apron depths worse than ever.

"Joe, be still," commanded Polly in her sternest tones. "If you don't, you will have to go into the Provision Room."

At these dreadful words little Davie's cheek turned quite pale. What had Joel done? But Phronsie's mind was all on her cake, and she continued to gaze at Polly in grieved astonishment, and to beg, "Please, Polly, give it to me now."

"See here, Phronsie," said Polly at her wit's end what to do, "you must be a good girl now, and do just as I say, else Mamsie will be so sorry when she comes home; so you must go and sit down in that chair till I go over to you."

To make Mamsie sorry was as much worse than the loss of any cake could possibly be, and Davie saying, "Yes, Come, Phronsie," and taking her fat little hand, the two children went over to the spot indicated, and climbed up to the chairs just as Polly had told them to; little David with an awful feeling at his heart that Joel was in trouble.

"Now, Joel," said Polly, mustering up as much cheer as she could, "you and I will go to the Provision Room and—"

The two children over on their chairs with their ears pricked up for every word, heard "Provision Room," and Davie screamed out, "Oh, don't make him go there, Polly!"

"Oh, we're going together," said Polly cheerfully, getting hold of Joel's hand. "Joey has something he is going to tell me."

"Ow!" exclaimed Joel, shrinking deeper into the apron.

"So come along, Joey." And away they went, Joel wiping off the tears on the back of one grimy hand while Polly held fast to the other.

"There, now." Polly sat down on the little stool in the middle of the old Provision Room, where, whenever the children were very naughty, Mother Pepper always had them sit alone until such time as she considered the punishment should be over. "You must tell me all about it, Joey." He had flung himself down on the earth floor, and buried his head in her lap.

"I tell you I've eat it," said Joel in smothered gasps. "Oh, dear me, boo—hoo!"

"Eat what?" asked Polly, still not understanding.

"The cake! I didn't know it was Phronsie's," mumbled Joel

in a fresh burst. "Oh! And it was on the floor, and—and— Oh, dear me! I was Mrs. Henderson's—Oh, dear me."

"Yes, I know," said Polly quickly, glad to help him over the hard places, "one of the hens."

"No, not the hen," snorted Joel in scorn, and raising his black head; "Dave was that, and I was the rooster—that big one, you know, Polly."

"Yes, I know," nodded Polly, quite pleased that he could be diverted even for a moment, "and so you picked up the cake from the floor. Was that it, Joe?"

"Yes," down went Joel's head again. "I didn't know it was Phronsie's, and now I can't give it back."

"Um, mm—" Polly was lost in thought for a minute. What could she do to make up for this dreadful loss? She never could get another piece of cake to replace it. Such windfalls as this one, which Mrs. Atkins had given her the other day, didn't happen often. And Polly, remembering how she had turned back on her way home from her errand to the store, when the wife of the storekeeper who lived in the ell had rapped with her thimble on the window, and then with the words, "I had comp'ny to tea las' night, an' I want you should have this to eat on th' way home, child," she had put the precious portion in Polly's hand, and Polly had run every speck of the way home, deciding to put it away to give to Phronsie sometime when it should most be needed, for the bit wasn't large enough to be divided between the three "children," as Polly and Ben always called the others. And now, only to think what trouble had come from it all!

"I've eat it," Joel kept saying in a steady refrain, and feeling it very cold comfort indeed to be brought to the Provision Room by Polly, with no help to give. "Oh, dear me!" he wailed on.

"I'll tell you, Joel," Polly exclaimed, and she gave a little jump from the stool so suddenly that he nearly tumbled over on his back, "what you can do. It will be splendid, I think. Now, understand, Joel, you oughtn't to have eaten up that cake when you found it. I gave it to Phronsie."

"Where'd you get it?" demanded Joel in great surprise.

So Polly related the whole story of the cake, only taking breath when Joel blurted out, "I wish Mrs. Atkins had given you a bigger piece."

"For shame, Joe," reproved Polly, sitting down on the stool again and taking both of his hands in hers. "She was very good to give me this. Yes, you shouldn't have eaten it up when you found it, but brought it to me. Never mind if you were the big rooster, the cake didn't belong to you. But now it is eaten up, why, it must be made up to Phronsie in some way. And I'll tell you how; but you've got to work because you ate the cake, you know."

Joel nodded his black head and wiped off the last tear. Since Polly was going to fix it, it was going to be all right, and Phronsie would be pleased. "Tell on, Polly," he begged eagerly.

"Well," said Polly, "you know Phronsie has been wanting a little pie ever since Mr. Beggs, the ragman, gave her that cunning little tin plate with the letters all around the edge. Now, if Mamsie will let us use the flour, I'll—"

"You'll bake her one," cried Joel in glee. "Oh, hooray!" he jumped to his feet and shouted.

David with Phronsie, their hands folded in their laps, sitting up stiffly on their chairs in the old kitchen, gave a great sigh of relief at that shout. Everything was quite right with Joel once more, to be sure.

"Well, but," said Polly, "you've got to work, you know, Joel."

"I'll make the pie," declared Joel, turning a somersault, "and roll out the crust, and everything."

"Oh, no, Joe," cried Polly in horror. "The very idea! Why, you never made a pie in your life."

"But I'm going to this time," declared Joel, pausing on the edge of another somersault and cocking up one black eye at her. "You said so yourself, Polly Pepper, that I'd got to work; so there, now."

"But I didn't mean in that way, Joel," said Polly. "Oh, dear me!"

"Well, how will I have to work then?" demanded Joel, getting up to his feet and regarding her with disfavor.

"Well, you know you ought not to have eaten up that cake," said Polly emphatically, "so, of course, you must work to pay it back. So you will have to pick berries, because there isn't anything to make a pie of but berries. And you must pick them."

"Oh, dear me, I don't want to," grumbled Joel, who had his own ideas of what he intended to do the rest of that day. And no berries could be found nearer than a mile-and-a-half hot walk.

"For shame, Joe," cried Polly hotly, "you've eaten up Phronsie's cake, and the only thing in this world I can think of to pay her back is to make her a pie on her own little new tin plate, and she can't have it if you don't go after the berries."

"I'll go—I'll go," promised Joel in alarm, his only fear now being that something would happen to prevent Phronsie from being paid back for her lost piece of cake, "but Dave's got to go with me to pick the berries."

"No, he hasn't, Joel," said Polly firmly; "not unless he really wants to. And you must pick all the berries for Phronsie's pie, anyway, and what Davie picks, if he really wants to go, must be brought home to Mamsie."

So Joel, quite relieved that Phronsie was really to have her pie, if Mamsie would let them have the flour, and quite as sure that Davie would go to pick berries if invited, pranced off at Polly's heels out of the Provision Room.

But the story was not told to Phronsie that day, for just as Polly ran over the rickety little steps into the old kitchen, a rap on the green door was heard. "There's our Mr. Beebe," screamed David, craning his neck to look out of the window. And Phronsie clapped her hands, and then they all rushed to the door. And there on the big flat stone was good Mrs. Beebe, and coming slowly up the path was Mr. Beebe, and there was the big black cloth bag hanging on Mrs. Beebe's arm, and Joel smelled doughnuts before she ever got into the kitchen.

"You dear, precious, little creeters, you!" exclaimed old Mrs. Beebe as they all surrounded her. "Get her Mamsie's chair, Joel, do," said Polly, "and I'll untie your bonnet."

"Let me," begged Phronsie, standing on tiptoe and putting up both hands. "I want to, dear Mrs. Beebe, I do."

"So you shall," said old Mrs. Beebe, smiling at her.

"Oh, Phronsie, you can't do it," said Polly in dismay.

"Oh, yes, I can," declared Phronsie. "I want to, I do."

"And so you shall, honey bird," declared Mrs. Beebe. So Phronsie was lifted up to the old lady's lap, where she was kept from slipping off by Polly holding on to her, while she fumbled among the black ribbon strings, every minute getting them more mixed than ever; Mrs. Beebe smiling above them, and protesting she wouldn't have anyone but Phronsie Pepper untie them for the world.

"Oh, dear me!" said Polly, the color rushing all over her round cheek. "Do let me help you, Phronsie. Joel, you come and hold Phronsie on to Mrs. Beebe's lap. Now, Pet, I'll show you how."

"No, no," protested Phronsie, shaking her yellow head,

"my dear sweet Mrs. Beebe wants me to untie it, and I must do it all by myself."

"She's mussing them dreadfully," Polly felt obliged to whisper over Phronsie's head into Mrs. Beebe's ear, but the old lady only smiled and said, "Never mind, I'll run a hot flatiron over 'em when I get home."

All this time Mr. Beebe had found a chair for himself, and sat down, blowing his nose on his big bandanna, and alternately entertained by little David and Joel, who ran back and forth from him to Mrs. Beebe, as the untying of the bonnet was in progress.

"She never'll get it done," grumbled Joel, unable to keep his eyes from the big black bag that still dangled from Mrs. Beebe's arm. It bulged generously, and the smell of its contents was getting into the very corners of the old kitchen. At last the bonnet was lifted from the old lady's head, and Polly bore it carefully off to lay on the big four-poster in Mamsie's bedroom.

"There, I did do it all myself," announced Phronsie, clasping her hands in much satisfaction, as she slipped to the floor.

"So you did, dear." Old Mrs. Beebe beamed at her and leaning over her she imprinted a kiss on the pink cheek. "Well, now, don't you want to see what I've brought for you?" and she slipped the handles of the bag from her arm, and opened its mouth.

"Yes, I do," said Phronsie, "very much indeed, dear Mrs. Beebe."

"Bless your heart, you shall, and Joel and David, too," said Mrs. Beebe. It was impossible for Joel to get closer to her than he at present was, and little Davie was wedged in the other side of Phronsie, as Polly came back from the bedroom.

"Now come, Polly," said old Mrs. Beebe, as she drew out from the bag a big clean cloth that, unrolled, displayed a good half dozen of the sugariest doughnuts of most ample proportions, "there's just one apiece, and one for your ma," she announced in huge satisfaction.

Old Mr. Beebe sat and laughed and mopped his face with his big bandanna all through the scene that ensued, as the children sat down on the floor and at once began work on their doughnuts, Polly first running to the closet to lay the two for Mamsie and Ben on a clean blue plate, and to shut the door fast.

"Oh, it's so good of you, dear Mrs. Beebe," she cried, dancing back to whisper this into the old lady's ear.

"Well, now, you sit down and eat yours, Polly, child," said old Mrs. Beebe. But first Polly had to run over to old Mr. Beebe's chair because he nodded to her mysteriously and beckoned with a long finger.

"I've got some pep'mint sticks in my pocket," he announced in a loud whisper, when she reached his side, "but Ma kinder thought 'twas better fer you to give 'em to th' children tomorrow, an' not on top o' th' doughnuts," and he smuggled a wad into her hand. So Polly had to run off and slip that into the cupboard, too. Oh, such richness, and lasting over until tomorrow! "Did ever anybody have such a dear, good Mr. Beebe, and such a dear, good Mrs. Beebe as we have!" cried Polly to herself as she tucked away her treasures. At last, there she was on the floor with the others and in the midst of the doughnut feast. And wasn't it a feast, though!

Joel was through first, every crumb carefully picked up and swallowed. Little Davie, having eaten quite slowly, was just on the point of breaking off part of his doughnut to give to him, when old Mr. Beebe called out, "Now, then, Joel, my boy, you come along of me: "I'm goin' out to look at my horse." So Joel clattered off with the old gentleman, well pleased with the invitation, and the kitchen toned down to quiet, only broken by Phronsie's soft cooing to herself between the bites from her doughnut. At last she laid it down in Polly's lap. "I'm going to get Seraphina and give her some," she whispered.

"Where's she goin'?" asked old Mrs. Beebe.

"She's gone to get her doll," said Polly as Phronsie ran into Mamsie's bedroom. When Seraphina wasn't played with, she was laid in the bottom drawer of the old bureau, where the precious red-topped shoes were kept. And, presently, out came Phronsie hugging Seraphina and telling her all about the doughnuts and good Mrs. Beebe, who was her own dear, sweet Mrs. Beebe, until the old lady sat back and laughed till the tears came, and David and Polly had finished their doughnuts. And, then, back came old Mr. Beebe and Joel, who was in a great state of excitement, whooping it all out as soon as he got within the door. "Mr. Beebe's going to take us to ride," he screamed, "can't we go, Polly—say, can't we—can't we?"

"Yes, do let 'em," said Mrs. Beebe, "I'm goin' to set an' be comfortable in your ma's chair, an' you go too, Polly," she added. "There's plenty of room, th' boys can set in the back o' th' wagon."

"Oh, I can't," said Polly, with a wistful glance out of the window at the big green wagon and the old white horse. "I've got to pick out basting threads."

"Can't you leave 'em, Polly?" asked the old lady kindly, with a glance at the flushed face.

"No," said Polly, pushing back the brown rings of hair from her forehead, "because Mamsie wants to take the coats home to Mr. Atkins today. I ought not to have stopped so long," she said remorsefully.

Old Mrs. Beebe gave a sigh, "I ain't any good at pickin' bastin's," she said. "My fingers is all thumbs at such work.

Well, Polly, you fly and get th' others ready, an' then sometime Pa'll come an' give you a drive."

So Polly flew to get Phronsie's things on. Joel already was in the big wagon hallooing for David to hurry up. And then Seraphina's bonnet must be tied on, for, of course, she must go too. And at last the three children, Phronsie carrying the remains of her doughnut to eat on the way, were off. Old Mrs. Beebe watched them from the window, and Polly hurried back up the path to fly to work over the basting threads.

XII

At the Parsonage

POLLY PEPPER drew a long breath and stepped up on the flat stone before the parsonage door. Even then it was not too late to turn and run home! But Mamsie—oh, that would never do, for hadn't Mrs. Pepper sent her with the blue bowl that had contained the little pat of butter, and her thanks for it! And if she, Polly, should turn her back on it all and run home, why, it would be such a dreadful thing and disgrace the Little Brown House forever. No, she must go through with it, and face Miss Jerusha, if, as she dreaded, that lady should come to the door. So she lifted the big brass knocker, and let it fall with a clang.

Heavy steps sounded along the oilcloth on the hall and the big door was thrown open. Yes, it was just as dreadful as she expected! There was the minister's sister.

"Go right away," said Miss Jerusha, shaking a long, bony hand. "Don't you know any better'n to come to this door?"

"My mother sent me, and—" gasped Polly, with shaking fingers hanging fast to the little blue bowl.

"Your mother?—well, didn't she know any better'n to have

you come to this door?" broke in Miss Jerusha with asperity;
"an' who is she, anyway?" all in the same breath.

"She's Mrs. Pepper, and oh—"

"Oh, are you one of those Pepper children who live in that
old brown house all down at the heel?" interrupted Miss
Jerusha.

"Yes," said Polly, with a warm little throb at her heart.
Wasn't it just the dearest place on earth, and what would
she give to be there now!

"Well, you go right away," commanded the minister's
sister decidedly. "You needn't come begging here. I declare,
if you hain't brought a bowl this blessed minute."

"Oh, we never begged in our lives," cried Polly in horror,
every bit of color flying from her round cheek. Then she
jumped off from the doorstone, only one thought possessing
her—to get to Mamsie.

"Jerusha, who is it?" The parson's wife came out of the
keeping room to the front door.

"Oh, some sort o' a begging person," said Miss Jerusha
shortly, and trying to slam the door fast.

"A begging person?" Mrs. Henderson being of another
mind about the big door was presently peering down the
path. "Why, it's Polly Pepper!" And she ran out after her.

"What nonsense!" sniffed Miss Jerusha, craning her long
neck after her.

"Polly," called Mrs. Henderson. But Polly's wild little
heart was urging her on so fiercely that she didn't hear anything else but those dreadful words that had been spoken.
So the minister's wife picked up her skirts and ran as she
seldom did since she was a girl. "Polly," she panted, at last
coming up to the flying little figure, "oh, do stop—for I really
—can't run any more." And Polly whirled around, her cheeks
still white and her brown eyes flashing.

"Oh, Polly." Mrs. Henderson, dismayed at the face, thought better of any idea of possible questions then and there. "Come," she said, taking one of the hands away from the little blue bowl.

"Oh, I can't," said Polly in a passion, and standing quite still, and she tried to pull away her hand.

But the minister's wife, not disclosing any idea of letting it go, but instead marching off toward the parsonage, Polly had nothing to do but to walk along by her side, over the flat doorstone again, and although she felt as if she must die in doing it, pass that dreadful figure of Miss Jerusha in the hall, till at last the two were standing in the study doorway.

"Well, Polly?" Parson Henderson laid down his pen. He was in the midst of his next Sunday's sermon, to be sure, but as he somehow couldn't work past that "Seventhly," he welcomed the interruption.

"Well, I never!" Miss Jerusha, stalking after, looked over the two. "To think of bringin' in that girl an' interruptin' you, Jotham!"

"Oh, I'm glad to see Polly Pepper always," said the minister gaily. He was away from his desk by this time, and with Polly's cold little hand in his was leading her to a seat, the minister's wife getting on the other side. Miss Jerusha sniffed, and made for a chair at the end of the room.

"Well, I never!" she exclaimed again, as she sat down heavily and she raised her long hands.

"Please let me go home," begged Polly faintly, and turning away her brown eyes from the big, square figure. "Oh, please, sir, do let me."

"Oh, Jerusha"—Parson Henderson held Polly's hand tightly as he turned to his sister—"I want to talk to this little girl now, so please go into the keeping room."

"How you can be so imposed on, Jotham, is more'n I

can see," Miss Jerusha snorted, but she got up from her chair, stalked out, and brought the door to with a spiteful little snip. If she was going at all, she would do it thoroughly.

When Polly Pepper was let out of the big door, she had a posy in one hand, and in the other, a paper bag holding half a dozen little cupcakes fresh from the parsonage oven that very morning.

"Now come again soon, Polly." Mrs. Henderson bent and kissed the rosy cheek.

"Yes'm," said Polly, with a happy little thrill, "and oh, thank you so much, dear Mrs. Henderson, for Mamsie's cakes, and the flowers." She gave a little hug to the posy and her brown eyes danced.

"I'm glad you love flowers so much, Polly," said the minister's wife, happy enough that she had cut her two precious rose-geranium blossoms. "Well, come again, child, when you can."

The dimity curtain in the keeping-room window was twitched away to admit a long face with its sharp eyes peering around the ruffled edge. But Polly didn't see it as she skipped happily down the path to the gate, and the minister's wife hurrying back along the hall to the study was not conscious of the "Mehitable" called too late.

"Well?" The parson who had recovered his pen laid it down again.

"Oh, Jotham," she shut the door and came around to his chair, "we must do something for that child—for all those children." She seized his well-worn sleeve and held it fast.

"I know—I know," Parson Henderson nodded thoughtfully, "and there's Ben. I must confess, Mehitable, I get to thinking of him so much it's hard to shake it off."

"But he is a boy," said his wife.

"Even boys can suffer," observed the parson dryly.

"Oh, I know, husband." Mrs. Henderson now gripped his coat collar and peered round into his face anxiously. "You know I think Ben Pepper has an awfully hard time, but, then, he can go out and work, and there's Polly—she must stay in and help her mother, and have no schooling and no fun; and then, Oh, dear me, there's that blessed little thing, Phronsie!"

"Yes, there's Phronsie," said the minister, with a twinge at the heart, "and Joel and David; we mustn't forget them."

"Oh, I don't forget them," cried his wife. "I can't for a single moment forget any one of those five poor little things. Oh, dear me, if only there weren't so many of them, Jotham."

"And Mrs. Pepper, we mustn't forget her, either," the minister drummed on his desk with troubled fingers; "for she has really the hardest time of all." And he got out of his chair, and, drawing his wife's arm within his own, began to pace over the well-worn carpet.

"Jotham," she clutched his arm with her other hand, "just think if I hadn't seen that child flying off! Just think!" She brought her anxious blue eyes up to his dark ones.

Parson Henderson's face dropped gloomily. "Yes, we ought to do something to make up for Jerusha." He brought the last out with a deep flush.

"Oh, don't look so, dear. You can't help it," cried his wife, with a remorseful throb at her unlucky words.

"I sometimes think," began the minister, then he stopped short.

"Don't think," she begged under her breath. "You had to do it, and it was just lovely of you, Jotham." She tried to get up on tiptoe to plant a little kiss between the troubled eyes. Failing of this, she dropped it on the rusty sleeve. "Don't, dear."

"Yes, there was no other place for her to go to, and she was good to Mother." But the dark eyes were still troubled.

"Yes, it was lovely of you to have her here," repeated Mrs. Henderson. "So don't think any more of it, husband," she implored.

"It's you who are lovely, Mehitable," he said with a sigh.

"Nonsense; and I shouldn't have loved you half as much if you hadn't looked out for your sister," cried his wife with spirit. "So don't let us worry any more about it. Besides, just think of her going away tomorrow!—and two whole weeks, Jotham!" She drew a long breath, and hugged her husband's arm tighter.

"Poor Mehitable!" he said, looking down at her. Then he laughed like a boy, it was so good to think of that tomorrow that Cousin Henry's invitation would bring about.

"Hush—hush!" said his wife, pinching his arm tighter. "I'm afraid she'll hear. Well, now, let us think about the Peppers. There isn't anything we can give them—" she broke off a minute, her gaze caught by a thin place in the study carpet, and she tried to step gingerly over it, guiding the parson askew—"and besides, Mrs. Pepper wouldn't take it even if we had any money."

"No indeed," said the parson with decision, "I can't think of that woman accepting money."

"Well—Oh, dear me!" Mrs. Henderson wrinkled her brows thoughtfully. "I do believe the first thing is to make Polly happy after this—this afternoon. Supposing I set up the attic, Jotham, tomorrow, and get her to help me," she brought up brightly.

"I thought that attic was in a perennial state of order," said the minister, bursting into another laugh. "I'm sure, Mehitable, you never have even a ladies' prayer meeting here without you first overhaul things up there, and sweep down the attic stairs."

Mrs. Henderson gave a merry little laugh, it was so good to see him cheery once more.

"Well, I'm going to set it up tomorrow, anyway," she declared. "There's a chest that isn't looked over, and ever so many things up there that ought to be seen to. And I'll ask Polly to come over and help, and then she can stay to dinner. You know Jerusha goes early in the stage—" she brought up with satisfaction.

"And why not ask her to bring Phronsie?" said the Parson. "The child can play around, and she can be with us at dinner, too."

"Now, how nice it is that you always think of the best things!" cried his wife, in delight. "Yes, that will be fine for tomorrow, and make Polly forget everything that wasn't pleasant, and we'll all enjoy it as much as those two blessed children. Why can't Peletiah run down now to the Little Brown House and invite them?"

"Well, he can start," said the minister grimly, with a vivid remembrance of Peletiah's usual rate of speed. "That's a good idea, wife." So Mrs. Henderson hurried out of the study. "Well, if Peletiah is slow, it's a comfort he's so steady; we can always find him when wanted," she reflected. And after many repetitions of the message to be delivered to Mrs. Pepper had at last fixed it in his mind, ·he set forth at a stolid pace for the Little Brown House.

"Somebody's coming!" cried Davie, hearing crunching on the gravel. "Joey, wait a minute!"

Joel, kneeling on the floor and pounding the cover on an old wooden box he was going to try to catch rabbits in, didn't hear, and gave a lusty blow with his hammer. "Gee—whickets!" as the nail—a crooked one—went in all askew.

"Do stop," begged Davie, with one ear on the door. And "Oh, Joel, how can you say such perfectly dreadful words!"

cried Polly, from the corner where she was trying to fix up Mamsie's workbasket that had been upset.

"There *is* someone coming," declared Davie, a little pink spot coming on his cheek; "there surely is, Polly," and he stood quite still to listen.

"Oh, no," said Polly with a little laugh, "it can't be, because we don't ever have calls, you know." She dropped a spool with a long white thread dangling from her fingers, down in her lap, and the laugh broke off suddenly. "I wish we could ever have calls; wouldn't it be perfectly elegant if we only could," she said wistfully.

"Oh, Polly, don't look so," implored little Davie, rushing over to her, while Joel hammered in another nail with a great bang. "Hoh! we do, too," he cried; "Mr. Beebe comes and Mrs. Beebe. I like her best 'cause she brings doughnuts."

"Oh, Joey, for shame," cried Polly, "to think only of what she brings us to eat!"

"They're good," said Joel, smacking his lips and laying down the hammer to think the better over the delights of good Mrs. Beebe's visits.

"I like Mr. Beebe," said David, turning off from Polly to announce it.

"So do I," said Joel, sitting back on his heels and flourishing his hammer. "He brings candy sticks."

"He brings candy sticks," hummed Phronsie, shaking off the little snips and shavings of wood from her gown and getting up from the floor where she had been crouching by Joel's side, she ran over to Polly who had now picked up the spools of thread remorsefully, and was hurrying away at fixing up the workbasket. "Oh, Polly, I want some pink candy sticks, I do."

"There, now, Joel, you see," said Polly reprovingly. "No, no, Phronsie, we can't have any today, Pet."

"But I want some, Polly, I do—very much indeed," said Phronsie gravely, and her little lips fell.

Polly threw down the coat and was just gathering her up in her lap, when she stopped suddenly. "There *is* somebody at the door. Oh, perhaps it is a call after all, children," and she drew herself up and felt elegant at once.

"I'll go," cried Joel, hopping to his feet.

"No, you mustn't, Joe," said Polly decidedly. "Davie heard it first—you must let him."

"Well, you said it wasn't anyone," grumbled Joel, but he stood still in his tracks.

"Well, and I didn't think it was," said Polly, pricking up her ears. "Yes, there it is—sure enough," as a soft, deliberate rap sounded on the old door. "Now, Davie, you open the door nicely and say Mamsie isn't home, but would they please to walk in." She patted his hair softly. "I'm so glad I put on Phronsie's clean pink apron," she said in great satisfaction.

Little David went softly across the kitchen floor, wishing Polly had let Joel go since he wanted to so very badly, and with fingers trembling from his great responsibility, he lifted the latch and pulled the old door open.

There stood Peletiah, the minister's son. Joel, crowding up behind Davie, took one look. "Hoh, 'tisn't anyone," he cried, terribly disappointed.

"Oh, Joel," exclaimed Polly, springing to the door, very much ashamed at such a reception to the minister's boy, and "Oh, Peletiah, do come in," she cried heartily.

"Yes, I'm coming in," said Peletiah, not a bit disturbed at Joel's words, "because my mother told me to." And he stepped slowly into the middle of the old kitchen floor, where he stood and regarded them all steadily.

"Won't you sit down, Peletiah?" said Polly with her best

company manner. "Joel, get a chair—" For Joel had turned on his heel to make tracks for his rabbit box again.

So Joel had to whirl around, but little Davie had seen his face. "Oh, let me, Polly," he begged, but Polly shook her head.

So Joel dragged up one of the chairs ranged against the wall, and pushed it back of the minister's son, but Peletiah paid no sort of attention to it.

"My—mother—wants—Mrs.—Pepper—to—let—Polly—and—Phronsie—come—to—the—parsonage—tomorrow—morning—and—help—her—and—stay—to—dinner," he said, in a singsong voice.

"What?" cried Polly, not believing her ears. Joel, who on furnishing the chair considered his hospitable duties all completed, was hurrying back to his beloved rabbit box when "stay to dinner" caught his ear, and he bounded back.

"My—mother—wants—Mrs.—Pepper—to—let—Polly—and—Phronsie—come—to—the—parsonage—tomorrow—morning—and—help—her—and—stay—to—dinner," said Peletiah again, not moving a muscle.

"Oh, goody!" cried Polly, clapping her hands. Then she thought of Miss Jerusha, and her face fell.

"Oh, didn't she want us? Say, aren't Dave and I going?" Joel plucked Peletiah's sleeve, and thrust his face eagerly into the midst of the group.

"My—mother—wants—Mrs.—Pepper—to—let—Polly—and—Phronsie—come—to—the—parsonage—tomorrow—morning—and—help—her—and—stay—to—dinner," said Peletiah again patiently.

"Oh, dear, dear, didn't she ask us?" cried Joel, terribly disappointed.

"My—mother—wants—" began Peletiah again.

"Yes, yes, we understand, Peletiah," said Polly, recovering her spirits that had fallen on account of Miss Jerusha, for surely the minister's wife would make her be kind to them; Polly could believe that, after today—"and aren't you ashamed, Joel?" all in the same breath.

"He keeps saying the same thing over and over," cried Joel very much disgusted, "and he doesn't tell about Dave and me a bit, and I know she wants us, too," he added in an injured tone.

"My—mother—wants—" began Peletiah once more.

"Yes, yes, thank you," cried Polly quickly. "Now, Joel, keep still. And we'll be so glad to go, Phronsie and I, that is, if Mamsie will say we may. And please tell your mother so, and, oh, thank her ever so much, please." Polly folded and unfolded her hands in a dreadful panic lest she might not be saying just the right thing, for it was the first time an invitation of this kind had come to her, and Mamsie away!

"And now you must stop and play with us," Polly hurried to say, for there were lively indications on Joel's part that he was about to return to the subject uppermost in his own mind. "Let's think," ran on Polly, wrinkling her brows, "what we want to do first."

"He can't play," said Joel with a sniff.

"Why can't we play Stagecoach?" proposed Polly, to save further remarks from Joel. "Come, boys, let's fix the chairs." And she bustled about to make things pleasant for their guest, little Davie running to help her, and Phronsie getting dreadfully in the way.

"He doesn't know how to play," said Joel loudly, supposing he hadn't been understood.

"Come on, Joel," called Polly, making such a rattle with the chairs that she couldn't be supposed to hear conversation. Peletiah stood quite still and looked at them all.

"There, now, we're ready," announced Polly, standing by the line of chairs set in the middle of the floor. "Oh, no, not quite—you must turn that one around, Davie."

"So I must," laughed little David, running to do it.

"I'm going to play Stagecoach," announced Phronsie in great glee, running over to stand in front of Peletiah and look up at him. "I am." And she smoothed down her pink apron with great satisfaction.

"Come, Peletiah," called Polly, at the head of the line. "Come, Joel!"

All the little Peppers rushed up to her, but Peletiah stood stock-still.

"Now, you know," said Polly, standing very importantly at the head of the line of chairs, "I ought to tell you, Peletiah, this is the way we play Stagecoach, because there aren't enough of us to play it the really truly way, so we put Going to Jerusalem and Stagecoach together. Now, come on, we're ready to begin." So Polly commenced to sing, as she slowly walked around the line, Phronsie pattering after, and then Joel and little David, all screaming at the top of their voices— "We're going to Je—ru—sa—lem, now won't you come with us? We're going to Je—ru—sa—lem, now won't you come with us?" and then suddenly, without a bit of warning, she cried, "we're going in a stagecoach," just as fast as she could say it, and the whole line broke into a wild scramble for the chairs, and everybody had a seat, for there was Peletiah standing in his same place, and looking at them all.

"I told you he couldn't play," said Joel, hopping off from his chair, but Polly was over by the minister's boy.

"Had you rather play something else, Peletiah?" she asked anxiously. Oh, if Mamsie would only come home, and how very dreadful it was, not to be able to do something for the minister's boy when dear Mrs. Henderson was so good to them! Polly racked her brains to think of just the right thing.

"Perhaps he'd like Sally Waters best," she said, looking over at little David. It was small use, she knew, to ask Joel.

"I like Sally Waters," said little David, coming up to her side, "ever so much, Polly."

"So do I," said Polly, glad of some help. "Well, now, Phronsie, we're going to play Sally Waters."

"We're going to play Sally Waters," said Phronsie, very much pleased and scrambling over to add herself to the group.

"I'm not going to play Sally Waters," declared Joel in a bad temper, and wishing the minister's boy would go home. "I'm going to nail on my box."

"No, no, Joe." Polly deserted the guest and ran over to whisper in his ear, " 'Tisn't polite when company is here."

"Well, he can't play anything," said Joel with a snort.

"Well, you must come over and help entertain him." It was a long word, and Polly was very much pleased when she brought it out successfully, so she ran back crying joyfully, "Well, now, come on for Sally Waters," as Joel dragged himself over.

"Well, children—" Mrs. Pepper's black bonnet appeared over their heads. They had been making so much noise no one had heard her come in. "I'm glad to see you, Peletiah, and what a fine time you're having!" And her tired face fairly beamed.

"Mamsie!" the little Peppers all shouted, all trying to get into her arms at once.

"Yes, Mother's home," said Mrs. Pepper with a long sigh, and she dropped a kiss on each little face.

"Don't push so, Joel," said Polly reprovingly, "and you're mussing Mamsie's bonnet."

"Well, Davie's pushing, too," grumbled Joel.

"Oh, I didn't mean to," said little Davie, but he did want dreadfully to get up close to Mamsie's neck, and be cuddled.

"Never mind the bonnet, Polly," said Mrs. Pepper with a little laugh. "And we mustn't forget Peletiah," she said.

"Oh, he won't play anything," said Joel in scorn, "not a single thing, and Polly's tried and tried."

"Joel," said Mrs. Pepper sternly. That made Joel hang his head in her gown.

"Oh, Mamsie," cried Polly radiantly, "you can't think what a perfectly splendid thing is going to happen, that is, if you will only say yes. Do, Mamsie, do—" and she threw her arms around Mrs. Pepper's neck.

"How can I until I know what it is," said Mrs. Pepper, bursting into a merry laugh. "And I think I best take off my bonnet first, Polly; then you can tell me all about it."

"Oh, so you must," said Polly, very much ashamed at her thoughtlessness. "Let me untie it, Mamsie."

"No, I'm going to untie my Mamsie's bonnet," said Phronsie with great decision, who always wanted to perform that office when Mrs. Pepper came home.

"Oh, Phronsie," said Polly, "Mamsie's so tired this afternoon, you better let me."

"No, I shall do it," said Phronsie, standing on tiptoe and fumbling at the black strings. "My Mamsie wants me to do it all by my own self."

"You better let her, Polly," whispered Mrs. Pepper over Phronsie's yellow hair.

"Then I'm going to make you a cup of tea," declared Polly, springing over to the stove.

"Yes, do," said Mrs. Pepper brightly. "How good it is to get home to you, children," she said, with a happy glance around the old kitchen.

"I'm going to do something for Mamsie," said Joel, pulling

his head out from the depths of Mrs. Pepper's gown. "I'm going to get her a chair." So he went over and pulled out one of the "Going-to-Jerusalem-in-a-stagecoach" line. "There, now, Mamsie, it's for you," he announced, dragging it up with a flourish.

"Oh, Joey, that's so good," she exclaimed, sitting down in it and drawing Phronsie to her lap where she could fumble among the black strings to her heart's content.

At this, little David's face became very sorrowful, and he was just going to hurry over to Polly, busy by the stove, for her to tell him what he could do for Mamsie, when Mrs. Pepper said suddenly, "Davie, you can take Mother's bag, and hang it on the nail." For when Mrs. Pepper went to help any Badgertown people with their sewing, as she had been doing on this day, she always carried on her arm a stout brown calico bag to hold her sewing things.

David laughed right out, he was so pleased, as Mrs. Pepper slipped off the strings of the brown calico bag from her arm, and he strutted across the kitchen to hang it on the nail by the window.

"Yes, I'm glad to see you, Peletiah," said Mrs. Pepper very heartily.

"My—mother—wants—Mrs.—Pepper—to—let—Polly— and—Phronsie—come—to—the—parsonage—tomorrow— morning—and—help—her—and—stay—to—dinner—" said Peletiah, all in one breath.

"Does she?" cried Mrs. Pepper. "Then they shall go; yes, indeed." And her black eyes shone with pleasure.

Peletiah at that started and moved slowly to the door.

"You tell your mother," said Mrs. Pepper, "that I am very much obliged, and that Polly and Phronsie will go."

"And Polly said to tell her that Phronsie and she would go

if you said they might. I must tell her that, too," said Peletiah precisely.

"Well, I have said they might go, so that is all you need to say, Peletiah," said Mrs. Pepper. "Only be sure to tell her I am very much obliged."

But Peletiah decided in his own mind as he went slowly off that he should give the whole of the two messages just as they came to him.

And the next morning Polly hurried to the parsonage with Phronsie, in a clean pink pinafore, clinging to her hand.

"Oh, dear me!" thought Polly, as she came in sight of it, and her heart sank with the dread of meeting a pair of sharp green eyes, and a long hard face, till she scarcely dared to look up. But she needn't have worried, for Miss Jerusha had been gone a whole half-hour, and there at the gate was the minister's boy waiting for her.

"I want to play what you did yesterday," said Peletiah.

"Oh—Stagecoach," said Polly with a gasp, bringing her brown eyes to bear on his face.

"Yes, and that other one," said Peletiah, "and I'm going to play it on Sunday because it's about Jerusalem."

"Oh, we don't ever play it on Sunday," said Polly in horror at the mere thought.

"I'm going to play it on Sunday because it's about Jerusalem, and Ezekiel is, too," declared Peletiah, in exactly the same tone as before, as Polly and Phronsie hurried up the path to the door.

There was the parson's wife waiting for them, and she drew the children in, Peletiah following solemnly; and in the big bedroom, that Polly had been in once before when she had come with a message from her mother to Mrs. Henderson, who was sick, they were told to lay off their things.

Oh, dear me, was ever anything so elegant as to go visiting and be treated like grown-up ladies! And what place could be so splendid as that bedroom with big pink flowers trailing all over the chintz curtains and hanging from the bed tester. Polly made slow work of getting Phronsie and herself ready to follow the minister's wife, her eyes were so busy.

"You like it, dear?" said Mrs. Henderson, smiling down at her.

"Oh, it's beautiful," sighed Polly, the color flying all over her face.

"It's be—yewtiful," hummed Phronsie, not knowing in the least what for, but because Polly said so. And the parson's wife laughed again and taking a hand of either little Pepper she led them out and closed the door.

"Now, then, Polly," she said, "what do you suppose I wanted you to come over for?"

"To help you," said Polly happily. "Oh, I'm so glad, dear Mrs. Henderson, please, may I?"

"Yes, indeed," said Mrs. Henderson cheerily, "but you never can guess what it is you are going to help about, so I will tell you. We're going to set up some things in the garret."

"Oh, may I go in the garret?" cried Polly, stopping short in her excitement, "and Phronsie, too—may we, may we?"

"Yes, indeed," laughed the parson's wife, quite as excited, "and we are going to do ever so many things up there. Fix up an old chest for one—dear me, I don't know what we shall find wants doing when we get up there."

"Phronsie, we are going up garret!" cried Polly, her eyes wide with anticipation. All her life she had longed to have a garret to go into to see its hidden treasures at least once; to play in one every day was beyond her wildest dreams. Now she was really to see one for herself!

Mrs. Henderson stopped to get a broom and a dustpan;

she already had a little whisk brush and a small brown-paper parcel in her hand.

"Oh, let me carry them," cried Polly eagerly.

"You may help," said Mrs. Henderson, giving her the dustpan and little brown-paper parcel, so Polly picked her way over the stairs, helping Phronsie up carefully.

"Well, here we are!" The parson's wife stopped to take breath at the top of the stairs, and set down her broom. "It wants setting up I think," she exclaimed.

"Oh, isn't it lovely!" cried Polly, her cheeks aflame, and peering on either side. How she longed to explore the dim recesses and cunning little hiding places under the big beams where the slanting roof ran down to the eaves. And what delightful chances of fun were hidden behind the broken-backed chairs and other dilapidated furniture set away for some convenient mending time! And those funny bundles of dangling things, she found out afterward they were herbs, hanging from the beams, and on nails along the wall! And oh! there was a big bluebottle buzzing like everything and knocking his head against the small-paned window.

"A spider has got him!" cried Polly, running over to set him free. And the fat little black spider, not liking that at all, ran off like lightning, till such time as she could dart out of her hole, and mend her broken web in which to catch another fly.

"Oh, dear me!" And then Polly was off, and Phronsie after her, to kneel down on the garret floor, where someone long years before had pasted strips of newspaper over the cracks.

"There's printing on it," she said, trying to read it, spreading her hands on either side. Phronsie immediately did the same.

"J-o-n-a; what is that, dear Mrs. Henderson?" for the rest was cut off.

"Why, that was the man's name," said Mrs. Henderson. "I suppose it was Jonathan," leaning over to read the old strip of newspaper. "And he was a blacksmith. See, Polly." She pointed to another strip. Sure enough. The whole word "blacksmith" was there, bold and plain!

"It's nice the whole word was saved, isn't it?" said Polly, patting it. So Phronsie had to crawl over and pat it, too.

"Did he live here?" asked Polly, finding it impossible to leave Jonathan, the Blacksmith, and sitting back on her heels to regard the minister's wife.

"No, I don't suppose he did," said Mrs. Henderson. "That strip was cut from an old newspaper; but perhaps he lived somewhere about here," she hastened to add, as Polly's face fell.

"I wish he had lived exactly here," said Polly with a sigh, and letting her gaze wander over the old rafters.

"Well, now, don't you want to see what I'm going to do first? And you are to help me." Mrs. Henderson was by this time over in the corner where a big beam ran down to the eaves, and tugging at an old hair trunk.

"Oh, let me help you!" cried Polly, springing to her feet and rushing over.

"Let me help," echoed Phronsie, getting up from the garret floor, and spatting her hands free from the dust, she ran to the corner, too, and the old trunk was soon dragged out and the lid with its great brass letters "S. H." was thrown back.

"Now, you see, Polly," said the minister's wife, down on her knees before it, Polly and Phronsie crouched on either side, "this trunk was my great-grandfather's, Stephen Hinsdale, and this is the reason why we keep so many old things in it. Just look!" She picked out one or two books whose leather backs flapped dismally. "They're fairly worm-eaten," she said, setting them on the floor.

"Oh, where are the worms?" exclaimed Polly in great excitement, and picking up a book to examine it intently. "Oh, do show me, dear Mrs. Henderson," she begged, Phronsie deserting her place to come around and look too.

"Oh, you can't see them," said Mrs. Henderson, "not the worms,—but there are the marks they've made. Well, never mind now, Polly, put it down, for I want to show you the rest of the things. I'm going to clear out this whole trunk." And she lifted out a red woolen cape very long and heavy, and all riddled with little holes.

"Now, only just look," she exclaimed in vexation, "the moths have nearly eaten this up, and I put camphor all round it. I do every spring."

"Oh, oh," cried Polly in great distress.

"I want to wear it," cried Phronsie. "I do." And she held out both arms.

"Oh, you couldn't wear it," said the parson's wife with a little laugh. "It was for a big woman; my grandmother, Polly."

"I want it," said Phronsie in a grieved little voice, and still holding her arms out straight.

"Oh, no, child." Then Mrs. Henderson rested both hands on the edge of the trunk, the old red cape dropping to her lap.

"I wouldn't wonder," she said, "if your mother could get you a little red coat out of that, Phronsie. Yes, you shall wear it, dear."

"Oh, I'm going to. I'm going to wear it." Phronsie gave a gleeful little shout and capered up and down the garret floor. "Put it on, I want it on," she begged, coming back to stand quite still.

"Oh, Phronsie, you can't wear it now," cried Polly with shining eyes at the thought of the little red coat that was to be made. "It would drag on the floor."

"Never mind," said Mrs. Henderson. So she put the old red woolen cape over Phronsie's shoulders, and it fell all around her, just as Polly had said, dragging on the floor. But Phronsie beamed perfect satisfaction, and she didn't want it taken off until the minister's wife said she would fold it up all ready to be taken home to Mrs. Pepper, which she did, and laid it in one of the broken-backed chairs. Then Phronsie sat down beside it to lay a soft little hand on it, and watch it, while Mrs. Henderson and Polly turned to the trunk again.

There seemed to be no end to the things that were in that trunk—an old waistcoat with brass buttons was drawn tenderly out, belonging to Stephen Hinsdale himself, and laid down beside the books and some old fans, and a high broken-toothed comb, and a piece of carved ivory.

"That," said the parson's wife, "was brought from India. I remember old Aunt Sally letting me play with it when I wasn't much older than Phronsie."

"Oh, may I hold it?" begged Polly, putting out a trembling hand.

"Of course you may, Polly," said Mrs. Henderson, dropping it in her hand, "and once I thought I'd lost it down the well."

"Oh, dear me!" exclaimed Polly, dropping the hand holding the carved bit of ivory to her lap.

"Yes, it was a dreadful moment." And the parson's wife drew a long sigh even now after all those years. "You see, I was naughty, and took it out in the yard to play, and another little girl who had come over to see me wanted a drink of water, and I wouldn't put down the piece of ivory, I was so afraid she'd snatch it, and I was helping to pull up the bucket when the little carved bit slipped right out of my hand."

"Oh, dear me!" cried Polly, turning pale with fright.

"And I shut my eyes, I was so scared. And Jane said—the

little girl's name was Jane—'There, now, that's because you wouldn't give it to me.' Oh, I remember it just as if it were yesterday, Polly Pepper."

"And did it go down into the well?" cried Polly in her distress, forgetting what her hand held tightly clasped in her lap, and leaning forward eagerly to scan Mrs. Henderson's face.

"No, indeed," cried the parson's wife with a merry laugh. "Look in your lap, Polly."

"Oh, I forgot," cried Polly, drawing a long breath of relief and opening her hand. "Wasn't I silly? But I'm so very glad it didn't go down into the well, dear Mrs. Henderson."

"No, it caught on a little green weed growing out between the cracks of the curbstone, and I screamed and my big brother came running, and he picked it out. But I was not allowed even to touch the little piece of ivory for a whole year."

"Oh, dear me!" said Polly sympathetically, and fumbling the small bit.

"Well, now, we must get to the other things," said Mrs. Henderson briskly. "I'm so glad you could come over and help me, Polly."

And Polly, feeling very happy at the thought of helping the minister's wife, laid down the little piece of carved ivory carefully against the other old treasures, and bent all her energies to doing what Mrs. Henderson told her.

"You see, Polly," said the parson's wife, when all the articles were drawn out of the chest, "we better turn it up on the side, and then we can brush it out."

"Oh, let me brush it out," begged Polly, jumping up to get the whisk broom.

"Well, you may," said Mrs. Henderson, picking up Grandfather's waistcoat to look it over, "and then you can roll up some fresh camphor. Dear me, I don't see how the moths do get in so!"

"Oh, what fun!" cried Polly, her brown eyes sparkling as she brushed vigorously away, sticking her head well within the old chest to poke out the corners.

"It's fun today because you are here, Polly, you and Phronsie," laughed Mrs. Henderson, feeling just about the same age as one of the children.

"I'm glad I'm here," said Polly, with a little thrill at Mrs. Henderson's words. "And I'm glad Phronsie is here, too, but she doesn't see all these perfectly beautiful things." And Polly pulled herself out to sit, brush in hand, and look over at her.

"Never mind," said the minister's wife hastily. "Phronsie is happy where she is. Don't disturb her, Polly."

So Polly fell to brushing away again.

"And now, Polly, you can do something more," said Mrs. Henderson, when the old chest was all brushed out, and set in position again. "And it will help me so much. You can roll up some little bits of this camphor," and she opened the brown-paper parcel she had brought up to the garret, "and put each of them in a piece of newspaper, and fold it into Grandfather's waistcoat,—I always mean to keep that, Polly, for I remember him in it—and then I can run down and see about my dinner."

This was the best of all, Polly thought, to be intrusted to take care of Grandfather's waistcoat all by herself, while the minister's wife was downstairs seeing to her dinner!

"The newspapers are over there." Mrs. Henderson pointed to the farther corner under the eaves. "I always keep a pile to wrap up things in." So Polly ran over and got them, and presently she was busy as a bee in the old garret, with Phronsie still sitting up close to the broken-backed chair, and humming softly to herself, and patting every now and then the red woolen cape.

And then when Mrs. Henderson ran up to see how things were getting on, she was so pleased! And she told Polly she could pack all the various articles back into the old chest, which delighted Polly very much. And then left alone once more, the big old chest all packed up, Polly seized the broom and swept every bit of dust from the old garret floor as far as she could reach, being especially careful to make it very clean over "Jonathan, the Blacksmith." And then just as she had nearly begun brushing down the stairs, up ran the minister's wife, with very pink cheeks after being over the kitchen stove.

"What a good girl you are, Polly Pepper!" she exclaimed. "Now, I expected to have to do those stairs myself." And she was so pleased, she almost let out a little secret that the parson had waiting for the two little Peppers. "Come, Phronsie," she called, "dinner's ready, child."

And then after Polly had washed Phronsie's face and hands, and after that her own in the big blue and white bowl in the big bedroom, and Phronsie's hair had been brushed, and Polly had made her own as neat as a pin, down they hurried, and if there wasn't Ben Pepper, sitting next to Parson Henderson, and watching sharply for them to come in!

Phronsie screamed right out, "*Bensie!*" and rushed over to him, and Polly ran and hugged him around the neck. "Oh, I'm so glad you've come!" she gasped.

"I thought I'd bring him, so I went over and asked Mrs. Pepper. Luckily, Ben had just come in from his work," said Parson Henderson with a little satisfied chuckle. "Now, then, Peletiah and Ezekiel, you let Ben sit between you."

Peletiah and Ezekiel solemnly made way for Ben Pepper

as their father had said. And down they all sat, except Polly, who helped Mrs. Henderson bring in the hot dishes.

When Phronsie saw Polly helping she tried to clamber out of her chair next to the minister to do the same. But the parson laid his hand on her. "No, no, child," he said, "you must stay and take care of me."

"Can I take care of you?" asked Phronsie, stopping instantly and looking up at him.

"Indeed you can," declared Mr. Henderson, heartily.

"Then I will," said Phronsie, settling back in her chair in great satisfaction. And presently there they all were, seven of them, the parson and his wife as young as the others, around the table, and the parsonage dinner was fairly under way.

"I've got a red cape, and it's mine," announced Phronsie, nodding over to Ben.

"Have you?" cried Ben in great surprise.

"I gave her Great-grandmother's cape," said the parson's wife, down the table-length to her husband. "It's dreadfully moth-eaten, but I think Mrs. Pepper can make her a little red coat out of the good part."

"I wish you'd give her all the rest of the old things," said the parson. "You get all tired out pulling them over."

"I've had a good time this morning, anyway," said his wife, and she smiled down at Polly.

And after dinner, when they really couldn't eat any more ham and eggs and baked Indian pudding, Peletiah came up to Polly.

"I want to play Stagecoach Jerusalem," he said, "and Ezekiel does, too."

"Oh," cried Polly, "I guess we can, now Ben has come, only—" and she looked at the dinner table, and all the dishes to be cleared off and washed and set away—"we've got to do these first."

"We're going to play Stagecoach Jerusalem," said Ezekiel, hurrying over to Ben, who had been looking on quite puzzled. "Peletiah said she did it, and everybody but you, over to your house yesterday."

"Oh," said Ben.

"What's that?" cried Mr. Henderson. So Peletiah went slowly over and told his father all about it.

"Wife," cried the parson, "as soon as Polly and you get those dishes done, why you and I will go in the Stagecoach Jerusalem." And his eyes danced like a boy's.

And sooner than anybody would think, every one of those dishes was washed and wiped, and set up on the dresser, or in the cupboard, and Polly brushed up the crumbs around the table. "There, now," she cried, "we're all ready!" And out they all ran into the big kitchen to get the stagecoach ready.

And presently the parson and his wife, and the three little Peppers, and the two Henderson boys had started on their journey to Jerusalem, and somehow or other Peletiah, who never seemed able to secure a seat, was at the last moment helped into one, Ben shoving him along.

"I'm here!" he cried, hanging on to the back of the chair. "I'm in Jerusalem!"

XIII

Company at the Little Brown House

POLLY sat down in despair just as Mother Pepper finished. As for Joel, he burst into a howl, and even little Davie sobbed softly to himself. Phronsie alone was just as sweet as ever, for she didn't know in the least what it was all about. While Ben, more distressed on account of Polly than loss to himself and the others, wrung his hands as he stood quite still, his blue eyes on Polly's face.

"No, it wouldn't be right for you children to go to the circus," Mother Pepper had just said. "There is only just so much money in the stocking, and it has to be saved for the things we must have."

She had poured out into her lap the ten-cent and five-cent pieces, and pennies, with two stray quarters, from the old black stocking that the children had brought out from its resting place in the old bureau in the bedroom, in the wild hope that she would say, "yes"—especially since Sally Brown, the next neighbor about half a mile distant, was going with her family.

"Oh, there's lots and lots of money," cried Joel, sticking his brown fingers in the little pile of coins to churn them about. "Oh, Mamsie!"

And "Oh, Mamsie!" echoed little Davie, with very red cheeks. How his blue eyes shone!

"And we've never seen a circus," broke in Polly passionately. "Never in all this world—oh, Ben!" With that Polly flung her arms around Ben's neck, and burst out crying.

Ben's ruddy cheek turned quite white. "Don't, Polly," he said hoarsely, and patted her back with an unsteady hand.

Mrs. Pepper took Joel's little brown hand in her steady one.

"She's going to give us some money, and we're going!" screamed Joel, in a transport, to the others. Phronsie, at this, stopped her capering about the middle of the kitchen floor to come up with wondering eyes.

"No, Joel," said Mrs. Pepper. Her voice shook, but she steadied it as she went on, and gathering up the coins she began to put them into the old black stocking again. "Mother can't let you have this money, for it wouldn't be right," she added firmly.

Then it was that Polly broke away from Ben's shoulder and sat down despairingly. And amid Joel's howls and little Davie's sobs the money was all shaken down into the toe of the stocking, tied up, and Mrs. Pepper went into the bedroom with it.

"Polly, you oughtn't to," said Ben, going over to her. Joel had thrown himself down on the old floor to give himself up to an abandonment of grief, and little Davie had crept alongside him to lay his wet cheek next to Joel's stormy one.

Phronsie stood still, looking from one group to the other in grave wonder.

"Oh, I know it," cried Polly gustily, as she began to cry and twisting her fingers dreadfully, "but we've—never—seen —seen—a circus."

"I know it," said Ben with a twinge. How many times, ever since he had seen the flaming red and yellow posters in Mr. Atkins's store, he had determined to take some of the money earned by chopping wood for Deacon Blodgett and doing chores at the parsonage, and go off to the circus with Polly—yes, he surely couldn't go without Polly, for he wouldn't enjoy it a bit without her! And then, every single time, he found himself bringing home that same money to put it into Mother Pepper's hand. And she had smiled and said, "Did anybody ever have such a comfort as you are, Ben!" And now Mamsie had gone into the bedroom so sorrowfully, and Ben shivered as he remembered how white her face was.

"Oh, you oughtn't to do so, Polly," he repeated hoarsely, and putting his hand on her shoulder.

"We—we won't—see—the el'funt," sobbed Joel in angry spasms, and kicking his well-worn shoes on the floor. Little Davie gave a great sob at that, not so much at the loss of a sight of the elephant, as that wasn't his particular choice of all the great wonders of this magnificent show, but the little white mice, who could do all sorts of tricks; hadn't he stood on tiptoe to spell all about the wonderful things they could do, when sent on an errand to the store. At all such times when there was a chance to get near the great posters tacked up by the side of the little boxes and pigeonholes running down one side of the store (for Mr. Atkins, besides keeping the general store, was also postmaster of the village), he had been lost to the charms of the rest of the great show. And

now he was never to see those dear wonderful little mice!
He snuggled up closer to Joel, and wound one arm around
his neck.

"And the snakes—the great big one that eats the camel,"
roared Joel, getting, in his anger, dreadfully mixed. "Oh—
oh!"—making his feet fly harder than ever.

"Polly, you see," said Ben, bending down to whisper in
her ear.

"I can't—can't—he—lp it—" said Polly gustily between
her fingers.

"Yes, you can." Ben shut his lips firmly together, and a
very disapproving look came into his blue eyes. Polly felt it
all over her miserable little body and her head sank lower
than ever.

"Mamsie's worried," began Ben, a dreadful feeling at his
heart as if the Little Brown House were going all to pieces,
since Polly seemed to be failing them all in this way—when
she sprang up, a rain of tears running down her flushed face.
"Oh, Bensie, I'm so bad and wicked," and she flung herself
into his arms.

"There, there, there," said Ben, giving her what he meant
for love pats on her shaking shoulder, "you aren't bad now,
you know, Polly."

"Yes, I am," said Polly in a smothered voice. "Oh, Ben, I
am."

"Well, you ought to stop now," said Ben, "or else you will
be bad, very bad indeed," he added decidedly.

"I can't, oh, I can't, Ben," said poor Polly, huddling up
against his neck.

"Yes, you can," said Ben, hating dreadfully to be cross, but
obliged to stand his ground, "for you'll make Mamsie sick if
you don't stop, Polly."

"Oh, Ben!" Polly gave a convulsive start and clutched him

firmer than ever. But the sobs stopped. "You surely will," said Ben more decidedly than ever, and seeing his advantage, "make our Mamsie sick, Polly Pepper."

"Oh, I won't, I won't," exclaimed Polly wildly, and raising her brown head. Ben was aghast to see her face with the tears from her brown eyes streaming over it, and he had an awful feeling to think he had been cross to her. But the next minute she brushed them all off with her hand and sprang across the old kitchen and into the bedroom.

"Now, then, boys," said Ben, going over to the little figures squirming on the floor. "You must get up this very minute. Stop screaming, Joe."

Joel at that rolled over on his back to look at Ben out of streaming eyes. "We can't—can't see—the el'funt," he cried, waving frantic little hands.

"Stop this minute!" said Ben sternly. Little David, at the sound of his voice so perfectly awful, wriggled himself loose from Joel and got up to his feet to look tremblingly at Ben.

"Never mind if we can't," said Ben stoutly; "that's nothing."

Joel, in the greatest surprise, wiped away the tears from his black eyes with the back of a grimy hand—"that was nothing, not to be able to see the elephant, oh!"—and he got up to his feet to stare into Ben's face.

"We can't see the el'funt," he repeated as loud as he could, supposing that Ben hadn't heard.

"Hush," cried Ben, pulling his sleeve, "Mamsie'll hear. Well, supposing we can't, that's not worth crying about."

"We can't see the el'funt," said Joel again, but this time to little David. But David was pressed up closely to Ben's side, so he didn't appear to hear the statement, and Joel, in a greater surprise than ever, was again reiterating it, when Polly ran out of the bedroom.

"Oh, boys," she began. She didn't dare look at Ben, but

somehow she seemed to feel his approval hop right down into a corner of her heart, "let's set up the kitchen. You must fix the mat, Joey. You kicked it up, and we must get it down straight before Mamsie comes back."

"We can't see the el'funt," began Joel in a loud, injured tone, hurrying over to her; Polly would hear him anyway.

"Yes,—yes, never mind," cried Polly, rushing about, straightening the chairs against the wall, and making a great to-do about fixing up.

"Never mind!" and *"that's no matter."* Joel whirled about in astonishment. Little David was down on the floor, pulling the braided mat straight, while Ben had run over to help Polly, and they were whispering away at a great rate.

"I'm going to do that," cried Joel, getting down to twitch the mat from Davie's fingers. "Polly told me to do it."

"Now, then," back came Polly and Ben together. "We must see what else we can do," cried Polly, in a twitter to provide something to keep the small fingers busy. And, "Oh, dear me! They'll begin talking about the circus if we can't find something more for them to do. Oh, Ben, I can't think of a single thing."

"Joel," said Ben, "I'm going to Grandma Bascom's; want to come with me, and Davie?" He edged to the door looking back as he spoke.

"Don't you?" Both boys sprang after him as quick as a shot, and none too soon, for out came Mrs. Pepper from the bedroom just as the door shut.

And then Polly told her where they had gone, and Mrs. Pepper sat down to the work so sadly interrupted when the plans to go to the circus were screamed out, and took up her needle to send it flying back and forth faster than ever on one of Mr. Atkins's coats. And Polly drew up the little stool at her feet and began to pick, with quick remorseful fingers, the basting threads out of another coat that was finished.

It wasn't till then that Phronsie deserted her place. "Oh, Polly," and she drew a long breath, as she came up to the side of the little stool, "what is it?" and she put her face in between the busy fingers and the basting threads.

"Take care," said Polly, "you almost made me break that, Pet. What do you mean, Phronsie?"

"What is it?" still demanded Phronsie in a puzzled way.

"Whatever does she mean, Mamsie?" cried Polly, wrinkling up her forehead and dropping the coat in her lap, so that the long white basting thread trailed off to the floor.

"Why, I suppose she's thinking of all you children, how badly you felt because you couldn't go to the circus, Polly," said Mrs. Pepper, with a keen glance from her black eyes on Phronsie's troubled face. "But never mind that now," she added quickly, seeing Polly's own. "Come here, Phronsie," she cleared her sewing out of her lap, and held out her arms.

Phronsie ran into them like a frightened rabbit. "What is it, Mamsie?" she cried, lifting her face.

"See here, Phronsie," said Mrs. Pepper, holding her very close; "look up at Mother," which really wasn't very necessary to say, as Phronsie hadn't taken her brown eyes from Mamsie's face. "Everything is all right; I want you to understand that, child. Mother says it's all right now."

"Is Polly right?" asked Phronsie, looking off at Polly's brown head, which was drooping just then.

"Yes, indeed," said Mrs. Pepper in such a hearty tone that Polly raised her head a little, "Polly is all right, Phronsie."

Phronsie drew a long breath. "And is Bensie all right, too?" she asked.

"Yes, Ben is all right, too," Mother Pepper answered.

"And is Joel all right?" Phronsie regarded her mother

closely again, but the look of fear had dropped out of her face, and she put up one little hand to her mother's cheek. "Is he, Mamsie?"

"Joel is all right, Phronsie." Then Mother Pepper smiled, "And Davie, too. Everybody and everything is all as it should be, child."

"Oh, I'm so glad," cried Phronsie with a little crow of delight, and patting her hands together. Then she slipped down from her mother's lap.

"It is, it is! Every single thing, and I'm glad," and she began to dance as hard as she could up and down the old kitchen.

"And now, Polly," said Mrs. Pepper, picking up her sewing again and sending a bright smile down to Polly, "you better fly at those basting threads as quick as ever you can," which Polly did, and when the boys came running in, with all thoughts of circus driven out of their heads, the old kitchen was as bright as ever, and fairly running over with good cheer.

Meantime, Mrs. Pepper and Polly had been talking, for Mamsie had cast about in her own mind very hard to discover some way to make up as far as possible to the children for their disappointment about the circus. It really seemed that its heralded arrival had driven all Badgertown people almost out of their wits with joy, to think it was coming to their village on the morrow. And all households were busily planning for some, if not all, of their members to attend the performances.

But one after another of the nice plans that presented themselves to Mrs. Pepper took money to carry them out, so, of course, that would have been as bad as to buy circus tickets. What could she do? "There must be some way, and I've got to find it," she said, stitching on, her lips pressed tighter together than ever.

At last she laid down her needle.

"Polly," she said, "how would you like to have company tomorrow afternoon?"

"*To have company!*" repeated Polly, dropping the coat to stare at her mother.

"I don't mean real company," Mrs. Pepper made haste to add, "but to play company. You know you said you'd like to, sometime when Ben would be home."

"And is Ben going to be home tomorrow?" said Polly. "I thought he was going to Mr. Henderson's to work."

"I shall tell Mr. Henderson he can't go tomorrow afternoon to the parsonage," said Mrs. Pepper calmly. "Would you like it?"

"If Ben can stay home, I'd like it, oh, so very much," exclaimed Polly joyfully, and deserting her stool, the coat flying off in a heap, she threw her arms around Mrs. Pepper's neck.

"Oh, Mamsie! You're just too good for anything!" Then off she ran to Phronsie, still spinning contentedly around by herself.

"Phronsie," she cried, seizing her and dancing away to keep step with the small feet. "We're going to have company tomorrow afternoon; we are, Phronsie Pepper!"

Phronsie tried to pull herself away from Polly, seeing which Polly stopped short.

"Oh, Polly," cried Phronsie breathlessly, and gazing up at Polly's face.

"Yes, we really and truly are, Pet, and Ben's to stay home, and play company, too." With that, she danced off by herself, while Phronsie hopped up and down and laughed to see Polly go. It was just at this moment that the three boys raced in.

"Halloa!" exclaimed Ben, out of his wits almost with joy

to see Polly so happy. For although he had diverted the boys from their distress, the fear of what Polly was suffering, and of Mamsie, too, had made him not sure of himself. He might rush off into the house to see how things were there, and then, of course, Joel and David would be sure to follow. And then —Ben had groaned and said to himself—it would be worse than before.

But now—why, there was Polly, capering away, her brown hair flying, and her cheeks red, and Mother Pepper over in the corner looking up to greet them with smiles.

"Hooray!" screamed Ben, at his loudest, "well, I guess I'm going to dance, too!" So he sprang over and grasped Polly's hands.

"Me, too," cried Joel, going after the others. But little Davie hurried over to Phronsie, hopping up and down and laughing. "Dance with me, Phronsie," he said, holding out his hands. And Phronsie put hers in them, and there they all were, the Five Little Peppers, skipping and spinning around and around the old kitchen. There wasn't any tune to go by, to be sure, for Polly was too out of breath to sing, but the laughter and scraps of chatter made a merry din, every bit of which sank down into Mother Pepper's heart, making it warm with contentment.

"Oh, dear me!" At last even Polly was forced to stop.

"Wasn't that fine!" cried Ben, his blue eyes shining. Joel had tumbled off to the corner where little Davie and Phronsie had sunk down to rest.

"I should just say 'twas!" declared Polly, "and, oh, Ben!" clasping her hands, "what do you think? We're going to have company tomorrow."

"What!" cried Ben in amazement.

"Our play company, you know," said Polly, seizing him by the front of his jacket with both hands, a favorite way of hers, when she had something very special to say, "we're going to have it tomorrow. Mamsie just said so!"

"Did she really, now?" cried Ben, his ruddy cheeks putting on, if possible, a deeper glow than the spin had caused.

Polly nodded her head delightedly, gripping his jacket tighter than ever.

"Oh, now, see!" exclaimed Joel, glancing over at them from his corner, "they're having secrets, Polly and Ben are," and he sprang up to his feet and plunged across the kitchen to them. "Tell me, what is it—tell me," he clamored.

"That's prime!" Ben was saying as Joel plunged up to them, and then, of course, little David and Phronsie followed fast.

"Oh, I think that's mean," protested Joel loudly, "not to tell us. You're always having secrets. What is it?" Then he laid hold of Ben's jacket, too. "I should think you might tell Dave and me," he whined.

"And Phronsie," added little David. But Ben didn't hear this, as Joel was making such a to-do.

"Well, you make so much noise, Joe," said Ben coolly, "that we can't tell you."

"Oh, I won't—I won't," promised Joel in a great state of excitement, and hanging tightly to Ben. "Tell us—tell us, what is it, Ben?" he screamed as much louder as possible than he had teased before.

But Ben burst into a hearty laugh, Joel revolving about him anxiously and teasing all the while.

"Oh, dear me! Do be still," cried Polly, seizing Joel's arm. "Don't you see, Joel, we can't possibly tell you anything while you're screaming so, and you couldn't hear it if we did." She shook his little arm. "Now, stop, and we'll tell you."

Joel's hands dropped away from Ben. "Will you, really?" he said.

"Yes," said Polly, "really and truly we will; we were going to tell you, Joel, anyway, and Davie and Phronsie."

"Goodness me!" exclaimed Ben, wiping his eyes and drawing a long breath, "has this dreadful noise really stopped?" and he pretended to be very much astonished.

"Yes," said Polly, laughing, "but it will begin again, I'm afraid, if you don't look out. Oh, children, just think," she clasped her hands, "we're going to have our company tomorrow afternoon. Mamsie has just said so!"

"*Our company*," screamed Joel, while little Davie stared, Phronsie standing quietly by Polly's side where she had run.

"Yes, our play company," said Polly. "You know we've been waiting till Ben could be home, and Mamsie says he is not to work tomorrow afternoon, and we can have it then; she just said so, while you were out of doors."

Joel took a good look at her face, then he tore himself away from the group to stand on his head in the middle of the floor. In this way he always gave expression to his deepest joy.

"Polly," screamed little Davie, shrilly, "can we really have it tomorrow, really, Polly?"

"Yes," said Polly happily, her brown eyes dancing, "as true's you live, Davie Pepper."

And little David ran, not to join Joel, but to Mother Pepper's chair. "Oh, I'm so glad, Mamsie," he cried, throwing himself into her lap on top of the coat she was sewing so busily.

When Phronsie saw him, she started for Mamsie, too, and precipitated herself in Mother Pepper's lap, the two children making a dreadful mix-up of the work. "Take me, Mamsie, too," she begged.

"So Mother will," declared Mrs. Pepper, casting aside the sewing as well as she could and bundling the two children into her lap; "there, now, here you both are"—little Davie constantly saying, "I am so glad, Mamsie."

"I am so glad," murmured Phronsie, though she didn't know in the least what it was all about, and swinging her feet contentedly.

"And now, Polly," Ben was saying over in their corner, Joel hanging on each word, "we must begin to get things ready if we're going to have all that company tomorrow."

"So we must," cried Polly with an important air, "because you see we never know how many are coming."

"That's so," assented Ben.

The Pepper children had long ago decided, on talking over this company afternoon, that whenever they could hold it, four of them should sit in state and receive, while one should knock at the door, and be ushered in as caller, with great ceremony. And after this call was ended, the one who had made it should slip into the seat of another, who should go out and be caller. And so turn about and turn about, till everyone had made a call, and again on a second round of visits if they wished. "For we can play it as long as we want to," Polly had said, smoothing down her calico apron in great delight.

"I guess you'll be glad to stop," said Ben grimly.

"Oh, Ben Pepper!" Polly exclaimed, "indeed, we shan't. Well, now for the first thing—we must dress up." She wrinkled up her forehead at that, and the delight dropped out of her face. "Oh, dear, what shall we do for clothes?"

"There's the feathers, you know," said Ben reassuringly.

The box of feathers was out in the woodshed, and carefully guarded as a great treasure, ready for just such a grand dressing-up as this company would require.

There were several beautiful ones that the roosters in neighboring barnyards had discarded, to be eagerly seized by

Joel and David. And one or two whole chicken wings, given by the parson's wife for the collection. And oh, best of all! two long, soft, flying ones, from Grandma Bascom's old feather duster that she was throwing away, and that Polly had run home with.

"Aren't these splendid," she had cried, waving them triumphantly as she dashed into the kitchen.

"Whickets!" screamed Joel, "oh, give them to me. I want them, Polly," making a dash for them.

"No, you won't, Joe," declared Polly, holding them high, "they must go into our feather box." And Ben, who happened to be on hand at that moment, seized them and carried them off to put them in safety. For, once in the Feather Box, no marauding fingers ever disturbed them, the three smallest little Peppers being in duty bound never to raise the lid until Polly or Ben said so.

"I know," said Polly, when Ben said, "There's the feathers," "but we can't dress up much in them." And her face, by this time, looked gloomy enough.

"Polly," said Ben, who couldn't bear to see her look so, "see here, don't you know how you pinched up a hat for Joel to play soldier with? Why can't you do some more?"

"But we don't want to be soldiers for company," said Polly, turning a surprised look on him that didn't lighten the gloom a bit.

"But don't you see," Ben whirled on her eagerly, "you can pinch up the paper into ever so many different shapes and stick the feathers in, and they'll be beautiful hats, Polly."

Polly stared at him out of her brown eyes. Then she seized his hands. "Oh, Ben, so I can," she cried, dreadfully excited. "I never thought of that, and we can have as many hats and bonnets as we want."

"As long as the feathers hold out," laughed Ben, well

pleased to see the effect of his plan, "and the paper," he added.

"Now, Phronsie and David," Mother Pepper was saying, when the jollity over Ben's plan of the paper bonnets and hats began to wax very high, "you'd better jump down from Mother's lap, and go over there."

"I'd rather stay here," said both children at once, snuggling deeper in her lap.

"But you see, Mother must sew now, else this coat won't be done. No, you run over," and obediently they slid down to the floor and scrambled off to the little group.

And the box of feathers was brought out from the woodshed, Joel and David being sent off to get it, which filled them with the greatest delight, and Ben ran to collect all the paper in the house that didn't have to be saved to light the fire with, Mother Pepper donating a stiff brown piece that had wrapped up some things given her by the parson's wife.

When Polly saw that donation, she was quite overcome. "That will make the most splendid hat of all," she declared. "I shall put the feather-duster plumes on that."

"Do, Polly," said Ben, "it'll be fine."

And then all the three younger children (the box of feathers being now on hand) were set to work to hunt for pins. "For we can't fasten the feathers on without," said Polly. And when this seemed a difficult matter—for pins cost money and were always carefully saved in the Pepper household—why, Mamsie came to the rescue, and said she would loan them some. But Polly must put them into the paper hats and bonnets very carefully so that they wouldn't be lost out, and return them all after the company had gone.

And Polly promised, you may be sure! "And the children better hunt for pins all they can, for you never know where a pin can be found," observed Mother Pepper wisely. And so the three younger ones got down to prowl in all possible and impossible places for the little slippery things, and Joel and David hunted with all their eyes for any little stray gleams of light in the dirt whenever they went outdoors.

And the next morning in burst Joel with a small paper box high in his hand. It hadn't any cover and if he hadn't made such a noise anybody might have heard something jingling within. "See what I've got!" he screamed.

"Oh, Joe, what is it?" Polly was pinching up a remarkable hat on which she was tacking a rooster feather. An old newspaper was at her feet that Davie was cutting up according to her directions. Phronsie was busy with the snips of paper and bits of the feathers that Polly broke off, under the belief that she was making for Seraphina the most beautiful bonnet in all the world.

"Umph, I guess I've got something you haven't got," screamed Joel, waving the box high, whereat some little things, very tiny, flew out of the box, making him sprawl immediately on the floor to hunt after them, when the rest of the contents promptly went out to join the first lot.

"Oh, dear me!" exclaimed Joel in the greatest vexation.

"I'll help you find them," cried David, throwing down Mamsie's big scissors and deserting the newspaper. Phronsie carefully laid down her paper snips and the bits of feathers. "I'll help you, Joey," she said, going over to get down and prowl by his side.

"Oh, they're pins," exclaimed little David, his blue eyes very big.

"Take care," said Joel irritably, "you're covering 'em all up."

"Where'd you get them?" asked David, picking up two or three. "Why, they're all crooked."

"She wouldn't give me any but crooked ones," said Joel, pawing the floor on every side.

Polly heard these words. "Joel," and she dropped the wonderful hat, "where did you get those pins? You haven't asked anybody for them—oh, Joel!" and she was over by the other children, consternation all over her face.

"Grandma Bascom gave them to me," said Joel, prowling away, "and now they're all spilled—"

"Grandma Bascom?" repeated Polly. "Oh, Joe, you didn't ask for them; Mamsie'd be so sorry."

"No," said Joel, "I didn't ask for one single old pin," and he cocked up one black eye at her, but he didn't stop working with his hands. "She asked me to stay and I told her I couldn't 'cause Dave and me was hunting for pins, and she said she'd got some only they were crooked—Ow—get away, Dave,—you're on my place—"

"Go on, tell what else she said," commanded Polly, beginning to breathe freer.

"And then she said I could have 'em as well as not, 'cause she was going to throw them away when she got round to cleaning out the drawers—"

"Are you sure?" asked Polly, as he began to regard his work again very closely.

"When she got round to cleaning out the drawers," repeated Joel in a very high voice to be the better understood.

"Well, I am glad," said Polly with a long breath, "that you didn't ask for them, Joe," and she ran back to her work with a light heart.

"I've found one," announced Phronsie, holding up a big pin; "I have, Joel."

"Well, put it in the box," said Joel. So Phronsie dropped the bent and twisted pin in the little pasteboard box, and then she had to get up to run over and tell Polly about it, before she hurried back to get on the floor and hunt alongside of the two boys for more.

"And I shall pin on the feathers from the duster with that very pin," Polly decided to herself as she worked busily away, "because Grandma gave them to us as well as the crooked pins!"

Meanwhile, during all this great and absorbing preparation for the grand affair, Mother Pepper was casting busily about in her mind how to get some refreshments for the company; but try as she would, nothing seemed to suggest itself, until the remembrance of the glass of blackberry jelly that Deacon Blodgett's wife had given her last summer, when making her fresh supply, came to her mind. There it was tucked away on the top shelf of the old cupboard. "Oh, I can't take that," said Mrs. Pepper to herself; "it's so good in case of sickness." But then—and she drew a long breath—would her little brood ever need it more than after this terrible disappointment that had threatened to make the Little Brown House the scene of despair? And surely when every household, in all probability, in the whole of Badgertown was to be drawn into the delights of the circus—all but hers—some sacrifices must be made to give what happiness she could to her children.

"They shall have it," decided Mrs. Pepper to herself. "Now, what else can I find for them?"

But nothing else appearing, no matter how hard she thought as she stitched away, she sighed. "Polly can bake some little biscuits," she said to herself, "to go with the jelly."

When the children were told that the precious glass of blackberry jelly was postively to be theirs for the feast to be prepared for the company, they were speechless with delight. Then came the great deliberation as to how to arrange it.

"We ought to have something to drink," said Ben, "seeing we can't have lemonade."

"Oh, Ben, we couldn't ever have lemonade!" exclaimed Polly.

"I said we couldn't," said Ben, "but we ought to have something; I thought folks always did when they had company, Polly."

"Oh, dear me, I know," said Polly, quite distressed at the failure to be like other folks, "but we haven't anything, Ben."

"Why can't we melt the jelly?" proposed Ben.

"Oh, Ben," Joel gave a loud howl. Then he flew over to Mrs. Pepper's chair. "Ben's going to melt the jelly you gave us—" he cried wrathfully. "Make him stop, Mamsie," he implored.

"Oh, I don't think he is, Joel," said Mrs. Pepper soothingly.

"He is—he is," declared Joel wildly; "he said so. Do stop him, Mamsie."

Meanwhile Polly's voice came pealing across the kitchen. Joel pricked up his ears. "How perfectly elegant!" she was exclaiming. So Joel flew back again, for things couldn't be as bad as he feared with Polly so joyful.

"And just think, Joey," she cried, as he came bounding up, "we're going to have the jelly melted and—"

"No, no, no!" roared Joel, interrupting.

"And we're going to pour it into the mugs and cups and drink it, and it will be just as sweet and beautiful as can be! And Ben thought this all out," added Polly proudly.

"Will it be sweet?" asked Joel.

"As sweet as can be," declared Polly decidedly.

"I'd rather have the jelly to eat on top of the little biscuits," said Joel grudgingly, yet he thought longingly of the beautiful mugful to drink.

"Oh, we aren't going to melt it all," said Polly quickly. "The very idea! We're going to save half to eat."

"Then I want to drink some," cried Joel, "and I'm going to melt it—Dave and me—"

"You can help, children," said Polly, bustling away, feeling very grand and important. Dear me, how much there was to do, to be sure, when company was expected!

And when at last the eventful afternoon arrived, there was a still further surprise in store for the five little entertainers of the company. In walked Grandma Bascom. "I thought mebbe you'd like this, Polly, to dress up in. My Pa brought it home from the Indies, an' you can keep it, 'cause th' moths has got into it," mourned Grandma, holding it up in her trembling old hands.

It was a yellowish, thin woolen shawl, dingy with age, with a wide border running all around it of flowers of various sizes, and in flaring colors that, strange to say, had not dimmed in the least all the while they had been in Grandma Bascom's possession. The children crowded around in speechless admiration as Grandma Bascom shook it out before their eyes.

"That corner goes up th' back," said Grandma, pointing to it, "an' Ma was alwus partic'ler to settle it that way, bein's th' flowers ran up so fur"—as they surely did! A most remarkable spray like nothing ever seen in a garden sprawled at its own sweet will almost into the middle of the shawl.

"There hain't no other corner got a sprig, so you can't make a mistake, Polly. An' be careful of th' fringe," which indeed was necessary advice, as this particular adornment to the shawl had become very tired in the lapse of time since Grandma Bascom's pa brought it from the Indies, and had dropped away, till here and there only a thread remained, looking very lonely indeed.

"An' don't stick your fingers in th' holes, child," cautioned Grandma, before she finally let it go into Polly's hands. "It beats me how those moths get into it, but if you don't ketch it on anythin', 'twon't tear no more."

"Oh, I'll be very careful of it," promised Polly, receiving the old shawl with fingers that trembled as much as Grandma's. "It's perfectly beautiful, but perhaps Mamsie won't let me wear it," she added, with a dreadful feeling that in that case the company would suffer a loss that could never be made up; "and then I'll bring it back to you, Grandma, when she comes home," she said loudly, for Grandma was so deaf.

"You ain't never goin' to bring it back to me," said Grandma, beginning to waddle to the door, and turning back —"I've give it to you, Polly."

"*You've given it to me!*" repeated Polly, in amazement, and her hands trembled so that the old shawl shook dreadfully.

"You've given it to Polly!" screamed Joel, huddling up to Grandma. "O my jiminy!"

Ben was not less excited, and the delighted babel that they all now set up pleased Grandma very much. She beamed at them all under the nodding frills of her cap border. "Yes, I've give it to Polly," she said. "It's got moth holes, and I sh'd be ashamed to wear it with them in; Ma never did. So Polly shall keep it to dress up in." And despite all the pressing invitations to stay and be part of the company to receive, Grandma waddled off down the lane to see to her hens and other necessary work left undone.

It was about a half hour after this. The old kitchen presented a very dignified aspect, suited for such a ceremonious occasion as it was presently to be the scene of. There on the table was spread the feast, two plates of little brown biscuits baked as nice as anyone could ever want, and on Mother Pepper's best blue willow saucer was half of the blackberry jelly. It had lopped down one side a bit, to be sure, as Polly turned it out of the glass, which was a great grief to her, but as Ben wisely suggested, "It will taste just as good, Polly," she tried to be comforted. And next to it was the row of mugs and cups of the blackberry juice, nice and pink where it had been pieced out with plentiful additions of water. Could anything be more magnificent!

And in front of the table spread with this feast was the row of entertainers, all obliged to turn their backs, because Joel would stare at the refreshments, and Polly said that was not polite, for he ought to look at the company.

Phronsie sat on her little stool in the middle, or as near as she could get to it, being between Ben and Joel, and little Davie was at the very end, and each head was graced with the most remarkable structure of hat or bonnet, from which floated, or stuck straight upright, as the case might be, some feather or a chicken wing drawn from their treasured box.

Polly was to be company first, and she now stood before the row, perfectly resplendent in a tall newspaper hat, from which perked out a rooster feather, and the yellow old embroidered shawl that Grandma Bascom's Pa had brought from the Indies, drawn across her shoulders. It had required all Ben's best skill to persuade the sprig of flowers to run where it should, and he tried several times to get it right, as Polly couldn't see her own back.

"It isn't exactly straight," he confessed at last, and pausing with a very red face, "but it doesn't matter, Polly."

"Oh, it must be straight," said Polly, feeling that it would be an awful thing if Grandma Bascom's shawl didn't look the same as when Ma wore it. "Do try again, Ben."

So Ben tried again, getting it worse than before. "The flowers won't come straight," he said, "and I can't make 'em." So Polly was forced to stifle a sigh and bear it as best she could.

"Now, children," said Polly, standing in front of the row

—Ben had taken his seat at the head of the line—"I'm going into the bedroom and—"

"What for?" cried Joel.

"Never mind," said Polly, all in a twitter, for she had a little secret kept carefully from all the others except Ben. It was impossible to keep it from him, for Polly and Ben told everything to each other. Mamsie had told her she might take her dark green silk parasol owned for many years and carefully kept rolled in tissue paper. And because no one was to carry it but Polly, and only once by her, the children must not be told, so Polly couldn't get it from the bureau drawer in the bedroom until the last minute.

"Now you must shut your eyes," said Polly, for there was no other way to get out of doors, after getting the parasol, than to come through the kitchen, and then they would of course see her, "and don't look until I say, 'How do you do!'"

"I don't want to shut my eyes," said Joel. "I want to see what you're going into the bedroom for."

"Shut your eyes, Joe," said Ben, leaning past Phronsie to give him a small nudge. So Joel shut his, especially as Ben, to set a good example, did the same. And little David, afraid he might see, put his two hands up over his face. When Phronsie saw that, she did the same thing, and then Joel, to be in the fashion, followed suit, and so did Ben, to keep the children in countenance.

But Polly couldn't find the parasol, for Mother Pepper took it out to mend a little break in the well-worn silk—afraid it might pull away more while doing duty for the company—and then she set the roll of tissue paper out on the counterpane of the big four-poster, telling Polly so. But Polly hadn't heard, being in such a fluster over the preparations; so she fumbled away, first in one drawer, and then in another, of the old bureau; even searching all through the lowest one where Phronsie always came to look at, and pat, her red-topped shoes.

"She's coming!" cried Joel, having a dreadful time not to take down his hands, but remembering Polly's command just in time.

"Well, you're not to look till she says, 'How do you do,'" warned Ben, as a small noise sounded over by the door. Then all was quiet.

"Oh, dear, I wish she'd hurry," grumbled Joel, and squirming dreadfully on his hard wooden chair.

Little David held his breath in delighted expectation, while Phronsie twisted her small fingers into her brown eyes. She wouldn't have seen for the world until Polly wanted her to, when a fumbling noise back of them struck upon all their ears.

"I guess Polly's thought of something she wanted to do to the refreshments," said Ben to himself, "though I don't see what it can be, for they look so nice." But if Polly wasn't satisfied, and still wanted to fix them over—why, it was all right; so he settled himself back on his chair.

But Polly seemed to be in a good many minds about the beautiful array of eatables, for the little clicking sound showed that the mugs and cups were being moved about; besides other noises that showed that something else was going on among the refreshments.

"What *can* she be doing?" said Ben to himself, more puzzled than ever, when—

"Oh!" screamed somebody. It surely was Polly, but she was in front of them. And the whole row, tearing away their hands —for it was impossible to keep their eyes shut after that— saw Polly, the perfect picture of astonishment, coming out of the bedroom, the old green parasol in her hand, and looking with all her eyes at the table back of them. Everyone whirled

around. There on the edge, in calm enjoyment, sat a monkey, resplendent in a smart red waistcoat adorned all down the front with shining brass buttons, and a perky little red cap, which, not forgetting his manners, he was pulling off with one hand. The other was cramming the last little brown biscuit into his mouth. The mugs and cups stood empty, and the blue willow jelly plate was licked quite clean.

"Oh—oh—oh—a monkey!" It was impossible for anything else to be heard. Joel choked, trying to say as he pointed with shaking finger to the company sitting on the table, "He's eat it all up," but even he could not get out any words. But Company didn't seem to mind the lack of a welcome in the least, peering about as he wrinkled up his brows for more refreshments. But there were none—that was plain enough to be seen.

So then what did he do but hop to the floor, and begin the most surprising antics possible, perhaps thinking it quite time for him to do something to entertain, who had been so well entertained himself; but more than likely with a view to being offered something further in the way of refreshment if he did his best.

And his best it was, for when the whole bunch of Peppers recovered from their astonishment, it was to burst into peals of enjoyment with eyes glued to the movements of a flashing red waistcoat and smart perky cap, as Company went through, from beginning to end, a most surprising list of accomplishments, turning up now and then a wrinkled little face to see if by any chance he was to be invited to have something to eat.

At last he got down to all fours and scrambled up to them. Little David gave a loud scream and clutched Polly about the neck, though, strange to say, Phronsie, the very one whom it might be expected would be frightened, leaned forward and put out her hand. "He's my sweet little monkey. I want him," she said.

The monkey, supposing at least a penny was in her hand, made her his grandest bow, and held out his paw, but, getting nothing, he gave the whole bunch of children a withering look, probably thinking that it was their funny curious head-gear (for they weren't nearly as fine as his smart red cap) that made them so queer, and turned and scrambled off to the door that he had left open a crack when he entered, and hurried out. And all they saw was a flash of red and his long tail slipping out.

"Oh, stop him—stop him!" roared Joel, plunging after him, with all the others at his heels. But, although they looked far and near, running down to the gate and out into the road, not a glimpse of him could be seen. And at last they were just turning back into the house when Sally Brown and her father and mother and four or five of the other neighbors came by in a big wagon.

"We've been to the *circus!*" screamed Sally from the back of the wagon, where she was crammed in among some other children. "And 'twas awful good," she added triumphantly.

" 'Twasn't either," declared another girl vindictively, in a louder scream. "The best monkey—th' one that does all th' tricks—ran away this morning, an' they couldn't fi-ind him—" Her voice pealed after her, as the wagon rolled on down the road.

"Oh, Ben!" Polly seized his coat. "It was our monkey, don't you believe?" she gasped.

"Yes," cried Ben, "I know it. Well, we've had the circus, after all."

XIV

In Doctor Fisher's Gig

"Do you think you know of a little girl, just about as big as you are, who would like to go to ride with me in my gig?" Doctor Fisher leaned over and whispered it into Phronsie's ear as she sat in the middle of the kitchen floor buttoning up her "red-topped shoes."

Phronsie dropped the little buttonhook, with a handle that looked exactly like silver, that old Mr. Beebe had given her when her new shoes were bought.

"Oh, I do—it's me—please take me!" She hopped to her feet. Ever so many of the buttons were in the wrong holes of one little shoe, while the other lay on the floor, the little buttonhook flying off to have a good time by itself.

"Oh, take me!" she begged very much excited, and standing on tiptoe.

"So I shall," cried the little doctor, beaming on her. "Oh, dear me, you'll have to get that other shoe on," with a glance of dismay. "Well, now I must button it up for you."

"Oh, no, no," said Phronsie, shaking her yellow head. "I must do it all alone by myself—I truly must." So she sat down on the floor and gravely set to work again, but the last little buttons positively refused to go in any holes at all.

"Now, see here, Phronsie," said Doctor Fisher at last, "you must let me help you, or you can't go. Don't you hear Dobbin telling us to hurry up? There, you put your foot right here, and I'll have those buttons where they belong in no time."

"Is Dobbin calling us?" asked Phronsie, the little hook pausing over a refractory button, to listen.

"Yes, indeed," little Doctor Fisher nodded vehemently. Just then the old horse waiting out by the gate gave a loud neigh. "Don't you hear him? There, now, says I." And he slipped the little buttons out of the wrong holes to begin afresh.

"Oh, no—no," protested Phronsie in alarm, pulling away her little fat foot. "Those are my very own buttons all done." And two tears ran down her round cheeks.

The little doctor viewed her with dismay, and pulled out his big bandanna to wipe away the tears that were now coming so fast. He was at his wit's end to know what to do next.

"I was going to say I'd take Polly, too, and she hasn't been to ride since her eyes got well," he said artfully, "but I can't, unless you stop crying and let me button up your shoes."

"Can't Polly go?" said Phronsie, struggling very hard to crowd the tears back, and wiping her cheeks with her fat little hands.

"No, not unless you stop crying and let me button up your shoes," declared Doctor Fisher firmly. "She'll have to stay at home, and, just think, she hasn't had a ride since her eyes got well," he repeated, quite delighted at his success so far.

"Then you may button up my new shoes," said Phronsie, smothering her sobs, and she stuck out her foot, and the little doctor speedily had all the buttons in the right holes. "Now, then, the other one." And then those buttons all flew into their places, and quicker than it takes to tell it, the little red-topped shoes were both fastened up, and Doctor Fisher was saying, "Now run and call Polly, child," which really wasn't necessary, for Phronsie was already on the way.

And then out flew Polly from the bedroom, her cheeks as red as two roses, and she raced up to Doctor Fisher. "Oh, I'm so glad— I'm going to ride! I am— I am!" just as if telling him a piece of news.

"Well, hurry up then," said the little doctor, bursting into a merry laugh, and quite as excited. So Polly flew off to get Phronsie's pink sunbonnet and her own, but presently back she came without them.

"Oh, I forgot we can't go without asking Mamsie," she said, and all the color flew out of her face, "and she's down to Mrs. Henderson's." And she clasped her hands in distress.

"You go right along," commanded the little doctor peremptorily. "I asked your mother on the way down here. I had to stop at the parsonage, and she said, 'Yes.'"

"Mamsie said 'Yes,'" shouted Polly, her brown eyes widening in delight, and seizing Phronsie, who had followed her closely, clamoring for her sunbonnet. "She did, Phronse, she truly did. There, come, Pet, and let me brush your hair." And she began to dance over to the bedroom, hurrying Phronsie along.

"I don't want my hair brushed, Polly," said Phronsie in a grieved tone, and stumbling along, Polly holding her hand closely.

"Oh, yes, you do." Polly by this time had her in the bedroom. "Misery me, Phronsie, Mamsie wouldn't ever want you to go to ride with your hair looking so. Why, it's just like a cat's nest," making the old brush fly busily over Phronsie's yellow hair.

"Will there be a cat's nest here in this very room?" asked Phronsie, peering out from the soft wisps falling over her face with wide eyes of astonishment.

"Yes," said Polly, in such a twitter over the promised ride she didn't think what she was saying. "Do stand still, or I never'll get through."

"Oh, Polly," Phronsie slipped from under the old brush, and pushed back the hair from her face, "then there'll be a little kitty!" And she clasped her fat little hands ecstatically.

"Whatever in the world!" exclaimed Polly, the old hairbrush sticking up straight in the air, "do you mean, Phronsie?"

"I'm going to have a little kitty," sang Phronsie, dancing away by the side of the old four-post bedstead. "Polly said so —a little kitty!"

"Phronsie," cried Polly, rushing after her, but Phronsie slipped off, her yellow hair streaming, and danced into the corner, "Polly said so—a little kitty!"

"Now, Phronsie," and Polly had her fast by the side of the big bureau, "you must just come out here"; and getting hold of her pink pinafore, Phronsie was soon in the middle of the bedroom. "Oh, make it a white one, do, Polly," she begged, dreadfully excited.

"What *do* you mean?" cried Polly in a great state of bewilderment.

"I want a white one," said Phronsie, but her lip drooped, and she looked ready to cry, for Polly's face certainly didn't look encouraging.

"If you'll tell me what you're talking about, child," said Polly, almost in despair, still holding the old hairbrush, "I'll—"

"You said there would be one," said Phronsie in an injured tone, and her brown eyes fastened on Polly with disapproval.

"Said there would be what?" gasped Polly.

"A cat's nest in this very room," said Phronsie, struggling

with her tears, "and I want—a little white kitty, I do, Polly!" Then she burst into a loud sob and flung herself into Polly's arms.

"Oh, dear me! Oh—oh!" cried Polly gustily, gathering her up, the old hairbrush flying off by itself. "Phronsie— Oh, dear me!"

"You said so, Polly." Phronsie, held tightly in Polly's arms, kept saying this over and over reproachfully.

"Oh, I know it," cried Polly. "Oh, dear me, I didn't mean there would really and truly be a cat's nest in this room, Phronsie."

"You said so," repeated Phronsie, and this time she wriggled around to look up into Polly's face with indignation.

"Well— Oh, dear me! I said your hair *looked* like one, Phronsie." Then Polly burst into such a merry peal of laughter that neither of them heard little Doctor Fisher come in from the kitchen.

"Well, I never!" he cried, setting his big spectacles straight to stare at them in amazement. Phronsie was, by this time, crying so that she didn't see him, but Polly did, and she sprang to her feet, upsetting Phronsie, the color rushing up to her brown hair. "Oh, I'm so sorry," she cried.

But the little doctor smiled kindly at her, and went over and picked Phronsie up.

"Heyday!" he cried, swinging her as high as he could, which wasn't much. "Well, now, don't you want to go to ride in my gig?"

But Phronsie was lost to all such charms and everything else. Polly had never told her anything that didn't come true before, so she wailed on bitterly, until Polly, quite pale now, had told the whole story, interspersed with many reproaches for her careless speech.

"Oh, if that's all," said the little doctor jubilantly, "I think I know exactly where to find a cat's nest, Phronsie."

"Is there a white kitty in it?" asked Phronsie, coming out of her sobs suddenly and brushing off the tears.

"Well, I don't know about the white one," said Dr. Fisher, racking his brains to remember if he had seen such a creature, and where. "But never mind," as the little face fell, "there will be some other cunning kittens in the nest, probably, and they're just waiting for some little girl who is going to be very good and not cry, and—"

"I'll be very good and not cry," announced Phronsie, struggling out of his arms, "and perhaps there's a white one there."

"Perhaps," said the little doctor, with a merry laugh. "And now hurry up your cakes, and get ready, or Dobbin won't wait for us much longer."

"I'll hurry up my cakes and get ready," sang Phronsie. So Polly ran and picked up the old hairbrush and the yellow hair was brushed, and the two sunbonnets tied on. Then Polly, feeling very important, locked the old green door and put the key in her pocket, and with a long breath of delight ran down the path after Doctor Fisher and Phronsie. "We are really and truly going to ride in his gig," she kept saying, over and over, to herself.

"You see," said the little doctor, when they were at last in the depths of the roomy old gig, and Dobbin was jogging down the country road, "I thought I'd go over to Miller's Corners this morning, because it's such a fine day. 'Tisn't very important, only the old lady expects me to call sometime this week." And he was just turning off, when a man on horseback, who seemed very much in a hurry, clattered up, calling out long before he got there, "Hey, Doctor—I want you."

"Now, what can have happened," exclaimed the little doctor, peering out with visions of dreadful accidents flying through his mind, as the man and the horse bore down upon the gig. "Well, what's wanted?"

"Mis' Granniss has got hurt," said the man, pulling up his beast so suddenly it seemed as if he must go over on his nose. "She hollered to me as I was goin' past to tell you."

"Sho—now, that poor woman!" exclaimed Doctor Fisher.

"Yes," said the man. "She fell over her stove, an' I guess she's pretty bad."

"I'll be there as soon as I can." The little doctor leaned over and took up the whip and gave Dobbin a cut, who, realizing from past experience a situation that required it, struck out his long legs so bravely that Phronsie, crowded into the middle of the seat, crowed gleefully at the pace as she clung closely to Polly with both hands.

Doctor Fisher, slipping to the edge of the old leather seat, gripped the reins tightly. "I have to, Dobbin," he said; "you must excuse me," whenever he applied the whip, and at last, after many turns down the country road and an occasional uphill, there they were at their destination, and Dobbin gladly stopped to draw breath.

"You can play about here, children," said Doctor Fisher, as he tied Dobbin fast to the worm-eaten post, and seized his medicine bag. So Polly and Phronsie hopped out of the gig, as the little doctor pranced off around the side of the house to the back door, this being evidently the best and quickest way to get into the house.

Polly drew a long breath and looked around. There wasn't anything very pretty about the place; everything was so run down at the heel. Even the old shed tacked on to the weather-beaten dwelling had almost split apart from its connection, as if to say, "I'd rather stand alone." And off on one side of the tiny yard where the grass sent up only occasional green spears was a heap of broken bottles, and old tin cans, and other refuse that seemed to have been there for years and years.

"Oh, dear me!" said Polly, under her breath. "Isn't it beyewtiful," hummed Phronsie, perfectly delighted. "He said we might play here, Polly."

Polly was just going to say, "Oh, we can't play in this dirty place, Phronsie," when she remembered Mamsie's words, "Make the best of everything," so she brightened up. "Let's go over there, Phronsie," pointing across the road to a couple of old oak trees.

"No, no," said Phronsie, shaking her head, "I want to stay here, Polly, I do." And she seized Polly's hand to drag her along. "Oh, there's a kitty!" And she dropped the hand and ran off.

"Don't touch her, Phronsie," called Polly, racing after, but too late! Phronsie already had in her arms a mangy, yellow cat, very dirty, and with big green eyes, now at their widest with fright.

"She'll bite you," screamed Polly. "Put her down, child," as she got up to Phronsie's side.

But Phronsie only hugged the dirty cat closer. "She won't bite me," she said. "Polly, she truly won't," as a small boy in a ragged pair of blue cotton overalls dashed out of the doorway and over the broken steps.

"You put down my cat, you girl, you!" he cried with a fierce jump at Phronsie, who was quite willing now to drop the yellow cat. But unfortunately the cat's long claws of one leg caught in Phronsie's pinafore and in trying to get away from the dirty hands of the boy, toward whom she seemed to have very little love, she put her claws on Phronsie's neck, and as she leaped over her shoulder, there was a long red mark left to show where she had sprung off.

"Now, you see, you've driven off my cat!" screamed the boy, anger all over his dirty little face, as the yellow cat leaped over the refuse heap and disappeared into a patch of scrub oaks.

"Oh, Phronsie," exclaimed Polly in distress, "just look at your neck," which was quite impossible for Phronsie to do, as the long scratch was up over the little pink pinafore ruffle. But it was there, Phronsie knew quite well, as it began to sting and ache. "It hurts, Polly," she said, putting up her hand to it, as she huddled up next to Polly's gown to get away from that dreadful boy.

"I know, child," said Polly soothingly. "Well, Doctor Fisher will fix it when he gets through in the house."

"He ain't ever goin' to get through, the doctor man ain't," said the boy, quite ready to hold conversation, visitors being few and far between. "Mother's got hurt, an' he's fixin' her up."

"Your mother's got hurt?" repeated Polly, her eyes widening in sympathy. "Oh, dear me, how?"

"Um—" the boy snapped his small mouth together impressively, "she fell over the stove, she an' the baby, but—"

"Oh, Polly, there's a baby!" screamed Phronsie, coming out suddenly from the folds of Polly's brown gown.

"Hain't you got a baby?" asked the boy.

"No," said Phronsie, "and I want one, I do."

"Huh—where do you live not to have a baby?" said the boy, in supreme contempt, and he swung on one dirty bare foot to come round again to stare at Phronsie with all his might.

"Oh, the poor thing," said Polly, thinking of that dreadful fall over the stove, "but I'm so glad the baby wasn't hurt."

"And I want the baby," cried Phronsie, excitedly tugging at Polly's hand. "I want it now, please, Polly."

"Come this way. I'm takin' care of her," said the boy, with an important air, striding off to the old shed, and Polly and Phronsie hurried after to find in an old box on top of a folded calico quilt, a small creature with very thin cheeks and big eyes gazing at them under a thatch of tangled black hair. She had something up at her mouth clutched in both hands, at which she was gnawing busily.

"Oh—oh!" screamed Phronsie, rushing over to the box and stretching out both hands. "Isn't she be-*yew*tiful! I want her, I do."

"Don't, Phronsie," cried Polly, trying to pull her away, but as well try to stop the wind. Phronsie was down on her knees by the box with both small arms around the baby, who immediately dropped her choice morsel and then roared because she couldn't get it.

"I'll find it," said the boy, and he gave a twitch to the dirty calico gown, and picked up the end of a corncob, where it had fallen down in the folds of the old quilt. "There." And he crammed it into the roaring mouth, when the two little hands, wildly pawing the air, seized it again. "I put some molasses on to it," he explained, as the baby began to suck it in great content. But she didn't take her big eyes from Phronsie's face.

"Oh, Polly!" cried Phronsie rapturously, "I want her, I do, for my very own baby—"

"Well, you can have her," said the small boy. "I'll give her to you."

"Oh, will you—will you?" cried Phronsie, hopping up from the dirty floor, in a transport. Then she clapped her hands. "Polly, he'll give her to me," she cried, her cheeks very pink.

"Oh, Phronsie," cried Polly, "he can't give her to you."

"Yes, I can, too. You don't know anything about it, you girl, you!" retorted the boy. "She's my sister, an' I guess I can give her away if I want to. You may have her," turning to Phronsie.

"He did say so, Polly, he did." Phronsie, now quite overcome with delight, began to hop up and down, singing, "She's my baby—she's my baby!"

"You're a bad boy," said Polly severely, "to want to give away your sister."

"No, I ain't bad either," said the boy sturdily. "I'm goin' fishin', an' I don't like that baby, an' I ain't a-goin' to stay home an' take care of her, so there." And without another word, he sprang out of the old shed, seized a snarl of fishing tackle on the ground just beside the door, and, although Polly called with all her might, he jumped over the broken fence, and raced off.

"Now, whatever shall we do!" cried Polly in great vexation. Phronsie neither heard nor saw anything but the baby, who was giving unmistakable signs of the most complete enjoyment in her old corncob.

"Well, I declare!" Little Doctor Fisher burst in upon them, his spectacles slipping to the end of his nose as he stumbled over the rickety steps. "Bless me, I didn't know where you had gone."

"Oh, Doctor Fisher," cried Polly, flying over to him, "there's a poor baby here—a perfectly dreadful one."

"Is the baby here?" cried Doctor Fisher, peering at the old box and its contents. Then he said, "Bless me" again and set his spectacles straight. "Where's that boy? His mother said he was taking care of it."

"He's run off," said Polly.

"Run off!" exclaimed the little doctor. "Well, I'd like to catch him," he added savagely.

"And he's given me the baby," declared Phronsie, springing up to seize Doctor Fisher's big hand. "He has—and she's whole mine, my very own—"

"The dickens he did!" exploded Doctor Fisher.

"Oh, dear me!" exclaimed Polly, "it's just as bad as it can be."

"I should think it was," said the little doctor gloomily. Then he pulled his long nose thoughtfully, which showed he was in great trouble in his mind.

"Oh, dear!" breathed Polly in the greatest distress, for it always grieved her dreadfully to see Doctor Fisher, who had saved her eyes and given her a new stove, troubled about anything.

"You see, Polly," said the little doctor, coming out at last from his perplexity, and standing up quite straight, "that poor woman is badly burned, her hands are, and *she* can't take care of the baby, that's plain. And there isn't anybody else to do it but that bad boy."

"Oh, he can't do anything," declared Polly vehemently. "Oh, don't make the baby stay with him!" And quite overcome with pity, she knelt down by the old box.

"Ah—goo!" exclaimed the baby, deserting the charms of the old corncob for a breathing space, Phronsie turning back from the little doctor to get down by Polly's side.

"Oh, dear me! Poor little thing!" breathed Polly; "nobody to take care of you except a bad boy and a cross old cat, and she's run away, too."

"Ah—goo!" said the baby, as if it were the pleasantest thing in the world to be left under such conditions.

"Oh, we can't ever leave her," said Polly, turning back,

one hand on the edge of the box, to look up in the little doctor's face, and her brow wrinkled in perplexity.

"No, of course not," said Doctor Fisher, just as decidedly, and his face cleared as he saw that Polly would help him out. "It will only be for two days, you know, until Mrs. Granniss's sister gets here. I'm going to write to her to come. Well, I shall take the baby up to Badgertown Center with me, and find a place for her somewhere."

And Doctor Fisher having quite made up his mind to do this, the next thing was to carry it out; so he skipped off, told the sick woman, sitting up in a big chair with her poor hands swathed in big bandages, all about it, and dashed out again before she had gotten out half her grateful thanks, picked up the baby out of its big box, packed all the children into the old gig, and away the gig rattled at Dobbin's heels down the hill to Badgertown.

"I'm going to send Miss Punderson to look after her till the sister gets here," Doctor Fisher pointed his thumb at the poor little cottage they had left behind, "but she wouldn't come if there was a baby in the house. Goodness me! she doesn't know any more about 'em than an old cat."

This made Polly remember about the cross, yellow cat at Mrs. Granniss's house. So she leaned around the baby in her lap, and said anxiously, "Phronsie has got such a dreadful scratch."

"What's that?" cried Doctor Fisher, pulling Dobbin up suddenly, to look into Polly's face. "What are you talking of, child?"

"Oh, the cross cat," said Polly, "at that house." Then she told the whole story, and Doctor Fisher made Dobbin stop entirely while he hung the old leather reins over his arm and examined Phronsie's fat little neck to his satisfaction.

"That will be all right in two or three days," he declared,

"so you won't know a cat ever touched you, Phronsie." And then he picked off the reins from his arm and clacked to Dobbin, and away they went faster than ever.

"Oh, I do wish we could keep the baby," said Polly, in a minute. "We could put her in the tub, and I'd wash her and comb her hair, and she'd be real pretty." And she pulled down the dirty calico gown in a motherly way.

"Oh, no, I'm going to wash her, Polly," said Phronsie in alarm, crowding up as closely as she could to the two. "She's my baby, and I'm going to do it."

"Well, I don't see how either of you can do it," said Doctor Fisher. "Your mother ought not to take her. No, I must get some other place—"

"Perhaps Mamsie will," said Polly quickly, with an awful feeling at the mere thought of having the baby go anywhere else. "I'll take care of her."

"No, no," protested Phronsie in a loud, injured tone, "I'm going to take care of her all by myself. She's my baby."

"Well, never mind," said Doctor Fisher, bursting into a laugh. "We'll fix it somehow. There, now, go on, Dobbin, and let's get this baby settled somewhere."

And as good luck would have it, as little Doctor Fisher hopped out at the post office to get the letter started to Mrs. Granniss's sister without delay, who should come along but Mrs. Pepper, just starting home with a fresh bundle of coats Mr. Atkins had given her to make.

When she heard the story, interspersed with Phronsie's pleadings to keep the baby, Mrs. Pepper looked at Polly.

"It must be as you say, Polly," she said, "for the extra work will come on you, and you don't get any time now to play."

"Oh, I wish you'd keep the baby," said Polly; "it'll be play to take care of her. Do, Mamsie," she begged.

"I'm going to wash her," said Phronsie, leaning out of the

old gig with flushed face, "and put her to bed, and comb her hair, I am, Mamsie."

"I will keep her," said Mrs. Pepper with a smile for Phronsie, but her glance rested on Polly's face.

"Then I shall drive you home," said little Doctor Fisher. "Get right in, Mrs. Pepper."

"Oh, no," she said, laughing, "the gig won't hold us all."

"I'll sit on the floor, Mamsie," said Polly, slipping to the floor of the gig, baby and all.

"Very well, then, I will hold the baby." So in got Mrs. Pepper, first handing in her bundle of coats next to Polly on the floor, then Polly handed up the baby, Phronsie crowding up closer than ever. Then in got the little doctor and away they all went, a gigful, with Mrs. Granniss's baby to keep for two whole days.

"It does seem so good, Mamsie," cried Polly, hurrying up the path to the Little Brown House with the baby, Phronsie running along by her side, protesting at every step that she ought to carry it as it was her baby, and Mrs. Pepper behind with the bundle of coats, "that we have a baby of our very own!"

"Oh, it's mine—my baby," cried Phronsie, pushing back her yellow hair to look up in Polly's face. "It's my very own baby."

"Well, never mind," said Polly, "it can be your baby, Phronsie, but you see I've got to take care of it. Oh, the key, Mamsie, it's in my pocket."

"I'll get it out," said Mrs. Pepper, running her hand in Polly's pocket, and drawing out the big key she unlocked the green door, and they all went in, Doctor Fisher peering around his old gig to watch them as he drove off.

"The first thing," said Mrs. Pepper with emphasis, "we must do, is to wash that baby, Polly."

"Isn't it," cried Polly with delight at the prospect; while Phronsie screamed, "Oh, I'm going to do it, I am!"

"So I'll get the tub all ready," said Mrs. Pepper, going into the bedroom to take off her things, and to make preparations for this new piece of work.

"Oh, Mamsie, I'm going to get the tub ready," declared Polly, hurrying after her.

"No, no," said Mrs. Pepper, with a glance at the face of the dirty little creature hanging on Polly's arm. "You'd better let me, Polly; she's used to you, now, and you must keep her for a while, else she'll cry."

Meantime, Mrs. Pepper was pulling out the tin bathtub, Phronsie hurrying over every movement in the greatest excitement and begging to help.

"You can get the soap, Phronsie," said Mother Pepper, bringing in the teakettle from the stove. "It's good you filled it up, Polly," she said approvingly, as she poured in the boiling hot water to the tin tub.

"And can't Phronsie get the towel, Mamsie?" said Polly, over in the corner where she had seated herself with the baby till the bath should be ready, Phronsie running off on happy little feet to get the soap.

"Yes, indeed," said Mamsie, pouring in cold water to the tub, and trying it with her hand. "Now, I do expect that baby is going to cry dreadfully, Polly," she said with a sigh. "Well, it can't be helped. That's a good girl, Phronsie," as Phronsie ran up and held out the soap, with a very important air. "Now go to the under drawer and get out a towel. Well, Polly, we're all ready; so you may hand her to me."

Mrs. Pepper had seated herself on a low chair by the side of the bathtub and held out her hands.

"Oh, Mamsie!" exclaimed Polly in dismay yet she did as she was bidden. "I thought I was going to wash her."

"Not this time, Polly," said her mother kindly. "Tomorrow you may. Oh, dear me!" as she rolled the baby over on her lap, and took out a big safety pin that seemed to have the whole duty of keeping the dirty little calico gown together. "Polly, we shall have to wrap her up in a quilt till I can wash these clothes."

"Can't she take some of Phronsie's things?" said Polly, hanging over the baby in the greatest distress. "Oh, dear me, Mamsie, can't she?"

"She can take my clothes," said Phronsie, poking her yellow hair in between her mother's busy fingers and the baby, who strange to say was so overcome by all this bustle, she really forgot to cry; "I'll go and get 'em."

"Come back, Phronsie," said her mother, as she clattered off. "No, probably the baby will want to go to sleep, after she's had a good bath, and Polly and I will have a chance to wash out her clothes."

"And I'm going to help wash 'em, too," declared Phronsie, getting back to her mother's chair and the scene of operations, just in time to see the Granniss baby lowered carefully into the tub.

As soon as the water touched her little thin legs, the baby took off her wide-eyed gaze from these strange folks who had so interested her, and glanced wildly off at nothing in particular, to give a loud, shrill scream and wave her pinched arms frantically about.

"Oh, Mamsie!" exclaimed Polly, turning quite pale, while Phronsie threw herself down by the side of the tub, the tears raining down her cheeks. "Oh, take her out, Mamsie, do!" she implored.

"It has to be done," said Mrs. Pepper, her lips firmly set together, while she soaped the baby, here and there, and sent gentle little splashes of water over its poor little body. "Phronsie, we've forgotten a washrag; don't you want to get it for Mother?"

When Phronsie saw there was anything to be done, she stopped crying and hopped to her feet, and presently back she came with the washrag. But then she commenced to cry and to plead again, "Oh, do take her out, Mamsie."

"I can't until she has had a good bath," said Mother Pepper. "And you don't know how good she is going to feel, Phronsie, when it's all done," she added cheerily.

"Is she?" cried Phronsie, through her tears.

"Yes, indeed!" said Mrs. Pepper, giving soft dabs with the washrag here and there. "Now, baby, you begin to look better already." And whether it was what the Granniss baby thought herself, or whether she liked the gentle touch and kind face above her and the feel of the water, no one will ever know. Certain it is, her screams died down to a low whimpering.

"She's better, isn't she?" whispered Polly, who had hardly dared to breathe, and leaning over with glad brown eyes.

"Decidedly," said Mrs. Pepper, lifting baby out to her lap, on which Polly had spread the towel. "Now, then, I must get her as dry as a piece of toast."

"Is she going to be as dry as a piece of toast?" said Phronsie, wiping off her own tears on her pinafore and crowding up as closely as possible to her mother's lap.

"Yes," said Mrs. Pepper, folding the little creature in the big towel and rubbing her gently, "just about as dry, and she likes it; now see."

"She likes it," repeated Phronsie in great glee, and clapping her hands. "Oh, Polly, she does!"

"Doesn't she!" cried Polly with shining eyes, for the Granniss baby not only didn't cry now, but she opened her mouth in a pleased little grin, and tried to pat her small, thin hands together when the ends of the big towel flew apart.

"Oh, Phronsie, she's trying to play pat-a-cake with you!" screamed Polly, quite enchanted at the happy state of things. "Mamsie, see!"

"Yes, I know." Mother Pepper nodded in satisfaction, then bundled the baby up in the towel closely. "Polly, I must give her one of Phronsie's little shirts," she said in a low voice. "There's no other way, else she'll take cold. Run and get it, child."

Polly started, then stopped and looked back. "Oh, mayn't Phronsie get it," she said, although she wanted to dreadfully.

"To be sure," said Mrs. Pepper, smiling approval. "Now, Phronsie, you may give her one of your own little shirts if you want to, because she's your baby, you know."

"Oh, I do want to," screamed Phronsie, "give one of my own shirts to my very own baby." And she ran as fast as she could, and pulled out the drawer to the big bureau where her clothes were kept, and raced back, waving it in the air. "Let me put it on," she begged, "do, Mamsie."

"No, Phronsie," said Mamsie, taking it, "I must do that as quickly as I can, so baby won't take cold." So the little flannel shirt was slipped over the Granniss baby's head, she still trying to play pat-a-cake, and then she was wrapped in a warm old quilt, and laid in the very middle of Mrs. Pepper's big four-poster. "Now, she must go to sleep," said Mamsie, "and you and I, Polly, and Phronsie too, will clear up these things, and make the bedroom all nice again."

The Granniss baby fully intended to protest about this arrangement, but she hadn't fairly begun, when her black eyes closed and she tucked her thumb in her mouth.

"She's asleep already," announced Polly, stopping to peep at the small heap in the middle of the big bed, on her way back after helping Mrs. Pepper to empty the tin tub out of the back door. "Hush, Phronsie, don't wake her up."

"I won't wake her up," promised Phronsie in a soft little whisper, "and I shall sit down and watch her."

"Do," said Polly in great satisfaction, dragging up a chair to the bedside. Then she went out into the kitchen and shut the door.

When Ben and Joel and David came home to dinner (they had all been to work at Deacon Blodgett's), there was the little old calico gown and torn petticoat of the Granniss baby's hanging on a line of string behind the stove and drying nicely.

"Oh, Ben!" exclaimed Polly, rushing at him tumultuously with hands uplifted, "we've got a baby."

"*A baby!*" ejaculated Ben in surprise. Joel and David who, in their joy at getting home, hadn't heard anything of all this, were capering around and crying: "Isn't dinner ready, Polly? Oh, we're so hungry."

"Hush!" warned Polly, flying over to the stove to get the hot baked potatoes. "You mustn't make such a noise. Yes, I'll get the dinner in just a minute, boys."

"Polly," Ben went over to her and seized her arm, "what *do* you mean about the baby?"

"I—oh—yes, there truly is, Ben," said Polly, getting down to pull the potatoes out of the oven; "I'll tell you about it in a minute." But Ben, although he dearly loved to have Polly tell him things, in this instance couldn't wait; so he started to find Mrs. Pepper, for she had gone into the bedroom and shut the door just a minute or two before the boys came home.

"Oh, you mustn't go in there," cried Polly, whirling around so quickly that two potatoes jumped from the dish she was carrying and spun off on the floor.

"Why not?" demanded Ben, stopping a minute and staring at her.

"Oh, dear me! There go those potatoes!" exclaimed Polly in vexation. "Because I told you, there's a baby in there."

"*A baby!*" repeated Ben again.

"Yes, yes, we've just got it," said Polly, setting down the dish, and then hurrying to pick up the two potatoes on the floor, "it only came this morning. Oh, Ben, don't you see." She ran up to throw her arms around him. "It's asleep, and the boys must have their dinner, and we mustn't make any noise, and—and—oh, I'll tell you all about it as soon as I cut the bread." And off Polly ran to get the big bread knife.

"There's one thing I want to know," said Ben, going after her with slow but determined steps. "I'll cut the bread, Polly; here, give me the knife." And he took it out of her hand. "Whose baby is it?"

"Oh, a poor woman's; she tumbled over the stove, and Doctor Fisher took us there, and we brought her home, the baby, I mean, at least Mamsie did," said Polly, jumbling up the words so fast that Ben wrinkled up his brows trying to understand it all. "Oh, dear me. Yes, yes, Joel, I'm going to bring the bread as soon as I can; do let me cut it, Ben."

"You two chaps will just wait until you can get this bread," said Ben, brandishing the big knife, and then cutting off the slices as neatly as possible; "come along and get the plate, Joe," as he piled them on.

"Whickets, I guess I will," exclaimed Joel, tumbling out of his chair, where he had been impatiently drumming on the table with his fork, Polly never allowing the boys to begin to eat dinner till they were all ready together.

"What did you say, Joel?" reproved Polly. "Oh, Mamsie wouldn't like it one single bit to hear you talk so."

"I won't," began Joel, seizing the bread plate so vehemently that a slice immediately flew off to the floor.

"Now, just see that!" exclaimed Polly in consternation, "and bread is so dear, we can't waste it."

"I'll eat it," said Joel, picking it up with eager fingers.

"Take care," warned Polly, "you're spilling all the rest." But little Davie fortunately having followed Joel away from the table to see if he couldn't help too in getting dinner ready, caught the bread plate just in time and set it straight.

"Oh, I didn't mean to," began Joel in distress.

"And you can't eat that bread after it's been on the floor," said Polly. "Dear me, Joe, what does make you act so!"

"I'll scrape it!" said Joel, giving up the bread plate to Davie, and suiting the action to the word he set to work on the slice.

"What's that!" he exclaimed suddenly, dropping the bread, knife, and all. Little Davie jumped, too, and even Ben started, it was such a funny little noise. It didn't sound like a cat exactly, and as the Pepper children didn't have any pets, it couldn't be one, of course.

"Oh, it's the baby, and she's awake!" Polly dashed off to the bedroom. "Come, Ben, and boys!"

It wasn't necessary to tell them to follow her, for all three were close to her heels, as she opened the bedroom door and dashed in. Mother Pepper was over by the four-poster turning down the old quilt, and Phronsie was scrabbling up the other side of the big bed.

"Mamsie," exclaimed Ben, after one look at the small face on the pillow, and he got close to Mrs. Pepper. "Oh, how can you take it?" pointing down at the bed, and he looked very grave.

"I know, Ben." Mrs. Pepper turned to get a good look at his face. "I know what you're thinking of, but, my boy, it was best, and besides it's only for two days."

"Oh, if it's only for two days," said Ben, drawing a long

breath; "only, Mamsie, you have to work so hard, and there's Polly." He couldn't get any further, and turned away to hide his face.

"Yes, there's Polly," said Mrs. Pepper in her cheeriest fashion. "Well, now, Bensie," and she laid both hands on his shoulders to turn him around again so that she could look into his blue eyes, "don't feel badly. I believe it won't hurt Polly, nor any of us, to look after that baby for a little while; trust mother."

"If I could only do anything to help," said Ben, looking helplessly down into the baby's little face, all wrinkled up as it began to yawn. Then it rubbed its fists into its eyes, preparatory to being wide awake.

Meantime, Joel and David were wild with delight, both boys scrabbling up on the bed by the side of Phronsie, and clamoring to know where it came from, and if it was really theirs, and how long it was going to stay, Phronsie all the while declaring it was her very own baby, and she was going to keep it always, till the bedroom was just a babel of sounds; and no one had a good chance to hear anything; and so of course no one did hear when the big green door opened, and somebody came in from the kitchen, until—"What you doin' with my baby?" struck into the general din, in a sharp, high voice.

Joel and David slid off the big bed and stared at the intruder and Phronsie screamed, for it was the ragged, dirty, bad boy that ran away from the baby, to go fishing. Now, having had very poor luck, he went home, and getting the news in a grateful burst from his poor mother, sitting up with bandaged hands in her chair, he had bounded out and somehow traced the baby to the Little Brown House.

"It's my baby!" he declared, with eyes flashing from his

dirty face, and squaring up to them all, "and you've stole her."

"Oh, how can you say so?" cried Polly, her brown eyes very stern. "And you ran away and left her."

"Well, you'd no business to take her," said the boy doggedly, but he dropped his tousled head and dug one set of toes back and forth across the braided rug. "She's my sister and I want her back."

"Don't let him have her, Polly!" screamed Phronsie, frantically clasping the little heap in the old quilt.

"Phronsie," said Mother Pepper. At the sound of her voice, the dirty boy lifted up his head and stared at her.

"And you ain't coming in here," declared Joel in a loud, wrathful key. "This is our Little Brown House, so there!" And he doubled up his small fists.

"Joel," said Mother Pepper.

"Well, you've got my baby," said the boy, whirling round at him, but he turned back to stare at Mother Pepper when she spoke again.

"Come over here," she beckoned to him. So he shambled around the foot of the four-poster, everybody making way for him, except Phronsie, and she was up on the side of the bed crouched close to the baby under the old quilt and trying to keep back the sobs since Mamsie had reproved her.

"Now, isn't it nice that your little sister has come to visit us for two days?" said Mrs. Pepper, quite as if everything had all been planned with the boy and his family a long while before, "and you're going to stay to dinner with us." Here Mother Pepper looked over at Ben.

"Oh, I'll help you," his blue eyes said, though he had to swallow pretty hard to keep the lump in his throat down.

"Hey?" said the boy.

"Yes, I said you were going to stay to dinner with us," said Mother Pepper calmly, lifting the baby, old quilt and all, as she spoke. "Dinner's all ready, isn't it, Polly? Oh, and, Ben, will you take him? I don't know what your name is." And she paused for a reply.

"Ira," said the boy, in a dazed way.

"Well, Ira, if you'll go with Ben, he'll show you where to wash your hands and face and—"

"And I'm going to show him, too," shouted Joel, his fists flying open, and running over to seize the other boy's hand, "and Davie'll come, too—" And off the four boys went.

"And, Phronsie, you may go and help Polly to get something for the baby," said Mrs. Pepper. "She can have your milk if you want to give it to her," with a sigh, to think how little there was in the cup, that always had to be eked out with water, "and some bread crumbled in it."

"Oh, I do, I do," cried Phronsie, slipping down off the side of the bed to fly after Polly. "I do want to give it to my own baby."

"And now, says I, we'll have our dinner," said Mother Pepper, going out into the kitchen with the baby.

Pelagie Doane